THE BEGINNING OF CIVILIZATION
Mythologies Told True

Book 5

THE PHARAOH AND THE GODS

Triumph of Egypt

Second Edition

by

Dennis Wammack

DCW
PRESS
A Boutique Publishing Company

Birmingham Alabama

The Beginning of Civilization: Mythologies Told True Series
The Pharaoh and the Gods: Triumph of Egypt, Second Edition
HCPB 250119

©Dennis Wammack, 2023, 2024, 2025
All characters and events in this work are fictitious.
All rights are reserved.

Hardback: ISBN 978-1-965619-06-3
Paperback: ISBN 978-1-965619-07-0
eBook: ISBN 978-1-965619-08-7

The Pharaoh and the Gods: Triumph of Egypt, Second Edition is the fifth in the six-book series, *The Beginning of Civilization: Mythologies Told True.*

For rights and permissions, contact Dennis Wammack, denniswammack@gmail.com. denniswammack.com

Cover design by the author using artificial intelligence resources.
Books are printed and distributed by IngramSpark, Nashville TN.
Digital format distribution is available through Draft2Digital.com.
Published by DCW Press, Birmingham, Alabama, dcwpress.com.

TABLE OF CONTENTS

The Appendix contains a Glossary of referenced names and places.

PART I. EGYPT

PART II. PHARAOH

THE PHARAOH AND THE GODS
Triumph of Egypt
Second Edition

1. Horus Wept
Year 150

Horus watched his sometimes lover priestess call forth his sometimes dead father. *What's it all about? Why do we live? What is at the other end of life? Why do we bow before the powerful? Seek the approval of fools? What is it we seek and what will we do when we find it?*

The sun rose higher into the sky. The adulation of the people became louder with each passing moment. The High Priestess did her job well. She had summoned Osiris from the land of the dead to be reincarnated as Ra, the Living Sun. *Dung! It's all dung! Droppings from a high-flying bird onto the heads of fools standing in cow dung trying to find meaning in their meaningless lives. I am barely a man and already the stench overwhelms me. Mother, Father, show me the way. I am lost. Show me the way.*

He tore his red-rimmed eyes from High Priestess Hathor, her arms upraised summoning Ra, and looked at Prince Djoser who stood captivated by the ceremony. *He is dead, Prince Djoser! You know that by now. But do you know that he is dead by my hand? But you would not care. His death gives the powerful the little ceremony you crave and the masses the big ceremony THEY crave. And it comes without cost to anyone except my father who bought it with his life and to me who bought it with blood-stained hands.*

He looked at the mindless, gathered multitude. *Mother Hathor will soon be telling me of the glory my father brings to the land. Uncle Djoser will be telling me how pleased Osiris would be with how everything worked out. Uncle Set will be pleased that both Father and Mother are dead. Or he will be furious they are still held in higher regard than him. And Mother Nephthys—how will you counsel me? To rejoice or to despair? And why should your words matter?*

Horus wept. *Father, I killed you so Uncle Djoser could create his unified, all-powerful kingdom. Did I kill you in vain? Will Djoser create the kingdom he believes he hungers for? A civilization to replace the one you lost along with Mother and Uncle Set and Aunt Nephthys and your mythological Queen Kiya. And if he does—what difference? And if he doesn't—what difference? You remain dead except in the minds of fools. Uncle Djoser knows exactly what he seeks. What do **I** seek? And why do I seek it?*

EGYPTIAN GODS: Osiris/Dionysus—Isis/Ariadne/Philyra, Horus, Set/Charon, Nephthys/Dexithea.
CANAANITE GODS: Anath, Astarte, Shalem, Shahar, Moloch, El.
OLYMPIAN GODS: Zeus, Dionysus, Hestia, Ares, Athena, Astraeus, Eos, Hermes.
OCEANIDS: Polydore, Lyris, Acaste, Eidyia, Dione.

2. What We Seek

High Priestess Hathor completed the sunrise ceremony as the sun completed its rise from the great river into the morning sky. She was satisfied. *I need a more dramatic ending. The people must be filled with ecstasy when they depart. The ending was acceptable, but I must make it even grander.*

Hathor dismissed her staff but called for a noon-time banquet to review the morning's activities. She wanted to give them time to reflect upon their glorious task and to consider how to improve upon it. A Nubian drummer informed her that Saqqar priests were gathering beneath the Mastaba to bow before her and seek entry into her service and, too, that Shaman Saqqar, himself, appeared to be on his way to the Mastaba. Hathor smiled with the self-satisfaction of total victory. *Great Lord Master God Osiris, after you vowed you would not cast me down from the heights, I swore to you that I would be the best priestess ever. I hope I have pleased you. I did my best for both you and Isis. I did my very best.*

Archer Hetephe approached Hathor and upon reaching her, curtsied. Both women knew that, since this morning's ceremony, their relationship had subtly changed. Hetephe was no longer the higher ranking, more powerful of the two.

Hathor nodded her head in recognition and said, "Archer Hetephe, you have brought greatness to your land. Prince Djoser, all Nubians, and all in the land of Kemet owe you a great debt. Thank you for the Nubians you convinced to join the service of Osiris and Isis. They made our ceremony a wonder to behold."

As the two women amicably discussed Hathor's successful conquest of Shaman Saqqar's hold over the dead and their Mastabas, the crowd parted to make way for the arrival of Prince Djoser and Queen Nima. Djoser held out both hands as a greeting to Hathor. Hathor did not accept his extended hands; she, instead, simply stared at him. Nima, immediately understanding what was at play, made quick calculations. Deciding, Queen Nima curtsied to High Priestess Hathor. Without unlocking her stare with Djoser's, Hathor nodded in recognition of Nima's curtsy.

Eternity waited as Djoser stared back, unblinking. *So, my little destitute trader girl has risen to the heights to where a prince must show subservience to her? How did you do this little girl? That I—Djoser, Prince of Kemet—must now bow before a common gutter girl? What would Friend Osiris have me do?*

Dionysus/Osiris, Ariadne/Isis/Philyra, Charon/Set, Hermes/Tehuti.
EGYPTIANS: Nebka, Djoser, Hotep, Khasek, Rocky
NUBIANS: Nima, Hetephe, King Kerma, Prince T'jaru, Prince Rafah.
CANAANITES: Phoenicia, Serket, Azazil, Jaffa | URFANS: Teumessian, Abram, Sarai, Terah

Deciding, Djoser broke his stare and nodded in subservient recognition to High Priestess Hathor.

Hathor returned a radiant smile, took his extended hands, and nodded back in recognition; but she did not curtsy. *I don't wish to dominate you, my Prince. But you must accept me as High Priestess to a god—as the one who will call forth the rebirth of Osiris every sunrise. I became what you wished me to become. Now, I am what I am. You will accept me for what I am and bow before me.*

Djoser tried to reaffirm his position as the ranking person, even over his mother, by praising the staff that attended to Osiris and the Word of Isis. But all who listened understood that Djoser was helplessly repeating that which Hathor had brought to pass. He ended his praise with a somewhat challenging, "And should the prince fear the High Priestess? Will Hathor wish to rule over all the land of Kemet?"

Hathor gently laughed as she replied, "Kings, queens, and princes are responsible for the care of living people and their land. I am responsible for the bodies of the dead waiting for their rebirth and for those living in the Land of the Dead. Lord Osiris entrusted me to be his High Priestess. I think not that powerful and high-born rulers have anything I desire."

"Except for more Mastaba's, jewels, and wealth—but only for the glory of the dead, of course!"

"But of course! I must prepare a place for your mother and father—and even you, my prince. That which you give to the priests and priestesses is that which you will have in the land of the dead."

"Does Hathor have all that Hathor desires?"

"No. But I work toward it every day—to increase the glory of Osiris and Isis—to make their story a common experience that will further strengthen the bond between all peoples of your land—of the upper kingdom and lower kingdoms. I shall strive every day to give the prince what HE wants—two kingdoms bound together as one united kingdom. Do my words please you?"

"Ever the little trader girl. Promising me everything I want while preparing to take everything I have. Your boss would be proud!"

She stiffened and haughtily replied, "My *Lord* Osiris *is* very proud!"

Again, Djoser laughed and replied, "I am sure he is! May I be dismissed?"

She nodded his dismissal and turned to chat with Queen Nima. Shaman Saqqar stood obediently to the side, waiting for his turn with Hathor.

As Djoser walked away, he nodded for Hetephe to join him.

Hetephe joined Djoser as he was walking down the Mastaba to the ground level. "May I join you, my prince?"

"Please do, Archer Hetephe. I am in need of pleasant, refreshing, female companionship."

"You just want someone to flick your Ibis, Prince."

"No, Hete. I want the pleasure of your company; *not* your exquisite Ibis flicking talents. Not right now, anyway. Right now, I need to clear my mind and find out how you and Hathor made this happen, and what it is I now want, and how to get it."

"Let's visit in the Mastaba of Chief Kemet—or Ptah as Hathor calls him. His Mastaba will be peaceful. I always enjoy visiting him. It will be a good place to clear your mind and make plans for your final, total, and complete conquest and unification of the upper and lower kingdom. 'Exquisite Ibis flicking talents,' you say."

Meanwhile

Set and Nephthys did not join the other Memphis powerful on the Mastaba of Osiris. Instead, they went to Hostess House for Set's morning meal of garnished cabbage. Anubis joined them. To the usual weight of Set's presence, Nephthys carried the burden of last night's death of her friend, mentor, hero, and confessor—Osiris—once named "Titan Dionysus of Everywhere" and with whom she had once lain.

As they sat in their post-meal ritual, Set looked up and became more animated. "Well, look who comes to join us—my young nephew Horus!"

Nephthys immediately looked and saw Horus approaching. Her heart quickened with compassion, sympathy, and sorrow. *Your father died, my son. Did he die well? I'm sorry. So very, very sorry. His mind had already died. It's for the best. But still, you loved him. As I did.*

Horus entered, looked around, saw Set, and walked over to their table. "May I join you?"

Set replied, "Yes, Nephew. Join us and tell us what happened."

Nephthys wanted to console Horus but remained silent.

Horus answered, "Father is dead, you know. He is now with Mother in the Land of the Dead. Does this please you?"

Set replied, "Yes. Yes, it does. Do you know when and how he died? Was it painful?"

Horus answered. "I killed him last night in time for Hathor to prepare for her morning ceremony. It was not too painful—for him, anyway. I smothered him with his wine-red pillow. He jerked a few times. I'm sure he knew what I was doing."

Set leaned forward with a touch of glee. "Did you hear that, Neph? Osiris was killed by his own son. How is that for betrayal? Our day starts well!"

Nephthys looked at Horus. They spoke but only with their eyes.

Anubis addressed Horus, "I'm sorry, Cousin Horus. You killed him, yourself? That must have been difficult but I'm sure Uncle Osiris thanks you for your compassion. His mind wasn't always right, and he knew it, I think."

Horus replied, "Thank you, Cousin. That's the nicest words I've heard all day."

Anubis reached out to lightly punch Horus's shoulder; an act of sympathetic male-to-male bonding.

Horus was a year older than Anubis, but they looked much like brothers and somewhat like Osiris. Something Set never noticed.

Nephthys offered, "When we get time alone, I would like to talk to you about it, Horus."

Horus replied, "Yes. Let's. After the sun sets. Down by the river. I would like that, too."

Set interjected, "You people can roll around in self-pity when I'm not around. Right now, let's celebrate with beers for everyone!!" Set held up his hand for four beers.

Horus said, "It is fitting that I drink wine, Uncle. And Mother Nephthys, too." Horus called to the server, "Make that two beers and two wines."

Anubis wanted wine instead of beer but thought twice and let the order stand.

EGYPTIAN GODS: Osiris/Dionysus—Isis/Ariadne/Philyra, Horus, Set/Charon, Nephthys/Dexithea.
CANAANITE GODS: Anath, Astarte, Shalem, Shahar, Moloch, El.
OLYMPIAN GODS: Zeus, Dionysus, Hestia, Ares, Athena, Astraeus, Eos, Hermes.
OCEANIDS: Polydore, Lyris, Acaste, Eidyia, Dione.

Set laughed a cackling laugh, "As you will! He is dead. Wine won't bring him back! Or his dead bitch whore. Beer—wine—urine—drink what you will!"

Horus reprimanded Set, "Mother was not a bitch, Uncle Set. She was a queen!"

"Yes, whatever. A queen. Can I at least call her a bitch queen, Nephew?"

"A queen, Uncle Set."

"Very well. A queen. A dead queen!"

The beer and wine arrived. Each toasted the moment with their own private thoughts.

Horus: *I will find you, Father. And you, Mother. Now I know what I want. This is what I want!*
Anubis: *We are all flawed. Uncle Osiris was the best of us, and he was somewhat insane. And now dead. I wonder if he is still insane.*
Nephthys: *I want you to be a human being, Set. Not even necessarily a GOOD human being. I have tried. I have failed. What can I do? I want to find the way.*
Set: *This is what I wanted and now I have it. Now, Horus, you little bastard child of Osiris and his bitch Isis, I can, at last, humiliate and destroy you.*

The Powerful

High Priestess Hathor and her contingent of Priests, Priestesses, and attendants hosted a Highsun meal for King Nebka, Queen Nima, and Chief Kerma. Shaman Saqqar was there as were Chief Kerma's two youngest sons, Rafah and T'jaru. Prince Djoser and a contented Archer Hetephe arrived late. The talk was animated and delightful. Hathor practiced being imperial. Osiris had once told her that people seemed to like an attitude such as that in their superiors. Politically knowledgeable, even more so than King Nebka, Hathor continually steered the talk toward the contributions of the Nubians in their grand sunrise ceremony. "I would not have the power to call Lord Osiris back from the land of the dead without the assistance of the Nubian drummers and announcers. Indeed, it is they who are key to calling forth the Living Sun."

Hathor, Nima, and Djoser took note that even Chief Kerma appeared to believe that Osiris had actually been called from the Land of the Dead and that the sun was now a living being. It wasn't that Chief Kerma thought about it on a critical level, he was told that this was what was

Dionysus/Osiris, Ariadne/Isis/Philyra, Charon/Set, Hermes/Tehuti.
EGYPTIANS: Nebka, Djoser, Hotep, Khasek, Rocky
NUBIANS: Nima, Hetephe, King Kerma, Prince T'jaru, Prince Rafah.
CANAANITES: Phoenicia, Serket, Azazil, Jaffa | URFANS: Teumessian, Abram, Sarai, Terah

happening by people who supposedly knew about these things. It must be so. More power to the Nubians who helped them do it.

Queen Nima thought, *If a Chief accepts this illusion as fact, what then of the masses? And my husband, do you believe this nonsense?*

Hathor continued her politicizing. "I am told, Chief Kerma, that the people of Memphis are angry with the Nubians because Nubians do not deem to visit our fair city. I am also told that the Hostess House in South Memphis has tried to convince your virile Nubian males to join them for food, beer, and dancing girls but none will come. How can Prince Djoser convince your subjects to favor us with their presence?"

Kerma replied, "The people of the upper kingdom are content with their home in the upper kingdom. We have no need for Memphis or the lower kingdom."

Hetephe, knowing the ambitions of her Prince Djoser, piped in, "I am at the Hostess House every quarter moon impressing the locals with my skills at archery. No Nubian male can defeat me; especially if I can get a beer in them before the competition. Tell them that, Chief Kerma!"

Kerma laughed. "What do they get after they defeat you Nubian Hetephe?

Hetephe did not miss a beat. "Why, they get *me*, Chief. High-born and right there on a table in front of everybody."

Djoser tensed but kept silent.

Hetephe continued, "A good chance to show how manly and virile they are in front of the locals!"

Kerma grunted what may have been a laugh.

"But if I defeat them, then they must dance naked through the streets of South Memphis and any woman who happens to desire a male defeated by a woman can have him—to the cheers of the other local women, I suspect. And Omari—he may want in on the action, too. Let's put a little pressure on my brother archers. They DO love a good competition!"

Djoser thought, *Go straight to their ego, my little archer woman. But you made that offer so easily. An occasional liaison is one thing—even with four at once—but you made this offer so very easily.*

Hetephe continued, "I have made my special friend, Prince Djoser, uneasy. He doesn't know if he wants me to make this challenge or not. It will certainly achieve his desire to bring our two kingdoms closer together. All I know is that a girl has got to do what a girl has got to do, and this girl has got to challenge every archer in the upper kingdom to come on the night of the full moon and try to win the right to plow her on a table in front of everybody!"

Hathor cleared her throat to distract from Hetephe's vulgarity. But still, Hathor owed her a great debt. She said, "It is done, Chief Kerma. Bring one hundred Nubian men and women to Memphis on the full moon. Your men can do whatever it is men do at Hostess House and your women can tour our trading shops. At sunrise, they can all mingle with the locals and witness the rebirth of Osiris as the living sun."

Chief Kerma grunted, "I will consider this thing."

Hathor, having tasted the elixir of total triumph, breathed deeply, and imperially said, "It is not for you to consider, Chief Kerma. The High Priestess of Osiris commands it!"

Kerma stared into the eyes of unblinking, unsmiling, Hathor. A queen and a prince had already capitulated. It was a bitter moment, but Chief Kerma nodded acquiescence. He felt no dishonor in doing so.

Prince Djoser thought, *I am well on my way to what I want, and this is a big step in my getting it—by the grace of two women.*

Prince Djoser praised the wisdom of Chief Kerma and asked, "Great Chief Kerma, may I have your permission to show your favorite son the glories and hidden places of Memphis?"

Kerma responded, "Yes, I would be pleased if Rafah learns all there is to know of Memphis."

I am sure you would, Djoser thought, but said instead to Rafah, "Come with me, Favorite Son Rafah. Let's start with the glory of the Mastaba of Osiris and Isis. You will be impressed by all that you see."

~

That evening, Nephthys found Horus looking out over the river. She joined him and asked, "Did Hathor ask you to do it?"

"No. But she ensured that I understood that it was needed for her to obtain all power over the dead. Everything was in place for the coming sunrise. It was her best chance to succeed. Kerma was observing, and every day Father lived, the power of his story diminished, diminishing her chances of success. Everything was perfect for a coming sunrise ceremony for Hathor to call Osiris to be reborn as the Living Sun—except Osiris still lived. Hathor could not call him from the Land of the Dead if he wasn't dead. Hathor wanted what was best for Osiris. Father wanted death to take him. He had lived too long."

Horus paused, "I understood these things. He was already near death. I helped him. He only twitched twice."

She moved closer to him.

He put his arm around her shoulder and asked, "Mother, how did you live and sleep with Uncle Set and counsel Father and raise me and raise Anubis as Set's son? It must have been difficult for you all these years."

She remained silent as they both looked at the beautiful moon hanging in silence over the great river.

Horus finally, quietly said, "I will find them all. I will understand why they lived—why they died—where they are—the meaning of meaningless. I shall!"

EGYPTIAN GODS: Osiris/Dionysus—Isis/Ariadne/Philyra, Horus, Set/Charon, Nephthys/Dexithea.
CANAANITE GODS: Anath, Astarte, Shalem, Shahar, Moloch, El.
OLYMPIAN GODS: Zeus, Dionysus, Hestia, Ares, Athena, Astraeus, Eos, Hermes.
OCEANIDS: Polydore, Lyris, Acaste, Eidyia, Dione.

3. To Conquer Sinai

The next Quarter-moon came. King Nebka sat in furious silence as General Khasek and Vizier Menka reported their failure to secure peace with the Sinai warlords.

Khasek: "Raids into Kemet are ongoing and growing more frequent."
Menka: "Men had been killed, children and women kidnapped and taken as slaves."
Khasek: "No single warlord can be identified. There are many."
Menka: "Livestock and grains had been taken."
Khasek: "They are now lying and covering for each other, daring us to take action. They have grown bolder and have no respect for the army of Kemet."
Menka: "Action must be taken."
Khasek: "Discipline must be restored and forcefully exercised."

The General continued, "We found and confronted six different warlords. They were indifferent to our demands that all raids into Kemet must cease. One warlord laughed at us and told us not to anger him; that we did not appear to have enough soldiers to fight our way out of his camp."

Queen Nima, Prince Djoser, and Shaman Saqqar sat behind the king listening.

They finished their report and sat in silence as the king considered what he had heard.

Finally, King Nebka said, "Your laughing warlord is correct. Memphis has enough soldiers to protect Memphis, even if Chief Kerma's ambitions grow to the attacking point. But to invade the Sinai and impose my will upon them is not possible. The enemy covers too much territory, is too mobile, and there are too many warlords to conquer. I can only conscript men to reinforce our border Nomes. There is no way that Kemet can conquer all of the warlords in the Sinai. We can only defend our border settlements."

With mounting frustration, the King broke into a coughing spell.

The general, vizier, and shaman waited until the king had recovered then all clucked in agreement. They began discussing a plan to recruit additional volunteers.

Prince Djoser asked General Khasek, "General, could not a hundred archers lay waste to the tribes of the warlords—with no loss of life to the archers?"

Khasek answered, "Yes, prince. But I have less than a dozen good archers. Chief Kerma has untold archers but obtaining any from the chief would be impossible. He needs them to reinforce his southern border with the Kush and he certainly doesn't want his archers available to King Nebka— just in case our relations sour. Training archers takes time, and we have little skill in that area."

Djoser said, "I have a friend, Father. May I pursue this problem with Archer Hetephe?"

The king replied, "One archer, no matter how expert, will not solve our problem, Son. But you may talk to her about our problem if you like."

Djoser asked, "General, would not conquering all of Sinai greatly increase the military power of Kemet?"

Vizier Menka answered for Khasek, "Not only increase our military power but we would have common borders with Canaan, with the Levant, with Mesopotamia, with all of the mature and growing powers in the east. We would become a significant trading power to all—plus we would control the turquoise mines in the Sinai. Shall we conquer the United Cities of Greece while we are at it, Prince?"

Djoser laughed, "No. They are our allies. Our Kingdom is safe as long as we remain allies with Greece. Besides Greece is not raiding our country and taking our people."

King Nebka coughed and said, "Our problem with the Sinai warlords has no solution."

Djoser thought, *Osiris taught me how to solve unsolvable problems. Break it into smaller problems and solve the smaller problems. The insolvable problem will take care of itself.*

He said, "I understand, but it will amuse Hetephe to be consulted."

The three men harumphed Djoser out of their conversations and continued their discussions.

Djoser smiled at his mother and asked, "May we visit, Mother? At Grandfather's Mastaba, perhaps."

EGYPTIAN GODS: Osiris/Dionysus—Isis/Ariadne/Philyra, Horus, Set/Charon, Nephthys/Dexithea.
CANAANITE GODS: Anath, Astarte, Shalem, Shahar, Moloch, El.
OLYMPIAN GODS: Zeus, Dionysus, Hestia, Ares, Athena, Astraeus, Eos, Hermes.
OCEANIDS: Polydore, Lyris, Acaste, Eidyia, Dione.

The queen and the prince excused themselves and walked the long concourse to Chief Kemet's Mastaba. Priest Hotep welcomed his mother and younger brother to the resting place of the mummified remains of Chief Kemet. Djoser walked to his grandfather's remains and bowed his head in silent reference. Finished, he turned to his mother and brother, and said, "Ahh. Perfect. The three of us together; a good time to speak of the unspeakable. Father's cough is not a good thing, Mother. How often does he do that?"

The queen did not want to discuss the king's illness, "He is still young. We do not need to talk of such things!"

Hotep replied, "The king does not wish to discuss his future Mastaba. He says there is ample time before he will need a Mastaba."

Djoser replied, "He is *not* young, Mother. He is old. His cough is not a good thing. We must make plans for his death."

Queen Nima replied, "This conversation has ended. I command you to cease such talk."

They talked on about how good Chief Nebka looked and questioned Djoser on how the Sinai might actually be conquered.

Djoser did not continue the subject of his father's eventual death, which for the sake of his kingdom had best be later than sooner. Djoser did, however, discuss the issue later in great detail with High Priestess Hathor.

~

That night, after leaving Rafah in Anubis's expert care at Hostess House, Djoser met Hetephe on Osiris's Mastaba at the table which had once been claimed by Osiris, himself. The priests, priestesses, and attendants went about their duties working around the two. High Priestess Hathor, herself, had welcomed the two and given her permission to enjoy the evening on her—rather—on Osiris's Mastaba. Hathor commanded that wine be served to her two distinguished guests.

After Hathor had departed and the wine served, Hetephe grew mellow and romantic. "It is so beautiful up here. We can see the moon over the great river and everything. It's such a pleasant evening." Her ankle accidentally brushed against Djoser's leg.

Djoser said, "I am still young and immature, woman."

"True. But you have such a lovely Ibis. I forgive you for your immaturity."

He laughed, "My sweet Hetephe, let us plot to take over the world."

"Oh, I would love to take over the world. What must I do?"

"Archers. I need one hundred Nubian archers—under your command—to wage war against Sanai warlord bandits. How do we do this?"

"Well, my best friend, High Priestess Hathor, who is indebted to me, has commanded one hundred Nubian to come to Hostess House at the next full moon to try to win my affection—my 'intimate' affection—are you jealous—I hope you're jealous—but anyway—just convince Chief Kerma to assign them to my command. There, you have it. What else?"

"Hmmm. I wonder why Chief Kerma would release them from his service?" Djoser paused and asked, "Who does Chief Kerma most fear? Who wants his Chiefdom?"

Hetephe answered, "Chief Kerma? Fear? Absolutely no one. And *everyone* wants his chiefdom. He had two of his older sons killed after they tried to dispose of him. The word in everyone's mouth is that the chief only trusts his two youngest sons because they are young and patient enough to let the chief die of natural causes before either tries to take over. He is grooming them both to be his successor. He says that he will let the stronger be anointed Chief. T'jaru isn't really interested in being chief. He is more interested in invading and taking over Kush. Rafah is infatuated with Memphis and if he becomes chief, he wants to make Nubia more like Memphis."

"And how does my little archer girl know what goes on in the minds of the Chief's sons?"

She giggled. "Oh, I have my ways!"

"Do you have a way to convince Chief Kerma to release a hundred archers to your command?"

She seriously considered the question. "Not a hundred but maybe fifty to T'jaru's command. Chief Kerma believes that he controls T'jaru. Commanding fifty archers would be a good experience for T'jaru."

"A hundred would be better, but fifty is a start. I believe Mother has just developed an overwhelming urge to visit Grandfather Kerma. Would you like to take a trip with us to see King Kerma in Abdju?"

EGYPTIAN GODS: Osiris/Dionysus—Isis/Ariadne/Philyra, Horus, Set/Charon, Nephthys/Dexithea.
CANAANITE GODS: Anath, Astarte, Shalem, Shahar, Moloch, El.
OLYMPIAN GODS: Zeus, Dionysus, Hestia, Ares, Athena, Astraeus, Eos, Hermes.
OCEANIDS: Polydore, Lyris, Acaste, Eidyia, Dione.

She pouted, "Will you be nice to me?"

"I may be young and immature, Archer, but I am not stupid. I value my life. Yes, I will be so nice to you that you will squeal with delight."

"Oh, I love squealing in delight. Let's go to Abdju after you make me squeal a little!"

Sunrise

Djoser watched Hathor's sunrise ceremony. Hathor continued to make incremental improvements each morning. The crowds grew and became trained in their appropriate responses.

Djoser gave his mother and father time to finish *their* sunrise ceremony and then sought an audience with his mother. He joined her for her morning meal and presented his plan to her. He finished with, "I see the big parts of the picture, but I don't know how to fashion the pieces together to present it to Grandfather. I don't know how to make him want to do this thing."

Queen Nima responded, "Let me see if I understand what you want. You want my Father to command fifty of his best archers to Memphis, compete in this little contest of Hetephe's, then follow Hetephe as their commander to a new outpost you are going to build on Middlesea, and, from there, build a highway to Canaan, and, as the opportunity arises, go into the Sinai and kill a lot of warlords for my husband. Yes, Son. I understand how you would not know how to make my father want to do this thing. Tell me. Why *would* Father want to do this thing?"

Tentatively, Djoser suggested, "Well, it would get one of Grandfather's competitor's out of the Upper Kingdom for a long time. The fifty archers would gain invaluable battle experience, and fifty battle-hardened archers would be a formidable force against the Kushites—or Osiris forbid—against the Lower Kingdom if Grandfather got adventuresome. And T'jaru would be tied up in the Sinai until Grandfather was ready to retire with twenty wives. Everyone would be happy."

Nima said, "Oh, I see. This is my father's retirement plan. How nice. And what will my son do if he someday becomes King of Kemet and is faced with an aggressive Upper Kingdom led by fifty battle-hardened archers?"

"Why, if I remember to ask nicely, The-Living-Word-of-Isis will command the archers into *my* service."

Dionysus/Osiris, Ariadne/Isis/Philyra, Charon/Set, Hermes/Tehuti.
EGYPTIANS: Nebka, Djoser, Hotep, Khasek, Rocky
NUBIANS: Nima, Hetephe, King Kerma, Prince T'jaru, Prince Rafah.
CANAANITES: Phoenicia, Serket, Azazil, Jaffa | URFANS: Teumessian, Abram, Sarai, Terah

They laughed, rose, embraced, and set off to do a day's work.

Next Morning

Djoser, Hetephe, and Queen Nima prepared for their departure to Abdju. King Nebka and his senior advisors arrived to hold council. The king asked Djoser, "So you believe you might be able to convince Chief Kerma to release fifty of his archers to my command?"

"Oh no, Father. The fifty archers will be under the command of Major Hetephe—a Nubian acknowledged by all as the greatest archer in the world. But Major Hetephe will be under *my* command—half Nubian and grandson of the chief. And I can't convince the chief of anything. That's why the queen—my mother, your wife, and his daughter—will do the convincing; accompanied by the prestigious Archer Hetephe. And as for reporting to me rather than to General Khasek, I hereby and forever pledge my allegiance to General Khasek's command but don't go touting that to Chief Kerma. Mother intends to insinuate that I will follow her commands, not yours or the general's."

General Khasek said, "If fifty Nubian archers decide to attack Memphis from the east, the bloodshed will be significant."

Djoser bristled, "General Khasek, Major Hetephe has proven her fealty to the concept of truly united kingdoms at every opportunity. Her services in bringing this dream to fruition are as great as yours. General, I will not have her loyalty to the kingdom questioned! Besides, you have trained your army well in their defenses against archers."

Khasek did not back down, "I question the loyalty of fifty Nubian archers led by an ambitious son of an ambitious chief!"

Hetephe broke in, "You are correct to be wary of my countrymen, General Khasek. But they will follow the guidance of Captain T'jaru who is under my command. As long as T'jaru remains loyal, there is no need for concern. It is my responsibility to be aware if his loyalty wavers at any time. I have been trained in observing changes in men plus I intend to handpick the women who accompany the archers as support staff and gossip at every opportunity. I am confident you could terminate any pre-planned insurrection before it began. You may assign one of your trusted advisors to be *my* second-in-command if you feel it necessary."

Vizier Menka said, "My king, this is an ambitious, dangerous plan but the rewards of a successful implementation outweigh the inherent danger. To

EGYPTIAN GODS: Osiris/Dionysus—Isis/Ariadne/Philyra, Horus, Set/Charon, Nephthys/Dexithea.
CANAANITE GODS: Anath, Astarte, Shalem, Shahar, Moloch, El.
OLYMPIAN GODS: Zeus, Dionysus, Hestia, Ares, Athena, Astraeus, Eos, Hermes.
OCEANIDS: Polydore, Lyris, Acaste, Eidyia, Dione.

subjugate the Sinai warlords would be a victory of unimaginable importance. Let them proceed as they will. The general and I will remain unobtrusive, interested observers."

Shaman Saqqar said, "My High Priestess looks with favor on Priest Hotep planning a trade route along the Middlesea shoreline to Canaan. Her requirement is that the story of Isis and Osiris must be told along the way to those who have not yet heard the good news. Priest Hotep intends to name the first outpost 'T'jaru,' assuming Archer T'jaru becomes captain of the Kemet fighting force in the Sinai."

Queen Nima offered, "Naming the outpost 'T'jaru' is a wonderful idea. That will please Father a great deal. But let's refer to a '*Nubian* fighting force,' not a '*Kemet* fighting force.' Naming the United Kingdom 'Kemet' still rankles my father. He considers himself an equal to Chief Kemet, but the United Kingdom is named 'Kemet,' not 'Kerma.' A king's jealousy, I'm afraid."

Djoser thought, *Mother, that is an interesting observation!*

The group talked for a while, then said farewells.

Major Hetephe led her group to the loading area where their chariots, wagons, and attendants waited. Hetephe would command the lead chariot, followed by Queen Nima and Prince Djoser. The entourage would wend through the streets of Memphis and South Memphis.

Djoser had sent word to Set that his delegation wished to stop at the House of Nephthys for the Queen to pay her respects to him and Nephthys for the outstanding work they both do in South Memphis. He thought, *A little spectacle for the people is always good—plus it's always good to feed Set's ego—plus Set will ensure his people line the streets to bow before the Queen and see the queen and the prince pay homage to Set.*

Hetephe solemnly waved to the staff of Hostess House as they passed by. *I need these people on my side when I compete with the Nubian archers. What if one accidentally defeats me? Djoser will be angry with me. He is already angry with me for even making the challenge. Oh, well, anything for my country.*

The streets were lined with residents paying their respects to their Queen and thrilled with the recognition of the high-born waving back at them. Several Hostess House working women were jumping up and down on tables enthusiastically waving to the Queen.

Dionysus/Osiris, Ariadne/Isis/Philyra, Charon/Set, Hermes/Tehuti.
EGYPTIANS: Nebka, Djoser, Hotep, Khasek, Rocky
NUBIANS: Nima, Hetephe, King Kerma, Prince T'jaru, Prince Rafah.
CANAANITES: Phoenicia, Serket, Azazil, Jaffa | URFANS: Teumessian, Abram, Sarai, Terah

The delegation proceeded to the House of Nephthys where the caravan stopped. Set and Nephthys were waiting on the front porch. The Queen was helped from her chariot and waited to greet her two loyal subjects. Djoser got down and stood with the four runners pulling her chariot. Hetephe joined him. Under her breath, she said, "Don't worry, my prince. I am the best there is. I cannot lose."

"Yes, archer woman. You *are* the best there is—at many things."

Set made a production of greeting the queen. Nephthys trailed three steps behind him and did not attempt to usurp the attention and adulation Set was receiving.

Djoser saw Anubis and Horus step from the house onto the front porch. He unobtrusively left the chariots to amble over and speak to the two young men. "Do you want to go on an adventure? We are going to Ogdoad City to visit Tehuti and then on to Abdju to see Chief Kerma. Get your things and join us. It will be great fun."

Horus morosely declined as Anubis excitedly exclaimed, "Yes, we would love to go. Cousin is wallowing in self-pity. This will be an opportunity for him to rejoin the living. I'll get our things." Anubis ran back into the house to pack, leaving Horus alone with Djoser.

Djoser said, "Your father would want you to go. Nephthys will be pleased if you go. I command you to go. You are going."

Horus laughed a bitter laugh, and, with sarcasm, replied, "I would be delighted to accept your gracious invitation—command—whatever."

"Good. Back wagon. Gossip with the attendants. That's where knowledge lives." Djoser turned to leave, hesitated, turned again to face Horus, and said, "Love is hard."

Horus quietly answered, "I know."

With greetings complete and everyone loaded, Major Hetephe began their long journey to Ogdoad City.

EGYPTIAN GODS: Osiris/Dionysus—Isis/Ariadne/Philyra, Horus, Set/Charon, Nephthys/Dexithea.
CANAANITE GODS: Anath, Astarte, Shalem, Shahar, Moloch, El.
OLYMPIAN GODS: Zeus, Dionysus, Hestia, Ares, Athena, Astraeus, Eos, Hermes.
OCEANIDS: Polydore, Lyris, Acaste, Eidyia, Dione.

4. Nubian Archers

Year 150, first month

The runner promptly delivered the Queen's message to Seshat in Ogdoad Town. Seshat had a full day to prepare her husband and the town for an official visit from their queen. As sophisticated as the citizens were compared to most cities outside of Memphis, the opportunities for excitement and pageantry were few. They were now beside themselves with excitement. A visit from the Queen coming so soon after the good news of the resurrection of Osiris overloaded their senses. Even Lord Tehuti, himself, as worldly, well-traveled, and sophisticated as he was, felt the stir of excitement.

There was to be a welcoming pageant—drummers, dancers, flags, singers, children in costumes, and all manner of entertainment. After the Queen met her loyal subjects, Lord Tehuti and Seshat would host a feast. A wonderful time was planned.

The children on the lookout for the caravan saw it coming down the highway and ran to tell the waiting citizens of Ogdoad Town. Hetephe saw the children depart and said to Djoser, who was riding in her chariot, "They know we are approaching, let's prepare for our reception."

The caravan stopped for the occupants to relieve themselves, put on proper dress, and return to their proper chariots and wagons. Major Hetephe donned her full Nubian Archer dress complete with a full-sized bow and arrows. The Queen donned her royal robe and placed her crown on her head. The prince, with much disgust, donned his official princely robe. Horus and Anubis looked at one another and shrugged.

Major Hetephe turned, looked at her caravan, and finding everything to her liking, commanded the chariot and wagon runners, "On to Ogdoad Town!" Although their entry into the city was festive, noisy, and exceedingly exciting, only two people fainted.

The receptions, speeches, entertainment, and introductions were flawless. The dignitaries finally retired to Lord Tehuti's house for their banquet.

Tehuti sat at the head of the long table with Queen Nima on the other end. The prince, Archer Hetephe, the queen's handmaidens, and the Ogdoad sat on either side. Each Ogdoad had been allowed to invite townspeople of their liking. The excited invitees sat quietly at a side table,

Dionysus/Osiris, Ariadne/Isis/Philyra, Charon/Set, Hermes/Tehuti.
EGYPTIANS: Nebka, Djoser, Hotep, Khasek, Rocky
NUBIANS: Nima, Hetephe, King Kerma, Prince T'jaru, Prince Rafah.
CANAANITES: Phoenicia, Serket, Azazil, Jaffa | URFANS: Teumessian, Abram, Sarai, Terah

overwhelmed with their great fortune to be invited. Horus and Anubis had each invited a young townswoman of their choosing to be their guest at the feast. The four had their own side table. Many citizens sat outside, with children in their laps, enraptured with the laughter and learned discussions coming from inside the home.

The queen praised Lord Tehuti and Ogdoad Town. Tehuti praised the King and Queen. Everyone at the head table praised everyone. The guests listened to all the praise in raptured silence. Anubis quietly interjected witty comments on the proceedings to his invited guest, an extremely attractive, full-bodied young woman. She hoped her smiles and laughter were appropriate for his comments, but she was far more concerned about not fainting, not wetting herself, and keeping her heart from exploding. Horus's companion, much more serious and detecting his sullen attitude toward the festivities, reached over, squeezed his hand, and smiled a sad little smile for him.

The feast ended and everyone retired to Tehuti's receiving room to mingle, chat, and drink. The queen's two handmaidens expertly stood on either side of the queen and discreetly controlled who chatted with her and for how long. Djoser and Hetephe charmed everyone they spoke with. Anubis and Horus retired with their guests to talk quietly in a corner.

Tehuti was excited. He told his guests, "I knew the gods would live forever! Osiris proves it beyond doubt! Him being called back from the dead every morning and all, to visit his admirers. I can hardly wait for my turn! Good old Dad, Zeus, is already up there in the sky. Everybody loves the sky, just like they love Dad. And Uncle Poseidon is living in the Ocean—everybody loves the Ocean—and Cousin Persephone painting the flowers and bringing up the crops and everything! It's all wonderful!"

Seshat said to Tehuti, "Dear, I believe Hathor invented that story about calling forth Osiris each morning. She needed power to subjugate Shaman Saqqara to her will. The story of Osiris and Isis, and of calling Osiris from the dead each morning, and him becoming the Living Sun were just convenient stories she thought the people might accept as truth and make her Gatekeeper to the Truth. She took a few kernels of truth and wove an elaborate hoax."

Tehuti shouted, "Don't be stupid, woman! High Priestess Hathor says it's the truth and a High Priestess knows about these things! And what about

EGYPTIAN GODS: Osiris/Dionysus—Isis/Ariadne/Philyra, Horus, Set/Charon, Nephthys/Dexithea.
CANAANITE GODS: Anath, Astarte, Shalem, Shahar, Moloch, El.
OLYMPIAN GODS: Zeus, Dionysus, Hestia, Ares, Athena, Astraeus, Eos, Hermes.
OCEANIDS: Polydore, Lyris, Acaste, Eidyia, Dione.

all of her Priests and Priestesses already waiting on Chief Kemet to return from the land of the dead? My friend Osiris just beat him to it!"

Prince Djoser interrupted, "Hmmph, Lady Seshat. Let's leave the discussion of religious details for another time. We have many citizens listening to our every word, and we don't want to confuse the issues with competing theological concepts."

Seshat knew she was being reprimanded and glanced at her stern-faced queen for further instructions. *They both want me to tell my people falsehoods. To let them believe this fantasy Hathor has created. How can this be? For leaders to let their people believe that fantasies are real.*

She responded, "Of course, my Prince."

Tehuti was elated the prince had backed him up, and continued, "Everybody knows that *something* has got to cause the sun to rise and the wind to blow and the tide to come in and the crops to grow! This explains everything! The gods cause everything outside *our* control. How can anyone *not* believe in the greatness and the power of the gods?"

Seshat frantically searched the eyes of her guests looking for anyone who appeared to know the truth. She found the gaze of Horus locked onto her. He nodded to her in recognition but held his finger to his lips to command her to remain silent.

Tehuti talked on. Repeating the stories again. Everyone listened and were comforted in knowing there were things greater than themselves.

Anubis and his guest retired to the riverbank to discuss things of great importance and for a closer inspection of the woman's body.

Horus invited his guest and Seshat to join him on the front porch to talk of cabbages and kings. Horus told them, "Kings must provide their people with the things their subjects need. Most people need gods more than they need food. People like Uncle Set, however, prefer a well-garnished cabbage. It is not for us to judge their needs."

Delightful conversations filled all of Ogdoad Town throughout the night and early into the morning.

The delegation rose late the next morning and visited with the powerful and leading citizens of Ogdoad Town. Prince Djoser played his people well, solidifying his concept of the upper and lower kingdoms being one unified people with common goals. "Osiris watches over *all* the people—he does not care about where you live, now does he?"

Tehuti proclaimed he and Seshat would most certainly attend the next possible ceremony calling forth the rebirth of his old friend and fellow god. Archer Hetephe explained that the ceremonies immediately after a full moon were generally the most elaborate, exciting, and well-attended. She told Tehuti, "You should plan on attending the next one! Plus, there will be an archery competition the night before at Hostess House that you will enjoy!" *Especially if some male accidentally defeats me!*

The caravan set off for Abdju after Highsun leaving behind an excited and even more faithful Ogdoad Town.

EGYPTIAN GODS: Osiris/Dionysus—Isis/Ariadne/Philyra, Horus, Set/Charon, Nephthys/Dexithea.
CANAANITE GODS: Anath, Astarte, Shalem, Shahar, Moloch, El.
OLYMPIAN GODS: Zeus, Dionysus, Hestia, Ares, Athena, Astraeus, Eos, Hermes.
OCEANIDS: Polydore, Lyris, Acaste, Eidyia, Dione.

5. Chief Kerma and the Gods

Chief Kerma and his city were sophisticated even by Memphis standards. Their culture was more nature-oriented than their neighbors in the north but their management and organizational skills, concern for the well-being and education of their people, and ability to feed and protect the citizenry were second to none. Their arts and cultural rituals competed with the Greeks. They prepared for the upcoming visit of state and prepared to greet their visitors—and political leaders—with pomp, ceremony, and a demonstration of the glory of the upper kingdom.

Queen Nima's caravan arrived. The people were extremely respectful and put forth their best effort and best face; plus they knew how to put on a show!

Neither the leadership nor the citizens had the puppy-like craving for affection from their betters that the citizens of Ogdoad Town did. Chief Kerma was chief because he maintained complex and realistic views and opinions about his kingdom and the world around him. *State visit? What do they want now? What can I get from them?*

Chief Kerma officially greeted Queen Nima with a large bear-hug. Nima was the principal reason the Chief did not declare war on the lower kingdom to add to his own lands. As long as Nima lived, the lower kingdom was safe. If she were to die, then new calculations would be made.

Prince Djoser waited his turn to greet the Chief. Djoser reinforced his kinship with the chief at every opportunity. Djoser's great fear was that the upper kingdom would not accept him if he ever became king.

After greeting his daughter, Chief Kerma turned his attention to the next dignitary, Prince Djoser. Kerma gave Djoser a half-hearted embrace. *My grandson continues to mature. He is only half Nubian, but my blood gives him great stature. He may not make the worthy ruler my strongest son would make, but I will wait and see.*

Djoser accepted—and noted—the lukewarm embrace, took the chief's shoulders, pushed him back with affection, stared into the chief's eyes, and warmly said, "My grandfather looks more powerful each time I see him. I dedicate my days attempting to become the man you are!" *Give Mother the fifty archers she will request, Grandfather. It is far more important than even she realizes. And she is a better ruler than you.*

Dionysus/Osiris, Ariadne/Isis/Philyra, Charon/Set, Hermes/Tehuti.
EGYPTIANS: Nebka, Djoser, Hotep, Khasek, Rocky
NUBIANS: Nima, Hetephe, King Kerma, Prince T'jaru, Prince Rafah.
CANAANITES: Phoenicia, Serket, Azazil, Jaffa | URFANS: Teumessian, Abram, Sarai, Terah

The rest of the day was spent with official speeches, festivities, and posturing. At some point, Queen Nima casually asked Chief Kerma to discuss some possible opportunities for the both of them at his morning meal. "Perhaps your son T'jaru and Archer Hetephe might be invited to join us."

Negotiations had begun.

Sunrise

Kerma's favorite five wives oversaw the preparation of the morning meal. The hog had been turning on the spit throughout the night. Honey, roots, fruits, nuts, herbs, and other garnishments were prepared with loving care. The chief lounged on his stack of animal pelts. His two youngest sons plus his five main advisors and support staff sat beside him waiting for an opportunity to be of service.

A young woman, partially clothed in a pure white sarong, met Queen Nima and her party at the entrance to the Chief's compound and led them to Chief Kerma. The woman constantly monitored the prince to ascertain if the prince showed any interest in her possible personal attention. Queen Nima sat across from her father. Djoser and Hetephe sat behind the queen, support staff stood behind them.

Nima began, "Good morning, Great Chief Kerma. Your hospitality is as great as your majesty. You are a wise and powerful ruler of your land."

"Greetings, Wise Queen Nima. We ate together and visited with the High Priestess after her Ceremony of calling Osiris to be reborn as the Living Sun. That was less than a season ago. So, will my wise daughter be direct and tell me what she wishes, or shall we play games with words until I decipher what she comes for?"

Nima laughed and replied, "Father, can not a daughter wish to enjoy the company of her illustrious father."

Djoser abruptly interrupted by saying, "Great Chief Kerma, may I speak to you directly and without fear?"

Kerma angrily responded, "Ask your mother, boy!"

Djoser did not lower his gaze and replied, "I ask the great Chief Kerma."

Kerma glanced at his daughter and thought, *Daughter, I may have your disrespectful son flogged to his death.*

EGYPTIAN GODS: Osiris/Dionysus—Isis/Ariadne/Philyra, Horus, Set/Charon, Nephthys/Dexithea.
CANAANITE GODS: Anath, Astarte, Shalem, Shahar, Moloch, El.
OLYMPIAN GODS: Zeus, Dionysus, Hestia, Ares, Athena, Astraeus, Eos, Hermes.
OCEANIDS: Polydore, Lyris, Acaste, Eidyia, Dione.

But he asked, "What says my daughter?"

Nima replied, "I commanded my son to speak for me when he is full well sure what needs to be said. He is direct and straightforward as are you."

Kerma glared at Djoser and said, "Speak!"

Djoser spoke. "Queen Nima comes to beg Chief Kerma for the allegiance of her youngest brother, T'jaru, into my service. I wish to spare her this humiliation by asking you directly myself. If you look upon the request with disfavor, then look upon me, not your beloved daughter." He stopped and waited for the Chief's response.

Kerma was confused and taken aback. Unsure of their motives, he temporized, and said, "I see. And why would she want this and why should I release my youngest son into your service?"

"She asks because I, Prince Djoser of the United Kingdoms, need his service. I *must* have his service because there is no one in either kingdom capable of accomplishing what must be done other than your son T'jaru."

Kerma snapped, "You talk in riddles, boy. Say it plain!"

Djoser snapped back, "The Upper Kingdom is constantly besieged by bandits and raiders from the Sinai. King Nebka has ample army to turn back a mass invasion, but he has no strength to eliminate ghosts in the night, raiders that pillage and vanish. My king has charged me with eliminating this scourge. It MUST be eliminated for the glory of the United Kingdom. I turned for advice from the finest archer the Nubian people have ever produced. You know her well—my advisor, Archer Hetephe. She laughed at my questions and said, 'That is simple enough. Bring me a great Nubian warrior with fifty archers. We will clear the Sinai of this vermin so that you may add it to the lands of Kemet. But my condition is this, the name of my kingdom must be changed. The name Kemet is distasteful in my mouth. After the glorious Nubian victory, the name of the united kingdom will be proclaimed, 'Egypt' in honor of the fertile soil given to us all by the great river from the Upper Kingdom.' "

Djoser paused, then continued, "Archer Hetephe will command all forces in the Sinai. I believe she can do what she says she can do." Djoser watched carefully as Kerma's pupils dilated with the name change demand. *You are hooked, Grandfather. Can Mother and Hetephe reel you in?*

Dionysus/Osiris, Ariadne/Isis/Philyra, Charon/Set, Hermes/Tehuti.
EGYPTIANS: Nebka, Djoser, Hotep, Khasek, Rocky
NUBIANS: Nima, Hetephe, King Kerma, Prince T'jaru, Prince Rafah.
CANAANITES: Phoenicia, Serket, Azazil, Jaffa | URFANS: Teumessian, Abram, Sarai, Terah

Djoser ended with, "Mother comes to beg. Major Hetephe comes to reason. I come to command!" *There we have it. I am committed. Does my insolence impress or infuriate you, Grandfather? I will know soon enough.*

The chief's nostrils flared. *COMMAND?!! Fifty archers? T'jaru? Why you little arrogant disrespectful ... I have now been commanded both by a Memphis Priestess and Nebka's son. I will kill you all!!*

Nima smoothly slipped in, saying, "My brazen son is not yet as accomplished as his grandfather with his words, Father. You taught him to speak his mind and to speak it plain. Forgive him for his poor choice of words. He is still young. May you and I walk together and talk privately—the daughter needs her beloved, wise father's counsel. Perhaps, Major Hetephe could join us and talk of the advantages that my father would gain from this plan."

Kerma stared into the unwavering eyes of the arrogant prince—deciding. *He challenges me in front of my advisors—should I kill him now or wait?—He IS my grandson—he DOES have a kingly bearing—He does not show fear.*

Kerma turned to his daughter and said, "I will leave the boy here and have him counseled in matters of respect. You may try to convince me of the merit of this ridiculous proposal! Let the girl come with us."

The chief rose and left with his daughter, who was all smiles and femininity, and with the archer, who was all business and reason.

Nima gave her best arguments.

"T'jaru is said to be ambitious. Perhaps too ambitious."
"You could rest easier knowing he is far away."
"He would gain invaluable experience for the future when you can make use of such experienced warriors."
"The timing of his return is whatever you wish it to be—sooner—later—whatever best serves you."
"Would you approve of the name 'Egypt' for the new land the Nubian archers will create?"
"You must approve of the new name—even command it. It would be a condition of service."
"T'jaru's victory would bring glory to all Nubians; to all Egypt!"
"A conquering T'jaru would bring glory to your name if you decided to retire and name him as your successor."
"How many wives and children and grandchildren and great-

EGYPTIAN GODS: Osiris/Dionysus—Isis/Ariadne/Philyra, Horus, Set/Charon, Nephthys/Dexithea.
CANAANITE GODS: Anath, Astarte, Shalem, Shahar, Moloch, El.
OLYMPIAN GODS: Zeus, Dionysus, Hestia, Ares, Athena, Astraeus, Eos, Hermes.
OCEANIDS: Polydore, Lyris, Acaste, Eidyia, Dione.

grandchildren do you have, now? Can you count them all?"
"Nubians are already an integral part of the Ceremony calling forth Osiris each morning. This would greatly increase Nubian influence and power in the lower kingdom."

Major Hetephe gave her best argument. "T'jaru will be under my command. I am under the command of my half-Nubian prince. That is the total chain of command. You already suspect that Djoser's allegiance is to his mother, not his father. It is Queen Nima that the prince goes to when he needs something done—like they are doing now. Great Chief Kerma, this will be a Nubian project. All the land of Egypt will know this. The Nubians will conquer Sinai for the glory of the new Egypt."

Nima said, "Please, Father. Consider this proposal. If not for your own glory, then for the glory of Egypt. If not that, then for the day when you decide to invade the land to your south with your battle-hardened archers and take the land as your own." She added, almost under her breath, "Or the land to your north."

Kerma glanced toward the two women. Archer Hetephe made no recognition of her queen's comments.

The chief walked with the women back to his quarters in non-committal silence.

That evening, young Nubian women danced vigorously for the pleasure of their chief, their distinguished visitors, and any Nubian man who might appreciate the art of the dance. The drummers drummed, the chanters chanted, the dancers danced.

Anubis watched one of the particularly attractive dancers that he had taken up with. She seemed to be dancing only for him.

Horus had taken up with the Shamans who were interested in the forces of nature beyond the knowledge of men. They were intensely interested in this new concept in the north concerning Osiris and a high priestess and the sun being a living thing. And a person sat with them with first-hand knowledge of this phenomenon and with a direct connection to the high priestess and the remains of Osiris in his Mastaba. Yes, they would be delighted to accept Horus's invitation to attend the upcoming post-full-moon sunrise ceremony and be introduced to this circle of power overseeing the dead. Their respect for Horus, although not even a Nubian, grew quickly.

Dionysus/Osiris, Ariadne/Isis/Philyra, Charon/Set, Hermes/Tehuti.
EGYPTIANS: Nebka, Djoser, Hotep, Khasek, Rocky
NUBIANS: Nima, Hetephe, King Kerma, Prince T'jaru, Prince Rafah.
CANAANITES: Phoenicia, Serket, Azazil, Jaffa | URFANS: Teumessian, Abram, Sarai, Terah

No mention of the Chief's conversations was made during the next day of festivities.

But an impromptu Archery Competition was arranged. Hetephe quickly picked out who would be the most accomplished archers, among them was her old friend Archer T'jaru. She made sure they all knew of her challenge to be held at Hostess House under the next full moon. "Defeat me and have me on a table in front of everybody!" She knew that it was the "on a table in front of everybody" that excited them. It wasn't her they wanted, it was the recognition of the conquest of an opponent with the resulting accolades and cheers of those that had lost—and as punishment to she who had dared dare them! Three archers shot excellent rounds. It took all of Hetephe's skill to lose to them. She flashed each a smile and asked, "Will you be competing for me at Hostess House?" The loss served two purposes; they would be overconfident, and their mind would be on her and not their archery when they competed. Whatever small chance they had for victory was now compromised.

She did not, however, lose to T'jaru. He shot an almost perfect round, but she could not be subservient to the man she hoped to be commanding. *He is a worthy competitor who on a good day might defeat me. But not today.*

She shot a perfect round. *I must command your total respect. Osiris help us all if you compete and defeat me.*

She tensed when he said, "I had not planned on competing at Hostess House, but perhaps I will. I believe that I can best you and I know full well that I will enjoy my prize."

That evening, the Shamans petitioned Chief Kerma for permission to travel to this sunrise Ceremony in Memphis. The story of Isis and Osiris was in the mouth of all Nubians. This story, in many ways, challenged the teachings of the shamans. There would be new knowledge to be acquired that the Shamans must understand and apply.

King Kerma questioned his Shamans about the entire Osiris stories. "Maybe Osiris is called from the dead, maybe not. It sounds to me like a convenient story for that Hathor woman to control the people. Can men really return from the dead? What about this 'God' business? What powers would such a person have, anyway?"

After the chief finally ceased his uninterrupted interrogation, the Chief Shaman cleared his throat and spoke. "Our chief asks the very questions

EGYPTIAN GODS: Osiris/Dionysus—Isis/Ariadne/Philyra, Horus, Set/Charon, Nephthys/Dexithea.
CANAANITE GODS: Anath, Astarte, Shalem, Shahar, Moloch, El.
OLYMPIAN GODS: Zeus, Dionysus, Hestia, Ares, Athena, Astraeus, Eos, Hermes.
OCEANIDS: Polydore, Lyris, Acaste, Eidyia, Dione.

we Shamans ask. We gather what knowledge we may wherever we can. What little we know comes from the knowledge that there are forces greater than ourselves. Every man who has felt the grandeur of a magnificent sunrise on the great savannahs full of antelope and their predators knows this. Whether these forces are spirits or gods or something else is unknown."

The oldest Shaman offered, "One of my wives tells the story of old man Babu who lived alone in their village when she was a child. Babu's father had been a mean man shunned by most of his tribe. After the man died, Babu would often stand up and dance an uncontrollable dance loudly saying unknown words. He would then fall foaming at the mouth and pass into unconsciousness. In the beginning, the Shaman thought that an evil spirit from the darkness fell upon Babu and that Babu wrestled the evil spirit. But then they thought perhaps it was Babu's mean father trying to return to life by taking over Babu's body. The people feared Babu, but Babu never brought harm to anyone. Whatever the cause did not return after Babu died."

Kerma said, "Was his chief a good chief? Did the chief punish those who needed punishment? Maybe Babu was being punished for taking advantage of others because his chief didn't punish him. Was Babu a good man?"

The shaman asked, "The chief was a good chief but who would punish a man if the chief didn't?"

Kerma considered and answered, "A spirit—an especially strong spirit— a spirit strong enough to be a god!"

The Shamans considered their chief's suggestion.

The chief Shaman quietly offered, "A spirit such as Osiris summoned from the Land of the Dead."

The men sat in silence considering that which had been proposed and all of its many implications.

Kerma added, "Kings have too many in their tribe to properly punish. They cannot possibly judge who needs punishment and what that punishment should be. Someone or something must punish these people. Perhaps it is a spirit or a god."

Murmurs of agreement rippled through the council.

Dionysus/Osiris, Ariadne/Isis/Philyra, Charon/Set, Hermes/Tehuti.
EGYPTIANS: Nebka, Djoser, Hotep, Khasek, Rocky
NUBIANS: Nima, Hetephe, King Kerma, Prince T'jaru, Prince Rafah.
CANAANITES: Phoenicia, Serket, Azazil, Jaffa | URFANS: Teumessian, Abram, Sarai, Terah

Chief Kerma walked to look out over the river before sunrise. *The Ceremony to call Osiris from the dead* **was** *impressive. My Nubian drummers and Chanters made it so. I felt a greater power than myself and all those gathered put together. It must have been the spirit of Osiris entering into me. Are you a wise and just spirit Osiris? A god? Will you punish those who need punishment and reward those worthy of reward? I have no control over you, but you may have control over me. Will you make me stronger? Weaker? Wiser? Even if I conquered the Lower Kingdom, it would be too many people for me to properly govern. Even now, my people are more than I can properly govern. Would you help me govern, Osiris? And what other spirits are there? And what other gods? Where lies the wisdom in this thing, Osiris? Help me find the wisdom.*

During the morning meal, Chief Kerma called his youngest son, T'jaru, to stand before those gathered together. The king said to T'jaru, "You are a worthy son. I give you a quest to bring glory to all Nubians. Return victorious from this quest and I shall name you chief of all Nubians, even over Rafah. If you are not victorious, then do not return! From this moment until the moment you are declared victorious, I command you into the service of Archer Hetephe. She is the Major warrior in the army of Prince Djoser. With you and fifty Nubian archers, she will rid the land of Sinai of thieves and murderers, from the unwise and unjust. Select fifty archers of your choosing. Are my orders clear?"

T'jaru was completely taken by surprise, but he knew not to stammer or appear confused. "My chief's orders are clear and wise. Major Hetephe is the greatest archer among us. I am privileged to serve under her command. I await my orders." He struck his heart with his fist and then turned to face Hetephe, who had just risen to her feet when Chief Kerma had said her name. T'jaru again struck his chest as a sign of respect and subservience.

Major Hetephe responded, in kind. *We have begun!*

Prince Djoser stood, bowed from the waist to Kerma, and said, "May I someday have the wisdom of the great Chief Kerma and the courage and leadership of the great Nubian Archer T'jaru." He asked the chief, "May I retire to my quarters and reflect upon the majesty of this day?"

Chief Kerma nodded permission. *All right, boy. Let time tell me the better man—you or T'jaru.*

EGYPTIAN GODS: Osiris/Dionysus—Isis/Ariadne/Philyra, Horus, Set/Charon, Nephthys/Dexithea.
CANAANITE GODS: Anath, Astarte, Shalem, Shahar, Moloch, El.
OLYMPIAN GODS: Zeus, Dionysus, Hestia, Ares, Athena, Astraeus, Eos, Hermes.
OCEANIDS: Polydore, Lyris, Acaste, Eidyia, Dione.

Queen Nima and her caravan departed from Abdju after Highsun. The caravan was followed on foot by Major Hetephe, Captain T'jaru, and fifty archers. Prince Djoser commanded the lead chariot. Beside him sat Anubis and Horus. Djoser and Anubis discussed the eventful trip to Abdju. Horus was silent; his mind filled with the deep discussions he had had with the Shamans late the night before.

Dionysus/Osiris, Ariadne/Isis/Philyra, Charon/Set, Hermes/Tehuti.
EGYPTIANS: Nebka, Djoser, Hotep, Khasek, Rocky
NUBIANS: Nima, Hetephe, King Kerma, Prince T'jaru, Prince Rafah.
CANAANITES: Phoenicia, Serket, Azazil, Jaffa | URFANS: Teumessian, Abram, Sarai, Terah

6. The Sinai

Hostess House Archer Competition
Year 150, first month, second week

Hotep had assumed his queen and prince would have success at Abdju. When they returned to Memphis, he and his son, Snefru, had quickly scouted the area near Middlesea and selected a campsite at the country's border to begin the road across the Sinai and on into Canaan.

This campsite would become a trade center and house all support staff. The support staff would be mostly volunteer women interested in such things and all it entailed. The road would be extended with the next camp being built one day's march from the last site. The base of Major Hetephe's operations would be moved to the second site after the archers had swept southward through the Sinai and neutralized the outlaw tribes and warlords. Captive children, women, and surviving men would be returned to the detention camp being built to the south of South Memphis. From this camp, interested Nomarchs could select immigrants for integration into their Nomarchy. Hotep estimated it would take two seasons to build the two camps and the road connecting them and he estimated that a total of twelve camps would be necessary on the trade route from Kemet to Canaan.

The project would take a minimum of two years to complete. When completed, the Kingdom of Kemet would establish a lucrative trade route to the Canaan cities in the east, eliminate the warlords from the Sinai, establish new towns along the way, gain two lucrative turquoise mines, plus add land to the Kingdom of Kemet. All that was needed was for Major Hetephe to do what Major Hetephe had told Prince Djoser she would do.

But first, there was a matter of Nubian Night at Hostess House and an archery competition. Without mention from Major Hetephe, Captain T'jaru forbade any of his men to participate in the competition. But Hetephe carried through with her promise of a competition. T'jaru and his men sat at their tables laughing and cajoling their brother archers. "Come on! Can't any of you men best this woman? We want to see you on top of her on that table! Come on!"

Hetephe was relieved that T'jaru and his men were not competing and that Djoser had not come. After it was over, and all the competitors were

EGYPTIAN GODS: Osiris/Dionysus—Isis/Ariadne/Philyra, Horus, Set/Charon, Nephthys/Dexithea.
CANAANITE GODS: Anath, Astarte, Shalem, Shahar, Moloch, El.
OLYMPIAN GODS: Zeus, Dionysus, Hestia, Ares, Athena, Astraeus, Eos, Hermes.
OCEANIDS: Polydore, Lyris, Acaste, Eidyia, Dione.

bested, Major Hetephe joined her command for a beer. She said, "Thank you gentlemen for not competing. I would have been so nervous, at least one of you would have defeated me."

Captain T'jaru responded, "I know."

Shortly thereafter, Prince Djoser and an exceedingly beautiful woman arrived by chariot. Djoser escorted the woman to Hostess Ba't at the Reception Desk and talked to Ba't for a while. The beautiful woman saw Hetephe seated at the archer's table, smiled, and gave her a small wave."

T'jaru saw the exchange and asked, "Who is that woman with the prince?"

Hetephe answered, "That's Red-Ribboned Woman Anath from the House of Ishtar. She is a favorite of the very rich men of Memphis. Maybe I should introduce you."

T'jaru did not respond but continued to stare at Anath.

After Djoser finished talking, Ba't turned and announced to her patrons, "Attention all you virile men out there! It has been brought to my attention that even though this is one of the biggest crowds Hostess House has ever had—Thank all of you handsome, virile Nubians—very few of our patrons have visited the House of Ishtar this evening. Ishtar is most upset! She had her daughters and their Class One, Two, and Three assistants prepared for a big night, tonight! The prince has considered this problem and tells me that most of our out-of-town guests are not familiar with the House of Ishtar and its services. As a public service, we are asking Red-Ribboned Woman Anath to describe what delights can be found there." Ba't extended her hand toward her older sister and said to her patrons, "Gentlemen, I introduce the lovely Anath!"

There was scattered applause from the locals. The Nubians were at a loss as to what was going on.

Anath began her presentation. The Nubians understood enough Northern Common to follow her conversation, but what she said hardly mattered. Her voice was liquid sex, promising delights from deep inside your mind, fantasies realized, warmth, understanding, oils, an overload of all of your senses. "For only a small gift, all of this can be yours—the expected value of the gift for each class of woman is posted at the entrance to the Men's Room. You will see that Class Three Assistants are quite reasonable. I and my sisters have retired for the evening, but our many assistants are still on duty and would favor the pleasure of your company this evening. Ask your Server if you have any questions. Good night, gentlemen. It was my delight to talk with you."

The prince escorted Anath back to the waiting chariot as the Nubians chattered away about what they had just heard.

After seeing Anath off, Djoser ambled to Hetephe's table and casually asked, "How many bested you?

Hetephe caustically replied, "All of them!"

The archers chuckled at Hetephe's insolence toward their Commander.

Djoser asked, "May I join you and your men, Major?"

Hetephe stood at attention and said, "Prince Djoser, it would be an honor if you joined your fighting men for a round of beer!"

The prince nodded and said, "At ease, Major. It will be my privilege to drink with the finest fighting force in the world!"

As one round became another and then another, T'jaru casually mentioned to Djoser, "That was an exceedingly desirable woman you entered with."

Djoser replied, "Anath is an exceedingly intelligent, accomplished woman. For your information, she asked me the name of the handsome man sitting next to Major Hetephe. And out of curiosity, how many archers did the major *actually* lose to in the competition?"

The bonding of warriors continued into the night.

Elsewhere, women shopped in the South Memphis trading houses, and Shamans were lost in deep discussions with Saqqar and his staff concerning life, death, resurrection, and the Land of the Dead.

Sunrise

High Priestess Hathor raised her arms to the horizon. Osiris came.

The Nubian Shamans were guests of Horus and Shaman Saqqar and had excellent viewing of the Ceremony. The Nubian Archers, as well as Rafah, were guests of Prince Djoser and, too, had excellent viewing. As a matter of fact, all visiting Nubians had excellent viewing locations as guests of King Nebka of the United Kingdom.

EGYPTIAN GODS: Osiris/Dionysus—Isis/Ariadne/Philyra, Horus, Set/Charon, Nephthys/Dexithea.
CANAANITE GODS: Anath, Astarte, Shalem, Shahar, Moloch, El.
OLYMPIAN GODS: Zeus, Dionysus, Hestia, Ares, Athena, Astraeus, Eos, Hermes.
OCEANIDS: Polydore, Lyris, Acaste, Eidyia, Dione.

High Priestess Hathor had ensured that this would be a memorable ceremony. Her Nubian drummers and announcers would be on special display for the glory of the Nubian people. They did not disappoint. The crowd was mesmerized. Five women fainted from excitement. Even the Nubians were carried away with the pageantry and the summoning of Osiris from the Land of the Dead. One could almost believe that rising before them was the rebirth of Osiris as Ra—the Living Sun.

Horus, as always, watched from beside the river sipping red wine.

After the Ceremony was complete, Djoser hosted a morning meal at the Mastaba of Osiris for Major Hetephe, Captain T'jaru, and their fifty archers. Djoser, Hetephe, Hathor, and Hotep had held intense discussions with King Nebka and his advisors on the image and perception they wished to project to the Nubians during this campaign. Truth must always be told or, at least, no outright lies should be told. The truth was simply this: They fought to create the land of Egypt! Egypt—a powerful nation that would incorporate the Upper Kingdom, Lower Kingdom, the Sinai, and someday the land of Kush. Egypt would be the most powerful trading and military nation other than Greece, itself. Egypt would be the "Home of the Gods."

The Nubian priestesses that had once been Lord Tehuti's handmaidens were charged with infatuating the archers—of ensuring the archers felt as if this were a Nubian conquest—of reinforcing the idea that the upper kingdom would be an integral part of the upper kingdom because of their triumphs—their victories. "Glory to the Nubians! Glory to Egypt!"

Djoser, Hotep, Hetephe, and T'jaru retired to Osiris's table to discuss plans for the war road and the forts. Rafah and Horus listened in. Noticeably absent were General Khasek and Vizier Menka—a strong statement that this would be a Nubian operation. Something of which Chief Kerma's son, Rafah, took silent notice.

Prince Djoser began, "Priest Hotep is in charge of building the war road and twelve outposts, complete with wells for drinking water, across the top of the Sinai ending at Canaan. He plans on completing a new fort with a connecting road every two seasons."

Priest Hotep said, "The first camp is the most important. It will be the point of our entrance from Egypt-to-be, across the Sinai, and into Canaan. The road will be our primary base of operations."

Dionysus/Osiris, Ariadne/Isis/Philyra, Charon/Set, Hermes/Tehuti.
EGYPTIANS: Nebka, Djoser, Hotep, Khasek, Rocky
NUBIANS: Nima, Hetephe, King Kerma, Prince T'jaru, Prince Rafah.
CANAANITES: Phoenicia, Serket, Azazil, Jaffa | URFANS: Teumessian, Abram, Sarai, Terah

Hotep nonchalantly added, "I will name the first camp Fort T'jaru. It will take time to grow into a proper city but by the time your conquest is complete, it should be a bustling trading and population center." Prince Djoser gave Major Hetephe naming rights for each of the remaining eleven forts.

Major Hetephe continued, "We have at least two seasons to complete our sweep to the south and return with our prisoners. What we do with the bodies of the dead warlords is our decision—return them—burn them—put them on display—whatever best suits our needs. Fort T'jaru will be completed by the time our Expedition is complete. We will return our captives there, then rest and regroup. Women, children, and men who are not seen to be a threat will be integrated into Nomarchies. Those dangerous or deemed to be a threat will be executed or imprisoned."

Discussions and planning continued into the morning and afternoon.

As they rose to leave, Djoser wondered, *Would you be pleased, old friend, that your table is once more the center of intrigue?*

The First Expedition
Year 150, second month

The day came the cry went out "Glory to Egypt!" and the First Sinai Expedition set off from the planned location for Fort T'jaru into the Sinai.

The Expedition consisted of fifty archers, a dozen wagons filled with supplies pulled by oxen and strong men, women skilled in treating the wounded, cooks, Anubis, and Horus. It was led by Captain T'jaru and commanded by Major Hetephe.

Prince Djoser, Queen Nima, Hotep, and Anubis stood and watched their hope for the new Egypt march toward glory—or as it was—toward war.

~

The campaign lasted three seasons.

They returned to Camp T'jaru with sixty women, seventy children, eighteen men, and four wagons filled with the fruits of war. They reported eighty males left hanging from scaffolds with signs saying, "We invaded the lands of Kemet."

There were no Nubian casualties.

Hotep already had the road toward the third fort well underway.

EGYPTIAN GODS: Osiris/Dionysus—Isis/Ariadne/Philyra, Horus, Set/Charon, Nephthys/Dexithea.
CANAANITE GODS: Anath, Astarte, Shalem, Shahar, Moloch, El.
OLYMPIAN GODS: Zeus, Dionysus, Hestia, Ares, Athena, Astraeus, Eos, Hermes.
OCEANIDS: Polydore, Lyris, Acaste, Eidyia, Dione.

Anubis went among the captured women, comforting them—giving them a shoulder to cry on.

Horus went among surviving men, talking of the death they had witnessed and feared.

After the celebrations, reports, festivities, planning, and feasting were done, Major Hetephe retired to the tent of Prince Djoser, removed her clothes, soaked in a tub of warm water, dried her body, went to him, and, in his arms, for a long time, cried.

The next morning, Djoser, Hetephe, Horus, Anubis, and four escort archers set off to return to Memphis leading the captives to the holding compound outside South Memphis. There the captives would be evaluated and resettled in various parts of the kingdom. Also, Prince Djoser and Major Hetephe would present their reports to the king and his council.

Death of a King
Year 150, fifth month

As Djoser and his group reached Charon City they were met by messengers from the Queen. The message was for Djoser's ears only, "Return to Memphis with all haste. King Nebka is dying. He will name you king of Kemet."

Djoser politely listened to the messenger and thanked him for his service. *Dung! Dung, dung, dung! This must not happen. This cannot be allowed to be! What can I do? None of this can be allowed to come to pass!*

He went to Horus and said, "There are high-level meetings in Memphis that I must attend. I am going to take Major Hetephe and go on ahead. You, Anubis, and the archers escort our caravan to the holding camp at a more leisurely pace. Don't fail me. I will see you in Memphis."

Djoser returned with Hetephe to the waiting palanquin. The carriers were experienced and well-conditioned, but Djoser volunteered to run with the carriers and only joined Hetephe in the palanquin when he could no longer keep pace with the running carriers.

Djoser used his running time to consider his situation and try to formulate a response to that which would undoubtedly happen. When, at last, he made the command to be carried in the palanquin, he was ready to discuss things with his only available counselor—Hetephe.

Hetephe understood the implications and offered some unhelpful suggestions. This, unfortunately, was not one of her areas of expertise. She might, however, be a helpful liaison between Djoser and High Priestess Hathor. Time must play out before Djoser had enough information to make decisions and commit himself.

Time played out.

"He is dead," Saqqar announced to the queen and others gathered in the room with King Nebka.

Queen Nima gasped, grasped her face, and quickly sat back down upon her chair beside her husband's body.

Vizier Menka solemnly said, "We must prepare his body for the afterlife, but he has no Mastaba; that is a problem. We must announce Prince Djoser's ascension to the throne immediately. Kemet cannot be without a king. I will make the announcement as soon as the body is prepared and Djoser gets back. He should be here by now, the messengers I sent to him will be flogged for their tardiness."

Saqqar said, "I will notify the High Priestess for her priests to begin preparing King Nebka for his journey. Let us see how she handles the absence of a Mastaba for him. She was remiss in not being better prepared. King Djoser must reprimand her!"

General Khasek was concerned about the coming relations with Chief Kerma. His subservience and allegiance to King Nebka had always been tenuous, cemented primarily by the marriage of the king to the chief's daughter, an arrangement no longer in place. He said, "King Djoser must proceed with extreme caution in this matter."

Soon, Hathor arrived escorted by five priests. She approached King Nebka's body and lovingly said, "Welcome my king, I have your new home prepared. It is stocked with your favorite food and drink. I will consult with Shaman Saqqar and select the very best Priest to protect your body and attend to your every need. Are you already visiting with your father? Has Osiris yet welcomed you? My priests will now take you to your Mastaba and prepare your body for the afterlife. This is a joyful day."

The Priests covered the king's body for transportation to his Mastaba.

Hathor's astonished audience listened to her words in silent disbelief.

EGYPTIAN GODS: Osiris/Dionysus—Isis/Ariadne/Philyra, Horus, Set/Charon, Nephthys/Dexithea.
CANAANITE GODS: Anath, Astarte, Shalem, Shahar, Moloch, El.
OLYMPIAN GODS: Zeus, Dionysus, Hestia, Ares, Athena, Astraeus, Eos, Hermes.
OCEANIDS: Polydore, Lyris, Acaste, Eidyia, Dione.

Hathor turned to Queen Nima and said, "There is sadness in you because of this, my Queen. The only sadness our king feels is that he will not be with you for a while. But even as Isis awaited Osiris, so waits Nebka for Nima." She turned to leave.

Nima said, "My husband doesn't have a Mastaba! He would never discuss it! Now, he has no place to rest!"

Hathor turned to Nima and softly said, "King Nebka's Mastaba awaits him. It is lovely and fully stocked for his afterlife. Such things are the concern of the High Priestess. Construction for the Mastaba for our new king is already planned, and we can now begin its construction. Allow us time to prepare King Nebka. I will return for you this evening and escort you to his Mastaba."

Nima was confused. She said, "This was never discussed!"

Hathor sweetly replied, "The king needs my full attention. Let me tend to him and I will return for you this evening. All will be made clear. Excuse me, great Queen Nima but I must go, now." Hathor turned and briskly walked to join her Priests and the remains of King Nebka.

The mourners were left in confusion, no longer sure how to proceed. Vizier Menka suggested, "We are all upset. Let's take some time to calm ourselves down and then plan the method and timing of Djoser's coronation ceremony. Surely, Djoser will arrive before the sun sets."

Vizier Menka asked Saqqar, "Shaman Saqqar, were you aware that King Nebka had a Mastaba waiting?"

Saqqar responded, "That is impossible. There has been no construction— no plans—no talk. The High Priestess plays some dangerous game."

Menka responded, "Well, at least she is accomplished at playing dangerous games. Let her game play out."

Nima sat in her chair, sobbing, "My husband is dead. My husband is dead."

General Khasek thought, *Yes, Queen Nima. You are no longer married to the king of Kemet, a most grievous problem!*

As Djoser's palanquin arrived on the outskirts of Memphis, the word in everyone's mouth was, "The king is dead!"

Hetephe moved closer to Djoser and said, "Djoser, I am so sorry for the loss of your father."

Djoser replied, "Thank you Hete. He was a great man, perhaps the greatest man this land has produced. I loved him, so. But I shall mourn for him in good time. This is not that time." *Well, at least they are not saying that I am to be king. Thank Osiris for small favors. Are you involved yet, High Priestess? Are you playing your part well?*

He continued, "Let's get to the palace council room. There will be chaos."

The runners took the palanquin directly to the Council Room. Djoser composed himself, put on his official, no-nonsense persona, and dismounted from the palanquin. He entered the council room unannounced, went directly to his mother, embraced her, and said, "He will be greatly missed, especially by my beloved mother."

She sobbed for a moment and told him, "You are to be king. That was his final wish. My son—the king."

He hugged her, stepped back, looked at General Khasek, and asked, "General, you understand the problem, I'm sure." He did not wait for a response as he asked Vizier Menka, "Has this been announced, yet?"

Vizier Menka replied, "No, but we ..."

Djoser cut him off, "Good! No formal announcement can be made until the announcement is formally approved by King Nebka. Have you considered the time, place, and wording of the announcement?"

Menka responded, "Prince Djoser, the king is dead. He cannot ..."

Again, Djoser cut him off, "I require Father's official approval of the announcement. It has already been drafted and is in the possession of High Priestess Hathor. I will have High Priestess Hathor present it to Father for his approval this evening. I propose the announcement be made by Hathor during the sunrise ceremony tomorrow morning. She will announce that King Nebka has entered the Land of the Dead to be with Osiris and Chief Kemet. The rumors are already out there. No one will be surprised but it's necessary to make it official."

Menka said, "Prince, the king is dead. He cannot possibly approve this announcement of yours. We must proceed ..."

EGYPTIAN GODS: Osiris/Dionysus—Isis/Ariadne/Philyra, Horus, Set/Charon, Nephthys/Dexithea.
CANAANITE GODS: Anath, Astarte, Shalem, Shahar, Moloch, El.
OLYMPIAN GODS: Zeus, Dionysus, Hestia, Ares, Athena, Astraeus, Eos, Hermes.
OCEANIDS: Polydore, Lyris, Acaste, Eidyia, Dione.

"The announcement is one which the king need not approve—only disapprove. If he disapproves, he can indicate this to High Priestess Hathor. And you are correct Vizier; we must proceed with haste. Everything must be announced during the Sunrise Ceremony. The King's death, the marriage, Father's proclamation naming our new king, and the coronation ceremony, itself. We have much to do in a short time!"

Menka asked, "What marriage?"

Djoser did not hesitate, "My mother's marriage to General Khasek, the man Father will undoubtably name as king."

Pandemonium erupted. Everyone said everything at once. Djoser listened politely and then broke in, "Good All of you now have it out of your systems. Now, let's get on with it."

He looked at his mother, "Queen Nima, you are to enter General Khasek's quarters before sundown—you had better hurry - and not leave until sunrise. Then, come directly to Osiris's Mastaba for the official marriage ceremony."

Nima was hysterical. This was all too much. She screamed, "What are you talking about? Marry Khasek? My son has lost his mind!"

Djoser commanded, "YOU ARE A QUEEN. BE A QUEEN. DO WHAT MUST BE DONE FOR YOUR PEOPLE!"

She screamed, "YOU ARE INSANE!"

In apparent fury, Djoser responded, "Was my father married to a FOOL? To a weepy-eyed woman who cannot handle her duties? To a pathetic example of a common uneducated, unenlightened, stupid hag of a woman? TELL ME NIMA OF THE NUBIAN PEOPLE—ARE YOU WORTHY TO BE A QUEEN?—WERE YOU WORTHY OF BEING MY FATHER'S QUEEN?—WHEN DID YOU CEASE BEING A QUEEN?!!!"

Hetephe sat in the corner, trembling at Djoser's fury. The men were speechless. Nima stared at her son with wide-eyed disbelief.

Djoser said, "All of you, calm down. You wouldn't discuss this eventuality with me. Did you think that I would not have a plan? Sit down, Mother. Everything is going to be alright. I came up with a plan and since it's the only viable plan around, it's the one we will go with." He looked at

Hetephe, and said, "Major, get Mother a glass of wine. Her last husband just died, and she will take a new husband tonight. Being Queen is hard!"

Djoser said to Khasek, "General, you *do* understand what Chief Kerma will do when he finds out his daughter is no longer married to the king, don't you?"

The general said, "There is a good chance he will invade the lower kingdom."

Djoser responded, "A likely probability. You will prevail but the loss of life on both sides would be significant."

He looked at his mother and asked, "Queen Nima, can you soothe all of this over with a visit to your father and casually mention that the old king died but that you married the new king so not much else has changed since you last saw him. That he simply must come and meet your new husband, the king."

Nima sat sobbing, but shook her head, "Yes." Hetephe arrived with the wine and sat on the floor beside her queen.

Djoser said to Vizier Menka, "Hathor will present the announcement to King Nebka this evening. If the King disapproves of the announcement, then we will go with somebody else, but High Priestess Hathor is very persuasive. I don't think he will disapprove."

Khasek was reflective. He said, "Prince, I don't know about any of this. I have never considered being king. I don't know how I would handle myself. You are the rightful heir. Even if it means war with Chief Kerma. We can probably defeat them. And marrying Queen Nima, I mean ..." He hesitated, "I don't know what I mean."

Djoser looked at him and said, "You need not bed my mother if there is no attraction between the two of you. Marriages of state are simply that. Consummation is not a requirement. You are a general because you have the bearing and intelligence of a king. If you are unsure of what words are to be said, that is why you have a council. A king can always buy time by deferring to his council. As for me, it is not yet my time. The Sinai must be conquered, the nation of Egypt must be created, and diverse peoples must be unified to become one people. After these things are done, after you are old and tired and your Mastaba complete, if I remain, then think kindly upon me. Can you do this thing, General Khasek?"

EGYPTIAN GODS: Osiris/Dionysus—Isis/Ariadne/Philyra, Horus, Set/Charon, Nephthys/Dexithea.
CANAANITE GODS: Anath, Astarte, Shalem, Shahar, Moloch, El.
OLYMPIAN GODS: Zeus, Dionysus, Hestia, Ares, Athena, Astraeus, Eos, Hermes.
OCEANIDS: Polydore, Lyris, Acaste, Eidyia, Dione.

General Khasek walked to Queen Nima, held out his hand, and said to her with stateliness, "I will not come to your bed. If I please you otherwise, you may come to mine. Now, we must hurry to my quarters, the sun nears setting."

She took his hand, rose, looked at him, smiled, and said, "I am Queen Nima of Kemet—a high-born Nubian. My king always pleases me." She left on the arm of General Khasek. She did not look at her son.

Djoser watched them leave, perhaps with a certain sadness, but then said to those remaining, "Alright, Council. Let's visit Hathor at Father's Mastaba and complete our planning for a big sunrise ceremony, tomorrow! It's the mastaba on the lower level, beneath Osiris's, the one she once called 'the Word of Isis' Mastaba. There has never been a body in that particular Mastaba. It first housed the Ark of Tallstone, then the Word of Isis, and now it will have a new occupant. She no longer needs the pretense that it houses the Word of Isis. She simply legislated that Isis's Word now lay with Osiris's body. She came up with an elegant solution to a complex problem. She will have already commanded Hotep to design another level on top of Osiris's to be King Khasek's Mastaba."

Meanwhile

As the drama of King Nebka's death played out in Memphis, Horus, Anubis, and the archers delivered the Sinai captives to the South Memphis holding camp. There, the prisoners were treated well because it was hoped that they could be integrated into Kemet Nomarchies, and Kemet treated its people well. Various cities and settlements had representatives to interview the captives.

The most desirable captives had been separated and designated as a gift to Chief Kerma as "the first captives of the Egyptian Army." They were separated from the others to wait for Djoser to escort them to the Chief.

Dyo and Dyowife from Ogdoad City were the first City Representatives to arrive at the holding camp. They strolled through the camp talking with the remaining "prisoners" explaining the type of person that might enjoy resettling to their city. The "prisoners" were surprised by the friendliness of these two people. In their own tribes, they had been treated as chattel expected to immediately obey every whim of their Warlord. They were not at all used to "civilized" people. To the person, everyone would be overjoyed to resettle in Ogdoad City. Dyowife laughed at their eagerness,

Dionysus/Osiris, Ariadne/Isis/Philyra, Charon/Set, Hermes/Tehuti.
EGYPTIANS: Nebka, Djoser, Hotep, Khasek, Rocky
NUBIANS: Nima, Hetephe, King Kerma, Prince T'jaru, Prince Rafah.
CANAANITES: Phoenicia, Serket, Azazil, Jaffa | URFANS: Teumessian, Abram, Sarai, Terah

and said, "At least wait until you hear from the representatives of New Port Kemet. They are on the water. You might enjoy that lifestyle better." It was beyond their comprehension that they were desirable citizens being offered a choice of where to relocate. Dyo and Dyowife selected half of the new immigrants to join them in Ogdoad Town.

Sunrise

All were in their places. The complete company of drummers and announcers knew what the High Priestess would say and were all prepared to repeat her words so that all gathered, no matter how far away, could understand. The crowd was expected to be massive. Djoser had retired to the river to watch. He knew he would find Horus there.

The time came. Hathor raised her arms to the horizon. "I call forth Osiris from the Land of the Dead to be reborn as Ra—the Living Sun." (BEAT)

Her words were repeated to the masses.

Osiris came.

Hathor said, "Osiris commands me to tell his people their king is dead!" (BEAT)

Her words repeated. A murmur ran through the crowd, "Our king is dead! We have no king!"

Hathor said, "Osiris commands me to tell his people that King Nebka was welcomed by Chief Kemet in the Land of the Dead. They rejoice in their reunion!" (BEAT)

Words repeated, the people were overjoyed, "Reunited! Father and Son are reunited!"

Hathor said, "King Nebka commands me to tell you he has given his people a new king!" (BEAT)

Words repeated, the crowd murmured, "King Nebka has named a new king!"

Hathor said, "Queen Nima takes King Khasek as her husband!" (BEAT)

Words repeated, the people were astounded, "General Khasek is to be our king? The queen has married him?"

Hathor said, "Osiris commands me to command you to look upon your new King and his Queen with awe!" (BEAT)

EGYPTIAN GODS: Osiris/Dionysus—Isis/Ariadne/Philyra, Horus, Set/Charon, Nephthys/Dexithea.
CANAANITE GODS: Anath, Astarte, Shalem, Shahar, Moloch, El.
OLYMPIAN GODS: Zeus, Dionysus, Hestia, Ares, Athena, Astraeus, Eos, Hermes.
OCEANIDS: Polydore, Lyris, Acaste, Eidyia, Dione.

The words were repeated as King Khasek and Queen Nima stepped to stand beside Hathor. The cry went out, "Hail, King Khasek! Hail Queen Nima!" Many in the crowd fell to their knees.

Hathor said, "Osiris is pleased with the king and with his people!" (BEAT)

The words repeated, cheers went up. Rejoicing. "Praise Osiris. Praise the king of Kemet!" There were many Nubians in the crowd. People bonded one with the other.

Horus quietly asked Djoser, "Was it difficult?"

Djoser responded, "Yes. Every moment of it!"

Horus asked, "Are you ready to mourn?"

Djoser choked up as he said, "Yes."

Horus turned and embraced his mentor-stepfather-uncle. "Love is hard."

Djoser wept.

After the sun had been called forth and Osiris reborn, a dry-eyed Djoser joined King Khasek and Queen Nima in their quarters for their morning meal. King Khasek greeted Djoser with, "Join us, prince. I have had a little time ...," he glanced sideways at contented Nima sitting quietly enjoying her meal, "... not much time but a little—to consider our parting conversation. You presented me with a complex plan to consider in an extremely short time. But I have considered the plan and discussed it with my wife. We are of one mind; your plan is the best we can do under the extremely unfortunate circumstances. None of us wanted the death of King Nebka but we have it and must deal with as best we can. The transition of kings needed to be accomplished as quickly and easily as possible so as not to cause Chief Kerma with his Nubian archers any concern. She and I plan to work as a team just as she and her deceased husband did."

Queen Nima smiled and said, "Our new king learns his new role well, Djoser. I taught him the king and queen's private rising sun ceremony this morning. He is quite accomplished. He has commanded that you and I deliver the Sinai captives to Chief Kerma. You will show me the captives later in the day. We will leave for Abdju for an impromptu State visit tomorrow morning after all sunrise ceremonies have been completed."

Meanwhile

Her reports delivered and responsibilities complete, Major Hetephe and her four escort archers left Memphis to rejoin her command, now to be based at the second fort on the trade route. Horus would travel with her as would Red-Ribboned Woman Anath.

Anath was interested in the nature of men who would actively pursue killing another human being, apparently without qualms. This was beyond her comprehension, but it spoke to the nature of the male and Anath must understand all there was to understand about the nature of the male. How can they purposely kill another man? Major Hetephe had described the horrors of what they did, but Hetephe took no pleasure in the doing. Besides, if allowed to join the expedition, there would be that handsome Captain T'jaru. Anath's mother and sisters discouraged Anath, but Anath was insistent that she be allowed to go. She had argued, "A two-month vacation away from what I do will do me good."

Anath was thrilled to be traveling with one of her favorite special friends, Horus. On their way out of Memphis, Horus began talking of things near to Horus's heart—death, dying, where do the dead go, do they still live in another place, can the living ever contact them, that sort of thing. Anath, as was her professional nature, was infatuated with every word out of any man's mouth. Anath, privately, was intensely interested in how any man could kill another man without qualms. Hetephe listened to the discourse, with interest.

Horus rambled on and on. "That which I believe closest to fact came from Father. He stated that he had neared death twice in his life, a place where he could decide to either release his body or to continue living."

He often told me, "Both times as I lay dying, the Light came to me and spoke. The Light was Queen Kiya and others who were dead. Both times the Light told me that I could release the prison that was his body and join them and become one with the Light. The choice was mine. If I chose to stay within my body, I would gain even more experiences which, when I finally shed this bodily husk, would bring even more joy and knowledge to The One—the Light that contains all things."

Anath gleefully responded, "Then Osiris died and became the light. He is reborn every sunrise as the Living Sun. What a beautiful story you tell, Horus."

EGYPTIAN GODS: Osiris/Dionysus—Isis/Ariadne/Philyra, Horus, Set/Charon, Nephthys/Dexithea.
CANAANITE GODS: Anath, Astarte, Shalem, Shahar, Moloch, El.
OLYMPIAN GODS: Zeus, Dionysus, Hestia, Ares, Athena, Astraeus, Eos, Hermes.
OCEANIDS: Polydore, Lyris, Acaste, Eidyia, Dione.

Horus opened his mouth to respond, then thought better of it. *That's not exactly correct, Anath. That's not even close to correct. But the simplicity of your understanding is probably all the understanding you want or need. Perhaps, on another day you will seek a deeper knowledge. I will wait for you as Father waited for me.*

He responded, instead, "Yes, Osiris is now the light, and he is one with Mother and all other things."

The three arrived at Charon City. The residents were overjoyed that Horus, himself, the son of Isis and Osiris, were in their midst. Everyone in Charon City adored Isis and Osiris. They begged him to stay the night with them, saying, "You can tell us the story of how Isis blew life back into the body of the dead Osiris so she could mount him and then give birth to you. It is a beautiful story always in the mouth of everyone in Charon City. Please stay the night!"

Horus had grown accomplished at nicely refusing such invitations but always saying, "I shall return another day and tell you many stories of my parents. You will be amazed!"

They continued to their next stop, T'jaru City, and then on to the next camp where they rejoined the Nubian Archers making final preparations for the Second Sinai Expedition.

The Second Expedition
Year 150, seventh month

The second camp was named "Camp Haboua," after the first archer to kill a Sinai warrior.

Major Hetephe briefed Captain T'jaru on the positive reception of their prisoners at the Memphis holding camp. All prisoners had been looked upon favorably. If there was a battlefield decision of "to kill or not to kill" then "not to kill" is the preferred outcome.

Anath stared with excitement at the archers as they prepared for the expedition where they would willingly go forth and kill other men. She was intrigued; plus, the killing would be led by that handsome Captain T'jaru—who even had a fort named after him. She asked Major Hetephe if she might be allowed to join the expedition. Hetephe replied, "Personnel decisions are made by Captain T'jaru. Ask his permission."

When she asked Captain T'jaru, he simply asked, "Can you cook?"

Dionysus/Osiris, Ariadne/Isis/Philyra, Charon/Set, Hermes/Tehuti.
EGYPTIANS: Nebka, Djoser, Hotep, Khasek, Rocky
NUBIANS: Nima, Hetephe, King Kerma, Prince T'jaru, Prince Rafah.
CANAANITES: Phoenicia, Serket, Azazil, Jaffa | URFANS: Teumessian, Abram, Sarai, Terah

She replied in a liquid voice, "Of course, I can cook, Captain. Anything a man could desire!"

Everything prepared, to the shouts of "Glory to Egypt," the Second Sinai Expedition set off to the south to eliminate more raiders from the Sinai.

Two days into the march, Scouts found evidence of a tribe. The archers prepared themselves. The tribe, estimated to be thirty warriors and their women and children, were soon tracked down. The archers waited until predawn to slip close and surround the camp so they could select their targets. The primary goal was to identify the warlord and kill him. Once the leader was dead, the remainder would be more prone to surrender.

Anath would be allowed to stand with Major Hetephe and Horus outside the circle of archers and observe the operation. In the predawn light, Anath felt an unusual emotion—childish anticipation!

Dawn broke. The archers crept nearer the camp and began selecting their targets; just now rising from their sleep. Their enemy had no archers, only swords, spears, and knives. Captain T'jaru selected the obvious warlord and motioned for the archers on either side of him to shoot their arrows at him upon his signal. All others would hold their arrows until T'jaru gave a second command. He would access the enemy's will to fight before he initiated a slaughter.

T'jaru then quietly issued the command, "Kill." Two arrows found their mark on the unsuspecting warlord. He fell to the ground. A Nubian skilled in Eastern Common, said in a loud voice, "Lay down upon the ground. If you are standing, we will kill you. Stand and die or lay down and live."

Twelve men grabbed their spears and swords and rushed, screaming, at the archers. They were immediately impaled with multiple arrows. The remaining men wisely fell to the ground to lie with the women and children.

The Nubian warriors began taking the remaining men and tying them to a heavy crossbeam. T'jaru and his two lieutenants walked to the nearest dying man and knelt to inspect him. Anath, uninvited, followed closely. T'jaru looked at the man—suffering, losing blood, no hope for survival— and nodded.

A lieutenant took his dagger and mercifully cut the man's throat. Anath stared in wonder at the sight—the blood flowing from the man's throat, the death gurgle as blood flowed from his wound and from his mouth—

EGYPTIAN GODS: Osiris/Dionysus—Isis/Ariadne/Philyra, Horus, Set/Charon, Nephthys/Dexithea.
CANAANITE GODS: Anath, Astarte, Shalem, Shahar, Moloch, El.
OLYMPIAN GODS: Zeus, Dionysus, Hestia, Ares, Athena, Astraeus, Eos, Hermes.
OCEANIDS: Polydore, Lyris, Acaste, Eidyia, Dione.

his look of terror—the sight of life leaving the man's eyes—she trembled with excitement. She asked, "Can ... can I do that?"

T'jaru looked at her in disbelief and asked, "You wish to deliver the death cut?"

Anath answered, "Y-yes."

T'jaru looked at his lieutenants who returned their Captain's gaze. One shrugged, "Why not?"

The lieutenant handed Anath his dagger. They walked to the next man and knelt to inspect him. T'jaru announced, "This one may live. Alert the medical people to attend to him."

Anath said, "No! ... I want to."

T'jaru studied the man. He decided. "Very well. Dispatch him."

Anath knelt and placed her dagger on the conscious man's throat. She stared into the eyes of fear—he pleaded for his life—she listened to his words with fascination—she slowly, gently forced the blade into the man's throat—blood began to seep out—he pleaded—she stared at the blood with continued fascination—she pushed the blade in deeper—her eyes widened—her lips parted—she slowly slid the dagger across his throat—listened to his death rattle—stared into his eyes as life left him.

She exclaimed, "I want to do another one!"

T'jaru said, "One more and that's all. You enjoy this too much!"

She replied, "Maybe two more, alright?"

T'jaru said, "Very well, two more."

After all the wounded men were inspected, four were allowed to live, and Anath was allowed to dispatch the remaining six.

That evening, around the campfire, after all prisoners—men, women, and children—were properly restricted, as the evening meal was being finished, Anath demanded of a lieutenant, "Gather all the dead bodies and lay them side by side by the fire. I wish to present Major T'jaru with a gift for the kindness he extended to me this afternoon. Major T'jaru shrugged, "Why not?" The lieutenant did as Anath commanded. Anath inspected the dead bodies and commanded, "Remove their clothes!"

By this time, Anath had the attention of Major Hetephe, Horus, and all other members of the expedition.

T'jaru said to his lieutenant, "Let's see where Red-Ribboned Woman Anath is taking this!"

The clothes were removed. Anath stared at the bodies with approval, her eyes widening, her breathing becoming more rapid. She walked and stood before T'jaru. She slowly let her clothes fall to the ground. Anath understood seduction and this would be the most demanding seduction in her storied career. She said to T'jaru, "Now, we will make love!" She walked to the dead bodies and lay across them, using them as her bed. She turned her head to stare into the eyes of T'jaru, "Please Captain T'jaru. Plow me. I need it so badly. Plow me, right now! Please!"

T'jaru was frozen, his mind racing. *I can't do that in front of my men. In front of everybody.*

He glanced at Major Hetephe for instructions.

She stared at him and then her eyes surveyed the archers; eyes wide with excitement and anticipation—and camaraderie! She nodded her permission.

Anath used her voice of liquid sex. With overpowering physical need, she said, "Please, my Captain. Plow me for the glory of Egypt. Please!"

The chant from his men went up, slowly at first, "Plow her! Plow her! Plow her!"

As he walked to T'jaru, Horus interjected, he wasn't sure why, "Do as she commands, Captain—for the glory of Egypt!" Horus pulled T'jaru up by his hands and led him to face the naked, eager Anath. She held out her arms to him, her legs wide. T'jaru removed his clothes and lay upon her. Anath received the thrusts of T'jaru as she writhed laying across the bodies of the dead men beneath her. For the first time in her life, Anath lost control. She threw her head back, her lips parted, her eyes open wide, her breathing labored. That which came upon her was not faked, no make-believe show for her client. Physical pleasure boiled up through her body to become an overwhelming emotional pleasure, and then through the entirety of her body to become a passion for life and pleasure and control and domination and killing and pleasure and sweetness and the pleasure of death, itself. The moan began deep within her body and rose with the earthquake of her shudders.

EGYPTIAN GODS: Osiris/Dionysus—Isis/Ariadne/Philyra, Horus, Set/Charon, Nephthys/Dexithea.
CANAANITE GODS: Anath, Astarte, Shalem, Shahar, Moloch, El.
OLYMPIAN GODS: Zeus, Dionysus, Hestia, Ares, Athena, Astraeus, Eos, Hermes.
OCEANIDS: Polydore, Lyris, Acaste, Eidyia, Dione.

Finished and exhausted, she felt T'jaru join her. She lay quietly beneath him and did not recite her usual ritual of, "How Great You Were."

Without emotion, she stared into the night sky full of bright lights. *I now understand the nature of men. I am changed. I am woman become man!*

She pushed T'jaru off her, picked up her dagger and a spear, and walked to the wagons where the wounded men were tethered. She approached the most belligerent and strongest of the survivors and said, "Kneel before me and yield your allegiance to the glory of Egypt!"

She did not understand his words, but was certain they contained the words "whore," "filth," and "never."

Horus joined them and offered, "He rejects your command."

She stepped close to him, placed her blade hard across his neck, and commanded, "YIELD!"

He spat in her face and glared at her.

The subtle smile began. The widening of the eyes began. The quickening of the pulse. The rapid breathing. She pushed her dagger harder against his throat and began the slow slice separating flesh from flesh, releasing his blood, creating the gurgle of death. She gathered his pulsing blood in her hands, used it to wipe the saliva from her face; gathered more and bathed her breasts and stomach in it; watched life leave him; caressed his falling body with her blood-soaked hands; and stared down on his corpse with satisfaction.

Anath stepped to the next prisoner, a man not much older than a boy. Covered with the blood of his leader, she commanded, "Kneel before me and yield your allegiance to the glory of Egypt!"

The boy-man stared back without fear. He spoke.

Horus told her, "I believe that he says that he is the youngest son of the greatest warlord in Canaan and that it is better to die by the blade of a great warrior than to surrender the honor of his Father."

She pushed the spear hard against his stomach.

The prisoner did not flinch.

She handed her dagger to Horus, and said, still staring at the boy-man, "Free him!"

Dionysus/Osiris, Ariadne/Isis/Philyra, Charon/Set, Hermes/Tehuti.
EGYPTIANS: Nebka, Djoser, Hotep, Khasek, Rocky
NUBIANS: Nima, Hetephe, King Kerma, Prince T'jaru, Prince Rafah.
CANAANITES: Phoenicia, Serket, Azazil, Jaffa | URFANS: Teumessian, Abram, Sarai, Terah

Horus obeyed and cut the ropes binding the prisoner.

Anath said to the boy-man, "If your father does not yield to me when I come for him, I shall kill him and his sons. I will kill his wives and his daughters. I will kill his men and their women and their babies and children. I will kill his dogs and sheep. When I come for your father, if he will yield and lay upon the ground as I come for him, all will live and be given a better life than he has given them. Tell your father, too, 'Anath the Dispatcher' *will* come for him!" With that, she handed him the spear, commanded, "NOW GO!" turned, and walked away to consult with Captain T'jaru.

Horus repeated her words to the boy-man and nodded toward the east.

The son of the greatest warlord in Canaan glanced at Anath walking away, turned, and began a fast trot back to his tribe.

By then, T'jaru had dressed and joined Major Hetephe by the fire to witness the birth of "Anath the Dispatcher."

The archers respectfully and somewhat fearfully separated to make a path for Anath to join her captain. She arrived and asked T'jaru, "Did I look foolish? I don't want to embarrass you by looking foolish. You *would* tell me, wouldn't you?"

Hetephe answered for T'jaru. "You did well, Dispatcher Anath. Very well!"

~

The campaign continued into the second season. Throughout the campaign and beyond, Dispatcher Anath earned and lived up to her new title. Horus studied the dispatch of each doomed man.

For the entertainment of his men, Captain T'jaru performed the ritual as best he could. His men were somewhat frightened by the climatic low-pitched howl of a female animal in the depths of heat. This, too, with amazement, Horus studied.

Major Hetephe did not approve of the ritual but did not forbid it. Her warriors were strengthened by it. *They are so easily entertained.*

~

The Second Sinai Expedition returned northward in the third season of the campaign and found the Trade Route and then Camp Haboua. There

EGYPTIAN GODS: Osiris/Dionysus—Isis/Ariadne/Philyra, Horus, Set/Charon, Nephthys/Dexithea.
CANAANITE GODS: Anath, Astarte, Shalem, Shahar, Moloch, El.
OLYMPIAN GODS: Zeus, Dionysus, Hestia, Ares, Athena, Astraeus, Eos, Hermes.
OCEANIDS: Polydore, Lyris, Acaste, Eidyia, Dione.

they would enjoy a quarter moon of rest and relaxation The archers unanimously approved naming the third fort "Fort Dispatcher Anath."

The expedition returned with three times as many prisoners as their first expedition. They were becoming more proficient and skilled in their scouting and in capturing prisoners alive.

Major Hetephe, with Horus and six archers, escorted the prisoners to the South Memphis Holding Camp. Most of the return was along the trade route. Transit was swift and easy, even with many prisoners. Transit from T'jaru City to Charon City was more difficult, but roads were in place, even if not up to the standards of the trade route.

They delivered their prisoners to the South Memphis Holding Camp. Representatives from the various cities were already waiting for the new batch of captives. Abdju and Ogdoad Town had taken the best of the lot from the first expedition. They would have more competition this time.

Talk of the Old Days
Year 150, eighth month

Horus always made time to visit Set and Nephthys. As demeaning as Set could be, he was familiar with the gods of old and could converse with first-hand knowledge about Zeus, Poseidon, Hades, Hestia, and the others. Plus, Nephthys was Horus's stepmother and once a favorite of his father's. Horus eventually decided that Nephthys had more intimate knowledge of the gods than even his Uncle Set. After delivering the prisoners and visiting Hetephe, Horus hurried to the House of Nephthys. He found his stepmother alone at home.

After exchanging embraces and warm greetings, Nephthys said, "Your Uncle Set is at Hostess House holding court with his admirers. Come, let's join him! He will be excited to see you!"

Horus replied, "He is never as excited to see me as you would like, Mother. No, let's stay here and visit. I have seen much since we last talked. I need your wise counsel on dark matters."

She laughed, "I am an expert on dark matters, Son. I will bring us a drink. What would you like?"

"A glass of Father's brown wine would be nice, Mother."

"Ah, a wise selection, Horus. Especially when we talk of dark matters." She left, returned with two glasses, handed one to Horus, sat in her chair,

Dionysus/Osiris, Ariadne/Isis/Philyra, Charon/Set, Hermes/Tehuti.
EGYPTIANS: Nebka, Djoser, Hotep, Khasek, Rocky
NUBIANS: Nima, Hetephe, King Kerma, Prince T'jaru, Prince Rafah.
CANAANITES: Phoenicia, Serket, Azazil, Jaffa | URFANS: Teumessian, Abram, Sarai, Terah

pulled her legs under her, leaned back, saluted Horus with her brown wine, and said, "Now, tell me of darkness."

Horus talked of Anath and her transformation from a delightful, high-class courtesan into a merciless instrument of war."

With that, Nephthys sat her brown wine down, embraced herself, slumped over, and began to cry. She sobbed, "I have not always been 'Nephthys'—whore to Lord Set. I was once an 'instrument of war.' It was horrible—horrible beyond belief. Go on. Tell me everything."

Horus, on unsure ground, described the birth of Anath the Dispatcher—the look in her eyes when cutting the throats of men—the sexual frenzy she experienced when laying upon the bodies of the dead as she fornicated with Captain T'jaru. He said, "This cannot be natural. She must be overtaken by some kind of force I cannot yet see."

Nephthys stopped sobbing, picked up her glass of brown wine, and said, "Your father surely told you of Olympian gods Hestia, Ares, and Athena. Perhaps, he did not tell you everything." They talked into the night.

Set returned late. Nephthys brought the men a brown wine and retired for the evening leaving the old and the young to visit.

Horus, armed with new knowledge of the old days, easily guided Uncle Set's conversation into the unholy perversions of the Olympian Gods.

Also, Set took a special interest in the exploits of "Anath the Dispatcher." *Nephew Horus appears to be fond of the little gutter girl who has become Ares-Aphrodite-Hestia incarnate. Interesting!*

Meanwhile

Major Hetephe delivered her report to King Khasek and his advisors. She noticed that Queen Nima sat close to the king and hung on to his every word.

The king's council had appointed King Khasek's youngest son, Sanakhte, to replace his father as general.

Nima was not especially pleased with this selection because when the time came, her husband would favor his own son over Djoser when deciding on who would become the new king. But Djoser surely knew something like this would happen when he pitched his little fit commanding her to marry Khasek and demanding Khasek become king rather than himself.

EGYPTIAN GODS: Osiris/Dionysus—Isis/Ariadne/Philyra, Horus, Set/Charon, Nephthys/Dexithea.
CANAANITE GODS: Anath, Astarte, Shalem, Shahar, Moloch, El.
OLYMPIAN GODS: Zeus, Dionysus, Hestia, Ares, Athena, Astraeus, Eos, Hermes.
OCEANIDS: Polydore, Lyris, Acaste, Eidyia, Dione.

Her son was sometimes too scheming for his own good. But she must admit, she remained queen and Khasek was a good king and even more dynamic than her dead, beloved Nebka. She would have kept Nebka as her mate, but a queen must do what a queen must do, and introducing Khasek to the intimate sunrise ceremony tradition was something a queen must do. *The ceremony always invigorates a king so. It is my duty!*

Major Hetephe's report was well received. King Khasek was more knowledgeable than Nebka on military implications. He asked, "Do you believe that Prince Djoser and yourself have a chance of winning this military operation? As you remember, I dismissed the suggestion as ludicrous. I would not even discuss it."

Major Hetephe replied, "And wisely so, my king. This forced Prince Djoser to refine his plan to the point of making it work. You drove him to succeed."

The king grunted, "I may be a military man, Major, but I recognize dung when I hear dung! Don't bring me dung!"

"Yes, my king. Actually, Djoser dismissed all of the council's advice. He knew what had to be done and why it had to be done, so he bypassed normal channels of command and will, I most fervently believe, be successful in ridding the Sinai of warlords, incorporating the Sinai into the kingdom of Kemet, and with your gracious approval of promises made, officially change the name of your kingdom to Egypt.—Sir!"

King Khasek looked at his council. "I wonder what words I should now say? I will defer that decision to my council!"

Uniforms

Meanwhile, as Nebka's priest hovered about, Djoser sat silently visiting his dead father in the Mastaba of Nebka. *It is going to succeed, Father. Hete and her army will clear the Sinai warlords within the year. Priest Hotep will finish the War Road and its fort. The Sinai will be added to your kingdom. I must visit Mother and reinforce that her husband MUST enthusiastically agree to rename his kingdom "Egypt." This is crucial. The name "Kemet" MUST be removed from the land. It is the only way your vast empire will congeal into one nation. And, too, you will add a magnificent trade route—Egypt will become the trading power of the world. And turquoise mines, did I mention that you will have unlimited turquoise? Hathor will like that—a girl can never have too much turquoise. But there are problems. There are always problems. I must go to Ishtar and tell her that her daughter will not return. That Anath is changed.*

That evening, after all meetings and briefings were complete, Djoser found Hetephe and asked, "Will you spend the night with me, Hete?"

She accepted the invitation without a double entendre or smart retort, "Yes, Prince. That would please me. May I bring my traveling bags to your quarters so that I can leave for the Sinai front from there?"

Djoser said, "Yes, of course. I have something I want your thoughts on."

Again, she resisted the temptation to be flippant, "I will hurry and get my things so we can have time to visit and things."

Djoser, too, resisted the temptation to comment on the "and things."

Within a short time, Hetephe sought entrance to Djoser's quarters. The guard permitted her entry.

"I'm here!" she called out.

He replied from the next room, "I'm in here, in my sleeping quarters!"

She took her things to his sleeping room. *Well, that didn't take long.*

Djoser was standing beside his bed motioning toward military clothing laid out on his bed. He said, "There are prototypes that I had our seamstresses create. If you like them, I will have them made for your entire Egyptian army. These are in your size!"

She looked in wonder and said, "They are gorgeous." She picked up a helmet with shoulder-length tricolored stripes of green, yellow, and red hanging on either side and the back.

He said, "The colors represent new life, indestructibility, and triumph. And look at the engraved copper piece across the front of the helmet. It's engraved 'First Egyptian Army.' and the four embedded rubies indicate your rank as a Major. T'jaru will have three rubies, and his lieutenants, two rubies. And look at the belt with the solid gold buckle. The two turquoise stones indicate that you participated in two campaigns. Everyone who participates in a campaign will get a turquoise stone to add to their own belt. An especially large stone will be awarded to indicate an act of outstanding valor. Do you like them? I can have a tricolored sash and dress made, also. Should I have a complete set made for your Command?"

EGYPTIAN GODS: Osiris/Dionysus—Isis/Ariadne/Philyra, Horus, Set/Charon, Nephthys/Dexithea.
CANAANITE GODS: Anath, Astarte, Shalem, Shahar, Moloch, El.
OLYMPIAN GODS: Zeus, Dionysus, Hestia, Ares, Athena, Astraeus, Eos, Hermes.
OCEANIDS: Polydore, Lyris, Acaste, Eidyia, Dione.

She stared at him unblinking, let her dress fall to the floor, and wiggled out of her undergarments. Without breaking her stare, she placed the helmet on her head and placed the belt around her naked waist. She said, "I will let you judge, Prince. How do I look?"

He gazed upon her body, looked into her eyes, and replied, "Magnificent!"

Without removing helmet or belt, she pushed him onto the bed and fell upon him.

Afterward, as she lay in his arms, their pillow talk was what one would expect. He whispered, "We still have Chief Kerma under our control. When Mother and I delivered the Sinai prisoners to him. He was highly pleased; especially since they were delivered under the Egyptian tri-color battle flag I had made on the way down. As Kerma was inspecting his new captives, Mother casually mentioned, 'By the way, I have taken a new husband. The last one died. The new one doesn't have the diplomatic finesse that I would like but he was our General and does understand military options, so I suppose that's an advantage. I want him to meet you as soon as possible. He can come here, or you can bring some of your wives to a Sunrise Ceremony and let us entertain you. Let me know which you prefer. Aren't these captives a good-looking group? I hope you are pleased with the work your Egyptian Army is doing.' Mother is so clever with words. Almost as clever as Major Hetephe!"

She asked, "When will the helmets and belts be ready? And add the tricolor sash and skirts."

He answered, "They will be ready upon our return with the next captives."

She reached up and kissed him under his chin, then on his chest, then on his stomach. She purred, "You lay there and fantasize about the clever words I could be saying instead of attending to some business that has come up."

Major Hetephe attended to business.

~

Late the next day, Horus joined Prince Djoser and Major Hetephe as they set off to return to the Sinai frontlines. The Third Sinai Expedition would be launched from Dispatcher Anath Camp. The major wore her new helmet and belt.

Dionysus/Osiris, Ariadne/Isis/Philyra, Charon/Set, Hermes/Tehuti.
EGYPTIANS: Nebka, Djoser, Hotep, Khasek, Rocky
NUBIANS: Nima, Hetephe, King Kerma, Prince T'jaru, Prince Rafah.
CANAANITES: Phoenicia, Serket, Azazil, Jaffa | URFANS: Teumessian, Abram, Sarai, Terah

They approached Charon City as night neared. Djoser said to Horus, "You promised to share stories of your Father with the people. This will be an excellent time to do so. I, myself, wish to listen and relive some old times. You agree, I'm sure!"

Horus was in no mood to share such stories, but he recognized a command when he heard one. He replied, "Yes, I will tell a few stories."

They arrived.

The Nomarch of the Glorious Scepter Nome was gracious and was becoming accustomed to all manner of traffic between Memphis and the War Road. Plans for a welcoming reception had already been planned, knowing that dignitaries might be coming through. The Nomarch had only to give the command to his staff. The word went out to the citizenry that, after evening meal, Horus would be in the city park telling stories of Osiris and Isis.

The crowd gathered in the park long before Horus, Djoser, Hetephe, and the Nomarch appeared. Torches illuminated the stage from which city productions were presented. All stood and bowed to the prince upon his arrival and then a cheer went up for Horus as he mounted the stage and faced the crowd.

Horus began. "As you love Osiris, so Osiris loves you and shines his love upon you every day." *This is dung, but Djoser says that dung is needed to make things grow.*

He continued, "His journey to become the Living Sun was long. It began when Olympian Zeus fell in love with Semele, a Princess of Greece. Zeus had never lain with a woman or even spilled his seed upon the ground. But when love-stricken Zeus gazed upon the innocent, desirable Semele, he knew exactly what to do and he did it with much vigor. Zeus remained hopelessly in love with Semele for almost an hour at which time he fell in love with and mounted the Oceanid Metis and impregnated her with Athena. Princess Semele named her son 'Dionysus,' after his father. Such is how my father began his journey. Does the story please you?"

A cheer went up from the crowd, "Another story! More!"

Horus felt his heart soften a little. He replied, "Very well, one more." He thought for a moment, and began, "My father was somewhat wild in his youth. As a child, he discovered how to ferment grapes into wine. He mastered the craft and found the effects wine could have upon the people.

EGYPTIAN GODS: Osiris/Dionysus—Isis/Ariadne/Philyra, Horus, Set/Charon, Nephthys/Dexithea.
CANAANITE GODS: Anath, Astarte, Shalem, Shahar, Moloch, El.
OLYMPIAN GODS: Zeus, Dionysus, Hestia, Ares, Athena, Astraeus, Eos, Hermes.
OCEANIDS: Polydore, Lyris, Acaste, Eidyia, Dione.

'It's both a blessing and a curse,' he often told me. He learned that he could get entire villages drunk on wine. He would play his Aulos and lead them through the streets in a drunken frenzy. They would couple with anyone nearby as the urge came upon them—in any combination available. He did not judge them. He provided the wine. They provided what came after. This he did for several years. Eventually, he met his half-brother, Heracles, a son of Zeus by Alcmene, the wife of a king. Zeus had tricked her into believing that he was her husband so that she would lay with him. My father and Heracles decided to travel to Tartarus where the Olympians lived and to meet their father. Father was named Dionysus back then. He loaded his wagon with wine and grape plants and set off with his friends, Seilenos and Marsyas, in the wagon pulled by Onos, his faithful donkey. There was much Aulos playing and wine drinking along the way. After many adventures, Father stood facing Zeus who refused to look upon my father as his son. Zeus aloofly told him to take his gift of wine, go away, and don't come back! Father, not at all distraught with his rejection, then sought out his paternal great-grandmother, Kiya; who happened to be the queen of all Tartarus. She not only graciously and lovingly heard my father's story but embraced him as one of their own and most certainly would accept his gift of wine. The entire Elder Titan family enthusiastically accepted my father and for the first time, he had a true family. Dionysus embraced the credo of the Titans and rejected that of their Olympian brethren. Zeus later discovered the delight of Father's wine and accepted Dionysus as an Olympian, which my father accepted but never fully embraced. There, you have the story of the youth of Osiris. Did it please you?"

The crowd stood and cheered, "Another! Tell us of your mother. Tell of Isis! More!"

Horus looked at Djoser for guidance. Djoser shrugged, "Why not?"

Horus said, "The short version, only the highlights and that will be all for this trip. Maybe more stories later. He began, "Mother was an Oceanid. In the beginning, her name was Philyra, and she was the assistant to the Chief of all Port Olympus Operations—who happened to be Olympian Hestia—the meanest woman to ever live."

The crowd cackled with laughter.

Horus continued, "Hestia had problems and since Hestia would not even speak to lower class people when she didn't have to, certainly not seek

Dionysus/Osiris, Ariadne/Isis/Philyra, Charon/Set, Hermes/Tehuti.
EGYPTIANS: Nebka, Djoser, Hotep, Khasek, Rocky
NUBIANS: Nima, Hetephe, King Kerma, Prince T'jaru, Prince Rafah.
CANAANITES: Phoenicia, Serket, Azazil, Jaffa | URFANS: Teumessian, Abram, Sarai, Terah

their advice, she sought the council of Dionysus—the most clever person she knew and of high class. Mother was sent to find Dionysus and command him to appear before Hestia. After all was done, Mother found herself replacing Hestia as Chief-of-Chiefs of Port Olympus with Hestia and the other Olympians being promoted out of lower-class society to become gods—a class so high, that they never had to deal with the lower classes again. The only point of contact between the Gods and the lower classes was Philyra's subservience to Hestia. Things went well enough until Hestia decided to get rid of Philyra by throwing her down the Port Olympus atrium into the pool far below. It never occurred to Hestia that you don't kill an Oceanid by throwing one into water, no matter what the height. Father found Mother. They sailed to Port Kaptara where Mother changed her name to Ariadne to escape Olympian revenge. Time and circumstance prevented Mother and Father from remaining together, so they went to their separate destinies. Mother, with the experience of a powerful executive, caught the attention of the King of Greece, whom she married. Father and his friend, Lord Charon, immigrated to Kemet where Lord Chron built the very city in which we sit, tonight. Then Charon amputated my father's hands and feet and sent them as a gift to Queen Ariadne, who was displeased. And from there, we all know the story of Isis and Osiris—Isis being the name given to Mother and Osiris being the name given to Father. Isis took the pieces, put Father back together, blew life back into him, mounted him, and—well, here I am!" As he finished the story, Horus held his arms wide.

The crowd stood, chanting, "Horus! Horus! Horus!" Although, some people began muttering, "Lord Charon cut off Osiris's hands and feet?"

Horus laughed a genuine laugh of happiness, waved, and stepped off the stage to join Djoser. Horus was replaced onstage by the Nomarch who said all of the appropriate things.

Djoser said to Horus, "Good work, Son. You are now quite the celebrity, and you did more good than you imagine, including renewing me. I needed those stories."

Major Hetephe stepped up, hit her chest with clenched fist, and said "Excellent stories, Shaman Horus!"

Horus basked in the pleasure of unexpected praise. *She called me Shaman!*

EGYPTIAN GODS: Osiris/Dionysus—Isis/Ariadne/Philyra, Horus, Set/Charon, Nephthys/Dexithea.
CANAANITE GODS: Anath, Astarte, Shalem, Shahar, Moloch, El.
OLYMPIAN GODS: Zeus, Dionysus, Hestia, Ares, Athena, Astraeus, Eos, Hermes.
OCEANIDS: Polydore, Lyris, Acaste, Eidyia, Dione.

From the background noise, Djoser overheard the words, "Our city is named after the one who dismembered Osiris. It should be named in honor of Osiris, instead."

Everyone wanted to talk with Horus, Prince Djoser, and the woman in the military uniform. The reception wore on into the night.

Sunrise

The three departed early for T'jaru City.

Along the way, Djoser reinforced the need for Horus to tell stories of Osiris to other communities. This would be necessary to preserve history while building Egyptian identity. *Plus, good therapy for Horus.*

Djoser said, "Horus, recruit some followers after every session. Tell them that you will meet with them whenever you are in their town. Teach them about your father and his beliefs. Make them assistant Shamans-in-training or something. A man can never have too many followers."

Horus grunted.

The three reached T'jaru City. It had grown by a few people. After evening meal, Horus told Osiris stories.

The three left T'jaru City at sunrise to journey on to Camp Haboua. Again, Horus told his stories.

The three left Camp Haboua at sunrise to join the First Egyptian Army at Dispatcher Anath Camp.

Major Hetephe's new uniform was looked upon with admiration. Excitement ran through the First Egyptian Army upon learning that they, too, would receive a similar uniform. They were being fabricated as they spoke. Dispatcher Anath was genuinely humbled when Captain T'jaru insisted that Anath, too, should receive a helmet and belt with turquoise stones.

Djoser continued eastward on the Trade Route to find Snefru, praise his progress, and tell him, "By the way, your grandfather died."

The Third–Sinai Expedition departed southward at sunrise the next morning. Horus accompanied them as an observer.

Dionysus/Osiris, Ariadne/Isis/Philyra, Charon/Set, Hermes/Tehuti.
EGYPTIANS: Nebka, Djoser, Hotep, Khasek, Rocky
NUBIANS: Nima, Hetephe, King Kerma, Prince T'jaru, Prince Rafah.
CANAANITES: Phoenicia, Serket, Azazil, Jaffa | URFANS: Teumessian, Abram, Sarai, Terah

7. The Third Expedition

Year 150, tenth month

The Third Sinai Expedition lasted two seasons and yielded wonderful results. Six warlords had been killed and most of their tribe had surrendered, due, in part to the fear that "Anath the Dispatcher" was coming for them.

The number of prisoners was so large that four archers were assigned to escort Major Hetephe, Prince Djoser, and Horus back to the holding camp in South Memphis.

The troupe spent the night at Fort Dispatcher Anath where Horus was greeted by three disciples who had already informed the camp workers that Horus would tell stories of Osiris after evening meal. The stories, as always, were excitedly received plus Horus gained another disciple. Djoser listened, with worry, to reports that at least one warlord, possibly two, had been seen observing the camp from afar. The camp had little protection against a determined attack, just a few male workers with a sword and spear. Djoser considered the reports and assured the inhabitants that he did not believe any warlord that had escaped the attention of the First Egyptian Army would be foolish enough to make their presence known but that he would find a way for some Kemet military soldiers to be stationed at each way station.

The troupe left for Camp Haboua at sunrise.

The attack came halfway between the two camps.

Hetephe surveyed the horizon and announced, "There are at least thirty men. Archers prepare and fire at will! Horus, take the captives and retreat toward Middlesea. Prince, try to make it to Haboua with the report in case we are all killed. All have your orders! Go! Now!"

The first of the bandits came into range. Major Hetephe and her four archers loosed their arrows. Four found their mark but only one bandit fell to the ground. *If they get into sword range, we will have to retreat!*

Driving them toward Oursea, Horus saw two captives look at one another and turn to rush back toward Hetephe and her archers. *Father, be with me!*

He removed his dagger, intercepted the closest man, and drove the dagger into his abdomen pulling the dagger upward, spilling the man's intestines

EGYPTIAN GODS: Osiris/Dionysus—Isis/Ariadne/Philyra, Horus, Set/Charon, Nephthys/Dexithea.
CANAANITE GODS: Anath, Astarte, Shalem, Shahar, Moloch, El.
OLYMPIAN GODS: Zeus, Dionysus, Hestia, Ares, Athena, Astraeus, Eos, Hermes.
OCEANIDS: Polydore, Lyris, Acaste, Eidyia, Dione.

into the sand. He removed the dagger and rushed toward the second man, who had stopped in confusion. Horus crouched and, motioning his dagger toward the sea, had the attention of the second man, who nodded "yes" and began a quick walk back toward Middlesea.

The archers had now downed twelve men and wounded six more. Hetephe commanded, "Separate positions. Make them commit to only one of us!" Her men ran from their tight formation to put thirty paces between them. The onslaught of bandits must now separate to attack only one of the archer's positions. In their momentary confusion, another four bandits went down. At this range, the arrows were fatal.

Hetephe went into "rapid-fire," killing only two but seriously wounding six more. In the end, only four bandits got through to attack the archers with their swords. The Nubians now had only their size, strength, agility, and short dagger with which to fight against men armed with swords. Three archers were killed. Only Hetephe and one archer remained standing. Major Hetephe commanded him, "Make sure all the scum are dead, prepare our warriors for transport to Camp Haboua." She then set off to find Horus and his fleeing wards.

Hetephe walked briskly to find Horus. She caught up with him at the edge of Middlesea where they had stopped. Major Hetephe commanded Horus, "Separate the captives into two groups, those who wish to settle in the land of Kemet and those who wish to return to the Sinai. Have those wishing to leave, travel east along Middlesea, and don't look back!"

Horus pointed to the man who had tried to escape and loudly commanded, "You! Take those who will follow you and leave! NOW!"

The man looked confused as Horus repeated his command and added, "This is your only chance to leave our company and return to the Sinai. CHOOSE NOW!" The man motioned to several of his friends and said, "Let's get out of here!" A dozen people, all men, followed him. As they left, Horus told them, "Anath the Dispatcher will follow close behind. Do not tarry!"

Major Hetephe commanded in a voice loud enough for all to hear, "Horus, take the men and travel westward and join the trade route closer to Camp Haboua. I will take the women and travel behind you with my archers protecting our flank. I don't want to attract another band of marauding warlords. If we do, then at least the men will get through safely

Dionysus/Osiris, Ariadne/Isis/Philyra, Charon/Set, Hermes/Tehuti.
EGYPTIANS: Nebka, Djoser, Hotep, Khasek, Rocky
NUBIANS: Nima, Hetephe, King Kerma, Prince T'jaru, Prince Rafah.
CANAANITES: Phoenicia, Serket, Azazil, Jaffa | URFANS: Teumessian, Abram, Sarai, Terah

enough. The men thought this to be an excellent plan. The women, not so much.

The troupe was divided into a group of men, led westward by Horus, and a group of women, led southward to the Trade Route by Hetephe.

Major Hetephe arrived at Camp T'jaru to be greeted by camp men armed with spears and swords. Horus had already arrived, and his male captives had been settled in at the holding barrack. The camp chief informed Major Hetephe that Prince Djoser had alerted the camp to portending danger and to be prepared to fight and that, although fatigued, the prince had immediately continued to Memphis. Horus had arrived with the captives sometime afterward and had told the camp chief to secure the captives in case of any additional problems. "So, here we are. What do we do now?"

She said, "Prepare my warriors for burial. I bury them here at sunrise—in Egypt."

~

Before sunrise, eighty foot soldiers of the newly formed Second Egyptian Army marched into Camp T'jaru. Their command was to defend the camps that would be converted into fortresses along the Egyptian War Road that had once been called a Trade Route.

The four warriors were given a full military funeral.

~

Hetephe and Horus delivered the captives to the South Memphis Holding Camp late that day. Hetephe said, "Meet me for morning meal at the Mastabas. We can go from there to give my report to the king."

Horus agreed and set off to the House of Nephthys.

Hetephe went to the prince's quarters in the House of the King. She let herself into his room and walked to the bed where he lay in exhausted sleep. She sat beside his bed and watched him sleep. *My young, little immature prince. How you have grown! I suppose we both have. Do you belong to me? No? Do I belong to you? No? To each other? Maybe. Have you grown greater than Osiris? Everyone does your bidding. Kings, Queens, Generals, Viziers, Shamans, the Nubians, the people of Memphis. And you don't even command them to do it. They do it because you suggest that it is the best thing to do. How do you do that? You are a dangerous man, my prince. Are women drawn to dangerous men? You neither know nor care. So, leave all that to me. I will take care of it.*

EGYPTIAN GODS: Osiris/Dionysus—Isis/Ariadne/Philyra, Horus, Set/Charon, Nephthys/Dexithea.
CANAANITE GODS: Anath, Astarte, Shalem, Shahar, Moloch, El.
OLYMPIAN GODS: Zeus, Dionysus, Hestia, Ares, Athena, Astraeus, Eos, Hermes.
OCEANIDS: Polydore, Lyris, Acaste, Eidyia, Dione.

She rose, removed her clothes, and climbed into his bed beside him. She nestled against him and took his arm to wrap around her. *Yes, my young, immature prince, leave all that to me.*

~

Hetephe rose without waking Djoser, walked to the river, and found Horus. The sunrise ceremony had just been completed. They talked for a while and then walked to the House of the King and announced to the guard, "Major Hetephe of the First Egyptian Army and Shaman Horus to report to the king and his council."

They were escorted to the meeting, which had not yet begun.

General Sanakhte saw Major Hetephe enter the council chambers and walked over to greet her. "Ahh, Major Hetephe. You live! Prince Djoser was not sure that your forces could fend off the large group of bandits that attacked you. He feared for your life and the life of your men—and Lord Horus. Welcome to both of you!"

Hetephe replied, "We lost four warriors. They were given a hero's burial. Most of the captives from the third campaign were successfully delivered to the holding camp. Your Second Egyptian Army arrived. Exciting events must be happening in these chambers. I had not considered that Prince Djoser does not know if we lived or died but he would have no way of knowing, I suppose." *Will he wonder whose underwear is lying across his face? He can figure it out.*

King Khasek announced, "We anxiously await your report, Major. I will send a courier to get the prince out of bed, so you won't have to give it twice."

Just then, Djoser entered, saying, "My apologies for my tardiness, King Khasek." He beamed at Hetephe, "You live! And Horus! Osiris answered my plea." Djoser walked to stand in front of his chair and awaited for the king to start the meeting.

King Khasek sat down at the head of the long table. Queen Nina sat on his left between the king and Vizier Menka. General Sanakhte sat on the king's right. Djoser sat in his chair against the wall as an observer as did his older brother, Priest Hotep.

King Khasek nodded to his Vizier to begin the meeting. Menka rose and recapped the last meeting, restating the extraordinary measures that had

Dionysus/Osiris, Ariadne/Isis/Philyra, Charon/Set, Hermes/Tehuti.
EGYPTIANS: Nebka, Djoser, Hotep, Khasek, Rocky
NUBIANS: Nima, Hetephe, King Kerma, Prince T'jaru, Prince Rafah.
CANAANITES: Phoenicia, Serket, Azazil, Jaffa | URFANS: Teumessian, Abram, Sarai, Terah

been implemented at the unending insistence of Prince Djoser and that the agreements could be rescinded at any time at the pleasure of the king. He said, "The basic fabric of our successful military has been restructured into a new and unproven structure. General Sanakhte will carefully and continually monitor the problems encountered by this restructuring."

Hetephe glanced at Djoser for any expression shedding light on the words she was hearing. He sat stone-faced.

Menka continued, "Major Hetephe must and will agree to the conditions of our understandings."

Hetephe went rigid.

Major Hetephe's command will be immediately transferred from Prince Djoser to General Sanakhte. Both Major Hetephe of the First Army and Major Khaba of the Second Army will be under the direct command of General Sanakhte ensuring all of Egypt's military might is under the control of one General.

Hetephe relaxed. *Djoser never intended to remain my commander. That was only for Chief Kerma's benefit. Who in the land of Hades is Khaba?*

General Sanakhte interrupted the Vizier, "Do you have a problem with that, Major?"

Hetephe stood to rigid attention, "It will be my honor and privilege to serve your command, General Sanakhte!"

Sanakhte said, "Good! At ease, Major."

She sat back down. *Men are so easy! But who in Hades is Khaba?*

Djoser's face may, or may not, have flashed a look of relief.

Major Hetephe was directed to give her full report on the Third Sinai campaign. Djoser listened to the details with rapt attention.

After the report, Priest Hotep said, "General Sanakhte, Major Hetephe, and Prince Djoser meet me in conference to discuss the Sinai Road construction in detail. We must convert a trade route into a war road. There are many details to be addressed".

A request from Priest Hotep was considered a direct command from dead King Nebka. "Yes," everyone agreed. "A plan must be completed post-haste."

EGYPTIAN GODS: Osiris/Dionysus—Isis/Ariadne/Philyra, Horus, Set/Charon, Nephthys/Dexithea.
CANAANITE GODS: Anath, Astarte, Shalem, Shahar, Moloch, El.
OLYMPIAN GODS: Zeus, Dionysus, Hestia, Ares, Athena, Astraeus, Eos, Hermes.
OCEANIDS: Polydore, Lyris, Acaste, Eidyia, Dione.

The principals retired to the war planning room. Djoser timed his exit to be with Hetephe's exit. He pounded his heart with his fist in greeting as he whispered, "Major Khaba is Sanakhte's younger brother. He is in the Sinai leading the Second Army. You will be expected to work closely with him. I will ask Hathor to request that Osiris help you."

She made no response.

They entered the conference room and Hotep called the meeting to order and said, "Snefru must immediately add fortifications to the existing camps. This will take at least two months. All new sites will be built as a fortress. At least one water well for each fortress must be constructed. Major Khaba's Second Army must provide adequate escort for those traveling along the War Road as well as defending the fortresses. I will discuss requirements for a defensive outer wall running the length of the War Road but that will be a major and costly undertaking. Military escorts will be required, at least for the short term. Major Hetephe, all these plans are being made because of one random attack on your caravan. Is it your feeling that we are overreacting to an isolated incident?"

She replied, "I lost four good men, Priest Hotep. A dozen captives were released back into the Sinai so they would not overpower my limited resources. Had this been a trade caravan rather than a military caravan, the slaughter would have been untenable. No, you are not overreacting. I can rid the Sinai of most of the warlords but where the opportunity for plunder exists, there must be preparation to defend it."

Discussions lasted throughout the day and into the night.

~

After the meeting ended, Djoser and Hetephe strolled to the stacked Mastabas to hopefully sit at Osiris's favorite table. Horus, Anubis, and Nephthys already sat there drinking wine. "Join us," Anubis called out.

Hetephe whispered to Djoser, "We must join them. I will be romantic later." They arrived at the table, Nephthys stood to embrace Hetephe, and then all sat down. Hetephe said, "It's always so beautiful up here. Almost as if there are no problems and sorrow in the world."

Horus muttered, "The only sorrow is that which the flesh brings."

Anubis exclaimed, "Cousin, flesh brings me great pleasure and joy. You should try it more often!"

Dionysus/Osiris, Ariadne/Isis/Philyra, Charon/Set, Hermes/Tehuti.
EGYPTIANS: Nebka, Djoser, Hotep, Khasek, Rocky
NUBIANS: Nima, Hetephe, King Kerma, Prince T'jaru, Prince Rafah.
CANAANITES: Phoenicia, Serket, Azazil, Jaffa | URFANS: Teumessian, Abram, Sarai, Terah

They bantered on about frivolous things.

Finally, Djoser asked, "Where is Lord Set? I have not encountered him in a long time."

Nephthys laughingly replied, "My husband wanders the western Red Land talking to every tribe he finds. He knows where all the oases lay. Set is becoming ever more determined to rise to the glory of Osiris. I am to be his Isis. The respect and adulation we both have in South Memphis are not sufficient for his ego. He has delusions of grandeur but is otherwise harmless to the prince. I humor his ambitions." She sipped her wine.

Horus added, "He hears of my growing following along the trade—I mean—War Road. I have disciples now, you know, just as you commanded me to, Prince Djoser. I did not realize how eager people were to hear the stories of my father and mother. They transferred their adulation to me. It's frightening. I am simply a son looking for his parents in the land of the dead. Hardly a person to follow around. This seems to anger my uncle. He has always been aloof to me. He grows more so— envious, even."

Anubis added, "Yes, my father wishes for me to travel with him much more than I do. He wants me to meet 'his people,' impress them, and lord my position over them. 'Anubis *is* the only son of Set and Nephthys,' he tells people." Anubis laughed a hearty laugh, "My heritage *does* get me untold attention at the House of Ishtar! What more could a man want?!"

Nephthys quietly offered, "Perhaps to save people from themselves."

Anubis said, "Father was impressed with Horus's telling of Anath's rise in status in the eastern lands. He may wish us to travel into the Sinai to witness this phenomenon. How dangerous is it? There aren't many beautiful women there, are there?"

They bantered on about frivolous things.

~

After much wine and warmth, Hetephe and Djoser retired to his quarters. Hetephe picked her underwear off the pillow, held them up for him to see, and said, "You never said anything about this little gift I left you."

He exclaimed, "Oh, are those yours?!"

She shoved him, forcibly, onto their bed.

EGYPTIAN GODS: Osiris/Dionysus—Isis/Ariadne/Philyra, Horus, Set/Charon, Nephthys/Dexithea.
CANAANITE GODS: Anath, Astarte, Shalem, Shahar, Moloch, El.
OLYMPIAN GODS: Zeus, Dionysus, Hestia, Ares, Athena, Astraeus, Eos, Hermes.
OCEANIDS: Polydore, Lyris, Acaste, Eidyia, Dione.

8. The Fourth Expedition

They named the fortress "Fort First Egyptians," in honor of the four archers killed in the service of the new land to someday be named "Egypt."

Major Khaba fussed at Major Hetephe, "Why not name it "Fort Second Egyptians" after *my* command? They are as important as *your* command."

Major Hetephe held her anger and sweetly replied, "You are correct, Major Khaba, and maybe your command is *more* important than my command—your father being the king and all. But you realize that *I* have naming rights. Would you like a fort to be named 'Fort Major Khaba?' Maybe that can happen someday. Let us both hope so. But for now, I estimate the Fourth Sinai Expedition will require two full seasons to complete. If you could release twelve of your men to my command, they would provide valuable support as we capture more and more nomads."

"I cannot possibly do that!" Major Khaba snapped back. "I need all of my men protecting the fortresses from invaders. Plus, we have morning drills to perform and numerous inspections. I'm afraid assigning men to you is out of the question!"

Hetephe replied, "Oh, how sad. Only *my* men will receive a turquoise stone to add to their belts. Your command will be left without any outward sign of accomplishment. And your men will not have any stories to share—like seeing Dispatcher Anath at work—and that ghastly ceremony she forces my captain to perform with her on the bodies of the dead. Well, those aren't sights for innocent eyes, anyway. I can make do with our usual support team. It's composed of mostly women, but I suppose they can do as well as the Second Egyptian Army Corps. But thank you for the consideration, Major."

Khaba sulked, then said, "Well, I will consider your request, but I am not making any promises."

With all seriousness, Hetephe replied, "The pressure of command is difficult, Major. You will be faced with many difficult decisions." *Maybe I should convince this dung-hole to go with us with the promise that he can replace T'jaru for the ritual. Hmm. That may not be a bad idea. Everybody wins!*

Hetephe departed to rejoin her command.

Fourth Sinai Expedition
Year 150, eleventh month

The Second Egyptian Army stood in perfect dress formation watching the First Egyptian break camp to set off on the Fourth Sinai Expedition.

Major Hetephe saw Horus talking to Anath and Captain T'jaru. The three glanced in the direction of Major Hetephe and started walking her way.

Hetephe thought, *Dung! This can't be good.*

T'jaru addressed Hetephe, "Sir! Shaman Horus informs me that you have a candidate to replace me for Dispatcher Anath's midnight ritual. The Dispatcher and I both agree this would have a positive effect on your command—and on myself. We would approve of such action. Sir!"

Hetephe stared at T'jaru. *Dung, Captain. I should not have mentioned that to Horus. Dung, dung, dung!*

She replied, "Very well, Captain. I will make inquiries." She marched to where Major Khaba stood with his troops. She briskly saluted her counterpart and said, "Dispatcher Anath has requested that you accompany her in her midnight victory ritual. She feels that this would boost morale in both of our Commands. The Expedition departs in a short while. I invite you to join the expedition with as many men as you can spare." She saluted again and turned to go.

Major Khaba excitedly asked, "Do you mean the ritual where she fornicates lying over the dead bodies?"

Hetephe turned and replied, "That very one, Major. She requires the most virile man available to plow her in front of as many warriors as can be gathered! It is for the glory of Egypt and is considered the most prestigious duty in my command."

Khaba replied, "I will place myself and twenty-four men plus one donkey-pulled wagon under your command and escort you into this Osiris-forsaken land."

Hetephe replied, "A difficult but wise decision, Major Khaba. Difficult but wise." *What a dung-head!*

~

The first encounter was difficult. The Warlord was not killed outright, and he was able to mobilize his men; well over a hundred. They had shields, the first the Nubians had encountered outside the army of Kemet. None of the men surrendered by lying on the ground. This warlord had been prepared and had trained his men well. As they charged and grew closer, Hetephe went into rapid-fire shooting at their unprotected legs. She wanted to slow them and buy time for her archers to deliver the fatal arrow. The last bandit standing had his sword in striking position but was impaled by a half dozen arrows. Major Hetephe commanded Captain T'jaru, "Send in the Dispatcher. She is to show no mercy!"

Hetephe noted that the Second Army had not positioned itself to defend her archers had the bandits breached her perimeter. They were standing in wide-eyed, open-mouthed amazement staring at what they had seen. She spoke to Major Khaba as she walked past him, "You are going to have your work cut out for you tonight, Major Khaba. Anath will be insatiable." *You command children, Major!*

As Anath did her work, several women stood and ran toward her with daggers drawn. The archers did their work.

Meanwhile, Major Hetephe inspected the captives, now bound by rope to the wagons. Several women screamed obscenities and spat in her face. The older boys glared at her, hatred in their eyes.

Later, the two majors and their captains met to review their situation. Major Hetephe commanded, "The Second Army must form a protective wall in front of the archers at our next encounter. The archers have no protection if the bandits get within sword-striking distance. If they have shields, our kill rate is reduced significantly. A hundred men with shields will have a real chance of overrunning us. The Second Army swordsmen will be our last wall of defense. With your superior equipment and training, you should dispatch them easily enough. The archers will offer whatever assistance they can with their daggers.

Major Khaba and his captain stared at one another. Khaba then asked Hetephe, incredulously, "You want my men between the bandits and the archers? But one of my men might be hurt!"

T'jaru glanced at Hetephe but Hetephe was ready. "Major, exactly how much training have you and your men had?"

Khaba replied, "Why, we need no training. I am the son of a king who was once a general. My command is from the very best families that

Memphis has to offer. All are high-born, intelligent, and educated. This killing experience is for the lower classes and the foreigners."

T'jaru winced at the word "foreigners."

Hetephe replied, "Ahh, yes. I understand. You take your men and enjoy the rest of your evening, Major Khaba. Prepare to do your duty at midnight for the glory of Egypt. We will talk more tomorrow morning."

~

At midnight, a still-shaken Major Khaba performed his duty to the delight of the watching men of the Second Egyptian Army. Anath was a forewarned professional. Afterward, Major Khaba was convinced that he had sated the insatiable.

Sunrise

In the pre-sunrise light, Hetephe coordinated her strategy with T'jaru, Anath, and Horus.

Major Hetephe greeted Major Khaba as he rose for the morning, saying, "Good morning, Major. I have a mission of the utmost importance that I thought you might wish to accept for yourself. If not yourself, then one of your most trusted lieutenants."

Khaba asked, "What type of mission?"

Hetephe said, "We cannot carry this many captives with us into the war zones. They will slow us down. Many must be led back to Fortress First Egyptians, immediately. I was thinking that you and two of your best men could escort the youngest, the girls and boys, back to the fort and then return in time to engage in the battles sure to come. This would be a great help to the campaign, larger turquoise stones would be in order."

Khaba replied, "Ahh, yes. I will be delighted to accept this command, but I would feel safer with six soldiers in case we run into trouble."

Hetephe responded, "A difficult but wise decision, Major Khaba. Haste is of the essence; in case we are attacked this morning."

Khaba replied, "Yes, yes. I will set off with the prisoners immediately."

Hetephe sat down with Horus and Anath to eat their morning meal as T'jaru selected the young captives to be returned to the fortress. The children's hands were tied together by one long rope so they could all be

EGYPTIAN GODS: Osiris/Dionysus—Isis/Ariadne/Philyra, Horus, Set/Charon, Nephthys/Dexithea.
CANAANITE GODS: Anath, Astarte, Shalem, Shahar, Moloch, El.
OLYMPIAN GODS: Zeus, Dionysus, Hestia, Ares, Athena, Astraeus, Eos, Hermes.
OCEANIDS: Polydore, Lyris, Acaste, Eidyia, Dione.

controlled by only two soldiers. Four older girls were tied by their waists so that each could carry an infant.

Hetephe nodded to T'jaru to begin. T'jaru led the remaining eighteen Second Army swordsmen to a captive woman. He handed the woman's binding rope to the soldier and motioned him toward Horus and Anath, who stood one hundred eighty paces apart. Eighteen Nubian archers sat in a row fifty paces in front of them. Horus met each captive woman and soldier and spaced them out with ten paces of separation, with the soldier standing behind the woman. T'jaru, with a sword rather than a bow, led the nineteenth woman to the middle of the line. He stood behind her, turned, and motioned his archers to stand.

Captain T'jaru looked toward Major Hetephe. Major Hetephe stood and in loud voice, commanded, "I, Major Hetephe of the First Egyptian Army hereby command each soldier of the Second Egyptian Army to behead the woman standing in front of you."

T'jaru gave the soldiers but a moment of stunned silence and then commanded, "That is a direct order, soldiers. To disobey a direct order will be punished by death. This is how it is done!" He raised his sword high, swung, and separated the woman's head from her body. He repeated, "I shall now walk to my Archers. When I reach them, I will turn, and any woman left standing will be killed as will the traitor standing behind her who refused to obey a direct order. Be merciful, soldiers, kill her quickly with one blow. That is a direct order."

T'jaru turned and began marching toward his archers. The captive women looked at one another in terror. Anath and Horus encouraged the soldiers on each end to raise their swords high and yelled—"Now! Strike!" They inexpertly did. The other soldiers panicked as T'jaru turned back toward them and the Archers raised their bows in unison. Their blows were neither swift nor merciful, but each soldier hacked at the woman in front of him. There was blood and screaming. Anath mercifully dispatched the several women who had only been hacked on. Six soldiers vomited.

Major Hetephe shouted to them. "Good work, soldiers. Now, kill the remaining women tied to the wagons." She hesitated and then added, "That is a direct order!"

After the bloody work was finished, after more vomiting of their morning meal, Captain T'jaru, by Major Hetephe's order, commanded, "I and

Horus are not accomplished swordsmen, but we will teach you enough to defend yourselves when attacked. We will teach you a few simple sword thrusts and how to use your shields. With a little practice, you will be at least as accomplished as those who are going to attack and try to kill you before this is all over."

Major Hetephe had her support staff strip the dead women and lay them on top of a male. She had a sign made and drove its post through the bodies of one of the men and woman. Upon it was written, "Anath found them! They did not surrender!" She stared vacantly at their handiwork. *What have I become? Osiris forgive me! What have I become?*

Major Khaba had not yet returned to rejoin his troops.

~

The fourth expedition was not burdened with prisoners; they had either been returned to base or had been killed. Hetephe met with her staff and advisors, including the Lieutenant from the Second Egyptian Army who had thrown up but otherwise demonstrated a modicum of military skill.

The group addressed many issues:
Horus: "Where did *they* come from?"
Hetephe: "They were experienced fighters."
T'jaru: "Shields, when did they start using shields?"
Hetephe: "Another encounter like that will cost us soldiers."
Anath: "Are the Swordsmen prepared to fight?"
Hetephe: "How do we best position our warriors?"

In the end, Major Hetephe commanded that the archers would be split into two formations, each fronted by nine swordsmen. They moved due south. The scouts would find them.

A scout scouting the southeast found them. He reported, "There is a camp less than a half-day march, due east. The warlord appears to have a tent that he sits under. I saw no swords and only a few spears. Most of the men appeared to be attending goats."

Major Hetephe commanded the expedition, "Due east."

After less than a half-day march, the scout reported back and said, "They are just over the horizon."

Major Hetephe commanded, "We will camp here. No fires. Maintain silence. We will attack just before sunrise."

EGYPTIAN GODS: Osiris/Dionysus—Isis/Ariadne/Philyra, Horus, Set/Charon, Nephthys/Dexithea.
CANAANITE GODS: Anath, Astarte, Shalem, Shahar, Moloch, El.
OLYMPIAN GODS: Zeus, Dionysus, Hestia, Ares, Athena, Astraeus, Eos, Hermes.
OCEANIDS: Polydore, Lyris, Acaste, Eidyia, Dione.

The troops assembled for deployment. Major Hetephe accompanied Captain T'jaru and his six most accurate archers as they crept to take the final assessment and finalize the killing of the Warlord. Horus was allowed to follow behind.

The camp was still sleeping. The tent obscured the occupants.

T'jaru offered, "I could have all archers unleash three successive arrows at the ten. The occupants would be dead before they woke up."

Hetephe countered, "No. We don't know who, or how many are in there. There are probably women and maybe children. We will follow normal procedures and wait for the warlord to appear."

T'jaru replied, "My six will kill him from this place on your command. I will position the others to await the probable attack. The camp looks peaceful enough. Perhaps Dispatcher Anath will have light duty this morning.'"

Hetephe replied, "Let us hope."

All were in position. All waited upon Hetephe's command to fire.

The sun breached the horizon. The tribes began to rise to meet the new day. After a few minutes, three children ran from the tent, followed by a woman. The woman turned and shouted back into the tent, "Get up, Old Man. It is time to begin our day."

Hetephe softly commanded, "Prepare your arrows!"

The old man walked from the tent and stretched, the woman between him and the archers. The old man laughed, and shouted after the children, "Be nice to the goats! They don't like to be frightened by playing children!"

Hetephe commanded, "Prepare to stand and fire!"

The woman moved to chase after the children leaving the old man exposed to the archers.

Hetephe commanded, "Stand and ..."

Horus whispered loudly, "Wait! Major Hetephe, may I advise you?"

Hetephe was livid. With wide eyes and labored breathing, she hissed, "And what does the Shaman wish to advise the Major?!"

Horus said, "Allow me and Anath to enter the camp. I can negotiate a settlement with no loss of life. If I fail, Anath and I may die but your attack will not be significantly compromised. This is the most promising situation we have encountered to allow such a negotiation. If I am successful, a new era of negotiated warfare will open up. This value of success far outweighs the risk of failure. I am convinced this is the correct tactic, Major."

She glared at him, her mind churning. Finally, she commanded the captain, "Send Anath to me. Tell her to prepare to accept a suicide mission."

The captain crawled away, then rose and ran toward the waiting forces. The message was relayed, and he escorted Anath back to the front line.

After a brief discussion between Horus, Anath, and Hetephe, it was agreed—only Horus and Anath would enter the camp—and they would be unarmed.

Hetephe said, "May Osiris be with you, soldiers!"

Horus said to Anath, "I want us to approach the camp carrying only your knife and wearing nothing but your helmet."

The two women gasped and considered what was just said, Anath responded by slipping out of her clothes and saying, "I am ready Horus. Use pretty words, alright?"

Horus said, "If we die, Anath, this was still the right thing to do!"

Anath laughed and said, "We all die, Horus. It's a rule."

They stood to their full height and began marching toward the camp.

Hetephe quietly commanded, "Archers, prepare for cover fire!"

The women in the camp saw them approaching in the distance. They called their children to them and all lay face down on the ground. The Old Man saw what was approaching and called several men over, embraced them, and shoved them face down on the ground with the women, children, and other tribesmen.

He turned toward Horus and Anath. When they were within talking distance, the Old Man said, "So, Anath comes for me! My people lie upon the ground as you command. They know and accept that they are now

EGYPTIAN GODS: Osiris/Dionysus—Isis/Ariadne/Philyra, Horus, Set/Charon, Nephthys/Dexithea.
CANAANITE GODS: Anath, Astarte, Shalem, Shahar, Moloch, El.
OLYMPIAN GODS: Zeus, Dionysus, Hestia, Ares, Athena, Astraeus, Eos, Hermes.
OCEANIDS: Polydore, Lyris, Acaste, Eidyia, Dione.

enslaved people. Do them as little harm as is your nature. If you need to hear the screams of war, hear my screams, not theirs."

Horus said, "I will accept your surrender and do no one harm. Our mission is only to rid the Sinai of warlords and bandits."

The Old Man said, "I am neither. We are simple Bedouins, Asair of the Desert. We neither plunder nor engage in war. We pay tribute to the warlords that require it of us—which is all of them. They keep us hungry and poor—but the desert provides for us well enough—or at least it did until Anath came for us. Now we shall be slaves in the Land of Kemet— or the Land of Egypt, if what the wanderers tell us is true."

Horus replied, "Egypt does not take slaves. We move our captives to live in our country—productive, happy, and free. We seek only to rid the Sinai of warlords and their bandits."

The Old Man laughed, and replied, "I see. You will move my tribesman from the land they know—from where we have lived since time began, from where we are productive, happy, and free. We must do as you command but we are not slaves. I am not wise enough to understand how moving my tribe from where we are to where you are going to take them accomplished anything at all. You will enslave my tribe, to resist results in the death of me and my people, so, do as you will."

Horus stared at the Old Man. *Short-sighted, ill-planned, unintended consequences—what were we thinking?—empty one land to populate another?—they cause no harm—they are not a threat—what can I do?—What can I say?*

Anath asked the Old Man, "Can you tell us where the bandits are?"

He replied, "They come and go as the wind blows them. If I knew where they were, my tribe would not be there. But everyone must eventually come to an oasis. I can certainly tell you where the oases are—all of them. Will you spare my tribe if I tell you where the oases are?"

Ananth persisted, "How do I tell the difference between bandits and Bedouins?"

He looked at her, shrugged, and said, "If you confuse me with a bandit, then I suppose you must kill us all, God Anath."

Anath looked at the old man and then at Horus. She asked Horus, "Can we tell the difference?"

Horus replied, simply, "Yes."

Anath brightly exclaimed, "Well, there we have it! These Bedouin people can stay on their land, and we can set up military camps close to each one of these oasis things and just kill the bandits. No more sending captives to South Memphis or killing innocent people!"

The old man looked hopefully at Horus and asked, "Is this possible Great Lord?"

Horus asked, "How do we find these oases?"

"Simply read the directions of the dunes. Use the stars at night when you travel. Know the direction of where the sun rises and know the landmarks. It is simple enough. The closest oasis is one march east and south."

Horus asked, "Do you have tribesmen skilled in finding these oases?"

The man replied, "From the time we are born, we learn to read the desert, Great Lord. Yes, all my sons and their sons can easily read the desert. Will my tribesman be enslaved?"

Horus said, "I will counsel with my people to decide our course of action."

The man exclaimed, "A feast! Tonight, we shall have a feast to celebrate your righteous decision! I will slaughter two goats. Return at sundown. My granddaughters will sing and dance for you! How many will come? It doesn't matter! All are welcome! I rejoice in this day!" He bowed to Anath and said, "You are just and merciful, God Anath. We shall sing your praises for all time, but the sun rises higher. Would you wish a cloth to protect your body?"

Anath and the man bantered on.

Horus stared at the camp and its people. *Do the right thing! Correct, Father? And what is the right thing? We have our orders! Clear the Sinai of its people! For the glory of Egypt! Capture them! Enslave them! Kill them! What is the correct thing to do? And how shall I ensure it is done?*

Eventually, he said to Anath, "Come, Dispatcher Anath. We will return to our council to decide the fate of the Bedouin and return tonight to seal that fate."

Anath left with Horus but turned to smile and gaily wave goodbye to the Old Man.

EGYPTIAN GODS: Osiris/Dionysus—Isis/Ariadne/Philyra, Horus, Set/Charon, Nephthys/Dexithea.
CANAANITE GODS: Anath, Astarte, Shalem, Shahar, Moloch, El.
OLYMPIAN GODS: Zeus, Dionysus, Hestia, Ares, Athena, Astraeus, Eos, Hermes.
OCEANIDS: Polydore, Lyris, Acaste, Eidyia, Dione.

Horus and Anath rejoined Major Hetephe and gave his report ending with, "I believe that I made us an appointment at a feast, tonight. You need a list of demands and concessions if any."

Major Hetephe's only comment was, "Dung!" She then led her troops back to the command base.

~

Hetephe, T'jaru, Horus, and Anath arrived at the Bedouin camp prepared for feasting and negotiations.

Hetephe realized that she was in an impossible situation. She intended to temporize, as best she could, until she could counsel with Prince Djoser. Her orders were to remove all warlords and bandits in the Sinai. These people were neither—but—they had the potential to become bandits. But for now, they were innocent people, presumably living peaceful lives in harmony with the desert and other tribes. *What to do? Dung!*

The Old Man rushed to greet his guests. He gave Anath a bear-hug, and said, "Welcome God Anath. You and your people will be the last to die if we are attacked by Mudhakhel and his bandits. Welcome!"

Anath introduced Major Hetephe, emphasizing that it would be she who made all the decisions.

The Old Man understood immediately and shifted his negotiation persona to Hetephe. Leading them to the feasting area for a night of delightful food, entertainment, and talk—posturing, probing, and difficult negotiations had begun.

Hetephe explained the goals of the Egyptian armies, ridding the Sinai of warlords and bandits—and creating a trade route to Canaan.

The Old Man enthusiastically supported these endeavors, but he would not pledge his fealty to any man, including the king of Egypt. However, an alliance with friends was certainly desirable. And, yes, The Old Man might be able to instruct three of his sons to serve Major Hetephe until her goals were met if Major Hetephe were to eliminate the scourge of Mudhakhel and his bandits. The location of all oases in the Sinai is well known to all Bedouin—there would be no problem leading Major Hetephe or her officers to any of them—and, yes, even known bandits must, at some time, camp at an oasis. And, "Yes, my sons certainly recognize the bandits."

Hetephe said, "The bandits that we eliminated were well-trained, well-armed, and had shields. Perhaps it was this Mudhakhel you speak of. If we take you there, would you recognize the tribe?"

The Old Man exclaimed, "They had shields? The only tribes that have shields are Mudhakhel and his bandits! You allowed me to offer my sons and my allegiance for something Dispatcher Anath has already accomplished! You are brilliant Major Hetephe! You will be my chief negotiator when I deal with my fellow Bedouins. At least you allow me to keep my wives and goats. You are as merciful as you are cunning! Mudhakhel has already been exterminated! What a glorious feast we are having!" He motioned to his three youngest sons, and commanded, "My sons, come and sit with me at our last meal together for a while. Learn the ways of Egyptian Commander Hetephe! She has much to teach you!"

The Old Man wished to leave and identify the bodies immediately after the feast, which they did, and it was. All made camp with the dead for the remainder of the night.

At first light, the Old Man set off to return to his tribe as the Egyptians set off to return to Camp First Egyptians. They were accompanied by the Old Man's three younger sons, a male goat, and six female goats.

Expedition Four Ends
Year 151, first month, second week

The return of the Egyptian troops caught the Camp First Egyptians personnel by complete surprise. They were not expected back for another full season—and they had no prisoners!

She was greeted by Major Khaba, who was delighted.

He said, "Ahh, Major Hetephe. You appear to be returning in complete failure—far too early and not one prisoner. It looks as if I should have torn myself away from my important inspection duties and returned to assist you. Oh, well. Perhaps next time."

She replied, "I look forward to you joining us on our next mission, although your first lieutenant has become a valuable resource. You were wise to train him so well. If you are not able to participate in a bloody combat mission, you can send him in your place. He will make an outstanding major someday after you are promoted to a staff position at Memphis headquarters; assistant to the general or even the king himself. Yes. You are very clever, but I see through you!"

EGYPTIAN GODS: Osiris/Dionysus—Isis/Ariadne/Philyra, Horus, Set/Charon, Nephthys/Dexithea.
CANAANITE GODS: Anath, Astarte, Shalem, Shahar, Moloch, El.
OLYMPIAN GODS: Zeus, Dionysus, Hestia, Ares, Athena, Astraeus, Eos, Hermes.
OCEANIDS: Polydore, Lyris, Acaste, Eidyia, Dione.

Khaba was pleased with himself, and giggled, "Staff position? Do you think so? Possibly so."

Hetephe responded, "Some of your men had a difficult time. You may want to use your experience to console them. They didn't always keep a straight row in their march."

Khaba was incensed. "Yes. I will speak to them and double their training. Perfect execution is so important in today's army! Thank you for the information, Major!"

She struck her heart with her fist and said, "I will give a general report to the camp after Highsun meal. Join us if you are interested."

As she departed, he called after her, "Yes. I will be there. Perhaps I can advise you on what you did wrong!"

Horus, Anath, and the Second Army First Lieutenant ate their Highsun meal with Horus's six camp disciples. Talk turned to the execution of the Warlord, his fighters, and the captive women. Details were given. The lieutenant described the emotions he experienced in the killing of the women. He had an appreciative audience—this was the subject that interested them all—death, dying, why, and what then?

Anath offered. "The way of Horus is to do that which is right. Because he led me and taught me what to do, an entire tribe was saved—maybe many tribes. I may never again get to escort anyone into the land of the dead. All because of Horus!"

Horus sat quietly eating. *"The way of Horus," Anath? Dung! You single-handedly and spontaneously created the plan that will save an entire people. I had no idea how to proceed. And you give me the credit? Hetephe will have to report—everyone will have to discuss, debate, find fault, revise, negotiate, and appear wise, but in the end, it will be this—that which you and the Old Man decided in the desert while you were birth-moment naked will come to pass. Anath—my prostitute lover—my cold-blooded killer—my innocent, loving child.*

After the meal, Major Hetephe gave her report to everyone in the camp. She ended with, "Major Khaba and I must return to Memphis immediately to give our reports to the king and his council. While we are gone, Captain T'jaru will instruct everyone in the camp on the art of swordplay and archery, including the women. If this is to be a War Road, then everyone on it must be prepared for an attack at any time. You will no longer be an archer or a swordsman, you will be an Egyptian warrior. I will return with expert instructors in these arts. Do the best you can. Help one another." She turned, looked at Horus, and said, "That is the way of Horus, I am told."

Horus did not respond. *Dung! I am up to my ears in dung!*

His disciples looked upon him with awe.

EGYPTIAN GODS: Osiris/Dionysus—Isis/Ariadne/Philyra, Horus, Set/Charon, Nephthys/Dexithea.
CANAANITE GODS: Anath, Astarte, Shalem, Shahar, Moloch, El.
OLYMPIAN GODS: Zeus, Dionysus, Hestia, Ares, Athena, Astraeus, Eos, Hermes.
OCEANIDS: Polydore, Lyris, Acaste, Eidyia, Dione.

9. The Cuckolding of Horus

They lay in Djoser's bed in Memphis. Their pillow talk was no longer double-entendres, giggles, and talk of Ibis flicking. It was focused.

She said, "Tomorrow's report to the king will be difficult. I don't even know my goals. Can you see the future yet? I need to know."

"The end is easy enough to see—combine the First and Second armies. Squads should be composed of both archers for long-range defense and with shielded swordsmen for hand-to-hand combat. Set up military camps near the oases and capture only the bandits that come there. Station squads at each fort to protect the fort and escort trade caravans over the War Road. Getting from this night to the end will be difficult. Now that you know your goals, how will you accomplish them, Major Hetephe?

She said, "I will let Major Khaba, Horus, and Anath tell me at tomorrow's meeting. Now that everything is solved, Prince Djoser, plow me!"

~

Meanwhile, at the House of Ishtar, Anath's mother and sisters listened breathlessly to her tales of the Sinai. Ishtar cackled with delight as Anath described cutting the throat of the mortally wounded men; her sisters gasped with sympathetic empathy as Anath described the life leaving their bodies. They all laughed joyfully at her description of making the very important, handsome Major T'jaru copulate with her as she lay upon the naked dead bodies of those she had escorted to the Land of the Dead. They listened appreciatively as Anath breathlessly told of her growing physical, emotional, and intellectual relationship with Horus—"He is so handsome—so smart—he has disciples in every camp that follow his every word—he is going to be sooo important one day."

Ishtar interrupted. "My daughter has a high rank and a title in the First Egyptian Army! She is the Dispatcher, and all men fear her. Can you dispatch Pig Omari for me? Place his head on our gate post; a gift for your loving mother!"

Anath replied, "No, Mother! I am a professional Dispatcher. A professional Dispatcher must never abuse her office for personal satisfaction! But I will consult with Horus on this matter if you like."

"No, let the pig live. He is old and slobbers a lot. Maybe living is a worse punishment than death. Anyway, he does not deserve the dignity of entering the Land of the Dead escorted by a professional Dispatcher."

The women giggled into the night.

~

And too, Horus had found the reassuring counsel of stepmother and sometimes lover Hathor rather than Step-mother Nephthys—who would be with irritating Uncle Set. Horus could visit them tomorrow.

Hathor lay nestled in his arms—or perhaps it was Horus who lay nestled in hers. Horus was bound to her by Hathor's certainties in her role as High Priestess to Osiris. Horus intellectually searched for that which Hathor already spiritually knew—the nature of death.

Horus lay whispering, "Anath says that she can sometimes see the light— the one Father talked about—the One, the All—inviting the soon-to-be-dead to come into it; to shed their body and at last, live! I don't know, Hathor. How can this be? Where do they go? Where do they live? How can we know?"

Hathor tightened her embrace. "Shhh, Horus. Don't fret. When I call your father to be reborn tomorrow, perhaps he will whisper secrets to you. But for now, let us enjoy the moment. It's all we have."

~

Earlier, Major Khaba had dined with his father and mother. The major told of his exploits and accomplishments at the front and that he fully expected to be awarded a turquoise stone of gigantic portions for his campaign belt. "Father, you will hear all the details in my report to the king at tomorrow's meeting. Is there any talk of an opening at headquarters for an efficient major, anytime soon?"

~

The next morning, the support advisors arrived early for the meeting. Horus and Anath found one another and sat down together against the back wall. Djoser and Hetephe arrived. Djoser took a seat midway down the council's table. Hetephe saw Major Khaba enter and motioned for him to sit beside her, which he gleefully did. Shaman Saqqara and Priest Hotep entered and sat on either side of the prince. General Sanakhte and

EGYPTIAN GODS: Osiris/Dionysus—Isis/Ariadne/Philyra, Horus, Set/Charon, Nephthys/Dexithea.
CANAANITE GODS: Anath, Astarte, Shalem, Shahar, Moloch, El.
OLYMPIAN GODS: Zeus, Dionysus, Hestia, Ares, Athena, Astraeus, Eos, Hermes.
OCEANIDS: Polydore, Lyris, Acaste, Eidyia, Dione.

Vizier Menka arrived and sat across the table from the prince. The scribes and support staff had long been in their places.

At last, the king and queen entered. All rose. Queen Nima wore her usual countenance of morning satisfaction as she stood behind the chair of the king. King Khasek sat down in the chair at the head of the table. All sat.

The king began the meeting. "I see that Major Hetephe returns more than a season earlier than expected and I understand she returns with no captives. None of this can possibly portend good news. Let's hear your report, Major Hetephe."

Hetephe rose and addressed the council. "Whether my report is received with joy or trepidation is beyond my knowing, King Khasek. I can only report. The council must judge its implications. But, if my king will indulge me a courtesy, I suggest that my counterpart, Major Khaba of the Second Egyptian Army be allowed to give his report first. His report may provide insights into the implications of my report."

Khaba was beside himself—to go first—he must take every advantage of this glorious opportunity.

King Khasek said, "Very well, Major Khaba. Present your report to this council!"

Trembling with excitement, Khaba rose and marched to the end of the council's table to face the king. "The conditions in the Sinai are extreme and challenging. I did, however, manage fourteen inspections and seven drills." He droned on for quite a while.

Major Hetephe made no expression.

After a long while, Prince Djoser interrupted. "Fascinating report, Major. This is the stuff of a possible headquarters position, someday. In the interest of finishing our meeting today, I would like to hear a few words from Major Hetephe."

Major Khaba huffed but sat down. *Everybody knows you're plowing her, but you shouldn't show favoritism!*

As Hetephe rose, she whispered to Khaba, "Excellent report, Major. It was obviously well received!"

Khaba puffed with pride.

Major Hetephe took her position to face the king. "King Khasek, the first section of my report will report the glory of both the First and Second Armies of Egypt and bring joy to our military leaders. It describes our intercepting and destruction of what I believe to be the largest and most dangerous warlord in the Sinai. His name was Mudhakhel, and he commanded over one hundred well-armed, well-trained bandit swordsmen." She described their close encounter and her tactical problems. She fielded questions from the council, especially over the response of the Swordsmen of the Second Army. She placated them with, "It was our first joint combat mission from which I was able to learn quite a bit. I instituted training exercises, and we became an integrated fighting unit when we positioned ourselves for the second attack which I will now report on." She did not pause for more questions.

She continued with the second portion of her report. She described positioning her troops, the subsequent reconnoitering mission, and the complex issues associated with her upcoming command to kill the tribal chief. "As I prepared to issue the command to kill, Shaman Horus presented me with a bold plan; a plan that could well result in the death of both Shaman Horus and Dispatcher Anath. But if his plan were successful, the very nature of our war in the Sinai would change and might give my king control over most of the tribes in the Sinai without another arrow being loosed. They call themselves Bedouins. I made a command decision counter to my standing orders. I will accept whatever punishment my decision merits. But regardless of your decision, I must extol the courage, foresight, wisdom, and merit of Shaman Horus and Dispatcher Anath. They are examples of the greatness that the Kingdom of Egypt is capable of producing. I am now ready for your learned and penetrating questions."

General Sanakhte and Vizier Menka began peppering her with questions.

Dispatcher Anath sat against the wall, flushed with excitement and pride over the accolades that Horus had received and even herself, as inadequate as her contributions may have been.

Horus sat coolly beside Anath. *Dung, Hetephe. You glossed over the fact that Anath spontaneously came up with the very plans you presented. I didn't do anything but say "Don't kill them without reason." How plowing hard is that?*

The questions lasted forever. Hetephe never flinched.

EGYPTIAN GODS: Osiris/Dionysus—Isis/Ariadne/Philyra, Horus, Set/Charon, Nephthys/Dexithea.
CANAANITE GODS: Anath, Astarte, Shalem, Shahar, Moloch, El.
OLYMPIAN GODS: Zeus, Dionysus, Hestia, Ares, Athena, Astraeus, Eos, Hermes.
OCEANIDS: Polydore, Lyris, Acaste, Eidyia, Dione.

Djoser added nothing to the discussion until the end, when he said, "From the sound of Major Khaba's report, if he has someone under his command that could fill his shoes, the major would make an outstanding addition to the command staff here in Memphis."

There were murmurs of agreement.

~

Queen Nima hosted evening meal for Djoser, Hetephe, Horus, and Anath in the royal dining room.

As they dined, Nima asked Djoser, "So, Son. What is it that shall come to pass?"

He laughed, "Well, after a couple of days of negotiations, and with a few well-timed suggestions, they will all decide that, yes, Khaba should be at headquarters. King Khasek is smart enough to know that Khaba will do less harm at headquarters than in the field. Their decision to combine both armies under the command of Hetephe will be more difficult—much more difficult. It would be helpful if the queen raised that possibility to the king on her marriage bed so that the king would be predisposed to this possibility. Organizationally, the commands *must* be unified but politically—well, there are many egos and fields of authority to reconcile. I must remain neutral on the subject and Hetephe must continually say 'Oh no, I am not worthy to command an army *that* large.' But, in the end, this must be done. Everything else is just details."

They finished the meal and Nima announced, "I wish to visit with sweet Anath. The rest of you go visit one another and plot to take over Canaan."

Nima said to a handmaiden, "Anath and I wish our very best wine."

Anath was beside herself. *Drinking wine with my queen. What could be finer?*

The queen said, "Ahh, Dispatcher Anath, I learn so little at these official meetings with the king and his council. That is one reason that I maintain such a large, delightful cadre of gossips. They know all there is to know about what is happening in my kingdom. Now tell me, sweet Anath, I understand that you can walk naked into a camp and make the bandits fall to the ground in fear before you. And you simply must tell me about this little ritual of yours lying on the naked bodies of the men you have escorted into the Land of the Dead. And I'm told that some in the Sinai are calling you a god? Tell me, Sweet Anath. Tell me everything!"

"My queen …,"Anath began.

"Oh, we aren't under scrutiny, right now, Anath. Call me Nima"

"My queen—I mean Nima—I mean—oh, dear, Nima. I am not at all used to this. I am just a Red-ribboned Woman who was drafted into the Egyptian army."

"Sweet Anath, if you are to be a god in the Sinai—if you are going *rule* the Sinai—we simply must teach you to accept your power. I will teach you everything! We are going to have such fun! Let's start by recognizing that Horus certainly has a place in the scheme of things but so does Anath. And Anath can move up in power without the least bit of help from Horus. But do keep him around to entertain and obey you. Good entertainers are sooo difficult to come by. I mean the ones that actually please you! Now, let's get started—always remember to act imperial— even if you don't feel imperial. You say that the bandits lay down in fear when you come for them?! How do you do that?!"

After much talk and wine, the queen and Anath joined the others sitting on the Great Concourse, plotting to take over Canaan.

Nima spoke to Horus, "Shaman Horus, my new friend, Anath, tells me that you are quite accomplished in many areas—that you are fascinating to talk to—and 'The Way of Horus' as she calls it, makes you sound as if you are a just and decent man. Your kind are so difficult to come by. But, still, you desperately need my friend Anath's guidance and advice; especially if you ever wish favors from her good friend, Nima."

Horus chatted amicably with his queen as he thought, *What is it you want from me, Prince Djoser?*

Prince Djoser nonchalantly listened intently as he observed Horus and thought, *Oh, nothing from you, Son. Quite a bit from Anath.*

~

The next morning, Horus rose early to visit his stepmother, Nephthys, and his Uncle Set. Nephthys was excited to see her son. "It's been so long, Horus. I worry for you so. You risked death to save others. I am so proud of you. Isis and Osiris are so proud of you. You carry on their flame."

Horus basked in the warm words of his stepmother. "Mother, I do the best I can, but I am lost and don't know where I am going or what I'm doing. Each morning, I ask Father to show me the way, but …" He paused,

EGYPTIAN GODS: Osiris/Dionysus—Isis/Ariadne/Philyra, Horus, Set/Charon, Nephthys/Dexithea.
CANAANITE GODS: Anath, Astarte, Shalem, Shahar, Moloch, El.
OLYMPIAN GODS: Zeus, Dionysus, Hestia, Ares, Athena, Astraeus, Eos, Hermes.
OCEANIDS: Polydore, Lyris, Acaste, Eidyia, Dione.

looked around, and asked "Where is Uncle Set? I'm sure he can tell me what I am doing wrong."

Laughing, she said, "He is in the western Red Lands with Anubis. They find wandering tribes for Set to impress with his knowledge of the gods of old times. He insinuates that he, himself, may be some kind of god. It amuses Anubis but he knows to remain serious when his father is busy impressing people." She stared at him a moment. "I am told that you have quite a following along the war road. Disciples in every camp listen to your every word."

"Yes. It is the prince's wish. 'Build a unified Egypt' has been pounded into my mind. The story of Mother and Father excites everyone. That I tell their gospel plus other stories about them plus I am their son builds some kind of mystique around me. I tolerate it. They are useful to the prince and, who knows, maybe even to me someday. Return with me, Mother. The people along the road would be elated to meet Great Nephthys of South Memphis, consort to Lord Set. We would have a wonderful time!"

"Oh, no. That will not happen. I have traveled farther and done more than any Telchine should ever hope for. I have a wonderful son and a wonderful stepson, and I am 'Nephthys of South Memphis.' Set no longer comes to me but I have lain with the most powerful men and women that have ever lived. It is enough. I am old and content. My time is done. I will rest now." She hesitated. "But Set might travel with you. He is jealous of all he hears about you from the East. He would enjoy strutting around with you; perhaps lording over you a little in front of the masses."

"He hated Mother and Father and takes it out on you and me, doesn't he, Mother."

"He hates himself and the world. It wasn't just your mother. It was the loss of everything he had ever accomplished; the loss of all the great things he had built. The Great Flood destroyed his life. So, ask Set and Anubis to travel the war road with you. It will do all of my family good."

~

Meanwhile, the king and his council met for five days; they discussed, planned, negotiated, proposed, re-evaluated, considered, and planned some more. Their final plan, including changes to the military structure, pleased no one except Prince Djoser.

Dionysus/Osiris, Ariadne/Isis/Philyra, Charon/Set, Hermes/Tehuti.
EGYPTIANS: Nebka, Djoser, Hotep, Khasek, Rocky
NUBIANS: Nima, Hetephe, King Kerma, Prince T'jaru, Prince Rafah.
CANAANITES: Phoenicia, Serket, Azazil, Jaffa | URFANS: Teumessian, Abram, Sarai, Terah

Minor-General Hetephe, commander of the unified First and Second Egyptian Armies, returned to Camp First Egyptians followed by an additional sixty Nubian archers and sixty Kemetian Swordsmen—all in full Egyptian army uniform. Assistant-General Khaba stood on the great concourse with King Khasek and General Sanakhte to watch them march smartly from the city.

Assistant-General Khaba was beside himself with delight. *Minor-General Hetephe couldn't keep her troops in a straight line if she had only two men.*

He was sure the king and the general noticed the uneven lines.

Dispatcher Anath marched with her command. Horus, Anubis, and Set trailed behind riding in a wagon pulled by oxen. Prince Djoser rode with them. He wished to make a personal inspection of the progress.

As they traveled toward Charon City, Set said to Djoser, "I seem to remember that Isis forbade me to return to Charon City. When she stripped me of my name, she also took my city."

Djoser replied, "That was long ago, Lord Set."

Horus chimed in, "Uncle Set, I give you permission to visit the city which bears your old name. Your punishment for what you did to Father is long ago forgiven."

Set said, "Ahh, so now the son of Isis tells me what I may and may not do! She is in the Land of the Dead but still taunts me through her son. The abuse I suffer is never-ending, isn't it, Anubis?"

Anubis answered, "Yes, Father. The world exists to torment you, but still, the common people love and worship you. Uncle Osiris and Aunt Isis caused all your problems and took everything away from you but they're dead now. So. let's go have a good time, all right?"

Set replied, "Yes, they're dead now and I am going to the city that I alone created. I wonder if they remember me?"

Horus thought *No, Uncle Set. They don't. But worse, they certainly remember, love, and worship Mother and Father.*

Set, riding happily in the wagon, continually strained to catch glimpses of Red-Ribbon Woman Anath marching imperially beside Minor-General Hetephe, Commander of the Unified Egyptian Army.

EGYPTIAN GODS: Osiris/Dionysus—Isis/Ariadne/Philyra, Horus, Set/Charon, Nephthys/Dexithea.
CANAANITE GODS: Anath, Astarte, Shalem, Shahar, Moloch, El.
OLYMPIAN GODS: Zeus, Dionysus, Hestia, Ares, Athena, Astraeus, Eos, Hermes.
OCEANIDS: Polydore, Lyris, Acaste, Eidyia, Dione.

Minor-General Hetephe and her command arrived at Charon City. The citizens gathered to see the pageantry of the glorious Egyptian Army marching through their city. Hetephe ceremoniously greeted the chief and dismissed her command to rest and mingle with the townspeople. "No fraternizing!"

The word quickly went out that Horus—and the prince plus some other people—followed close behind. Excitement was palpable. The Disciples of Horus gathered and prepared a reception for their soon-to-be arriving guest. "Surely he will stop and visit with us."

Soon, the oxen-drawn wagon appeared. Anubis motioned excited children to climb into the wagon with them and complete the ride into town. Several clambered onto the wagon but were old enough to recognize Horus. They sat and stared at him with silent, wide-eyed awe. Djoser tried to banter with them, but the children had chased the wheels and unexpectedly caught the wagon.

Set stood and began waving and nodding to the crowd, like a monarch waving to his subjects. Many waved back but most eyes were on either Horus or Djoser.

The wagon pulled to the front of the Main building where they were effusively greeted by the Nomarch and his wife. Proper greetings were made.

Djoser said, "Yes. We would be delighted to take advantage of your city's hospitality with an overnight stay." And also, "This is Lord Set, once known as Lord Charon. He founded this city of yours and it is his namesake. He comes to visit you from his home in South Memphis, where he is held in the highest regard—even higher than myself—and I am a prince. He is also loved and admired by the tribes in the western Red Lands. He is a man of great importance!" *Self-importance, anyway.*

Set puffed-up with pride.

The Nomarch replied, "Yes, yes. But you bring us Shaman Horus, himself, the only begotten son of Isis and Osiris. He must tell us the gospel again, after our evening feast. And then, as many more stories as he will tell. Come and mingle with your people, Prince Djoser. Bring your friend Set, if you like."

Dionysus/Osiris, Ariadne/Isis/Philyra, Charon/Set, Hermes/Tehuti.
EGYPTIANS: Nebka, Djoser, Hotep, Khasek, Rocky
NUBIANS: Nima, Hetephe, King Kerma, Prince T'jaru, Prince Rafah.
CANAANITES: Phoenicia, Serket, Azazil, Jaffa | URFANS: Teumessian, Abram, Sarai, Terah

The Nomarch led Djoser into the crowd to mingle as the Disciples of Horus gathered around Horus.

Set was still processing all that he had just heard and seen. Once processed, he filled with fury.

Hetephe assembled her command to continue their march to Fort T'jaru.

~

That evening, after receptions, visiting, and feasting, Horus ascended the stage in the city park and told the story of Isis and Osiris to the enthralled crowd. Djoser watched as Set fumed for a while and then walked away. Anubis waited a few minutes, then followed his father. Horus wisely decided *not* to tell the story of how Set amputated the hands and feet of Osiris, telling instead, the story of how Set and his father led the Ogdoad from the city of Urfa to settle in this very place. Their opinion of Set went up greatly after the telling. Horus answered many questions concerning this story, expertly sidestepping the question, "Why did Set leave his city?"

Anubis had calmed his father. They sat together in the far corner of the crowd watching the unwashed slobber over Horus. Set mentioned to anyone who came into listening range, "Horus is an exceptionally talented young boy. I have taught him a great deal but although he *is* talented, I fear that I still best him in many ways."

Rocky, the city's chief Disciple of Horus, had taken an interest in Set and sat listening to him try to engage any passing person. At that point, Rocky asked Set, "In what way can you best Horus?"

The question took Set by surprise. He was not expecting anyone to question him. His mind raced for something he was superior at. "Well, I can remain underwater much longer than Horus. Many think of me as an honorary Oceanid, I can stay underwater for such a long time. It is a small thing, of course, but still, it is only one of my many superior talents."

"A contesting!" Rocky exclaimed. "A contesting between the old, wise, accomplished Set and his young protege, Horus. Tomorrow morning! I will prepare everything! A contesting in our great pool. Who can remain underwater the longest? You will bring excitement to Charon City. Everyone will be there to watch. Well, all the young people, anyway. Our old are not that interested in contesting's. I will inform Horus. Tomorrow morning after morning meal—in the city park pool!" Rocky scurried away

EGYPTIAN GODS: Osiris/Dionysus—Isis/Ariadne/Philyra, Horus, Set/Charon, Nephthys/Dexithea.
CANAANITE GODS: Anath, Astarte, Shalem, Shahar, Moloch, El.
OLYMPIAN GODS: Zeus, Dionysus, Hestia, Ares, Athena, Astraeus, Eos, Hermes.
OCEANIDS: Polydore, Lyris, Acaste, Eidyia, Dione.

to inform Horus and all his friends; "There will be a contesting between Horus and Set! How exciting!"

Rocky informed Horus of the challenge Set had made. "You will accept it, won't you? It will bring our young people such fun and excitement and add to your reputation!"

Horus laughed. "And after he defeats me? What then, my friend? Don't let him fool you. Uncle Set may be old, but he is in perfect physical shape. It's one of his vanities. And swimming underwater? Back in the day, he would swim with the Oceanids, and they were excellent instructors, especially in the ways of water. No, my friend. Uncle Set has made a challenge that he can beat me at. My reputation must bear the beating."

Rocky replied, "Well, do the best you can, Lord Horus. That's your way. But the word is already in everyone's mouth—'Set will contend with Horus after morning meal in the city pond.' " The disciple laughed. "Our hero Horus, defeated by an old man who wanders the western Red Lands! Oh, the embarrassment!"

Horus laughed. "Yes. Oh, the embarrassment!"

The evening passed and everyone retired to their sleeping quarters.

Set was incensed because he was being shown to a guest house to room with Djoser while Horus was being escorted up the stairs to his nemesis's old room. *Oh, the unfairness of life!*

Horus entered his father's old room on the third floor. Bloodstains remained on the floor where Set—then Charon—had cut off the hands and feet of Osiris—then Dionysus—in an act of horrible revenge. *Uncle Set—why? I should accept defeat. It will make Uncle Set feel good about himself and cost me nothing. Should I accept defeat graciously, Father? Or, let myself drown rather than let him defeat me?*

Horus lay down upon his father's bed. Perchance to sleep. Or to think.

After the moon was past its highest and everyone was sleeping, Horus rose from his bed and walked to the city pond where the reeds grew.

~

Sunrise came.

Many inhabitants knelt toward the east. In Memphis, High Priestess Hathor would soon be invoking Osiris to return to life as Ra—the Living

Sun. After the sun had fully cleared the horizon, the people rose and went to their morning meal. After the meal was completed, many citizens, especially the young, excitedly gathered at the city pond for the great contest between Lord Horus and his still-powerful uncle, Lord Set. After a short time, the crowd parted. Prince Djoser and Rocky led Set and Horus to the pond.

Djoser had arranged for three drummers to lead their way. *Building excitement never hurts!*

After arriving, Djoser made a grand show as he explained the rules of the contest. *Building excitement never hurts!*

Set was in his glory. After Djoser finished speaking, Set stripped off his clothes and struck a pose so that the crowd could admire his old, but still superb, body.

Horus watched, shook his head in apparent resignation, and removed only his shirt. "I'm not competing with that body!" he exclaimed loudly for the merriment of the crowd.

Set smirked.

Per the rules, the men entered the water. Horus drifted toward the area where the reeds grew. As they waited for the command to submerge, Horus discreetly removed a reed from his pants.

The signal was given. The men fell to their knees, their heads completely underwater. No one noticed a reed casually rising from the water.

Wagers had been made. The crowd screamed for their favorite. Women watched with fascination. *Men are such children. They never grow up, do they? But that Set is handsome, isn't he? If he wins, I will most certainly go and congratulate him! He will need someone to dry him off, anyway.*

The drummers acted as metronomes. One beat per average heartbeat. After one-hundred-twenty beats, the spectators began watching in earnest. Could they make it to one-hundred-eighty beats? "Yes!" Any moment now, one would rise from the water! Two-hundred-forty beats! They are both well-trained! Three-hundred beats! "Unbelievable!"

At four hundred twenty beats, Set's gasping head appeared. He was sure that he had defeated Horus and was surprised when he saw no sign of him. Set looked at Djoser, who simply shrugged. Set excited the water and

EGYPTIAN GODS: Osiris/Dionysus—Isis/Ariadne/Philyra, Horus, Set/Charon, Nephthys/Dexithea.
CANAANITE GODS: Anath, Astarte, Shalem, Shahar, Moloch, El.
OLYMPIAN GODS: Zeus, Dionysus, Hestia, Ares, Athena, Astraeus, Eos, Hermes.
OCEANIDS: Polydore, Lyris, Acaste, Eidyia, Dione.

frantically searched for Horus. He did not even notice the three women busily drying the water off his body.

Djoser offered, "Maybe he drowned rather than let you defeat him, Set. The boy *is* strong-willed, you know!"

At six hundred beats, Rocky panicked and rushed into the water to save his beloved teacher, Horus.

Horus felt Rocky's hands pulling him to the surface. Horus discreetly let the reed disappear into the surrounding water. Horus stood tall, looked around, and casually asked, "Did I lose?"

The crowd was ecstatic. They shouted the praises of both men. Set stared at Horus with disbelief. Horus looked at Set and simply shrugged as he and Rocky departed through the adoring crowd. Several young women followed closely behind.

The prince allowed the festivities to continue through the noon meal after which the oxen-drawn wagon, with its passengers, resumed its journey to Fort T'jaru.

Set was not pleased.

~

Minor-General Hetephe was busily reorganizing the fort's chain of command, layout, and personnel to the new military concept supposedly created by Assistant-General Khaba at Headquarters.

Anath saw the wagon approaching in the distance and started to run to it so that she could enthusiastically greet Horus but stopped herself as she remembered her queen's admonishment: "Imperial!" She stopped herself and waited patiently for the wagon to arrive. She did allow herself to give a little wave and a big smile to Horus, but that was all. While waving, she caught a glimpse of Set staring at her from the back of the wagon. *Was that a flash of interest in me, Lord Set? You haven't shown any interest in me for a long time!*

The wagon arrived. Horus jumped down and rushed to embrace Anath. He had been away a long time and only Anath could ease his distress—intellectual, emotional, and physical.

Anath eagerly accepted his embrace but over his shoulder, she saw Set watching them—an intensity in his gaze. She smiled him a little smile. She huskily whispered to Horus, "Welcome back, Shaman Horus, I and your disciples have been eagerly waiting for your return. I have missed you."

Horus uncharacteristically gushed an emotional response. He looked forward to the comfort of her naked body against his in the night.

Djoser and Set walked up to the couple. Djoser said, "Dispatcher Anath, Lord Set is here to monitor our progress on the eastern front. I have been telling him of your contributions to our effort. How a warlord will lay on the ground in fear as you walk toward them clothed only in your helmet and military belt. You are another of Ishtar's daughters who has climbed to the highest rank in my land. Perhaps you could give him a tour and explain our operations. Just don't be modest when describing your contributions. Minor-General Hetephe holds you in high regard."

Anath had only a split second to decide which of her many smiles and greetings she should extend to Set. *I am to be imperial—but even to Lord Set? I am no longer a Red-ribboned woman, I must not be inviting—I am Dispatcher Anath, to be feared.*

She flashed her inviting smile as she said, "I will be delighted to give Lord Set a tour of Fort T'jaru." She turned to Horus and said, "I am eager to visit with you tonight, Horus." She gave Horus her Red-ribboned smile, full of promises, and then led Set into the fort.

Set took note of everything; including who got what smiles.

As Anath escorted Set through the fort, Minor-General Hetephe broke away to speak to him. She finished by extolling what a powerful woman Anath was becoming in the Redlands with the Bowdoin chiefs.

Set, seeing an opportunity, mentioned, "Is that so? I, myself, am the most powerful figure in the western Redlands. Many tribesmen confuse me with Zeus. Something I discourage, of course, but still, sometimes they address me as God Set. Perhaps soon, we will have a God Anath in the eastern Redlands. We would make quite a pair, wouldn't we, God Anath?"

Anath smiled her Imperial smile.

Hetephe excused herself. She was anxious to greet Prince Djoser. As she departed, she said, "The Prince and I will be dining late this evening, Dispatcher. You and Lord Set join us at our table!"

Anath replied, "We will be delighted to join you, Major." *But Horus just got here. I haven't been with him in a long time!*

EGYPTIAN GODS: Osiris/Dionysus—Isis/Ariadne/Philyra, Horus, Set/Charon, Nephthys/Dexithea.
CANAANITE GODS: Anath, Astarte, Shalem, Shahar, Moloch, El.
OLYMPIAN GODS: Zeus, Dionysus, Hestia, Ares, Athena, Astraeus, Eos, Hermes.
OCEANIDS: Polydore, Lyris, Acaste, Eidyia, Dione.

The guided tour continued.

Horus visited with his disciples, but he kept looking for Anath. *Is she still showing Uncle Set the Fort? Uncle cares nothing for forts. He must have found an appreciative audience somewhere. Of course, Anath adores him and wants to please him. But Nephthys said that Set doesn't care for women anymore, just an occasional male. He probably found out what high regard Anath commands here and is reflecting in her glory—trying to outdo her glory. Tell Anath about the underwater contest, Uncle Set. Tell her about that.*

"Do you agree, Lord Horus?" one of the disciples asked.

Horus broke from his thoughts. "I'm sorry. I was thinking of something else. What was the question?"

Meanwhile, Set and Anath were dining with Hetephe and Djoser. Set kept aggressively refilling Anath's wine glass. "I am told that God Anath is an extremely valuable resource, Prince Djoser. Do you remember when Anath was just a little poor girl without hope? How I—well, *you* and I— gave Anath and her family everything they have today? Do you remember that, Anath?" He rubbed his ankle against her leg.

She flashed him her full-on, Red-ribboned Anath smile. *Don't be hurt, Horus. I have a duty. I must do what I must do. Forgive me.*

"Why, yes, Lord Set. My family owes everything that we have to you."

~

Having been informed that Anath would be retiring with Lord Set for the night, Horus walked to the beach and sat staring at the ceiling of heavenly lights. *It's my fault. I should not have defeated him this morning. Dung! But I must face life without blinking. Tomorrow, he will tell me that he plowed you tonight—many times. But you, my love, are not plowing—you are giving love—sharing love— providing warmth, comfort, and peace. Set is the savior of the House of Ishtar. Give unto Set what is Set's. Moan for him, my love. Writhe under his touch. It costs you nothing, nor me. Moan for him, my Sweet.*

Horus wept.

~

Meanwhile, Anath entered Set's room and dutifully undressed for him. She had lain with Set many times in the early years and still remembered the things that excited him. She knew her duty, she knew her profession, and even though she was now the highly respected Anath the Dispatcher, her debt to Set could never be repaid. Set had not only saved her from the gutter, but he had also saved her mother and sisters. He had made them all most high. Set would certainly receive her Class One performance.

After they finished, she lay in the crook of his arm whispering things a girl was supposed to whisper at a time like this.

Set stared at the ceiling—thinking. Finally, he said, "I may take you as my concubine."

Her heart froze with fear. *No, Lord Set. Do not ask this of me!*

"Nephthys is old and no longer good in bed. You re-invigorate me. I am a god in the western Red Lands and with you by my side, I will become a god in the east. We will both become gods. You will be held in higher esteem than your sister, Hathor."

I am bound in affection to Horus, Lord Set. Let Horus and I have our happiness. I owe Horus so much. He completes me.

"I will be all-powerful and will bring you men to sacrifice and dispatch to the land of the dead. I shall watch you cut their throats and then you and I will copulate on their dead bodies. We will swim in their blood."

When I am with Horus, I do not desire those things, Lord Set. Please, No.

"Already, I have great power—over Djoser—over the king and queen—over my weak, weepy-eyed nephew, Horus. I know you care for him. As you should. As a loving woman cares for a stray and wounded dog she comes upon. I know, too, that your first allegiance is to your duty. And being a concubine to the most powerful god in the world is your duty."

I don't care that he is not powerful, Lord. The people love him as do I. He brings them hope, as he does me!

"You know how powerful I am, Dispatcher Anath. Do you like powerful men? Do you like them on top of your body? Feeling their power pouring into you? Filling you? Washing over you? Do you, Anath?"

"Y-yes, my Lord." *I do.*

"Then it is settled. You must perform one task for me to make it so. One simple task and I will make you the honored concubine of the most powerful man to ever live. You must bring me a gift—a special gift!"

EGYPTIAN GODS: Osiris/Dionysus—Isis/Ariadne/Philyra, Horus, Set/Charon, Nephthys/Dexithea.
CANAANITE GODS: Anath, Astarte, Shalem, Shahar, Moloch, El.
OLYMPIAN GODS: Zeus, Dionysus, Hestia, Ares, Athena, Astraeus, Eos, Hermes.
OCEANIDS: Polydore, Lyris, Acaste, Eidyia, Dione.

"A gift, my Lord?" *A gift?*

"Yes. A gift worthy of the glory and power of God Set and God Anath."

Yes. It must be a worthy gift.

"Bring me an eye from Horus."

An eye from Horus?!

"He need not know you took it or that I have it. Feed him enough of my cave mushrooms and he won't know what happened. Let him plow you tomorrow night and feed him the mushrooms. When he is delirious, place this spoon in the corner of his eye and jam it in. The eyeball will pop right out. Take it and bring it to me. I will place it on my nightstand to watch us plowing each other with great vigor. Would that excite you?"

"I should not do such a thing, my Lord. *Yes. It would excite me!*

"I will be all-powerful, Anath. You will be my consort. I shall plow your body with all my power every night! All that, plus it is your duty; your obligation to me!"

"I don't know, Lord Set. I don't know what to say." *But I do, Lord Set. I do know what to say.*

Anath moved her fingers exactly where Set would want them moved. She said, "Perhaps you could help me decide."

He took her.

~

The next morning, after the sun had risen, Anath and Set walked into the dining area. Anath saw Horus eating alone at a table in the far corner. She tried to divert Seth, but it was too late.

Seth called out across the room, "Nephew, may we join you for morning meal? I have a fantastic appetite this morning!"

Anath had never known how much Seth needed to dominate Horus—to lord over him—to humiliate him—to hurt him. Set described last night's intimate details. "She moaned and writhed in ecstasy under my body as I plowed her. She begged me, 'Just one more time!' I granted her entreaties several times."

He is being horrible to Horus! And I didn't beg. I just asked.

She also saw how Horus handled himself, never reacting to Set's taunts. *He doesn't even fight back.*

She decided the best she could do was to remain quiet and let men be men. She attempted but could not hide the warm glow that encompassed her body.

She finally said to Horus, "I would like to see you on the beach after Highsun, my love, I will bring food and wine. We can talk."

Horus looked at Set. "Will that be satisfactory, Uncle?"

"Why, of course, Nephew. The better for Anath to compare us, don't you think?"

The morning wore on.

~

She met him on the outcrop of rocks on the beach. They sat on the rocks, and she said each word that she should say as she poured wine for him and fed him fruits and bread. She did not try to seduce him, or him her. They simply talked of meaningful things and sipped wine—and ate fruit and a special sweetbread. Before the cave mushrooms took his mind, she told him that she would leave him on the beach alone with his thoughts. She understood that Set had come between them but that she had lain with many men and Set was just one more—even as Horus had been just one more. She had affection for Horus, but things change—they must always change—they should not see each other again. She talked until Horus became incoherent. She stretched his immobile body across a rock, removed the spoon, and drove it into his eye. Horus could no longer differentiate between pain and ecstasy. Perhaps they were the same. She carefully wrapped the eye, looked at Horus's motionless body, and felt no urge to kiss him one last time or reflect on their time together. She shoved his body in between the rocks and returned to Set. She placed the eye of Horus on the night table staring at their bed. Anath teased herself out of her clothes for Set's excitement.

Soon enough, the all-seeing Eye of Horus watched Set's powerful body cover the all-too-willing body of Anath.

~

Late in the evening, Horus's followers found Anath and asked where they might find their beloved leader. He had not shown up for their appointed

EGYPTIAN GODS: Osiris/Dionysus—Isis/Ariadne/Philyra, Horus, Set/Charon, Nephthys/Dexithea.
CANAANITE GODS: Anath, Astarte, Shalem, Shahar, Moloch, El.
OLYMPIAN GODS: Zeus, Dionysus, Hestia, Ares, Athena, Astraeus, Eos, Hermes.
OCEANIDS: Polydore, Lyris, Acaste, Eidyia, Dione.

meeting. Anath explained that they had met on the beach at Highsun to eat and talk and that she had told him that she would no longer come to him and that she had left him alone on the beach, crying.

The followers hurried off to the beach to find their teacher.

~

It took three days for Horus to recover.

Djoser joined Horus and his six disciples for morning meal. "You look good in that eye patch. It makes you look even more manly."

Horus said, "A man without his woman, as I understand. I don't remember much about our meeting but the word in everyone's mouth is that Anath is now Set's concubine and that a seabird ate my eye."

Djoser replied, "Yes. Yes, she is. I'm sure she knows Set cares nothing for her. She is only a tool for him to gain more power. But she went to him, anyway. Trading a good man for an uncaring man. Who can understand the mind of a woman? And the sea bird, I'll withhold judgment on that!"

"The eye must be my own fault, Uncle Djoser. The distraught accident of an angry, grieving man mixed with too much wine. And Anath did what she had to do. She owes Set her and her family their existence. She will be good for him. She was good for me for a long time. Now is a good time for me and my disciples to walk to Fort Haboua. We are closer to the Land of the Dead when we are alone with one another. It will be an opportunity for my Fort T'jaru disciples to meet and mingle with my Fort Haboua disciples. I plan on telling many Osiris stories at Fort Haboua after the evening meal."

Djoser said, "I will be leaving for Fort Haboua at high sun tomorrow. Lord Set is coming with me. She did what was necessary, Horus. May I tell her that you understand and agree with her decision?"

"Of course. Tell her whatever words you think will fill her with joy. She deserves that. Will he bring Anath with him?"

"There is talk of that possibility. Will you still be there when we arrive? "

"Then no, she might feel awkward, for some reason. We will already be on our way to Fort Dispatcher Anath."

"You are conceding defeat?"

"I was defeated. I cannot help Anath in this thing. I certainly don't want to burden her. She is becoming God Anath of the Sinai. That's what you and your mother wanted. Someone to unify the Bedouins and bind them to your concept of Egypt. I am sure that Set would like to be God Set of the Sinai. You will want that, too—for the glory of Egypt."

"For the unification of Egypt, Horus."

"When the time is right, tell Anath how proud I am of her. She has done well. I will most certainly be gone from Fort Dispatcher Anath before they get there. It will be her time of glory. My presence would spoil it as she shares her victories with Uncle Set. I am sure we will meet again, Prince Djoser."

Before he turned to leave, Horus said, "Soon, Father. I will see you soon." He turned and departed.

Djoser watched him leave. *So, a bird pecked your eye out? Does either of us believe that? You, of course, have no choice but to believe it. The truth would be unbearable. Soon, Son. I will see you soon.*

The Way of Horus
Year 151, first month, second week

The nights became the days became the seasons.

Major Hetephe established commands at each fort with the capability of providing a military escort to all caravans traveling between Forts.

The three sons of the Old Man showed Captain T'jaru the location of all the oases. T'jaru set up a camp away from each but close enough that they could attack a warlord when so alerted by the friendly Bedouins. The test was easy enough. Was the tribe armed or not? If not armed, they were protected citizens of Egypt. If armed, Anath came for them.

Anath's reputation continued to grow as did Lord Set's. Set had the knack for sucking off the respect of one person onto himself—of insinuating that, well, he would not actually call himself a god even though he had been personally acquainted with them all—Zeus, Ares, Athena—"Anath is very much like God Athena, isn't she?"— Poseidon, Hestia, and, of course, his very best friend—Osiris. The tribesmen began calling him El Set—the high lord of the Red Lands—consort to God Anath—bringer of warfare and lovemaking. Anath occasionally, not often anymore, but

EGYPTIAN GODS: Osiris/Dionysus—Isis/Ariadne/Philyra, Horus, Set/Charon, Nephthys/Dexithea.
CANAANITE GODS: Anath, Astarte, Shalem, Shahar, Moloch, El.
OLYMPIAN GODS: Zeus, Dionysus, Hestia, Ares, Athena, Astraeus, Eos, Hermes.
OCEANIDS: Polydore, Lyris, Acaste, Eidyia, Dione.

occasionally, got to enthusiastically perform her signature lovemaking ritual sandwiched between those she had dispatched and the great El Set.

Farther east, Horus and twelve of his disciples walked the war road, telling stories about Osiris, discussing the nature of death, and, too, explaining what was required to walk the Path of Kiya—which he now referred to as the "Way of Osiris"—which was rapidly becoming the "Way of Horus."

Horus had finally overtaken Snefru, who was completing the ninth of the twelve forts. Horus convinced Snefru to scout ahead and identify the locations for Forts ten, eleven, and twelve; especially twelve. Horus wanted to establish his presence at the twelfth Fort to make contacts in Canaan and begin laying the groundwork for its eventual completion. Prince Djoser had dictated that the name would be Fort Rafah in honor of the new chief of the Nubians. Fort Rafah would become the gateway to Egypt—destined to become a major trading city—maybe THE major trading city.

That, plus the religious thought in Canaan was fresh and fertile ground for his pursuit of finding the Land of the Dead.

That, plus he would be a year away from Anath.

Dionysus/Osiris, Ariadne/Isis/Philyra, Charon/Set, Hermes/Tehuti.
EGYPTIANS: Nebka, Djoser, Hotep, Khasek, Rocky
NUBIANS: Nima, Hetephe, King Kerma, Prince T'jaru, Prince Rafah.
CANAANITES: Phoenicia, Serket, Azazil, Jaffa | URFANS: Teumessian, Abram, Sarai, Terah

10. Canaan

Year 151, eleventh month

So it was that Snefru, with Horus and his twelve disciples, entered the land of Canaan.

Snefru announced, "Well, this appears to be the border between the Sinai and Canaan. We will build Fort Rafah on the Sinai side."

"How can you tell this is the border?" asked Horus.

"Because we are a day's march from where we will build the eleventh fort and I'm tired of walking."

"We are defining the border of Egypt and founding what will become a great city because you're tired of walking? Shouldn't we look around or something?"

"I agree. You go look around. I'll rest here and wait for you. Leave your disciples with me to set up camp."

"The sun is setting. Let's do it your way."

"Good decision. You prepare a meal for us. Your disciples can drive some deep shafts for me."

"Yes, I suppose you need to make sure you can build water wells in this Osiris-forsaken place."

Sunrise

The sun breached the horizon as Snefru asked Horus, "Is your father alive yet? I don't understand exactly when he returns to life. Hathor will just now be preparing to call him. The ways of gods are beyond my understanding."

"Yours AND mine. But your father is the high priest to Chief Nebka. Surely, you understand these things."

"I do understand. My grandfather is dead. Your mother and father are dead. They will stay dead forever. Sorry to tell you. The powerful need to give the unpowerful hope and happy stories so that the powerful can stay powerful. Sheep must have shepherds. There is no harm in it, I suppose. Maybe some good."

"Are you sure they're dead, Snefru? Maybe they're just where we aren't."

EGYPTIAN GODS: Osiris/Dionysus—Isis/Ariadne/Philyra, Horus, Set/Charon, Nephthys/Dexithea.
CANAANITE GODS: Anath, Astarte, Shalem, Shahar, Moloch, El.
OLYMPIAN GODS: Zeus, Dionysus, Hestia, Ares, Athena, Astraeus, Eos, Hermes.
OCEANIDS: Polydore, Lyris, Acaste, Eidyia, Dione.

"Save the dung for your disciples, Horus. They are dead. Forever dead. That's why we have wine—to make this life worthwhile while we live."

"The living only have the moment, my friend." He paused. "What did you find out from your deep shafts?"

"Great news! All four showed indications of water. And I only went four shafts into the sand. This place will work well. I just wonder how far we are from civilization. We can't have a trading city without trading partners."

"I'll send three disciples due south, three others to the southeast, and I will take Rocky and the others east along the coast—although the coast appears to turn toward the north from here—or at least to the northeast. We will all travel for three days and then turn around and come back with our reports. If we don't find any people, let's just turn around and tell Djoser to forget about it."

"Three years out of my life and 'just forget about it?!' I don't think so, young Horus. Go find me some trading cities!"

"Yes, old Snefru!"

Rocky and the other disciples began stirring. Morning meals were eaten. The expeditions set off to discover the world.

~

On the third day, Horus with four disciples found their city.

Jaffa was a bustling seaport town with a large population. It appeared to be a perfect trading city for the someday-to-be-built Fort Rafah. Their mission was to scout the area and identify its usefulness to Fort Rafah. What manner of people lived here? Were they war-like, farmers, or traders? Which gods, if any, did they bow to? How were they likely to respond to an Egyptian fort being built two days to their west? Who were their neighboring towns and villages? What manner of food and drink did they consume? And on and on. The four would spend the evening in town and then two disciples would return to carry what information they gathered back to Snefru. But, regardless, this city would validate Snefru's decision for the location of the twelfth fort.

They walked the city. It was not the size of Memphis or even South Memphis but it was large enough to provide an evening's entertainment. Late in the evening, a young woman appeared out of nowhere, smiled, and offered them wine. Horus nodded at his youngest disciple and said, "You know where we are camped." The disciple disappeared into the night with the young woman. Horus said to the remaining two, "I hope he doesn't get his throat cut. Either way, we will have learned something." They found a building from which music emanated. They entered it to find wine, women, and song.

The people inside appeared to be congenial. Most happy to talk about anything at all, loudly and with full cups of wine.

The three men saw a vacant table which they went to. They did not need to motion for service, the young woman appeared immediately. "What would you boys like?"

Rocky glanced over his shoulder to see what "boys" she was talking to.

Horus said, "We are from Egypt out to see the world and don't know what you drink around here. What would you recommend?"

"Out discovering the world, huh? I'll bring you big boys some big cups of wine but be careful, wine can make you wild and crazy! God Dionysus made it so!"

Horus said, "Excellent! I'm sure we will enjoy it." *It is both a blessing and a curse!*

Rocky stared at her backside as she walked away. Her purple dress covered her rear; most of it, anyway.

They listened to the nearby conversations and understood most of the dialects. Only one conversation between four gigantic men was not understandable, but even there were a few common language words.

The waitress brought their wine—*big* cups of wine.

Horus asked, "What city should we explore after we leave this fine city?"

"Well, DON'T go southwest to Rusalem—that's where I'm from. Nothing happens in Rusalem. Maybe go north to Megiddo—some say it's the biggest city in the world, maybe bigger than even Damascus. I bet you boys could find some real trouble to get into in Megiddo."

Rocky laughed. "If YOU are from Rusalem, *something* must be happening there. What's it like?"

EGYPTIAN GODS: Osiris/Dionysus—Isis/Ariadne/Philyra, Horus, Set/Charon, Nephthys/Dexithea.
CANAANITE GODS: Anath, Astarte, Shalem, Shahar, Moloch, El.
OLYMPIAN GODS: Zeus, Dionysus, Hestia, Ares, Athena, Astraeus, Eos, Hermes.
OCEANIDS: Polydore, Lyris, Acaste, Eidyia, Dione.

"It's like nothing you want to know about. God Shalem of Nightfall rules the city. He and his consort God Shahar of Sunrise fill the night sky with their babies every night. It's supposed to keep everything peaceful! But over in the nearby valley town of Tophet, they sacrifice baby girls every Winter Solstice by throwing them on a fire. How peaceful is *that*?"

Horus thought, *If I remember Mother Dexithea's teachings of the old days correctly that sounds like Astraeus, Eos, and the abominable Ares.*

He asked, "So why didn't you go to the big city of Megiddo?"

"Too expensive. This is a port town full of sailors. A girl can make a good living here humpin and pumpin."

"Am I supposed to know what 'humpin and pumpin' means?"

She touched his shoulder, smiled, and said, "I get off work, soon, sweet honey. Come home with me and you can find out."

He laughed, "I don't want to ruin our friendship." He changed course. "It sounds like you have a lot of gods around here."

"We've got gods comin' out our anus, honey. Every pitiful town has a god, usually more. Everybody worships their own god. I guess it's because we are a big trading port. Everybody brings their gods and leaves 'em."

"Ever heard of Osiris?"

"Naw, is he one of your Egyptian gods?"

"Yes, he is our major god. Maybe I can tell you his story one day."

"You drink, I listen. That's the rule 'round this place!"

"Well, then—another wine for us all—and when we finish, my friend Rocky will be extremely interested in finding out what 'humpin and pumpin' means."

Her attention shifted to Rocky. She felt his biceps and asked, "Are you this big all over, honey? "She stooped to look under the table, rose, and exclaimed, "Never mind. I saw the size of those feet! I'll get your wine, right now!" She hurried off to get their wine.

Horus said, "Find out about the sailors. Where they're from—their nature, whether respectful or argumentative. If she knows, find out what they trade and what countries they're from. Casually mention that

Dionysus immigrated to Egypt and changed his name to Osiris. Don't mention my name."

She returned with the wine.

Horus stood, picked up his wine, and said to Rocky, "I'm going to wander into the crowd and find somebody from Megiddo. I'll see you tomorrow back at camp. Do your duty. Find out about humpin and pumpin."

Rocky said, "Yes, Master!" He then turned to Purple Dress and asked, "What time do you get off work, exactly?"

Horus scanned the crowd of mostly men. *Which of these talkative fellows might be from Megiddo? Easy enough to find out.*

He asked, in a loud voice, "Anybody here from Megiddo?"

There were. All talkative.

Horus and his disciples found their way back to their camp before sunrise. Fortunately, none got their throat cut.

~

They slept late. It was well after sunrise before they rose to eat their morning meal and compare notes from the night before.

The highlights of Rocky's report were, "Humpin and pumpin mean exactly that. She was a wealth of information about the sailors. She is a follower of Dionysus and was excited to learn he went to Egypt and became Osiris. She cried over the beauty of the story of Isis and Osiris and will share the story with all her friends who are also followers of Dionysus. Wine is how they support themselves, you know."

Horus reported on Megiddo and then said, "I'm going to Rusalem. The rest of you go on to Megiddo. Let's meet back here in four days and then head back to Snefru. We will have a lot of information."

They finished their meal and set off on their separate ways.

It was late afternoon when Horus found the town of Rusalem. It lay in a beautiful land—a plateau in the mountains surrounded by valleys and mountains. Toward the east were a sea and a great river. To the west lay Middlesea. Horus entered through a city gate. The town itself wasn't much of a town; low stone walls protected a few buildings surrounding a large square fronted by what might be a temple of some kind. Its only water

EGYPTIAN GODS: Osiris/Dionysus—Isis/Ariadne/Philyra, Horus, Set/Charon, Nephthys/Dexithea.
CANAANITE GODS: Anath, Astarte, Shalem, Shahar, Moloch, El.
OLYMPIAN GODS: Zeus, Dionysus, Hestia, Ares, Athena, Astraeus, Eos, Hermes.
OCEANIDS: Polydore, Lyris, Acaste, Eidyia, Dione.

supply was from a spring in the nearby valley. *It's certainly peaceful. Too peaceful for a young woman with ambition, I suppose.*

Horus walked through the square and entered the temple. An old man was busy cleaning around the altar and jumped with surprise at the sound of Horus's voice. "Hello, Father. You have a peaceful temple here."

The man turned to greet Horus. "I am priest to God Shalem of Nightfall and his consort God Shahar of Sunrise. Welcome, stranger. We do not get many visitors in Shalem."

Horus introduced himself and made small talk making sure to compliment the gods on their peaceful town. *"Peace" seems to be the operative word in Rusalem.*

Horus was offered and accepted a cup of honeyed milk The priest joined him as they sat down at the nearby offering table where Horus turned the conversation to the religious aspects of the town and shared his commitment to the Egyptian God Osiris, of which the priest had never heard but was quite familiar with the Greek God Dionysus. The priest was delighted to hear the gospel of Isis and Osiris who sounded like very nice gods for the kingdom of Egypt.

Horus then said, "I was told of the town Tophet and their Winter Solstice Festival. Could what I heard be true?"

"Oh yes, yes. They are horrible people, not peaceful at all. Every Winter Solstice they sacrifice their young to those horrible gods, Ares and Demeter. It's best not to travel to Tophet, Friend Horus!"

"I journey to learn of all the gods of Canaan; especially unpeaceful gods such as Ares and Demeter. Are the people warlike?"

"No, you will be safe enough, but they are not clean or hospitable to strangers or especially nice. We limit our contact to trade for food. Their crops *are* bountiful."

Horus continued the conversation for a while and then left the priest to walk the town and talk to its inhabitants. *I wish I had asked the name of the woman in the purple dress.*

He camped on the edge of the city and rose at sunrise to travel to Tophet. He passed women working in the fields, who ignored him, and then came upon an unwalled town with a large square surrounded by uncared-for buildings. Men sat in the square. They also ignored him.

Dionysus/Osiris, Ariadne/Isis/Philyra, Charon/Set, Hermes/Tehuti.
EGYPTIANS: Nebka, Djoser, Hotep, Khasek, Rocky
NUBIANS: Nima, Hetephe, King Kerma, Prince T'jaru, Prince Rafah.
CANAANITES: Phoenicia, Serket, Azazil, Jaffa | URFANS: Teumessian, Abram, Sarai, Terah

He entered a large run-down building, which might be a temple, and was met by a gruff man. "Whaddya want, stranger?"

Horus introduced himself and told his story as the gruff man stared at him without much interest.

Gruff Man responded, "We don't trust strangers much around here. You might not want to be around after the sun goes down. Som' of th' boys might not like you bein' here. But Yeah, we got a ritual. We mostly starved before that Urfa Missionary came through and taught us what to do to make sure we got good crops. We do it and now we always have good crops. God Ares and God Demeter is real good to us."

"What is your ritual?"

The man took interest because Horus had expressed an interest. "Oh, I'm in charge of it. I guess you could say that I'm the Priest around these parts. Around Solstice time, I pick out the prettiest girl around—I usually get one that idn' bleedin' yet cause she probably hadn't been messed with yet —and you want to give God Ares a girl that hadn't been messed with. The day before, I get her nice and drunk, so she won't fight and embarrass our town. I get three of our boys just turned men, so they'll be nice and eager. Then I throw each one of 'em on top of her and let'm fill her with their seed. Then I finish her off, myself, real nice like. After it's over, I gut each of the boys while the girl watches and then we throw her on top of our big fire. God Ares and God Demeter are thrilled with their offerin'. We been gettin' good crops ever since."

"Do they all scream a lot?"

"Oh, yeah. They scream real good. That's what God Ares likes—people screamin' an' all—with guts on the ground—girls burnin' to death on the fire screamin' real loud."

"That's interesting, but I hear God Ares has been kicked out as a god in Greece. I hear that God Demeter much prefers a grown experienced woman and she had rather see the woman and the three men, plus yourself, to live to see the bounty of the crops she sends you in the spring. That's what I hear, anyway. But I do know that the more progressive cities in Greece have taken on this new model, and it works better for them— they always get really good crops."

"You don't say. Well, I'll remember that if we ever have a bad crop. A grown woman, you say. How many times does she need to be humped?"

EGYPTIAN GODS: Osiris/Dionysus—Isis/Ariadne/Philyra, Horus, Set/Charon, Nephthys/Dexithea.
CANAANITE GODS: Anath, Astarte, Shalem, Shahar, Moloch, El.
OLYMPIAN GODS: Zeus, Dionysus, Hestia, Ares, Athena, Astraeus, Eos, Hermes.
OCEANIDS: Polydore, Lyris, Acaste, Eidyia, Dione.

"Once by each of the young men but three times by the most virile man around, I guess that's you."

"You don't say. Hey, do you want some honey-milk while you're here?"

Horus accepted the drink. They visited for a while. Horus left Tophet well before sunset.

When he was out of sight of the town, he stepped off the path to relieve himself. As he was finishing, he felt a sting on his ankle that made him double over with pain. He looked at his ankle and saw a yellow scorpion the size of his hand scurry off. *Dung! That can't be good.*

He considered his options. *I can rest in Rusalem. They are a lot more friendly. They probably have an ointment for this kind of thing.*

He continued his walk to Rusalem. Halfway back, his throat became itchy. Soon after, it was hard for him to breathe. Soon after, he became lightheaded. Soon after, he vomited. Soon after, he fell to the ground unconscious.

~

The Universe mused, *Time? What is time but the mind's attempt to separate all that happens into smaller sections that might be somewhat understood? Time passes? Time stands still? There is no time? What do you think is the nature of time, Horus? Here? In this place?*

And death? What is death? What do you think the nature of death, Horus? Here, in the blackness.

Within the blackness that was the darkness of his mind, the white light formed and waited motionlessly in the center of his brain—waiting to be acknowledged.

Horus thought, *I have failed in all things—I am nothing—forgive me!—I am not worthy of forgiveness—but forgive me.*

At last, he noticed the white light within the blackness within the darkness. The light began to grow larger. It grew larger than his mind and encompassed all that was. The white light was beautiful beyond knowing.

The light segued into his father's face and spoke to him. *"I am the One and the All. My son, you please me greatly. Your experience shall add to the One's experience as will your knowledge."*

The light changed again, into a woman's face. *Mother?*

"I am the One and the All, my son. Even here I long to hold you, to touch you, to be you, and you to be me. Release the body you wear and join me."

The light became his father. *"You have found that which you sought, my son—the Land of the Dead. Except know this, all that has ever been still exists at the moment that it existed. You have only to shed the body that surrounds you and then become the One with All others. Every moment that has ever been awaits you. At this moment, you are neither dead nor alive. The choice is given to you to decide. Choose well, my son."*

The light grew dimmer and then was gone.

Resurrection
Year 151, twelfth month

He thought, *I have much left to do! I choose life!*

His eyes opened. He stared into the soft compassionate eyes of a young woman.

She said, "Your fever's gone, and you're not shakin' anymore. I dint think you were gonna make it but you gonna live."

Over her shoulder, Rocky's head appeared. It said, "You gave us quite a scare, Master. Welcome back. I'll give you our report on Megiddo, later."

The woman prepared to leave and said, "Rest. I'll get you some broth. You haven't eaten in a quarter-moon."

"A quarter-moon?"

Rocky told him, "You were incoherent for a long time, Master. After you did not return on the fourth day, I came searching for you. The priest and his granddaughter had taken you in. Without her skills in this matter, you would be in the Land of the Dead, right now."

The woman returned with the broth. "Sit up. Eat this. I'll feed it to you."

Horus obediently sat up and ate his broth. Then he slept.

She woke him before sunset. "You slept enough, Mister Horus. Now we gotta watch Grandfather call the children of Shalem and Shahar. It'll bring you some peace. Let's get outside, right now!" They went outside and sat against the temple wall facing out toward the square.

EGYPTIAN GODS: Osiris/Dionysus—Isis/Ariadne/Philyra, Horus, Set/Charon, Nephthys/Dexithea.
CANAANITE GODS: Anath, Astarte, Shalem, Shahar, Moloch, El.
OLYMPIAN GODS: Zeus, Dionysus, Hestia, Ares, Athena, Astraeus, Eos, Hermes.
OCEANIDS: Polydore, Lyris, Acaste, Eidyia, Dione.

The square was already filled with townspeople sitting on blankets, facing away from the temple toward the setting sun.

The priest stepped from the temple, held his arms toward the setting sun, and, as the sun disappeared beneath the horizon, began singing a lovely song of peace. One by one, the children of Shalem and Shahar began appearing in the night sky. It was a beautiful evening. Horus felt a strange sensation. Sitting beside the young woman whose name he did not know—he felt peace.

The ceremony was completed; the people began going back to their homes. The young woman rose as the priest turned to enter his temple and said, "Visit with ma' new friend, Grandfather. Mister Rocky told me Horus is a very important person. I'll get us somethin' to drink and then listen to you two men talk about importan' things."

She disappeared into the temple as the priest sat in the chair she had left. As Horus and the priest talked of important things, the young woman returned, gave them each a large cup of honeyed milk, and sat on the ground at her grandfather's feet—to drink her drink and learn of important things.

The drink finished; the priest rose. "It's been a peaceful evening, Mister Horus. I enjoyed our conversation. But I'll leave you and Serket to yourselves, now. The evening, like you and Serket, is still young." He kissed his granddaughter on the cheek as she rose to retrieve the drinking cups. He said, "I'll fetch you more drink. You stay and talk to our new friend. I understand he's very important." He left to retrieve more drinks.

Horus said, "Serket. That's a lovely name."

"You tryin' to flatter me, Mister Horus. I like that."

He laughed. They bantered on.

The priest interrupted them when he brought them drink and told Horus, "Oh, your friend Rocky said to tell you that he'll be introducin' himself to the women-folk in town and that he is camped at the gate. Find him when you're ready to go." He bid his final goodnight and left them.

Horus asked, "Where were we?"

Serket replied, "You were flatterin' me."

Horus smiled at the innocence of Serket. He had not felt such warmth since his early days with Anath. The wonderment—the trust—the eagerness of thought—the warmth. He had been a long time away from warmth.

They happily bantered into the night.

~

The priest always rose before sunrise. He enjoyed watching the arrival of Shahar calling her children back from the night sky. It was so extremely peaceful. He walked by the cracked door of his granddaughter's bedroom. He did not look inside. *Best not to see.*

He sat by the temple door watching the dawn. His granddaughter did not join him as she usually did. He allowed himself a passing bit of sadness. When she finally did join him, much, much after sunrise, there was a glow about her that reminded him of the glow of Shahar calling to her children, those that she so greatly loved. *The day will bring what the day will bring. Don't fret. To worry is not to trust Shalem. Accept whatever comes. There will be peace.*

He asked, "Is our guest still sleeping?"

She replied, "He didn't wake up when I got outta bed—I mean—yes, I saw him still sleeping when I passed by his bed. He's still tired, I imagine."

The priest asked, "Does he please you?"

Serket sat in silence for a long while. Rather than replying, she rose and embraced her grandfather. In tears, she answered, "Yes, yes. He pleases me great."

Much later, Horus appeared at the temple door, stretched, and asked, "Priest, may I counsel with you?"

The two men counseled.

Afterward, the priest found his granddaughter and asked, "Serket, are you sure you wanna leave with a man you don't even know?"

"But I know him, Grandfather. I listened to his screams and mutterin's when he was die'n. We talked a whole lot last night before we—ah—got to our beds. Bad things chase him. I'll make myself worthy to be his disciple. But if'n not, I'll still bring 'm peace. What higher joy than to bring a person peace? After we—ahh—I mean—he asked me to go with'm on

EGYPTIAN GODS: Osiris/Dionysus—Isis/Ariadne/Philyra, Horus, Set/Charon, Nephthys/Dexithea.
CANAANITE GODS: Anath, Astarte, Shalem, Shahar, Moloch, El.
OLYMPIAN GODS: Zeus, Dionysus, Hestia, Ares, Athena, Astraeus, Eos, Hermes.
OCEANIDS: Polydore, Lyris, Acaste, Eidyia, Dione.

his travels. In his own way, he's tryin' to bring peace to tha' world. That's what he told me. Maybe I can help him do that. Will you bless me?"

"He will bring you pain, not peace, Serket."

"He has already taught me more'n I could ever learn in Rusalem, Grandfather. He's already teachin' me to talk real good. He taught me that everybody talks a little different in every town. He can teach me to talk like the people in whatever town we're in—just like a Oceanid. When I come home to Rusalem, I can talk like we do in Rusalem and when I'm in Memphis, I can talk like they do in Memphis. I'll sound real high class and smart even tho I'm from Rusalem."

"What's an Ocea-nid?"

"I don't rightly know but they talk real good."

He laughed. "Well, if you'rn gonna travel the world with some strange man you just met, you should talk real good, I guess."

Serket was filled with love and peace. She stood, took her grandfather's hands into hers, and asked, "Will you bless me, Grandfather?"

He stood, placed his forehead on the top of her head, and gave her the blessing of Shalem. He ended with, "You can always come home, child. Here'll be peace for all time."

Serket spent the rest of the morning saying farewell to everyone in Rusalem, ending with "May peace be with you."

After the noontime meal, Serket left the peace of Rusalem to travel the unpeaceful world of Shaman Horus and his disciple, Rocky.

~

Serket walked between Horus and Rocky as they walked in the general direction of Jaffa.

Serket said to Rocky, "Mister Rocky, you talk almost as good as Mister Horus. Where'n you from?"

Under his breath, Horus said, "Almost as well as Master Horus."

Serket repeated, "Almost as well as Master Horus. Wher'n—I mean—where are you from?"

Rocky answered, "I am from Charon City, not too far from Memphis."

She said, "That must be why you'n—I mean—why you sound so much lik'n—like—Mister—I mean Master Horus."

Rocky replied. "Oh, Master Horus cultivates that accent of his. It's high Egyptian with a mixture of High Greek and some old-world inflections thrown in. The Oceanids taught him what would sound impressive to the high born in Memphis."

"So, if I can learn to talk like Mister—Master Horus, I'd sound impressive to high-born people?"

Rocky corrected her, "Say 'speak like'—don't use contractions—speak faster."

She repeated, "If I learn to speak like Master Horus, I might sound impressive to high-born people?"

Rocky laughed. "Yes, Student Serket, you most certainly would!"

They walked on. Serket kept talking hoping that Horus would continue to "learn her."

During their talking, Serket said, "Phoenicia went to Jaffa not too many yars—years—ago."

Horus became focused, "Phoenicia—that means purple, doesn't it?"

She said, "You used a contraction, Master Horus. But yes, she was named Phoenicia because she always wore the purple dress our mother made her. Mother worked in the dye factory in Jaffa and she snuck off—sneaked off?— stole some of the dye. Mother came home every quarter moon to see Phoenicia and me but then Mother quit comin' back. Nobody ever found out why. But when she got all growed up—I mean—after she become a woman, she put on her purple dress and went off to Jaffa to find Mother, but Phoenicia never come back, neither. Her purple dress was too little by then, but it was all she had. I hope Phoenicia didn't—did not—die."

Horus said, "Rocky may have met your sister in a wine house. Tomorrow, you and he go and find out if it *is* Phoenicia and what happened to your mother. You said they make that purple dye in Jaffa. Purple cloth is an extremely valuable trading material. The Jaffa Portmaster can tell me how much they export."

EGYPTIAN GODS: Osiris/Dionysus—Isis/Ariadne/Philyra, Horus, Set/Charon, Nephthys/Dexithea.
CANAANITE GODS: Anath, Astarte, Shalem, Shahar, Moloch, El.
OLYMPIAN GODS: Zeus, Dionysus, Hestia, Ares, Athena, Astraeus, Eos, Hermes.
OCEANIDS: Polydore, Lyris, Acaste, Eidyia, Dione.

They arrived in Jaffa and found the other two disciples patiently waiting. They all discussed new knowledge they had obtained. They agreed that tomorrow the two disciples would carry this knowledge to Snefru, who was hopefully still laying out the twelfth fort, that Rocky and Serket would search for Phoenicia, and that Horus would visit the port. It was a plan. Osiris always loved a plan.

Sunrise

They rose and bowed their heads toward the rising sun. Horus said a few words of greeting. They ate their morning meal and were off on their day's adventures.

Horus

Horus made his way to the dock. Rocky had gleaned enough information from the woman in the purple dress to give Horus enough talking points to sound knowledgeable. At the least, he would make contacts for when the real Egyptian traders came calling.

It was a good-sized port, at least the size of New Port Kemet. Horus strolled the grounds for a while looking confident and then was ready to enter the main port building. He entered and was confronted with a burly man sitting at a desk looking extremely busy. Horus said, "My name is Horus. I am from Egypt and wish to meet the Portmaster. Can you make this happen?"

The burly man slowly looked up and replied, "I can make anything happen. Why should I *want* to make that happen?"

"So that you will keep your job and so that I won't come around there and beat your worthless butt."

The man stood in fury, glaring hatred.

Horus sweetly replied, "Now that I have your attention, kind lord, my name is Horus, and I would be most appreciative and would be indebted to you if you would introduce me to your worthy Portmaster. We in Egypt have heard so many wonderful things about how well-run Port Jaffa is. You, kind lord, are undoubtedly partly responsible for this."

The man continued to glare as he tried to decide how to proceed with this arrogant dung-head. "Very well—Horus of Egypt—Portmaster Polydore will reduce my pay if I kill a potential client. You aren't worth it, anyway."

Dionysus/Osiris, Ariadne/Isis/Philyra, Charon/Set, Hermes/Tehuti.
EGYPTIANS: Nebka, Djoser, Hotep, Khasek, Rocky
NUBIANS: Nima, Hetephe, King Kerma, Prince T'jaru, Prince Rafah.
CANAANITES: Phoenicia, Serket, Azazil, Jaffa | URFANS: Teumessian, Abram, Sarai, Terah

"You are merciful and kind. Thank you."

The burly man disappeared into an office in the rear of the building. In a few minutes he returned, said "Straight back," sat back down at his desk, and went back to his work.

"Thank you, so much." Horus walked straight back into the office and was met by an attractive, efficient, older woman.

She greeted him, "Horus—you're the son of Dionysus and Queen Ariadne, aren't you? There can't be that many Horus's in Egypt. Come in. Sit here by my desk." She motioned toward a chair as she sat down at her desk. "My name is Oceanid Polydore, I'm the port master here. How is Prince Djoser? I haven't seen him in—oh my goodness—a long time."

Horus was pleased. They chatted and reminisced about old times.

Polydore was certainly interested in news from the West—"It's to be renamed Egypt, is it?" "You're building a trade route across the Sinai?" "You really believe you can eliminate these marauding warlords?" "When can you arrange a trade delegation?" "I will set a meeting up with Chief Jaffa the Eighteenth. The chiefs love the name 'Jaffa,' for some reason."

"I believe I can ask Prince Djoser and his assistants to arrive on the new moon after the one coming up. Will that be satisfactory?"

"Yes, that will be fine. Perhaps we can meet for evening meal if you remain in Jaffa. I enjoy revisiting my youth."

"There is a wine house a few streets down. It's a bit rough but not as bad as many I have passed by. Sundown?"

"This is a port town in Canaan, Lord Horus. It's a rough city. I will meet you there at sundown."

Serket and Rocky

Rocky took Serket to the wine house, but it was not yet open. They stood there for a moment. "Well, I know where she lives. I suppose it will be all right to go to her quarters."

"How do you know where she lives, Shaman Rocky?"

"Well, you know. She got off work and everything."

"Do you mean that you went home with her?"

"Well, you know."

"Oh!"

They arrived at the house where the purple-dressed woman had a room and entered it. Rocky walked to the door of the room where he had stayed and knocked.

A woman's voice from within answered, "Come back later, I'm busy!"

Rocky replied, "We are sorry to disturb you. This is Rocky. Serket of Rusalem is with me. We will leave and try to find you at the wine house when it opens."

The voice replied, "Wait a minute!"

Muffled voices were heard from within and shortly, the door opened, a half-dressed man came out, said "Hello," and scurried away.

"You can come in, now."

Rocky and Serket entered the room where the woman stood beside her bed in her night clothes. The room contained only the bed, a table, and two rickety chairs.

The woman said, "I am ashamed, Sister. I am without peace."

Serket said, "I am here, Phoenicia, we will find you peace." The two women ran to the other and embraced."

Phoenicia sobbed, saying, "Mother is dead, Serket. They caught her stealing snails and then all the men humped her until she died, and they threw her body into the sea. She died because I wanted a purple dress. Forgive me, Serket. Our mother is dead because of me."

Serket said, "Shalem still brings his children out each night at sunset and Shahar still calls them home before the morning sun. We all knew that Mother would be dead when she did not return home. So, it is. Don't be upset. She is at peace, now."

Rocky sat at the table as the sisters cried some more and talked some more and cried some more. When they were finished, a kind of peace had settled over the room.

Horus did not find Rocky and Serket until close to sunset.

Dionysus/Osiris, Ariadne/Isis/Philyra, Charon/Set, Hermes/Tehuti.
EGYPTIANS: Nebka, Djoser, Hotep, Khasek, Rocky
NUBIANS: Nima, Hetephe, King Kerma, Prince T'jaru, Prince Rafah.
CANAANITES: Phoenicia, Serket, Azazil, Jaffa | URFANS: Teumessian, Abram, Sarai, Terah

Rocky took Horus aside and whispered, "They're sisters—their mother was killed for stealing snails that make that purple dye—they had a nice talk—Phoenicia is working tonight—Serket is taking her savings tomorrow and buying Phoenicia new clothes—Serket wants to eat at the Wine House tonight so she can get to know her sister's work—I'll fill in the details, later—All right?"

Horus replied, "Yes. I'm meeting the Portmaster there tonight. You two go ahead and find us an out-of-the-way table for four. I will find you after I meet the Portmaster."

Horus walked the streets and timed his arrival at the Wine House as the sun set. Polydore arrived moments later. He said, "I hope you don't mind but I told two friends we would meet them. Rocky is one of my followers. Serket is a young woman who saved my life after a scorpion sting. We brought her to Jaffa to meet her sister who is a server here."

"How cozy. A great big group hug. This promises to be an interesting evening, Lord Horus."

"To be called 'Horus' would be nice."

"Well, then, I'll be 'Polly.' But only when I'm not at work. Understood?"

"Yes, Polly."

She laughed. They entered the Wine House. Horus saw Rocky and Serket in a back corner. Serket saw them and waved. Their evening began.

The conversation began pleasant enough and became more pleasant as the evening wore on.

Horus: "This is Serket. She is from Rusalem."
Polly: "You saved him after a scorpion bit him, I understand."
Serket: "Yes, it was a Yellow Scorpion. The worst. 'If it's yeller, it'll kill a feller.' This is my sister, Phoenicia."
Polly: "Love the purple dress, Phoenicia. So do the men, I imagine."
Phoenicia: "Yes, but I'm buying another dress tomorrow. Serket is going with me."
Serket: "Lord Horus is teaching me to speak proper talk."
Polly: "He is, is he? I'm an Oceanid, you know. Teaching is what Oceanid's do best."
Serket: "Could you teach me and Phoenicia how to talk proper?"
Polly: "I would be delighted. I haven't had eager students in years. Do

EGYPTIAN GODS: Osiris/Dionysus—Isis/Ariadne/Philyra, Horus, Set/Charon, Nephthys/Dexithea.
CANAANITE GODS: Anath, Astarte, Shalem, Shahar, Moloch, El.
OLYMPIAN GODS: Zeus, Dionysus, Hestia, Ares, Athena, Astraeus, Eos, Hermes.
OCEANIDS: Polydore, Lyris, Acaste, Eidyia, Dione.

you need work? I can always use motivated workers, but Phoenicia would make a better living here with that short dress and all these men."
Serket: "Oh, yes. That would be so exciting! Phoenicia, too! We are trying to find peace for my sister. What do we do?"
Polly: "Come mid-morning. Tell Burlyman you have an appointment. You will work during the day, and I will teach you at night."
Horus: "That's really his name?!"

They chattered into the night and then retired to their quarters; Serket with Horus, Rocky with Phoenicia. Polly was met at the door by Burlyman who escorted her safely through the city to her home, where he left her.

Sunrise

Horus nodded to the rising sun, spoke to his father, and prepared morning meal for Serket. Rocky and Phoenicia would be joining them shortly.

Serket rose, walked to Horus, and embraced him. "Good morning, Lord Horus. I will miss you, so much."

"Are you sure you want to stay in Jaffa, Serket? I won't be back for almost two seasons. There is much of the world to show you."

"I can have a real proper job in Jaffa and maybe save a shekel. I will be here with Phoenicia. She needs me right now. And we both get to learn how to talk real proper. I want to be worthy when I see the world with you, and besides, Jaffa is a really big city for a girl like me."

They talked and laughed and kissed. Rocky and Phoenicia arrived. They ate their morning meal, talked, said goodbyes, and, with joy and peace, set off on their new adventures.

Dionysus/Osiris, Ariadne/Isis/Philyra, Charon/Set, Hermes/Tehuti.
EGYPTIANS: Nebka, Djoser, Hotep, Khasek, Rocky
NUBIANS: Nima, Hetephe, King Kerma, Prince T'jaru, Prince Rafah.
CANAANITES: Phoenicia, Serket, Azazil, Jaffa | URFANS: Teumessian, Abram, Sarai, Terah

11. Port Jaffa

Year 152, first month

Horus and Rocky returned to Fort Rafah. His other disciples plus Snefru were hard at work laying the cornerstones defining the layout of the Fort.

They met and talked for a while. The trade potential at Port Jaffa was significant. "Can you go ahead and finish this fort next?" Horus asked.

Snefru replied, "Your most stupid idea, ever, Lord Horus. Without a road connecting this place to Fort T'jaru, trade here would be useless. No, with a lot of luck and hard work, maybe I can have much of the road well on its way in two seasons but even that will be difficult. No, five seasons to complete the road without any new forts, then we can worry about the remaining three forts."

Horus said, "Complete the road by the full moon after next—*and* Fort Rafah! The prince will want it completed for his negotiating team."

Snefru laughed. "We'll see. Let's return to Memphis at sunrise. We both have a lot to do and not much time to do it."

On the way back, Snefru made mental notes on the landscape and estimated what would be necessary to quickly build the road over the sometimes-desolate landscape. They stopped for one day to inspect the progress of the construction of the tenth fort. It must be completed and populated soon because the Tenth Sinai Expedition would be planning on this being their new base of operations when they completed their tenth mission. Horus was relieved that Anath and Set would be someplace in the Sinai, and he would not have to greet them.

They all journeyed to the ninth fort where Snefru left Horus behind to spend a night visiting his disciples and tell the locals stories of Osiris. At the eighth fort, Snefru had told the residents that Horus was on his way. Upon learning of this, several Bedouin tribes had come to the fort solely to hear these wondrous stories.

Snefru arrived in Memphis two quarter-moons before Horus, but Horus had told many stories of Osiris and Isis.

Year 152, second month

Horus finally arrived back in Memphis and went directly to his stepmother and sometimes lover, High Priestess Hathor. They shared wine as she

EGYPTIAN GODS: Osiris/Dionysus—Isis/Ariadne/Philyra, Horus, Set/Charon, Nephthys/Dexithea.
CANAANITE GODS: Anath, Astarte, Shalem, Shahar, Moloch, El.
OLYMPIAN GODS: Zeus, Dionysus, Hestia, Ares, Athena, Astraeus, Eos, Hermes.
OCEANIDS: Polydore, Lyris, Acaste, Eidyia, Dione.

listened with complete attention to the stories of his adventures and of the people he had met. And, too, his stories of the many gods in the land of Canaan and her excitement that Horus was meeting some success introducing Osiris into that True-God forsaken land. She sympathized over the loss of his eye but confessed that the patch made him look more manly than ever. They talked into the night. He considered her invitation to lay with her but, in the end, decided, for some unknown reason, that it would not be appropriate.

The next morning, Horus stood by the great river and watched as High Priestess Hathor called forth the Living Sun. *It is a spectacle, I must admit. The people are always impressed. Are you impressed, Father? Do you care?*

As the sun cleared the horizon and the ceremony ended, Horus went to the King's House to find Djoser and catch up on the status of things. The guard said, "Prince Djoser is entertaining Chief Rafah at Hostess House."

Horus thanked the guard and walked to Hostess house.

He arrived at Hostess House to find Djoser sitting alone at "his" table. "Do you remember me, Great Prince? A humble servant of your realm?"

"Come, my son. Join me. I'm afraid our friend, Chief Rafah, will be awhile. He has eight wives—two of them visiting Mother—and still, he wishes to frequent the House of Ishtar. He is infatuated with one of them—Astarte, I believe."

They gossiped for a while and talked of Portmaster Polydore; an acquaintance of Djoser's from long ago. Then Djoser said, "Myself, Rafah, Menka, General Sanakhte, and you will be our trade delegation to Jaffa. We haven't had a trade delegation in a long time. The Greeks simply renew our standing agreement. This will be our first foray into soliciting trade from foreign cities since the days of King Nebka. It isn't trade with Jaffa that concerns me. It's that any decision made at Jaffa will ripple through all subsequent trading partners. I want us all at Jaffa so that nothing will be overlooked. I have King Khasek's permission to refer to us as Egypt while we are in Canaan and make any formal agreement under that name. Chief Rafah is my ally and friend, now, and I intend to keep it that way by all means possible."

"Take Astarte with us."

"As a member of the delegation?"

Dionysus/Osiris, Ariadne/Isis/Philyra, Charon/Set, Hermes/Tehuti.
EGYPTIANS: Nebka, Djoser, Hotep, Khasek, Rocky
NUBIANS: Nima, Hetephe, King Kerma, Prince T'jaru, Prince Rafah.
CANAANITES: Phoenicia, Serket, Azazil, Jaffa | URFANS: Teumessian, Abram, Sarai, Terah

"Anath and Set are out there someplace killing warlords. Astarte and Rafah could complement them and make a strong connection to the Sinai, Canaan, and the Upper Kingdom."

"I knew that I had trained you well, boy. Just like I told your father I would. By the way, I'm still upset about how it worked out with Anath. I know Anath was extremely important to you. Set can be as abrasive as any Olympian god."

"She remains on my mind, even now, Father. But as I understand it, I wasn't man enough for her—not dominating enough to be a real man. But the Rusalem woman I met brings me a peace of which Anath was not capable. I will avoid Anath and Set if I see them together. I can handle either one separately but not the two at the same time."

"I will keep that in mind, Horus. Here comes the carriage. It's probably bringing Rafah. You try to discreetly bring up the Astarte suggestion."

The carriage arrived. The Hostess House attendant helped Astarte descend—all eyes were immediately on Astarte. Astarte saw Djoser and Horus and excitedly waved to them. She waited for Chief Rafah to descend to take her arm and escort her to Djoser's table.

Horus rose, embraced her, and asked, "Do you want to go on a grand adventure to a foreign land, Astarte?!"

"Oh, yes, that would be fabulous! May I bring my Chief?!"

~

Meanwhile, for two quarter moons, Snefru consulted long hours with his father. They visited the quarries and significantly increased the output of road-building materials. They visited the port and recruited sailors to join their road-building project—there would be endless beer provided. They cut corners, obtained additional draft oxen, and called in a lot of old debt. But in the end, although all forts would not be complete, by the full moon after the next, there would be a trade road and an entrance fort between Egypt-to-be and the lands of Canaan.

The Egyptian Trade Delegation
Year 152, fourth month

Horus and Rocky arrived in Port Jaffa late in the day a quarter-moon before the new moon. They wanted time with Serket and Phoenicia before Horus officially introduced himself to Portmaster Polydore and then,

EGYPTIAN GODS: Osiris/Dionysus—Isis/Ariadne/Philyra, Horus, Set/Charon, Nephthys/Dexithea.
CANAANITE GODS: Anath, Astarte, Shalem, Shahar, Moloch, El.
OLYMPIAN GODS: Zeus, Dionysus, Hestia, Ares, Athena, Astraeus, Eos, Hermes.
OCEANIDS: Polydore, Lyris, Acaste, Eidyia, Dione.

presumably, to Chief Jaffa the Eighteenth to co-ordinate the Egyptian negotiating delegation to be arriving the morning after the new moon.

They first went to the Wine House, but Phoenicia no longer worked there. Then they went to Phoenicia's room, but Phoenicia no longer lived there. "Whaddya want? She don't live here no more. I do!"

Their remaining option was to inquire with Portmaster Polydore. Burlyman semi-graciously greeted them with, "Are you here to see Portmaster Polydore or those new women?"

Horus said, "I don't want to interrupt the Portmaster. Are either of the new women available?"

"Yeah. Out on the patio. That way," he said pointing toward the back.

The two men looked at one another and made their way toward the back. Double doors opened onto a new, bustling patio filled with sailors drinking beer. Women in short dresses ran from table to table keeping the beer flowing. One motioned for the two men to come sit at the table she had just cleaned. They went and sat down. "You boys want a beer? What kind? Greek or Crete?"

Horus asked, "Do you serve wine?"

"Oh, yeah, Baby. Not a sailor, huh? What about you, Honey?"

Rocky replied in his best gruff voice, "Beer for me, Honey." He looked at Horus, shrugged, and added, "You gotta Phoenicia workin' here?"

"Yeah, you want me to go get'er?"

"Yeah, tell'r Rocky's come a'callin' "

The server hurried off but quickly returned saying, "The boss'll see you in 'er office. She's got your drinks 'n there." She pointed to an enclosed room at the end of the patio.

The two men, still at a loss of what was happening, rose and walked to the door to the office and knocked. A voice from within said, "Come in and close the door behind you."

They entered.

Before the door closed, Phoenicia was all over Rocky. Serket breathlessly took Horus's hands into hers, and remembering her language training, said, "I have missed you a great deal Horus, and so much has happened.

Dionysus/Osiris, Ariadne/Isis/Philyra, Charon/Set, Hermes/Tehuti.
EGYPTIANS: Nebka, Djoser, Hotep, Khasek, Rocky
NUBIANS: Nima, Hetephe, King Kerma, Prince T'jaru, Prince Rafah.
CANAANITES: Phoenicia, Serket, Azazil, Jaffa | URFANS: Teumessian, Abram, Sarai, Terah

We do not deserve our good fortune, but we work hard every day to earn it." She looked at Phoenicia, still all over Rocky, and said, "Phoenicia, Dear, you and Rocky can use our resting cot if you like. We promise not to watch."

Phoenicia backed off, stared at Rocky, and forgetting her language training, explained, "I don't have to pump and hump no more Rocky an' Polly gave me an Serket jobs 'cause Serket got to build a servin' patio for the sailors an' I get to run it an' I got six wom'n doin' what I tellum t'do an' they do real good an' ev'rbody loves our patio and love workin' here cause I don't make 'em hump and pump less they want to an' it's real wond'rful here rocky an' I got new dresses an everthin'."

Phoenicia, having gotten it all out, suddenly remembered her new station in life and language training. She stood back and said, "I hope you have been well, Master Rocky. My sister and I have been given extraordinary opportunities which we have embraced. Do you like our new patio operation?"

Rocky replied, "You are an amazing woman, Phoenicia. I am fortunate to know you."

With that, Phoenicia was, once more, all over Rocky.

Soon enough, there was a knock on the door and a voice said, "Ladies, it's me, Portmaster Polydore. May I come in?" As Phoenicia hurriedly straightened her clothes and hair, Serket responded, "Certainly, Portmaster. We are visiting old friends. Please, join us!"

The door cracked and Polydore slipped in. "I don't want to interrupt reunions, but I wish to invite you and your guests to join me on your patio for our evening meal. It would be an honor for our Greek sailors to dine with the son of Queen Ariadne and Titan Dionysus."

The two women looked puzzled. Polydore added, "Isis and Osiris."

Phoenicia responded, "Oh! Why, yes. That is exceedingly gracious of you, Portmaster. I will have our cooks prepare something worthy of the occasion. You prefer fish, as I remember. I will begin preparations."

Phoenicia walked from the room, picked up a silver bell, and rang it. The six serving women immediately finished what they were doing and scurried to line up in front of Phoenicia. Phoenicia said, "We are extremely fortunate to have important dignitaries from Egypt dining with

EGYPTIAN GODS: Osiris/Dionysus—Isis/Ariadne/Philyra, Horus, Set/Charon, Nephthys/Dexithea.
CANAANITE GODS: Anath, Astarte, Shalem, Shahar, Moloch, El.
OLYMPIAN GODS: Zeus, Dionysus, Hestia, Ares, Athena, Astraeus, Eos, Hermes.
OCEANIDS: Polydore, Lyris, Acaste, Eidyia, Dione.

us this evening. I cannot ask you to exceed your normal level of hospitality because you already maintain the highest level of excellence possible. I ask only that you maintain your impeccable standards, this evening. Because of the added pressure, there will be a little extra in your next pay. As you were."

The women smiled at one another and hurried back to serving with their "impeccable standards."

Phoenicia went into the kitchen to plan an impeccable meal with her impeccable cooking staff.

Polydore, Serket, and the men stood in the office listening.

Polydore said to Serket, "You have created a little whirlwind. I don't want to cross her."

Polydore then said to Horus, "And Builder Serket is not to be crossed either, Lord Horus. I gave her an impossible task because I could not find a man willing to tackle it—build me a patio on the dock for my sailors to enjoy while they are in port. That a woman could accomplish this in 'women-are-for-humping' Jaffa would make Mother Metis herself proud—extremely proud. Serket went from having no resources and no knowledge to completing this thing in less than two quarter moons. It's still unbelievable, and yet, we will be dining on it this evening."

Serket quickly added, "It was Master Burlyman that taught me how to talk to the workmen—what to say and how to say it plus some words good girls should never hear—certainly not speak." She giggled. "But I did make up some new words. They don't like being called a woman's-bloody-rag-excuse-of-a-man, but they can't talk back because Master Mad-dog had already explained that, if they did, he would personally build them a second rectum. They seemed to respect me a little bit more after our discussion of what I expected from them. At any rate, they built this wonderful patio for me."

Polydore laughed. "Burlyman is my bodyguard. The only way I got this position was because Sea Captain Mad-dog Burlyman told Jaffa the Eighteenth what a pond-scum-excrement of a port he had here. Jaffa was willing to listen but became upset when Burlyman recommended me, a woman, for the Portmaster post. They negotiated but I was the First Assistant Portmaster at Port Graikoi for Zeus's sake. I was eventually offered the position here but with Burlyman as my bodyguard. Jaffa males have no respect for a woman, especially a woman with power and no protector. I will leave you three to catch up, but I expect you to join me at my table after sundown."

Rocky jumped in with, "I'll sit on the deck and drink beer and watch the activities."

The two left together, leaving Horus and Serket, at last, alone.

Sunset

Polydore walked to her table overlooking the patio and sat. A server rushed over to bring her wine and bowls of fruit and nuts. Polydore nodded her appreciation and motioned for Rocky to join her.

Soon the door to Phenicia's office opened and Serket stepped out followed by Horus. Polydore rose, which attracted the sailors' attention. As Horus reached her table, Polydore announced, "Gracious and respected sailors of the world—especially those of you from the ports of Greece—I am honored to present to you 'The Falcon'—Horus—son of the Great Queen Ariadne of Greece and Titan Dionysus of Everywhere. Gentlemen—Shaman Horus of Egypt!"

Under his breath, Horus asked Rocky, "Do we have any shekels?" to which Rocky nodded, "Yes."

The sailors stood and held up their beer in salute.

Horus raised his fist into the air in acknowledgment and exclaimed, "Sailors of the world—you are the lifeblood of civilization. In gratitude, Egypt is buying your next beer!" No proclamation could have been more well received.

Phoenicia watched from the kitchen as her staff continued their impeccable service. In passing, her most competent and aggressive server leaned over and whispered, "You got ever' thin' goin' real good, Chief Phoenicia. I an' the wom'n can take over now if you'n wanna go eat wi' th' high-class people."

Phoenicia looked wistfully toward Polydore's table. The woman went on, "Ya gonna larn to trust us or what?!" and walked away.

As the woman again passed by, with an order, Phoenicia said, "Take over for me. You are chief in my absence." Phoenicia walked to Polyvore's

EGYPTIAN GODS: Osiris/Dionysus—Isis/Ariadne/Philyra, Horus, Set/Charon, Nephthys/Dexithea.
CANAANITE GODS: Anath, Astarte, Shalem, Shahar, Moloch, El.
OLYMPIAN GODS: Zeus, Dionysus, Hestia, Ares, Athena, Astraeus, Eos, Hermes.
OCEANIDS: Polydore, Lyris, Acaste, Eidyia, Dione.

table and inquired, "May I join you? This is an excellent learning opportunity for my staff."

The service was impeccable, the food delicious, the patio raucous and rousing. A good time was had by all.

After the dining was over and after Horus had bought another round of beer, the six—Burlyman followed twenty paces behind—walked the sandy beach. Polydore had kicked off her shoes and was more mellow than she usually allowed herself to be—perhaps a little inebriated—but not too much. She was surrounded by sophisticated and sophisticated-to-be friends she could talk to who would almost understand. "The time of the Oceanids has ended. We can't even walk the beaches unclothed anymore. Men everywhere take that as an invitation—a demand—to mate with you. That would not be so bad, but they have no respect for us as a human being—they see us only as a mating machine—to satisfy their vulgar male fantasies. They don't understand that we are our own person—with our own hopes and female fantasies—totally unlike theirs. We will not have it! We decided long ago when Great Mother Metis passed that we would accept no more Sisters into the Sisterhood. There weren't that many wishing to join us after the Elder Titans were killed, anyway. The world is changing but we Oceanids have no intention of changing with it. We shall pass into nothingness with our dignity and our ideals unpolluted by the growing coarseness of people. Phoenicia and Serket thrill me to my bones because they are what all people could become when given the opportunity. Why cannot this be the destiny of our kind? Why, instead, do we get the peoples of Canaan and beyond—those that follow the teachings of the madmen from Urfa—those that worship the Olympian gods of old? You Egyptians—whatever you call yourselves this season—live in your own little world of a civilized people. You do not even see what is growing around you, but we Oceanids see it. Even in Greece, the Titan Muses tell history true and unchanged. But the Greek poets and philosophers hear truth and then change truth to fit their ideas of what the truth *should* be—what they *want* truth to be. And when they are done, only their male fantasies remain." She grew silent and pensive.

No one spoke for a long while.

Then Horace quietly asked, "No more Oceanids?"

~

The next day, Mad-dog Burlyman introduced Horus to Chief Jaffa the Eighteenth. "Yeah, I'm usually around. Just bring your people by and let's see what we can work out. I hope Egypt is rich. I could use some more trade around this place. That port is my only source of stuff. The port is run by some woman, you know! A woman, for Zeus's sake. What in the dung is this world comin' to?"

Horus recognized that an invitation to an official reception would not be forthcoming. He complimented the Chief on something or the other and left the meeting. He exchanged glances with Mad-dog, who merely shrugged. Horus met Rocky on the Port patio.

Polydore had been looking for Horus's return and walked out to greet him. "How did your meeting go?" Horus merely blankly stared at Polydore. She responded, "Oh!"

The three talked for a while. Horus would leave immediately to meet the Egyptian delegation at the site of the twelfth fort. The delegation needed to know what awaited them in Jaffa. It would not be at all what any of them were expecting. Polydore asked if Assistant Serket could accompany him as an observer. Port Jaffa might well be the major beneficiary of any trade agreements. Serket could provide Polydore with first-hand insights into possible negotiations.

As Horus left, Polydore said, "Port Jaffa would be delighted to host a reception for our distinguished visitors the night of the full moon. I will have Patio Chief Phoenicia begin preparations. Make your friend Rocky available to my Patio Chief. She will need to know their preferences in food and drink."

~

Horus and Serket walked the primitive trail between Jaffa and the future site of Fort Rafah. Horus felt the strong need to meet Djoser before the trade delegation arrived at Port Jaffa to forewarn them of the nature of their upcoming negotiations. The Egyptians were expecting formal talks, not the "yeah-whatever" reception that awaited them. Horus and Serket spent their walking time discussing the nature of death, achieving internal peace, and the influence of the gods on the actions of people.

Djoser, Snefru, and Priest Hotep were already at Site Twelve monitoring the completion of the Great War Road. The road had been completed a

EGYPTIAN GODS: Osiris/Dionysus—Isis/Ariadne/Philyra, Horus, Set/Charon, Nephthys/Dexithea.
CANAANITE GODS: Anath, Astarte, Shalem, Shahar, Moloch, El.
OLYMPIAN GODS: Zeus, Dionysus, Hestia, Ares, Athena, Astraeus, Eos, Hermes.
OCEANIDS: Polydore, Lyris, Acaste, Eidyia, Dione.

full two days before the Trade Delegation was expected to arrive at the fort at the end of the Egyptian road. Priest Hotep, himself, had accompanied his son on the final inspection trip. They were both elated at their results and praised the workmen incessantly. There were three more forts to complete, of course. And the road might never be completely finished. They were now discussing protective walls running the length of the road, additional water wells, and other improvements that would be necessary as trade increased along the road. Snefru had arranged for a small ceremony when the delegation arrived so that the prince and other dignitaries could celebrate the triumph of the workers who had made such a wonder as this possible and in so short a time. There would undoubtedly be some type of formal dedication ceremony after the three remaining forts and niceties to this one were completed, but completing the road itself was a major cause for celebration. Plus, they had constructed a rudimentary, but serviceable, Fort Rafah.

Horus and Serket arrived but Horus would wait until Snefru and Hotep had their moment of glory before approaching Djoser with his concerns.

Everyone said all the proper words to all the proper people. Everyone admired that which had been built and bragged about their ease of transit all the way from Memphis. Here was Egypt's road to even greater glory and wealth. So it went into the night.

Sunrise

Horus bowed his head to the rising sun. "Good morning, Father. The world is worse off than when you left us. I fail so quickly. Have a bright day!" He was joined by Serket as he prepared their morning meal.

Djoser arrived and said, "May I join you? I have yet to be formally introduced to your interesting friend who is much lovelier than Anath."

Serket coolly responded in her highest-class dialect, "He is trying to flatter me, Shaman Horus. Should I ignore him or flatter him back?" *God Shalem, let me speak my best. Don't let me sound like a low-born person. For the sake of Horus, be with me!*

Horus answered, "Flatter Prince Djoser, Assistant-Portmaster Serket. He is easily flattered, he likes it, and he may be of use to us one day."

Phoenicia had taught Serket that batting your eyes at a man was the surest way to maintain his interest. *I hope I am not appearing too forward.*

Dionysus/Osiris, Ariadne/Isis/Philyra, Charon/Set, Hermes/Tehuti.
EGYPTIANS: Nebka, Djoser, Hotep, Khasek, Rocky
NUBIANS: Nima, Hetephe, King Kerma, Prince T'jaru, Prince Rafah.
CANAANITES: Phoenicia, Serket, Azazil, Jaffa | URFANS: Teumessian, Abram, Sarai, Terah

She batted her eyes and replied, "And Prince Djoser is as lovely as Shaman Horus."

Djoser replied, "Assistant Portmaster Serket, you don't sound to be a native of Canaan. Are you from Greece, perhaps?"

He thinks I'm from Greece! Are you pleased with me, Horus? He thinks I'm from Greece.

The three talked on until Djoser finally asked, "All right, Horus. Why are you meeting me here?"

Horus explained the coarseness, lack of organization, and lack of sophistication of Chief Jaffa. "I can't imagine what he can offer you. I don't know that he even knows what his people have for trade."

"Hmmm. So, what trade they have must be through the port and the Chief looks down on women. Tell me again about the city of Megiddo."

The camp was coming to life. Djoser bid a pleasant day to Horus and Serket and walked to the beach to think.

Another day was spent in Fort Rafah-soon-to-be. There was more bragging about what Snefru and his men had created plus Djoser made time to discuss the situation in Jaffa with his advisors.

Serket attempted to join in the business discussions of the men but continually found herself entertaining Astarte who was fascinated with Serket's accent or lack thereof. Astarte was also interested in what Serket thought of Horus's sexual prowess. "My sister Anath loved Horus until Lord Set seduced her away from him. She loved Horus's mind. Horus was all right in bed, but nothing like Lord Set. Gods are so dynamic. I never thought Horus was that interested in coupling, anyway. Does he come to you often?" And on and on.

Serket discovered that an occasional "Is that so?" in a high-born accent was always an acceptable response.

The Egyptian Trade delegation set off for Jaffa immediately after sunrise.

~

The delegation arrived in Jaffa in a late afternoon and set up camp at the edge of town. They were pleased that the Port would host a reception.

EGYPTIAN GODS: Osiris/Dionysus—Isis/Ariadne/Philyra, Horus, Set/Charon, Nephthys/Dexithea.
CANAANITE GODS: Anath, Astarte, Shalem, Shahar, Moloch, El.
OLYMPIAN GODS: Zeus, Dionysus, Hestia, Ares, Athena, Astraeus, Eos, Hermes.
OCEANIDS: Polydore, Lyris, Acaste, Eidyia, Dione.

Polydore did the best she could to obtain local dignitaries—there simply were no local dignitaries other than Chief Jaffa the Eighteenth who Mad-dog Burlyman had personally invited with great force of personality. Polydore did track down two farmers who grew olives and grapes. They were both surprised that they were being invited—commanded—to attend a fancy reception for some high-born visitors from Egypt. They, plus the owner of the dye-making facility would be the Canaan trade representatives. All Port employees of any potential rank would also be attending—much to their delight. For a Canaan back-country town such as Jaffa, Polydore was almost pleased with her guest list. Burlyman was tasked with ensuring Chief Jaffa showed up—sober.

Meanwhile, upon arriving in Jaffa, Djoser requested that Horus give him and Rafah a tour of the city. Djoser was a head taller than most of the Canaanites. Rafah was a head taller than Djoser. The Canaanites were not in a major trading area. They had not been exposed to such an exotic person before—an ebony black giant that strode their city as if he were their chief. Both Djoser and Rafah were sizing up the town that would be the closest "major" town to Fort Rafah and the town through which most trade would probably flow. They were both concerned with what they had to work with. Horus showed them the nicer wine house where he had met Phoenicia and the coarser wine houses preferred by Chief Jaffa.

The sun set; the three men went directly to Polydores' reception. Horus entered first and alerted Polydore of the princes' and chiefs' imminent arrival. She formed a receiving line headed by herself, then Chief Jaffa, the purple-dye manufacturer, and the two farmers. The two farmers were at a loss as to what was going on. The manufacturer was not much better off but he had the business sense to take his cues from Portmaster Polydore as he detected large profits in the making.

Patio supervisor Phoenicia greeted the prince and chief at the door and exchanged pleasantries. She led the two men to be introduced to the Jaffa dignitaries. "Portmaster Polydore, with great pleasure, I introduce Prince Djoser of Egypt."

"Welcome to our city, Prince Djoser. I understand you and your delegation hope to create a significant trade presence in our fair city. I believe that you will be delighted to meet the fine citizens of Jaffa who can make this happen."

Djoser responded appropriately.

Dionysus/Osiris, Ariadne/Isis/Philyra, Charon/Set, Hermes/Tehuti.
EGYPTIANS: Nebka, Djoser, Hotep, Khasek, Rocky
NUBIANS: Nima, Hetephe, King Kerma, Prince T'jaru, Prince Rafah.
CANAANITES: Phoenicia, Serket, Azazil, Jaffa | URFANS: Teumessian, Abram, Sarai, Terah

Phoenicia then introduced Djoser to Chief Jaffa who was not at all sure what to say.

Djoser said, "You run a major city, Chief Jaffa. How do to keep it running so smoothly?"

Jaffa knew he had to say something—anything, "Well, I inspect the wine houses all the time. I have a lot of wine houses that need inspecting. You can find women at the wine houses. Any kind you want."

"Well, that sounds interesting. Egypt might have a market for wine. We must discuss what you would want in exchange for your wine." Djoser chuckled. "But not women, evidently. You appear to have a sufficient quantity of women."

"Yeah, but they're mostly humpers and pumpers."

"Oh? Do you have a wife or consort, Chief?"

"Nah, I get all the women I want in the wine houses."

"Well, perhaps we can discuss that in the future. So nice to finally meet you, Chief Jaffa. I will join you later in the evening."

Phoenicia then introduced the prince to the dye manufacturer, who had been listening to the exchange between the chief and the prince. "Greetings, Prince Djoser. Ma name's Murex and I own the finest purple dye-making place in Canaan. Do you people like purple cloth? I'm the man who can get it for you!"

"Ahh, Lord Murex. I am pleased to meet you and, yes, I believe our Egyptian traders will be most interested in your dyes. Is it difficult to manufacture?"

"Oh, Yeah. I got over a hun'ert wom'n out in the water all the time findin' the right snails. But they steal my snails all o' the time but I mak'm real sorry that they steal from me. Yeah, real sorry! But I get the job done an' I can make all the dye you can use."

"Let's meet tomorrow morning to work out the details."

"Yeah, around Highsun. I should be up by then."

"Excellent Lord Murex. I look forward to it."

Phoenicia moved the prince down the line to the first farmer and then the second. The farmers were surprised to find that an olive crop and a lentil

EGYPTIAN GODS: Osiris/Dionysus—Isis/Ariadne/Philyra, Horus, Set/Charon, Nephthys/Dexithea.
CANAANITE GODS: Anath, Astarte, Shalem, Shahar, Moloch, El.
OLYMPIAN GODS: Zeus, Dionysus, Hestia, Ares, Athena, Astraeus, Eos, Hermes.
OCEANIDS: Polydore, Lyris, Acaste, Eidyia, Dione.

crop might have significant value to the Egyptians. "Yeah, great Lord. I would luv findin' out 'bout sellin' to you."

Thus, negotiations began.

Beer and wine flowed. The local dignitaries were infatuated with a party such as this. They were all treated "real good" and "real important."

Djoser pulled Rafah aside and hurriedly said, "Become best friends with Jaffa. When the subject of 'humpin women' comes up, extol Oceanid Polydore as probably 'the best humpin a man can get' and 'she's smart, too.' Tell him you intend to 'get you some of that unless somebody beats you to it.' Make him salivate for her."

Djoser then found Polydore, leaned over, and whispered, "You are to become Consort and Chief Whore to Jaffa the Eighteenth. Rafah will plant the seeds of desire tonight. Are you all right with that?"

She looked at him with surprise and asked, "Do I have a choice?"

"You always have a choice, but it's the right thing to do and Oceanid's always do the right thing. Meet me on the beach after this is over. We will talk, then."

As Rafah made his way to become best friends with Jaffa, Djoser took up with Lord Murex, who had never been called "lord" before. Djoser found out that Murex was originally from Sur, which was way up north. They know how to make purple dye "real good." Murex had traveled down the coast until he found a good supply of shellfish from which he could make his own dye. Djoser extolled Murex's wherewithal to initiate and accomplish such a great endeavor. Djoser allowed how "We are going to have a great future together!"

Vizier Menka became friends with the lentil farmer; General Sanakhte with the olive farmer.

Serket, Phoenicia, and Astarte mingled with everyone. A good time was had by all.

~

Djoser stood barefooted in the moonlit water—waiting. She kicked her shoes off and came to him. They walked silently down the beach until they were out of sight of the stragglers still drinking on the dock patio. Out of sight, he told her to pull off her dress.

"Pull off my dress, Prince Djoser? I thought you were giving me to Jaffa."

You are an Oceanid, Polydore. How long since you walked unclothed down a beach?"

"Too long." She pulled off her dress and dove into the water. She swam out a long way and then returned.

He sat waist-deep in the surf waiting for her return. "Will you consider my request?"

She slid down into the surf and sat down in front of him, pressing her bare back against his chest. He put his arms around her to warm her from the cold water. She asked, "Why is it the right thing to do?"

He tightened his embrace. She pressed more firmly against him. "The normal reasons—to spread civilization—to turn coarse, uneducated people into a more sophisticated people—specifically, in your case, to train an uncouth, slobbering male into a man worthy to be called 'chief.' All that plus Egypt needs a competent government in Jaffa—Jaffa is the gateway into the Sinai. Chief Jaffa can still be chief, but you must be his administrative assistant who makes the decisions and does all the work."

"I do the work. He gets the glory. Typical. What makes you think I can become his beloved consort and assistant?"

"An Oceanid is persuasive. A determined Oceanid is a force of nature."

"Do you think I will be able to stand being touched by that pig?"

"You tell me."

"Oh, a penis is a penis, I suppose. All penises are nice. Fun to play with— pretty to look at—wonderful functionality. They have only one problem—every one of them is attached to a male. That usually ruins the entire experience. Present company excluded, I'm sure."

He laughed and laid his lips upon her shoulders.

She coolly asked, "What else?"

"Oh, you promote Serket to Port Master. You build Phoenicia a gigantic warehouse where she can be your chief trader and store dyes, lentils, and olives until Egyptian caravans show up with wood, feathers, crocodile skins, and such for trade. It will be your repository for all manner of trade goods including what you can bring in from Megiddo. You will have a

EGYPTIAN GODS: Osiris/Dionysus—Isis/Ariadne/Philyra, Horus, Set/Charon, Nephthys/Dexithea.
CANAANITE GODS: Anath, Astarte, Shalem, Shahar, Moloch, El.
OLYMPIAN GODS: Zeus, Dionysus, Hestia, Ares, Athena, Astraeus, Eos, Hermes.
OCEANIDS: Polydore, Lyris, Acaste, Eidyia, Dione.

port plus a terminal for caravans. You convince Rocky to be her chief negotiator. Traders will think he's the supervisor and are dealing with a man rather than a woman. We are in the hinterlands, Oceanid. It may take a while to bring the men up to minimum standards."

"And you think seducing me will make me agree to do these things?"

"Oh no. I returned you to the sea. The seduction is complete. Whatever follows is up to the Oceanid."

"All we ever required was respect, you know. Respect us and we are yours. "There is no respect for a woman in this land. I don't know if that can ever be changed."

"An Oceanid and the Sea. It is enough, I think."

She was silent for a moment. "Yes. It is enough." She turned and tilted her head upward so that his lips could find hers.

~

The next morning, the port women and Astarte met for their morning meal.

Polydore casually announced, "There will be changes."

No one responded.

She spoke again, "I have been directed to seduce Chief Jaffa into being my plaything and my becoming the administrative assistant for the city of Jaffa."

The women each began excitingly talking simultaneously; each listening intently to what every other woman was saying.

Finally, Serket asked, "But who will be Portmaster?"

Polydore replied, "Why, you will, Serket. Who else?"

"But I want to follow Horus and hear his teachings, and we are quite close."

Polydore sighed. "My Sweet Serket. Life is long. You will have time enough for that, later. But for now, Port Jaffa needs you, Canaan needs you, Egypt needs you, and I need you. Such opportunities are rare. I must insist you accept the position."

"But ..."

Polydore held up her hand for silence. "You are too talented to follow some man around listening to him talk nonsense!"

"But he brings me peace."

Polydore said, "And *you* can help bring civilization to this Osiris-forsaken land. Will you do what is right or what brings you peace?"

Phoenicia and Astarte both agreed.

Astarte: "He's just a male. There are men everywhere for the taking!"
Phoenicia: "You can be someone of importance."
Astarte: "You can make a difference in the lives of people."
Polydore: "You must accept the position. You must!"

Polydore said, "Well, that's settled. Now, Phoenicia, I have an even bigger task for you. And Red-ribboned Astarte, I may need your help with Chief Jaffa."

~

The Egyptian Trade delegation spent several days in Jaffa firming up agreements. There were no documents to be signed, only the binding word of men.

Polydore and Astarte properly seduced Chief Jaffa. Jaffa realized that high-born women were more accomplished and interesting than women available to any man for a smile and a gift.

Polydore: "Astarte will not always be available, but I will always be around for you, and I can advise you on things."
Astarte: "Would not a large trading building built beside the port add to your glory and riches?"
Polydore: " I have just the people to manage it. Rocky and his consort."
Astarte: "Stop staring at me that way! Your gaze is getting me too excited!" *Men are so easy!*

Horus did not travel with the delegation to Megiddo. He, with Serket, traveled instead to Rusalem.

She said, "Oh, Horus. What have I agreed to? Being with you is the only thing I want in life. You bring me such peace and wisdom. I'm sorry! I'm so sorry!"

"I will be with you in Jaffa every full moon. I can live in Jaffa and travel the war road one season and travel to Canaan every other season. The

EGYPTIAN GODS: Osiris/Dionysus—Isis/Ariadne/Philyra, Horus, Set/Charon, Nephthys/Dexithea.
CANAANITE GODS: Anath, Astarte, Shalem, Shahar, Moloch, El.
OLYMPIAN GODS: Zeus, Dionysus, Hestia, Ares, Athena, Astraeus, Eos, Hermes.
OCEANIDS: Polydore, Lyris, Acaste, Eidyia, Dione.

Urfa missionaries have been busy in Canaan sowing half-truths and outright lies. There is much to explain to the people about the nature of their gods. Our separation will make our time together all the sweeter."

"You will be surrounded by lustful, willing women. I am afraid of losing you to one of them."

"I have no need of a woman but you."

"Even that Anath woman that Astarte is all the time telling me about? The one that 'cast you into the dung pile after Lord Set took her away from you? It's all right if you go to her. Just don't tell me about it."

He laughed. "Especially, Anath. She was my love until Set poisoned us against one another. If I did lay with her and didn't tell you, Uncle Set most certainly would—in great detail. But let us not talk of unpleasant things. Let's enjoy our time together while we have it. This looks like a good place to enjoy our time!"

She looked around and agreed, "Yes, this is a wonderful place to do it!"

After they had finished, she lay in his arms as they stared up at the children of Shalem and Shahar coming forth in the evening sky to fill the heaven. They were at peace.

He said, "I will visit your grandfather and your people tomorrow, but I must travel to Tophet the day after. The Winter Solstice is less than two seasons away. I must do what little I can do to alleviate their horrible Rite."

"The burning of the maiden and the disemboweling of the men?"

"Yes. But the burning and the disemboweling are for the pleasure of God Ares. Persephone would be pleased with only the plowing—and it would please her even more if the woman were a willing volunteer receiving lovers of her own choosing. I must convince their chief of this. I will tell whatever lies I must."

"Truth is always better."

"They believe the lies told by missionaries from a tyrant using lies to maintain his own power and glory! Yes. Truth is best when people believe truth to be truth. But they need their fantasies to get through life. Sometimes those who bring light are stoned to death by those who prefer darkness. So it is. I will tell a smaller lie to mitigate the bigger lie." He paused. "It is so peaceful lying here with you."

Dionysus/Osiris, Ariadne/Isis/Philyra, Charon/Set, Hermes/Tehuti.
EGYPTIANS: Nebka, Djoser, Hotep, Khasek, Rocky
NUBIANS: Nima, Hetephe, King Kerma, Prince T'jaru, Prince Rafah.
CANAANITES: Phoenicia, Serket, Azazil, Jaffa | URFANS: Teumessian, Abram, Sarai, Terah

"Yes, a peaceful lie." She rolled over to be on top of him and gazed lovingly into his eyes.

The children of Shalem and Shahar played across the night sky.

EGYPTIAN GODS: Osiris/Dionysus—Isis/Ariadne/Philyra, Horus, Set/Charon, Nephthys/Dexithea.
CANAANITE GODS: Anath, Astarte, Shalem, Shahar, Moloch, El.
OLYMPIAN GODS: Zeus, Dionysus, Hestia, Ares, Athena, Astraeus, Eos, Hermes.
OCEANIDS: Polydore, Lyris, Acaste, Eidyia, Dione.

12. Winter Solstice

Year 153

The Holiday Season begins a quarter-moon before the Winter Solstice and continues a quarter-moon after the Winter Solstice. In Memphis and other towns throughout Egypt, families that could, would gather for gift-giving, feasting, prayers, and reflections on their past year because the days grew ever shorter, and Ra grew ever weaker. If Ra did not recover his strength at the Winter Solstice, then all days would end. But at the end of all things, those that could, would be with family. Homes were decorated with greenery signifying hope and reminding Ra of all the beauty he brought to his lands.

The Mastabas would be flurries of activity with priests and priestesses decorating them with festive greenery and red berries. This time of year, the people of Memphis were allowed to come and pay their respects to those who currently lay dead and to reflect on life.

The pressure on High Priestess Hathor was immeasurable. It was her responsibility to call Osiris from the Land of the Dead each morning. Osiris had always come to her call. But he did not rise as high in the sky as he should—the days grew darker and shorter. The Winter Solstice would be the day of reckoning. How high would Osiris rise the next day? Would he rise higher than the morning before? Her astronomers would tell her immediately after Highsun if he had risen higher. If she were worthy to be High Priestess to God, if she performed her duty, if Ra did rise higher in the sky at Winter Solstice, then the mood during the subsequent quarter moon would shift from reflective contemplation and familial love to one of relief and celebration—of drinking, and perhaps of wild abandon.

And all things depended upon one woman—the once little hostess girl named Hathor, now the powerful High Priestess to Osiris, who was charged with calling forth Ra—the Living Sun.

~

On this first evening of the holidays, Prince Djoser joined his mother and her husband in the king's seasonally decorated study for a glass of fruit-wine. Outside, singers were singing songs of winter's beauty and of spring's hope.

Dionysus/Osiris, Ariadne/Isis/Philyra, Charon/Set, Hermes/Tehuti.
EGYPTIANS: Nebka, Djoser, Hotep, Khasek, Rocky
NUBIANS: Nima, Hetephe, King Kerma, Prince T'jaru, Prince Rafah.
CANAANITES: Phoenicia, Serket, Azazil, Jaffa | URFANS: Teumessian, Abram, Sarai, Terah

Djoser brought with him a festively wrapped large package. He made a show of presenting the package to his mother. "For my beloved, glorious mother—Queen of Kemet!" He handed her the package.

Nima was excited. She exclaimed, "For little me! Whatever can it be!"

"Something which attempts to match your exquisite beauty but fails ingloriously!"

"Should I open it now?!"

"As soon as I get my drink!" The attendant served him a fruit-wine. "Now!" he exclaimed.

She tore into the package and gasped with delight. "It is beautiful beyond words, Son! Where did you find such a thing?!"

"The linen is Egyptian. The dye is Canaanite. Canaanite linen is poorly made but by trading our linen with their dye makers, this is what we can achieve. The Greeks will trade their first child for bolts of this. And you, Mother, have the very first bolt. The color is quite royal, don't you think?"

She unfolded a length of the purple fabric and wrapped it around her body.

King Khasek commented, "It may be more comely on you than pure white, Nima."

She ran to embrace Djoser and then commanded her handmaiden, "Send for my seamstress. I wish to wear a gown made of this fabric this very night. I must find out if it is more comely than pure white on me!!" She twirled with the linen wrapped around her.

King Khasek laughed at his wife as he walked to Djoser and asked, "Will Minor-General Hetephe be joining us this season?"

Djoser replied, "She wishes to stay with her troops as long as she can. Most have been given a two-season leave to return home and rest. Their progress has been slowed because Snefru keeps getting called away from building his forts and Hete doesn't want her troops to outrun their supply lines. But her new strategy of simply controlling all oases is working well. We may never have the Sinai army at full strength again. She hopes to return to Memphis in time for the big ceremony so she can pump some arrows into Osiris's rump in case he has grown too lazy to do his job."

EGYPTIAN GODS: Osiris/Dionysus—Isis/Ariadne/Philyra, Horus, Set/Charon, Nephthys/Dexithea.
CANAANITE GODS: Anath, Astarte, Shalem, Shahar, Moloch, El.
OLYMPIAN GODS: Zeus, Dionysus, Hestia, Ares, Athena, Astraeus, Eos, Hermes.
OCEANIDS: Polydore, Lyris, Acaste, Eidyia, Dione.

Nima said, "Don't be disrespectful, Son. One never knows who one is influencing."

"You are correct, as always, Mother. But, with Horus being gone, Hathor may need extra attention. She takes her responsibilities far too seriously. She has begun to believe her own fabrications."

"Her responsibilities are serious. As serious as ours."

King Khasek cut in, "And if we all perform our responsibilities to the best of our abilities, this time next year, we shall all be together—all of our goals will have been met—all our projects completed—there will be peace and good-will across the land." He hoisted his fruit-wine into the air.

Nima and Djoser returned the salute with, "To eternal peace and goodwill!"

As he drank, Djoser thought, *Will hope and dreams never die?*

~

Sunrise, the second day of the holidays, Hathor and her staff performed their ceremony magnificently. The people of Memphis and their out-of-town guests were elated. They lined up in an endless line to visit the Mastaba of King Nebka. Of these, one in ten was invited to visit the Mastaba of Chief Kemet. Of these, one in ten was invited to visit the glory of glories—the Mastaba of Osiris—of God, himself.

With the ceremonies complete and the post-ceremony duties done, a priestess led Nephthys to join Hathor. The two women embraced and sat down at Osiris's favorite table for morning meal.

Hathor said, "We are both without Horus. Some woman has turned his heart away from family and friends to become her plaything."

Nephthys laughed. "Our son will be no woman's plaything, nor will his heart turn away from those he loves. It is my Set that has abandoned friends and family. He is in the Sinai with that Anath woman trying to become a god of some kind—El Set, he calls himself—'personal friend of God Zeus'—as if Zeus even knew that my husband existed."

"Red-ribboned Anath mistreated Horus horribly, I am told."

"Set mistreats them *both* horribly. Anath simply isn't aware enough to know that she is being used by Set to humiliate Horus. She believes Set and Horus fought for her favor, and, to her disappointment, Set won. She is so wise in the way of men but so blind to that. But Djoser tells me the Serket woman brings our Horus peace and joy. I hope this is so."

"Hete told me this Serket is becoming a powerful woman in both Canaan and on the war road. Chief Jaffa traded many goods to obtain a fast horse for her from the far east. Serket rides it to a fort when a person has been stung by a deadly scorpion. If she arrives in time, she has the potions and knowledge to save the person's life. They say that she then goes through the camp calling to the scorpions and that they come to her. She gathers them and takes them deep into the desert so that they will be safe from the dangers of men. Hete will not swear this to be true, but men saved by the hand of Healer Serket swear they have witnessed it."

Nephthys raised her fruit-wine toward Hathor in salute, and said, "To peace and joy!"

Hathor responded in kind. "To peace and joy!" *I shall tell Isis that her son has found a consort worthy of him! It will bring her happiness!*

Rusalem

Serket stood leaning against Horus as her grandfather welcomed the children of Shalem and Shahar as they began twinkling into the evening sky. He thanked them for sharing the wonder of their love, and the peace that their children brought to all people who looked upon them. This would be the longest night of the year. How thrilled they must be to sparkle and play for so long a time.

Horus, Serket, Phoenicia, Rocky, and the grandfather ate a long, celebratory evening meal. The old man had both his granddaughters with him—and they were both successful in the big, important city of Jaffa.

Horus again told of the conversation he had had with the Chief of Tophet and how he was hopeful but unsure if he had convinced the chief to change his Fertility Rite to what "God Persephone now desires" rather than "the old way that the missionaries had described."

The grandfather said, "Men of reason and goodwill will always do that which is right!"

Horus raised his cup of honey, milk, and herbs to the old man in salute, "To men of reason and goodwill!"

The four young people raised their cups and repeated his words.

EGYPTIAN GODS: Osiris/Dionysus—Isis/Ariadne/Philyra, Horus, Set/Charon, Nephthys/Dexithea.
CANAANITE GODS: Anath, Astarte, Shalem, Shahar, Moloch, El.
OLYMPIAN GODS: Zeus, Dionysus, Hestia, Ares, Athena, Astraeus, Eos, Hermes.
OCEANIDS: Polydore, Lyris, Acaste, Eidyia, Dione.

"And now, a gift for our grandfather!"

The two women jumped up and pulled a festively wrapped package from behind them.

"A gift? Whatever for? What is it?" the old man asked.

"Open it!" both women squealed.

Their grandfather slowly and carefully unwrapped his gift. It was a large flask. He looked at them quizzically.

They all answered at the same time:
Rocky: "It contains wine."
Serket: "It brings peace."
Horus: "Drink it slowly and carefully."
Phoenicia: "It is both a blessing and a curse."
Serket: "It will make you feel warm and safe."
Horus: "Drink it carefully."

The four spent the evening introducing the old man to this new drink. The evening grew late. Most of the villagers had retired for the night.

The old man spoke of days past. "Your mother was a beautiful woman. She changed when your father was killed in the great raid from the valley. There was much hunger, then. The rains had not come that year. People were starving. They came from the valley for our food. Our men defended Shalem as best they could. Our only weapons were our farming tools. They took most of our food and retreated. Your father was clubbed to death. He fought valiantly but he was a man of peace, not of war. He died in the arms of your mother. You were both so young."

The old man got a catch in his throat. His granddaughters moved and sat at his knees.

He continued, "My daughter was without a husband. We were a poor town and we had lost most of our food. She went to the city to find work in order to feed us. She returned every quarter moon with food. As the seasons wore on, she began losing her beauty and began looking older than she really was. She loved you so much. She began bringing home small amounts of a beautiful powder. She kept it safe until she had enough to color a dress for Phoenicia. The dress was much too large when you were a child, but you grew into it as you became a woman. Then, one day, your mother did not return on the quarter-moon, or any quarter-moon ever again." The old man tried to choke back a sob but couldn't. His voice broke on "ever again."

His granddaughters rose and hugged him, saying things granddaughters should say to a crying grandfather.

Horus watched. *Perhaps the wine was not a wise gift.*

He rose, walked to the old man, pulled him to his feet, grasped his shoulders, stared into the red-rimmed eyes, and said, "You raised your daughter to be a good woman. Her husband was a good and valiant man. Their goodness and valor live on in their children. Be proud and thankful for all that you have accomplished. You have raised your granddaughters to become successful, loving women. You and they bring much peace into a world in much need of peace. The children of Shalem look down upon you and rejoice. Go to bed and sleep well this night. Rejoice in living it."

The old man shook his head in acquiescence. His granddaughters led him to his bed, tucked him in, and sang a lullaby. He slipped into a peaceful sleep.

The women rejoined the men. They finished their wine.

Phoenicia said to Rocky, "I have had a most eventful night, but I am ready for bed, now."

She and Rocky retired to the girl's old bedroom.

Horus and Serket found an isolated area where they could stare up into the sky. They laid out a sleeping blanket and undressed. Serket was not interested in looking at peaceful lights in the sky. She was interested in Horus. Horus was surprised by the intensity of her lovemaking. After she was sated, she did not roll off his body but positioned her body to lay on his. She whispered into his ear, "So much sadness. Why is there so much sadness in the world?"

He whispered back, "Because there are so many people."

He held her tightly as she drifted into sleep. He stared into the peaceful sky trying to come up with a more useful answer than "because." *Well, Father. It is a reasonable question. Is that the purpose of death? To relieve us of sadness? Of pain? of our own inhumanity? What says the dead? And in the valley— what do they do even as I lie here? Did I accomplish good? Did I make the valley a better place?*

EGYPTIAN GODS: Osiris/Dionysus—Isis/Ariadne/Philyra, Horus, Set/Charon, Nephthys/Dexithea.
CANAANITE GODS: Anath, Astarte, Shalem, Shahar, Moloch, El.
OLYMPIAN GODS: Zeus, Dionysus, Hestia, Ares, Athena, Astraeus, Eos, Hermes.
OCEANIDS: Polydore, Lyris, Acaste, Eidyia, Dione.

He slipped into a fitful sleep. The distant sound from the valley awakened him. Serket still used his body as her bed and her comforter. He stared into the peaceful sky. The moon had passed its high point. The rites in the valley would be nearing completion. The sound began as a child's scream of fear but soon turned into a girl's scream of agony. Oh, how she could scream! And scream and scream and scream.

He lay listening to the valley, holding Serket, staring into the peaceful sky.

Memphis

She gathered her priestesses, priests, and support staff well before sunrise. *I must show no fear. I must exude total confidence. To show fear is unworthy of me, my country, and my god. I shall call forth Lord Osiris and he shall rise higher.*

She spoke to them with supreme authority. "On this day, you will each perform your duties for the glory of Egypt and its people. You shall reveal the glory of Isis and Osiris. You will call forth life—hope—dreams—the future of the land—the future of Egypt—the future of our kind. On this day—in this place—for you—and only for you, will Osiris rise—he will hear the entreaties of the keepers of his Mastaba. And on this day, he will rise—he will rise higher than yesterday. He will be invigorated—stronger—for he will hear the voices of his people. Because their voices shall be strong and glorious. On this day—in this place—you shall call forth the renewal of all life—you shall call forth Osiris—Ra, the Living Sun! YOURS IS THE GLORY. GO TO YOUR STATIONS!"

Dressed in their robes of office—in bejeweled crowns—in necklaces and bracelets covered with colored and precious stones—in the absolute finest of linens and leather—the glory of Egypt went each to their station. Below them, in silence stood the waiting people of Egypt—all ranks—all stations—all manner of people—some on their knees in reverence—some tightly grasping the hand of the person beside them—waiting.

Waiting ended.

Hathor stepped forward and with raised arms and a loud voice, called forth Osiris to become Ra—the Living Sun.

~

Horus woke in the morning light. Serket was already visiting her grandfather as he bid farewell to the children of Shalom and Shahar. His villagers had gathered for the daily ceremony of thanks.

Dionysus/Osiris, Ariadne/Isis/Philyra, Charon/Set, Hermes/Tehuti.
EGYPTIANS: Nebka, Djoser, Hotep, Khasek, Rocky
NUBIANS: Nima, Hetephe, King Kerma, Prince T'jaru, Prince Rafah.
CANAANITES: Phoenicia, Serket, Azazil, Jaffa | URFANS: Teumessian, Abram, Sarai, Terah

Horus watched them all with tenderness. The sun had breached the horizon, and the old man was giving thanks for the peace the children had brought the village of Rusalem. The villagers turned to one another and expressed their friendship to everyone around them.

After all were settled and eating their morning meal, Horus went to Serket and told her, "If I leave now and don't slow down, I can make it to Memphis before the next quarter-moon. I wanted to spend this time with you and your people, but I would like to spend at least a day with my mothers. I hope you understand, Serket."

"Understand? You will always do that which is tight, Horus. My understanding is not required. But ... I understand. It brings me peace that you came to Rusalem to be with me and my family during such an important time. Tell your mother I hope to meet her one day."

He packed, bid farewell to his friends, embraced Serket, and set off on a fast pace back to Memphis.

~

Horus trotted and walked as fast as could, stopping only for rest, for five days and nights. Finally, in the distance, he saw the great skyline of Memphis. He stopped to savor the moment. As he rested, he heard the hoofbeats of a galloping horse in the distance behind him. *Hoofbeats? How many horses are there in Egypt?*

He did not turn around to look.

Soon, the horse pulled up beside him and a voice with the accent of a high-born Greek woman inquired, "Nice man, I have been told that scorpions infest yond town. Do you know if this could possibly be true?"

"Not only true, Great Lady, but scorpions that are not at peace. They have requested I rid the place of all humans so that they may once again live in harmony with the great river."

She laughed at him and dismounted. "You are funny, Horus. 'Rid the place of all humans.' You couldn't really do that ... *could* you?"

"No, Serket. I could not! What are you doing here?"

"You are not pleased to see me? Polydore said she would manage the port for me! Shalom carried me as fast as she could to be with you and meet your mother. We thought you would be pleased!"

He immediately embraced her and whispered endearments into her ear.

"That's much better, Horus. And I promised Polydore to relocate many scorpions for you. It is to be Chief Jaffa's gift to the prince. Now, take me to your city and introduce me to your mothers."

They turned to go and, for the first time, Serket noticed the skyline of Memphis. She stopped and stared in wonder. "Is that a city or a mountain? Oh, Horus. It's so big!"

He took her hand. "And it is all for your pleasure, my great lady. Don't forget to use your pretentious accent when you speak to people—except to Mother Nephthys—she invented that accent."

He led her to meet his mother. Shalom followed closely behind.

They arrived at the gates of the city. Horus procured grooming and care for Shalom. The attendants were infatuated with the creature. Most of their wards were some form of cattle. Shalom was the center of attention.

Horus led Serket wide-eyed through the streets of Memphis. "I will give you the great tour of Memphis, tomorrow. I wish to spend the rest of our day with Mother Nephthys. I have three mothers, you know. We will visit Mother Hathor, tomorrow. Mother Isis is with Father—so I am told."

Her mind was overwhelmed by the time they reached the House of Nephthys.

Nephthys was thrilled to see her stepson and he had bought his friend Serket to meet her. Nephthys bubbled over with joy as she talked to the two of them. She finally inquired about the health of her husband.

Horus answered, "Uncle Set and—his friend—have taken up residence in Fort Kerma, Mother—that's the ninth fort on the war road. They both go on all of the military expeditions. Dispatcher Anath doesn't want to miss her chance to deliver a death stroke, although the need has become increasingly rare. But Uncle Set, I'm told, wants to be seen as her mentor and inspiration. That, plus he gets to perform the fireside ritual with her in front of everyone. His reputation grows as does Ananth's. It helps his ego, I am told."

Serket exclaimed, "Is Lord Set your *husband*, Mother Nephthys?! But he and that Anath woman are always ... I mean ... they don't behave like ... I mean ... Lord Set is married?!"

Dionysus/Osiris, Ariadne/Isis/Philyra, Charon/Set, Hermes/Tehuti.
EGYPTIANS: Nebka, Djoser, Hotep, Khasek, Rocky
NUBIANS: Nima, Hetephe, King Kerma, Prince T'jaru, Prince Rafah.
CANAANITES: Phoenicia, Serket, Azazil, Jaffa | URFANS: Teumessian, Abram, Sarai, Terah

Nephthys laughed. "Set is not known for his faithfulness, Sweet Serket. I knew that before I became his ... 'faithful consort' is a better description than 'wife,' I suppose. Set will do whatever Set must do to gain greater glory and adulation. It is his nature. His people in South Memphis consider him to be a god as do the nomads in the western Red Lands. He is now working on the Sinai and even Canaan. My husband is quite the celebrated man. He wishes to challenge Osiris, himself, as the supreme god of Egypt."

Serket offered, "Your son is the better man, Mother Nephthys. Horus is a good man doing good works. He has many followers."

They talked on until time to retire for the evening. They retired early because Horus wanted Serket to attend Hathor's Sun Rise Ceremony. "It is a ritual unlike anything you have ever seen."

~

All three rose well before sunrise. They were all of rank and could have stood beside Prince Djoser on the Grand Concourse to witness the rebirth of Osiris. Horus preferred the spot by the river from where he had experienced the first resurrection. He wanted, for some unknown reason, for Serket to experience what he had that first sunrise—for her understanding of the weight he carried, perhaps for her forgiveness.

But Serket was overwhelmed by the size of the city—by the sheer number of the people in the streets—by the magnificence of the setting—by her new accidental station in life.

The predawn light appeared and bathed the scene in a surreal light. Eventually, the drummers and announcers began taking their positions between the Mastabas and the main street.

The sun was moments away from breaching the horizon. The priestesses and priests stepped forward in the full dress of their office—and then— wearing her crown of the gigantic red stone and full dress of her office stepped High Priestess Hathor. She raised her arms and with a loud voice called forth the rebirth of Osiris.

Drummers drummed and announcers repeated her words so that all people could hear. Only seven people fainted. Serket was big-eyed and mesmerized. Osiris shined down upon the people he so loved.

EGYPTIAN GODS: Osiris/Dionysus—Isis/Ariadne/Philyra, Horus, Set/Charon, Nephthys/Dexithea.
CANAANITE GODS: Anath, Astarte, Shalem, Shahar, Moloch, El.
OLYMPIAN GODS: Zeus, Dionysus, Hestia, Ares, Athena, Astraeus, Eos, Hermes.
OCEANIDS: Polydore, Lyris, Acaste, Eidyia, Dione.

After the Ceremony was complete, Horus escorted Nephthys and Serket to the Mastaba of Osiris to visit with his mother Hathor. Serket could hardly contain herself. *Just imagine! Me visiting with the most powerful people in the world! Which accent should I use?!*

Hathor greeted them at the Osiris table. Djoser was already there, fruit-drink in hand. He said, "Horus! Welcome home, my son! And you have brought the lovely Serket. A wonderful morning! Greetings, Nephthys. I'm sure you are happy to have your son home!"

Horus embraced his Mother Hathor. Serket subconsciously noted that the embrace was longer and more intense than one might expect.

Nephthys accepted embraces from Hathor and Djoser and then said to Djoser, "What have you done with my young son Anubis, Prince? He doesn't return home, anymore."

Djoser laughed. "Since Lord Set has forsaken South Memphis, the women of Ishtar House have replaced him with Anubis as their Protector. I understand he has benefits."

"The Oceanids are correct! All men are pigs!" Nephthys exclaimed.

Hathor said, "Enough of that! Introduce me to your friend, Horus. Are you worthy of her?"

Serket made multiple instantaneous decisions. She curtsied—but not too deeply. She smiled—but not too greatly. She spoke using her middle-class accent. "I am privileged that Lord Horus will acknowledge me as his friend. He speaks of you highly very often. I feel I already know you."

Hathor answered, "Do not be concerned, Lord Serket. Horus learns quickly. He will become worthy of you soon enough."

Hathor, Serket, and Nephthys chatted amicably.

Djoser finally exclaimed, "Enough of this. High Priestess, give Serket a tour. Introduce her to Osiris. Horus and I can catch up while we drink and eat morning meal. Join us when the tour is over."

"Yes ... Master!!!" Hathor replied.

Djoser added, "Please!"

Hathor smirked and said, "That's better, Prince Djoser." She led the two women toward the Mastaba as Djoser and Horus sat down at the table

Dionysus/Osiris, Ariadne/Isis/Philyra, Charon/Set, Hermes/Tehuti.
EGYPTIANS: Nebka, Djoser, Hotep, Khasek, Rocky
NUBIANS: Nima, Hetephe, King Kerma, Prince T'jaru, Prince Rafah.
CANAANITES: Phoenicia, Serket, Azazil, Jaffa | URFANS: Teumessian, Abram, Sarai, Terah

and talked of the progress in the east. The women eventually returned and joined Djoser and Horus.

Djoser brought up the lingering but heated dispute between himself and Hathor. "The eastern frontier will soon enough no longer be our frontier. Fort Rafah will formally become the easternmost point of our land. Osiris will rise over Fort Rafah before he rises over Memphis. Hathor must move the ceremony from Memphis to Fort Rafah!"

Hathor retorted with fury. "I told you there will be no further discussion of this matter. I will not hear of it! Osiris will be called to life as he rises over the great river of Memphis. I am his High Priestess and that is my command."

Horus responded, "Have both my stepparents forgotten how to reason?! It will not be Osiris rising over Fort Rafah, it is only the sun on its way to High Priestess Hathor to be imbued with Osiris—the stuff of life. There is no conflict with a priest at each fort welcoming and encouraging the sun along its way to be given life by Hathor. I have followers in every fort, any one of which would be delighted to be sanctified by the High Priestess with the right to greet the rising, but not yet living, sun. I, myself, as the son of Isis and Osiris, would be delighted to perform this greeting at the sunrise after the Fort Rafah Winter Solstice Festival."

Hearing his proposal, Djoser and Hathor stared at one another in slow understanding. Djoser became ecstatic. "What a wonderful concept! The entire ceremony is strengthened and improved upon and brings the entire Sinai into the celebration of Isis and Osiris!"

Hathor remained imperial. "Bring me three candidates from each fort. I will instruct them on what will be required of them. They must be suited with proper attire and sanctified into the priesthood—or maybe just some type of assistant priesthood rather than full priesthood. I will discuss this with my priests and priestesses."

So it was, that Horus found himself an integral part of the great "Winter Solstice Dedication and Naming Ceremony" whereupon the fragmented kingdoms of Kemet would become the mighty united kingdom of Egypt.

EGYPTIAN GODS: Osiris/Dionysus—Isis/Ariadne/Philyra, Horus, Set/Charon, Nephthys/Dexithea.
CANAANITE GODS: Anath, Astarte, Shalem, Shahar, Moloch, El.
OLYMPIAN GODS: Zeus, Dionysus, Hestia, Ares, Athena, Astraeus, Eos, Hermes.
OCEANIDS: Polydore, Lyris, Acaste, Eidyia, Dione.

13. Egypt

So it was, Osiris was renewed to live another year.

So it was, the seasons passed.

So it was, the great War Road of Egypt and its forts were completed.

So it was, life was lived, people went about their duties, and civilization advanced in small, everyday ways.

So it was, that in the twelfth season, all Royalty and its court left Memphis to travel to Fort Rafah leaving behind only the holy Priestesses and Priests of Osiris to call forth Osiris for his people.

~

Astarte was beside herself with anticipation. She hardly knew which invitation to accept. Either would increase her international social recognition. She could attend the dedication and renaming ceremony with Set and her Sister Anath, or she could attend the event with the up-and-coming Chief Jaffa and his Consort Polydore. *Which invitation should I accept? Which will help me the most? This is all so exciting. Whatever will I wear?*

Serket swept all the forts for scorpions and removed them far inland for the safety of all concerned, including the innocent scorpions.

Horus and his new right-hand man, Azazil, met with Horus's followers in each fort extolling them on how to be helpful to the visitors who would be unsure of how to behave in such an environment. And now, Horus had three official docent-priests in each city—ordained by the High Priestess herself, to greet the rising sun and encourage it on its way to the great river—there to be imbued with life. Horus was ordained into full priesthood since he would be responsible for his docent-priests.

Polydore, Serket, and Phoenicia made a temporary tent camp midway between Jaffa and Rafah so that they could juggle their responsibilities between the two towns. All three still had heavy responsibilities in Jaffa but were expected to also support the great Winter Solstice Dedication. Serket did have Shalom, her horse, which was a lifesaver, especially when they discovered that the horse was happy enough to carry all three at one time. Rocky was doing well with port operations and the adjacent newly completed Egyptian Trading Center.

Polydore had obtained fireworks from Greece.

Dionysus/Osiris, Ariadne/Isis/Philyra, Charon/Set, Hermes/Tehuti.
EGYPTIANS: Nebka, Djoser, Hotep, Khasek, Rocky
NUBIANS: Nima, Hetephe, King Kerma, Prince T'jaru, Prince Rafah.
CANAANITES: Phoenicia, Serket, Azazil, Jaffa | URFANS: Teumessian, Abram, Sarai, Terah

~

The king's caravan had already left Memphis in order to visit and inspect each fort along the way. Vice-King Rafah, his wives, and his court traveled with King Khasek and Queen Nima. They would arrive in Fort Rafah two full days before the naming ceremony to be performed at the moment of Winter Solstice.

Everyone would be at the ceremony which was little more than a quarter-moon away. People were already arriving. Fort Rafah would be closed to all but the highest-ranking dignitaries; Chief Rafah, himself, the king and queen and their courts, and emissaries from Greece.

Jaffa was filled with visitors from as far away as Megiddo and Damascus plus traders from Greece and the important ports. Each fort along the way would be housing dignitaries from Kemet and Nubia. It was all extremely exciting.

~

Set and Anath, too, were invited to Fort Rafah for the great ceremony as was Astarte who met them saying, "I am so excited to attend the great ceremony as your guest, El Set. Sister Anath and I must coordinate our ensembles to maximize the impact that your presence will have on those gathered. We three will have to privately celebrate before and after and maybe during the ceremony. I may be able to get us some purple ribbons. We would all look so good with a touch of purple."

~

Horus was in Tophet, talking with the chief. "I am told that God Demeter was disappointed to hear that her representative in your Winter Solstice festival was thrown into the fire. She shuddered at the thought it might be her. She almost did not send the rains she was so upset. God Ares was delighted, of course. But personally, I don't care for Ares. He is too bloodthirsty to be of interest to a sophisticated, civilized man. By the way, I am friends with priests and priestesses to many gods. Try the plan that I proposed to you last year, I can probably get a representative from God Demeter to stop by and personally thank you. A chief must always do what he thinks is best but at least consider my plan. Try it. If it doesn't work out well, you can always return to the old-fashioned way."

"I don't like change! It's too much trouble! You can go now!"

EGYPTIAN GODS: Osiris/Dionysus—Isis/Ariadne/Philyra, Horus, Set/Charon, Nephthys/Dexithea.
CANAANITE GODS: Anath, Astarte, Shalem, Shahar, Moloch, El.
OLYMPIAN GODS: Zeus, Dionysus, Hestia, Ares, Athena, Astraeus, Eos, Hermes.
OCEANIDS: Polydore, Lyris, Acaste, Eidyia, Dione.

Horus courteously paid his respects and returned to Fort Rafah.

Upon arriving, he was relieved to learn that Serket was not there. Because Anath and Set were.

Set saw Horus arrive at the eastern gate, "Nephew Horus! Over here! Come join us! We haven't seen you in a long, long time. Come! I will find us a table at the cafe. We can visit!"

Horus waved to them and walked over to join them. Anath embraced him—tightly. They found a table. Set talked—about his conquests—about his fire ritual experiences with Dispatcher Anath—in great detail—about their growing power and recognition throughout the Sinai and even into Canaan. "And what have you been doing, Horus? Have you found a woman to replace the extremely talented and enthusiastic Anath that I seduced away from you?"

Anath cast her eyes downward and sweetly smiled at the recognition of her talents.

Horus started to speak but a flash of insight stopped him. He redirected the entire conversation. "I have failed at one of my projects, Uncle Set. It will take a much better man than I to accomplish that which all men of good-will would want to be accomplished, and the glory it would bring with it."

Set was instantly on alert. "Oh! And what project is this, Nephew Horus?"

Horus explained the Tophet issue. "Tophet is less than a day's run. A real man could be there and back in less than three days."

Set was hooked, "A contesting, Horus. I challenge you to a contesting over this Tophet thing!"

Horus said simply, "I accept."

~

The evening of the next day, Set and Anath arrived outside the village of Tophet. Anath removed her clothing except for her Egyptian Army Helmet and her belt with a dagger.

She posed and asked, "How do I look?"

"Terrifying and ravishing, God Anath. Absolutely terrifying and ravishing!"

She giggled.

Anath entered the village twenty paces in front of Set. She was noticed immediately. A woman ran running to tell the chief of this unbelievable sight. The chief walked out of his hut to stare at the approaching Anath—naked but for helmet and belt—and dagger.

She shouted, "I am Dispatcher Anath. I have come for you! Lie upon the ground and live or remain standing and die!" She did not slow her pace.

The chief looked around in total confusion. He had heard of this apparition, but he thought it was only tales told to frighten the weak.

She did not slow. She pulled her dagger from her belt and motioned him onto the ground.

Nervously, he thought, *This is only a woman! She is trying to frighten me! I will not have it!*

She broke into a trot. Her dagger in the kill position.

He fell prostrate onto the ground.

Anath stopped and called out, "El Set, he is wise. He wishes to live and waits for you!"

Set came marching in. He stopped in front of the prone chief and said to Anath, "Show him absolute power, God Anath!"

Anath walked to the prone chief, sat down over his neck, and urinated on him.

Set explained how God Demeter was displeased with the way the chief conducted his Winter Solstice ritual and the way that the chief would conduct it in the future. "You will obey, or God Anath will return for you, and she will not be kind and merciful as she is now."

The chief grunted something.

Set commanded, "The chief understands and agrees, God Anath. You may return to your killings!"

Anath rose and marched back out of the village. Set followed.

~

Serket had arrived at the fort and sat with Horus and Azazil at the Fort Rafah Cafe.

EGYPTIAN GODS: Osiris/Dionysus—Isis/Ariadne/Philyra, Horus, Set/Charon, Nephthys/Dexithea.
CANAANITE GODS: Anath, Astarte, Shalem, Shahar, Moloch, El.
OLYMPIAN GODS: Zeus, Dionysus, Hestia, Ares, Athena, Astraeus, Eos, Hermes.
OCEANIDS: Polydore, Lyris, Acaste, Eidyia, Dione.

Set and Anath triumphantly entered the east gate. Anath saw Horus and gaily waved but she and Set continued to their quarters for Set to celebrate his obvious victory-to-be.

Horus remarked, "I believe that Uncle Set has accomplished my goal for me. It will probably cost me a victory in a contesting, but such is the price of doing good. It will be difficult for you when you meet them, Serket, but remain at peace and Uncle Set's words will not harm you. In the meantime, what a glorious day!"

~

Prince Djoser arrived in the morning to oversee the reception for that afternoon's arrival of the king's caravan. He met with local officials and was pleased with their preparations.

Arriving, too, were Polydore and Phoenicia who set up residence in Horus and Serket's quarters.

None of the four had official duties at the upcoming Winters Solstice Dedication Ceremony. Horus would have a major role in the Sun Rise Ceremony the next morning and the three women would play major roles in Chief Jaffa's reception welcoming the king and his court to Canaan, three days after the solstice.

Prince Djoser saw the four eating their Highsun meal at the cafe and asked to join them. Serket was pleased but Phoenicia was thrilled. *I'm going to get to eat with a real prince!*

They chatted away. Horus brought up and explained his Tophet contesting to Djoser in detail.

Djoser remarked, "Set never gives up trying to beat you, Son. I'm sorry, but that is his nature. Nephthys is traveling with the queen. I will find time to take her to this village after the Solstice ceremony and find out what happened to the celebrants If the chief lets the woman live, Nephthys can give him 'warm greetings from Demeter.' Nephthys is a Telchine, you know, and she *does* love giving a dramatic performance."

The time grew near for the king's caravan to arrive. Everyone in the fort went to their assigned positions for the welcoming festivities. The drummers began drumming. The singers, singing. The flags, waving.

The caravan arrived. Everyone had a wonderful time.

Dionysus/Osiris, Ariadne/Isis/Philyra, Charon/Set, Hermes/Tehuti.
EGYPTIANS: Nebka, Djoser, Hotep, Khasek, Rocky
NUBIANS: Nima, Hetephe, King Kerma, Prince T'jaru, Prince Rafah.
CANAANITES: Phoenicia, Serket, Azazil, Jaffa | URFANS: Teumessian, Abram, Sarai, Terah

Winter's Solstice, Year 154

The sun sunk below the horizon. The official festivities began.

Upon the stage, addressing all those gathered, Major Hetephe introduced her Captains, their men, the fort commander, his permanent base defense staff, his caravan escort soldiers, and Dispatcher Anath. Also introduced were the old man's three sons who were instrumental in securing all oases. She ended with General T'jaru.

And then, on the stage, Vizier Menka introduced the local support staff with their managers and local residents.

The Vizier was replaced by Shaman Saqqar who extolled the fact that this was the location where the sun would first enter Egypt on its way to Memphis for Osiris to be reborn. He then introduced Horus who introduced his docent priests who would greet the sun each morning.

The evening wore on.

Djoser mounted the stage, told a few jokes, and announced that, by his reckoning, this was the One Hundred Twenty-fifth Anniversary of the First Winter Solstice Festival first held at Tallstone. He then introduced the great architects of the war road, Hotep and his son, Snefru. He praised them lavishly and then introduced the construction personnel who were present. And then, finally, the moon approached its highest position of the night; Horus introduced Queen Nima and the great King Khasek— who would now speak.

All retired from the main stage except for King Khasek, who had long practiced the speech he now gave. The fort astronomer signaled the king, "Sixty heartbeats to the Solstice." The king ended his speech, inserted a long pause, and then announced, "I proclaim the Kingdom of Kemet to be no more. The name of our glorious, unified lands from this moment forth shall be—'EGYPT!' "

Although the evening ceremonies had been long, the crowd erupted into a frenzy of excitement.

There would be fireworks and celebrations throughout the night.

Standing at the back of the stage, Hetephe took Djoser's hand and tried to look into his face, which was hidden in darkness, which was good.

She could not see his tears.

EGYPTIAN GODS: Osiris/Dionysus—Isis/Ariadne/Philyra, Horus, Set/Charon, Nephthys/Dexithea.
CANAANITE GODS: Anath, Astarte, Shalem, Shahar, Moloch, El.
OLYMPIAN GODS: Zeus, Dionysus, Hestia, Ares, Athena, Astraeus, Eos, Hermes.
OCEANIDS: Polydore, Lyris, Acaste, Eidyia, Dione.

PART II. PHARAOH

14. The Way of Horus

Horus did not sleep the night of the naming of Egypt.

In the predawn light, he went directly from the parties to his position at the east Gate of Fort Rafah. His three docent priests stood on either side of him as the remainder of his disciples gathered behind them. Many onlookers gathered just inside the gate.

Horus raised his arms toward the east, the sun breached the horizon. "Welcome back to your homeland Great Sun—bringer of light and life. We of Egypt love you, greet you, and will escort you along your way to the great river where the High Priestess waits to call forth Osiris—to imbue you with life, once more, so that you shall become Ra—the Living Sun!"

One woman fainted but it may have been from a night of festivities and wine-drinking rather than from hearing the words of Horus. But then again, maybe not.

~

The day was spent recovering, resting, and having private celebrations. There was another, more informal reception that night. Set, with Anath, searched for and found Horus and Serket. "Nephew Horus! Over here! Bring your lovely whore and join us for talk, drink, and celebration."

Horus thought, *Remain at peace, sweet Serket. Words cannot hurt us.*

Words, of course, can hurt you but Set's salacious soliloquy was interrupted when Djoser and Nephthys walked up.

Djoser said, "Greetings Lord Set. You remember Nephthys—your wife!"

Set and Nephthys exchanged uncomfortable greetings. Anath innocently exclaimed, "Don't worry Mother Nephthys. I'm taking really good care of our Set."

Set started to comment, but Djoser's glare made him reconsider. Djoser smoothly interjected, "Your wife and I are going to the village of Tophet in the morning to visit their chief. Horus told me about the good work you may have done there. You know how I love good work; makes for a peaceful people."

Dionysus/Osiris, Ariadne/Isis/Philyra, Charon/Set, Hermes/Tehuti.
EGYPTIANS: Nebka, Djoser, Hotep, Khasek, Rocky
NUBIANS: Nima, Hetephe, King Kerma, Prince T'jaru, Prince Rafah.
CANAANITES: Phoenicia, Serket, Azazil, Jaffa | URFANS: Teumessian, Abram, Sarai, Terah

Set began to explain how his presence would ensure all went well but, in the end, Djoser and Nephthys would go to Tophet alone.

The next morning, Serket accompanied Djoser and Nephthys to Rusalem to introduce them to her beloved grandfather. Djoser was impressed with the tranquility of the grandfather and his villagers. *I need to find out how he does it.*

Djoser and Nephthys then traveled on to Tophet. The villagers were excited to see another two, high-born strangers in their village. They certainly remembered the last two, as did the chief. He came from his hut armed with a sword and dagger. He stared at the two wondering how to proceed. *At least they aren't the last two that were here!*

Djoser quickly said, "Peaceful greetings from God Demeter, great chief of Tophet. We come to hear of your recent celebration. Will you counsel with us?"

He decided. "Yeah. You can come sit on one of my sitting rocks. The wench can stand behind you!"

Djoser said to Nephthys, "Oh, joy! Confidant to the great God Demeter, herself, you may stand behind me as I hear of the chief's accomplishments!"

Hearing the name of Demeter, the chief remembered Horus's promise and reconsidered his approach. "Maybe the wench—I mean—confi'nt can sit with us if she wants to."

Nephthys answered, "I prefer to stand. Thank you."

Djoser said, "Introduce me to your woman celebrant from your celebration." *If she still lives.*

The chief looked around at the gathered villagers and motioned for a woman to come and join them.

The woman's eyes grew large as she tentatively approached the council of high-ranking people.

The chief said, "This here's the wom'n that got humped."

Djoser said to the woman, "I understand you got some good humping. Would you agree?"

The woman gushed, "Oh yes, great lord. I was mightily satisfied!"

EGYPTIAN GODS: Osiris/Dionysus—Isis/Ariadne/Philyra, Horus, Set/Charon, Nephthys/Dexithea.
CANAANITE GODS: Anath, Astarte, Shalem, Shahar, Moloch, El.
OLYMPIAN GODS: Zeus, Dionysus, Hestia, Ares, Athena, Astraeus, Eos, Hermes.
OCEANIDS: Polydore, Lyris, Acaste, Eidyia, Dione.

"And which three men accommodated you?"

She was puzzled, "Accom'd me? You mean, who humped me?" She brightened up and pointed to three younger, fit men standing and watching.

Djoser exclaimed, "Gentlemen, my congratulations on your fine humping abilities that so greatly pleased God Demeter."

The woman excitedly continued, "After they got done, my chief finished me off. He humped me real good."

Nephthys exclaimed, "Excellent. It is exactly as God Demeter explained it to me. She was extremely pleased with the unadulterated pleasure her surrogate brought to her. She commanded me to give this gift to show her pleasure to the chief of Tophet."

The chief did not understand half the words the woman—'confid'nt'—said, but he understood the gold necklace she was presenting to him—heavy gold strands with semiprecious stones hanging from it—of greater value than his entire village. The chief stood up in awed silence.

Nephthys asked, "Whatever is the matter? Do you not like God Demeter's gift for your considerate sacrifice to her pleasure?"

The chief fell to his knees, head bowed, and said "Can I offer three women to God Demeter next year?"

Nephthys replied, "Would they all be willing women?"

"Oh yes, great Confd'nt. We will hold contests to see which woman most wants the humpin and let'm pick out the men they want to do it!"

Nephthys replied, "That would be most satisfactory, Great Chief. God Demeter will look forward to all of the pleasure you will be providing her. By the way, why did you change your procedure?

"You mean, why didn't we jus' throw 'er in the fire when they got done like we usually do?"

"Yes. Whatever made you realize what pleased God Demeter the most?"

The chief answered, "Some real nice man came through by the name of whore-us and told me to. I did't change last year cause I don't like change but he came back through again this year an' tol' me again so I decided to try it. He tol' me God Demeter might sen' somebody jus' like you if she

Dionysus/Osiris, Ariadne/Isis/Philyra, Charon/Set, Hermes/Tehuti.
EGYPTIANS: Nebka, Djoser, Hotep, Khasek, Rocky
NUBIANS: Nima, Hetephe, King Kerma, Prince T'jaru, Prince Rafah.
CANAANITES: Phoenicia, Serket, Azazil, Jaffa | URFANS: Teumessian, Abram, Sarai, Terah

was happy with the change. Ah'm glad I did it but I almos' did't cause this dung hole and his whore-friend came by and thretn'd me. I almos' sac'erficed a girl this year jus' t' show'm. That's why I had the spear ready cause I figur'd they'd come back to kill me. Ah'm glad I didn't let'm get the best o' me. It worked out real nice."

Nephthys answered, "Very nice, indeed, and I will ensure that you aren't bothered again by that dung-hole and his woman. It was very nice meeting you, Chief. Keep up the good work. Shall we leave these good people to reflect in their glory, Prince Djoser?"

Djoser replied, "Yes, indeed, Confidant Nephthys. Our work here is done. Good day, Great Chief."

After the pleasantries were completed, Djoser and Nephthys left the villagers admiring the chief's new necklace.

When they were away from the village, Djoser inquired, "All that talk back there got me excited. Do you want to go into the woods and let me hump you real good?"

Without breaking stride, she glanced sideways at him and snorted, "The Oceanids are correct! All men are pigs!"

They continued their return to Rusalem as Djoser reflected and muttered to himself, "Yes. Yes, we are."

Djoser Unmoored

"The Way of Horus" was simply "The Way of Queen Kiya" repackaged and refined through the experiences of his father, Osiris, plus his own experiences—"Do that which brings the most good." The complexities of modern life usually resulted in decisions yielding good, bad, and unintended consequences.

Prince Djoser found delight rolling around in the good consequences; Priest Horus found despair rolling in the bad; Vizier Menka was left with repairing the unintended; the king took credit for the good and blamed the bad on Zeus.

Horus's scattered followers found themselves coalescing around the newly formed docent priests in each fort. The three resident docents gave structure and social meaning to their value system of "the way Horus would do it" or, as it eventually became known, "the Way of Horus." They began taking their roles in society more seriously than simply wine-drinking friends sitting around discussing the improbabilities of human existence. They began taking a more active role in ministering to the sick, needy, and all others suffering some form of despair. People began consulting them when they needed advice. Tying them all together into one cohesive unit was the regular visits by their beloved teacher and mentor—Horus.

Horus did the good work his mother and father would want him to do, but always, his obsession remained, *Is there actually a "Land of the Dead." If so, where is it? How do I talk to the dead? Was my scorpion sting experience real or simply a hallucination of a fevered mind influenced by Father's stories?*

His knowledge was anecdotal, but his father had believed the dead still lived somewhere in some form. The details were sketchy—"shed your body" plus "the White Light will come for you." Hardly the stuff of true knowledge. Still, he searched—visiting every Shaman and everyone who dealt with the deceased. All the while ministering to the downtrodden and gaining disciples along his way.

Azazil, Rocky's replacement, traveled with Horus into ever-expanding territories. Every village, city, and camp Horus and Azazil visited had one or more gods the townspeople respected and sometimes worshipped. Benign interpretations of the fabled Demeter, Zeus, Dionysus, or Aphrodite were the most common. However, many of the implementations were counterproductive for the well-being of most of the ordinary residents—this relationship had invariably been influenced by missionaries from the ancient city of Urfa.

Rocky now managed the Egyptian Trade Center in Jaffa. Phoenicia set prices, found buyers, scheduled distribution, and managed operations but Rocky talked to the traders offering what Phoenicia instructed him to offer. Rocky was best friends with all the traders.

Phoenicia's Trading Center, coupled with Serket's Port, coupled with Polydore grew Jaffa into a city of regional importance rivaling even Megiddo and Damascus; the cities on old established major trade routes.

Set achieved his desire to become considered a god in the Sinai but was continually frustrated by Horus's ongoing successes. Plus, Horus had defeated Set in all but one contesting. Horus never mentioned this indignity, but Set remembered every defeat and was sure that Djoser was aware of each one. To be bested by the son of his hated enemies Isis and

Dionysus/Osiris, Ariadne/Isis/Philyra, Charon/Set, Hermes/Tehuti.
EGYPTIANS: Nebka, Djoser, Hotep, Khasek, Rocky
NUBIANS: Nima, Hetephe, King Kerma, Prince T'jaru, Prince Rafah.
CANAANITES: Phoenicia, Serket, Azazil, Jaffa | URFANS: Teumessian, Abram, Sarai, Terah

Osirus festered in his soul. The seduction of Anath was Set's only triumph over Horus. This relationship was described in exaggerated prurient detail every time Set crossed paths with Horus. Horus graciously declined several invitations to watch. Polydore, as a matter of course, taught all her female students the "Art of the Forceful No." This knowledge was put to use when Set found Serket alone and aggressively attempted to couple with her. She declined, first with the "Gracious No" and then with the "Forceful No."

Minor-General Hete retired with honors from the Egyptian Army. She was replaced by Major T'jaru. There were military parades in Memphis. Everyone came. She continued to practice her archery every day. Except for perhaps Artemis, Hete was the best archer in the world and intended to stay that way.

Djoser had accomplished all he had set out to do—creating a degree of affluence along with a feeling of self-worth in South Memphis—building roadways to make travel within the kingdom easy and comfortable—establishing a common religious ideology unifying the people — solidifying the relationship between the Upper and Lower Kingdoms—bringing the eastern Red Lands under control—renaming the kingdom with a name embraced by all Egyptians—establishing a great trade route to the lands outside Egypt.

The day came as he and Hete sat at the Mastaba drinking wine with Hathor and he realized he had accomplished all his goals and had no plans past this point. He raised his cup to Hathor in salute and said, "We brought a little wine. We brought a little joy!"

Understanding his melancholy, Hathor replied, "King Khasek will probably name his son his successor—maybe you, but probably Sanakhte. You and Hetephe could go explore the world. Go find Horus."

He replied, "Maybe we can go find some horses to import. I like horses. I had one once. Its name was Pony."

They sat together in silence and sipped their wine.

The days had become seasons.

~

Six seasons after the last Winter Solstice Festival, Djoser and Hete arrived once again in Fort Rafah.

EGYPTIAN GODS: Osiris/Dionysus—Isis/Ariadne/Philyra, Horus, Set/Charon, Nephthys/Dexithea.
CANAANITE GODS: Anath, Astarte, Shalem, Shahar, Moloch, El.
OLYMPIAN GODS: Zeus, Dionysus, Hestia, Ares, Athena, Astraeus, Eos, Hermes.
OCEANIDS: Polydore, Lyris, Acaste, Eidyia, Dione.

On their way from Memphis, they had visited each fort along the war road seeking to identify and resolve problems and strengthen bonds with Memphis. Because of his known association with Horus, Djoser was in high demand to meet with the docent priests and discuss weighty subjects; including reports of Urfa missionaries being seen along the war road.

Hete was in high demand to visit the military personnel and discuss various strategies and protocols for defending the forts and escorting the increasing number of trade caravans between forts.

Fort Rafah was no exception. "There have been reports of raids on our turquoise mines. How should we address this problem?"

They remained in Fort Rafah for a quarter-moon before continuing to Jaffa, where Serket maintained their home.

Djoser and Hete's arrival in Jaffa was met with jubilation and receptions. Prince Djoser remained a favorite of the local people and ex-Minor-General Hetephe was well known for her leadership in ridding the Red Lands of the warlords and bandits that had plagued the good people of Canaan. All that, plus El Set and God Anath were said to respect and honor both Lords, even if neither were a god.

Serket held a reception at the port cafe. Chief Jaffa the Eighteenth and his consort, Polydore, were the hosts. Everyone but Horus was there.

Chief Jaffa was flanked by Polydore and Astarte. He said to Djoser, "My port is overflowing with goods that would trade well in Megiddo and Damascus. Perhaps your road builders could be retained to assist in building a trade road from Jaffa to Damascus through Megiddo."

Djoser glanced at Polydore's face as the chief conversed. She appeared to be a woman in love. A woman, at least, filled with the pride of her man transforming from a small-town, drunken, ne'er-do-well to a sophisticate who could chat with a prince of Egypt on a presumably equal basis.

Astarte was thrilled to be hanging onto the arm of the most powerful local man available while he was talking to what might well be the most powerful man in the world. Astarte smiled a lot at both, her imagination running wild.

Set and Anath hung around the periphery until they could slide into Chief Jaffa's circle. Set gushed, "Prince Djoser, my friend! How good to see you!

Anath and I have been missing the excitement of the big city of Memphis!"

Djoser replied, "Hello, Lord Set. You are doing well, I understand."

Set replied, "Oh, yes, indeed. Becoming a god has been strenuous on me, having to plow God Anath on the corpses of her victims, in front of a large audience is taxing but her following demands it of us."

Djoser snapped, "Don't be crude, Set. It's unbecoming!"

"One does not tell a god what to do, Djoser. We do as we wish."

"I'm telling you, Set. Don't be crude."

Astarte became excited. *Men fighting!*

The other members of the circle immediately tensed. Cool-headed Polydore interjected, "Lords! Please. This is *my* party. Don't ruin it for me! El Set, tender ears may be listening to us. Let me request that we don't discuss matters of sexuality, tonight."

Set replied, "Since you ask so nicely, I will grant your request."

Djoser thought, *Set, have you gone mad?*

Polydore discreetly head-motioned Phoenicia who came rushing over and arm-pulled Djoser from the chief's circle into Rocky and hers. "Prince Djoser, you simply must tear yourself away from these wonderful people and join us commoners."

Astarte stared after the prince wondering if she should stay where she was or follow the prince. She looked to her sister Anath for guidance. Anath was content to stay with the chief.

Rocky nodded to Djoser in recognition. "Lord Set is becoming increasingly demanding. Even Horus is beginning to lose patience with him. He physically attacked Serket once, you know. She handled him well enough, but Lord Set is not one to forget a slight."

Djoser replied, "He is taking this El thing seriously?"

"Oh, yes. Very seriously. He is trying to pass Horus in importance and adulation by the Canaanites. Anath is referred to as a god because, well, she is an overpowering force to be feared. Set takes his association with her to build up his own image. He refers to himself as El—a god. Set wants to be thought of in the same terms as Zeus. I fear Horus is fighting

EGYPTIAN GODS: Osiris/Dionysus—Isis/Ariadne/Philyra, Horus, Set/Charon, Nephthys/Dexithea.
CANAANITE GODS: Anath, Astarte, Shalem, Shahar, Moloch, El.
OLYMPIAN GODS: Zeus, Dionysus, Hestia, Ares, Athena, Astraeus, Eos, Hermes.
OCEANIDS: Polydore, Lyris, Acaste, Eidyia, Dione.

a losing battle explaining to people that the gods of old are not powerful, supernatural people in the heavens, but just obnoxious, powerful humans who were wiped out by the great flood. Evidently, honoring and worshiping gods makes Canaanites feel better about life in some way."

"Are these local gods revered in the same way as Isis and Osiris are in Egypt?"

Rocky laughed. "We need several flasks of wine and a long evening to discuss *that* subject, Prince Djoser. But no. Egyptians consider Isis and Osiris to be more real and to be greater beings than the gods of old. Canaanite gods are more transient, interchangeable, and disposable, and may still be living. In some cities, like Rusalem, their gods are part of the fabric of the city. But Megiddo is overrun with gods. It drives Horus to tears, sometimes."

Djoser asked, "Does Set really believe he can command me?"

"Lord Set hasn't quite made it to the top, yet. You can ignore him, at least for now, but certainly if God Anath commands you to do something, it will be best to do it, immediately!"

Djoser was indignant. "I AM A PRINCE OF EGYPT! Anath is a ... a ..."

Rocky interrupted, "A living god. A very powerful living god with the power to do Zeus only knows what. Chief Jaffa obeys her. Everyone in Canaan obeys her. You might be able to get away with disobedience but don't turn your back on one of her rabid followers. I overheard in a wine house someone say that he has, himself, seen Anath shoot lightning bolts out her anus. That he serves and will protect Anath with his life!"

Djoser signaled for another wine. *May Osiris protect us!*

Phoenicia said, "You two are far too serious. Let's go find Hete and slip down to the beach!"

Serket saw them leaving and asked, "Is this an escape so you can go kiss, or may I join you?"

Phoenicia replied, "You're jealous that you're missing out on something. It's not our fault you can't hold on to a man!"

Serket snapped back, "*My man* is very important and is out trying to save the world. Thank you, very much!" She turned to Djoser and said, sweetly, "Horus would not have journeyed to Byblos had he known you were coming. Prince. He hungers to be in your presence and talk of meaningful things. He and Azazil are out in search of wisdom. I expect him back within two quarter-moons. Will you still be here?"

Djoser replied, "Byblos? That's even more northern than Damascus, isn't it? On the coast, if I remember correctly."

"Yes, my Lord. They are a great seafaring people. They mingle freely with the Greeks and the Mesopotamians. Horus believes these peoples to be more sophisticated and learned than the tribes and cities in Canaan and even Egypt. My Horus seeks the Land of the Dead, but still, he tries to comfort and rehabilitate people as he seeks."

"I need to do those things, too. Where are they? Maybe we could join them." Djoser looked at Hetephe and asked, "What about it, Hete? Want to go on an adventure? I'll buy you a horse!"

"Sure. We don't have enough adventure in our lives, and I would love to have a horse like Serket's."

Djoser became excited. "What about you three? If we find him, you will have somebody to kiss on the beach, Serket!"

Serket replied, "No, thank you. He will come back to me. You will find him if you travel up the coast. Horus leaves followers and disciples everywhere he goes. They can help you."

The five walked to the beach and bantered about good things. Rocky and Phoenicia *did* fall behind for a while. They may have kissed.

As the reception closed, Djoser pulled Polydore aside to thank her and inquire, "Oceanid, tell me of your sisters in Riverport."

She stared at him for a moment, and replied, "I have no sisters in Riverport. I am so glad that you are enjoying your visit. Good night," turned, and briskly walked away.

~

The next morning, Djoser went to Set and Ananth's quarters. He did not knock. He walked in, saw them, and said, "If either of you ever pulls that 'I am a god' dung on me again, I will have both your names stripped from the history of Egypt and have you killed the moment you step through the gates of Memphis! Am I understood!"

With impotent fury, Set replied, "Yes, Prince Djoser. I understand.

EGYPTIAN GODS: Osiris/Dionysus—Isis/Ariadne/Philyra, Horus, Set/Charon, Nephthys/Dexithea.
CANAANITE GODS: Anath, Astarte, Shalem, Shahar, Moloch, El.
OLYMPIAN GODS: Zeus, Dionysus, Hestia, Ares, Athena, Astraeus, Eos, Hermes.
OCEANIDS: Polydore, Lyris, Acaste, Eidyia, Dione.

Becoming aroused, Ananth replied, "Yes, my great and powerful Lord Prince. I understand!"

~

Djoser and Hetephe visited Jaffa for a quarter moon, then goodbyed their stately goodbyes and set off to find Horus.

As they left Jaffa, Djoser said, "Follow the coast! Ask anyone, 'Which way is Horus?' It's a good plan, don't you think?"

"Sure, it's a great plan. Maybe we will find a horse."

They had a leisurely, enjoyable journey, meeting and talking to strangers, stopping and laying on the beach. Hetephe, no longer a professional soldier under the direct command of the Prince of Egypt, could now return to one of her favorite hobbies—ibis flicking.

Reunion

A quarter moon later, they found Horus surrounded by followers as he performed a sunrise ceremony in a coastal village south of Byblos. Horus and Hetephe waited at the edge of the gathering until the ceremony was complete. Horus engaged in conversation with the crowd until he looked around and saw Djoser. Horus stopped mid-sentence, said, "Excuse me for a few moments," and walked to face his stepfather. They stood in silence until Horus broke and embraced Djoser. The two men exchanged the greetings of two old friends reunited after a long time apart. Finally, Djoser broke the embrace and said, "When you are finished with your friends, find us in the village common area. We can spend the rest of the day catching up." With that, Djoser and Hetephe left the gathering and found a table in the park-like area of the village where they set up house.

Djoser wanted to start their day with a fruit-wine, but Hetephe insisted that wine would make her think of ibises. They could only drink Bitters this morning. "Maybe later."

After a while, Horus joined them, "Azazil is discussing the nature of gods with two that are interested in such things. Few are interested but we are pleased to find two in a village this small."

Djoser said, "Their understanding of what a god is and isn't appears to be somewhat fluid in this land."

Horus replied, "That's true for Canaanites. I am finding that Mesopotamians may have a more advanced but still misunderstood concept of gods. The Phoenicians understand all of it but don't care about any of it. Let's go to Byblos. There is a woman there said to have survived the great flood. I think Byblos may have an archery field. Hete will be pleased."

Byblos

Arriving in Byblos, Hete was thrilled. "This is a *big* city. Where are you going to be? I'm going to find the playing fields. A city this size will have playing fields!"

They walked by an outdoor cafe. Djoser said, "We will be here at sunset. Don't let anyone beat you, Hete! And if they do, stay off the table!"

She snorted and walked off to find an archery field.

Horus, Djoser, and Azazil continued into an older residential neighborhood. Horus stopped in front of the oldest house. He said, "She lives alone and will enjoy talking about the old days." They walked to the door, knocked, were soon greeted by the woman, allowed in, seated in her best chairs, and each was served a sweet drink and fruit. Introductions were made and chit-chat ensued. After a while, Horus gently said, "Grandmother, Stepfather Djoser is interested in the great flood and the problems it caused. I told him that you were there when it happened."

She sat in silence for a moment. Djoser noticed her eyes become moist. She said, "Yes, I was there. My family died that day. My friends died. My chickens died. Our animals died. Everything died but me. I was still a young woman, untouched by a man."

She became silent, her eyes more moist. She continued. "The Oceanids warned us. They went house to house telling us to take all we could carry and move to higher ground. That within three days, the sea would rise higher than the Olympian Godhouse; that our world would be underwater forever; that a wall of water would come and destroy everything in its path; 'take what you can and move to higher ground!' They were Oceanids but, still, no one believed them. They told us that the children of Cronus had done grievous things and were going to be punished by Oceanus and not even God Poseidon himself could stop the judgment that was coming for them. She told us that the remaining Titans grieved over the destruction they would cause but that the Olympian Gods must die. She

EGYPTIAN GODS: Osiris/Dionysus—Isis/Ariadne/Philyra, Horus, Set/Charon, Nephthys/Dexithea.
CANAANITE GODS: Anath, Astarte, Shalem, Shahar, Moloch, El.
OLYMPIAN GODS: Zeus, Dionysus, Hestia, Ares, Athena, Astraeus, Eos, Hermes.
OCEANIDS: Polydore, Lyris, Acaste, Eidyia, Dione.

said, 'Take what you can and move to higher ground!' She knew no one but I believed her. She turned to go but turned back toward me and took a vest from her bag. She looked at me and said, 'When it comes, put this on, run into the sea, and lie face down.' She touched my cheek and said, 'I hereby make you an Oceanid. Be brave, my sister.' Then she turned and left us. Even then, I wanted to cry. I believed her. As my parents scoffed at what they had heard, I went into our barnyard and sat with my chickens, feeding them grain out of my hand, and letting them climb over me. I sang songs to them and told them that everything would be all right; that those who followed the path of Queen Kiya need not fear evil. Two days passed. It came late in the night. I was already in bed asleep, but you could feel it coming—hear it coming. I put on the vest and ran outside. The moon was full and bright. What I saw was higher than the sky. No matter how high I looked, it was higher. I wanted to say goodbye to my chickens, but they would be sleeping—my parents would be sleeping—the world would be sleeping. It would be better if no one woke. I put on the vest and ran to the sea. It was rising even as I ran to it. I looked up at the wall of water one last time and lay down in the water. I thought, 'I am an Oceanid. I will be brave,' and was washed away from my world forever." She choked an ancient sob and said, "There you have it. The vest I wore raised me to the top of the water and held me there. There was nothing to see but water. I was delivered to dry land before Highsun the next day. Only I and endless, ruined things were left on that dry land." She stopped talking.

Horus looked into the woman's eyes. She did not see what was before her but only what had been. He said, "I am here, Grandmother. You are not alone." He reached and took both her hands into his.

She snapped out of her reverie and smiled at him. "You are a nice young man, Horus. You don't understand but you at least pretend to."

"I can never experience what you did, Grandmother. But I want to hear of it—to try to understand—to at least come close to understanding."

She continued, in the present, "Two Oceanids found me late that day. They had three other people they had found. One of them could not walk without help; one babbled incoherent words. The Oceanids took us south down the new shoreline toward a tent city their sisters had built. They called their city 'El's End.' We walked for three days and found thirty more survivors on our way. We entered El's End and found thousands of homeless people there; too many for the Oceanids to feed and take care of. As the days passed, I was taught to fish so I could take care of myself and others, too. One day a nomadic tribe from the east came and told of an uninhabited fertile land between two great rivers farther to the east. Lord Jarmo had been a powerful farmer. He led those who would follow toward the east. They, like everyone else, had nothing but their lives. There were no families—nothing—all had been left behind under a stade of water. That which the Titans had given to us—lost. I remained here at El's End—or whatever they call it these days. The name changes so often."

Prince Djoser quietly asked, "Byblos. They call it Byblos these days. What do you think caused the flood, Grandmother?"

She laughed. "I already told you, young man. Were you not listening? Oceanus sent the flood to kill the children of El. The civilized world just happened to be in his way. Of course, the young people these days are saying that the gods sent the floods to exterminate mankind because they were displeased with us—at least that's what the missionaries from Urfa say. I feel that I went from being the victim to becoming the culprit. Such are the minds of men, I suppose. Most men have left the path of Queen Kiya to worship gods they don't even know. The young ones have never even been taught her path—told what is right and what they should do. I am told that this nice young man Horus is trying to teach them." She cackled. "Good fortune with that, my son."

Horus kept the woman engaged for a while longer. She was enjoying reliving her life with men who were interested.

Nightfall approached. Djoser looked into his traveling bag for a gift to give the woman. "Do you like wine, Grandmother?"

"Oh, yes. Far too much. It is a curse. I gave up wine and men long ago. I have been happier ever since!"

Djoser laughed. "Well, I have Red-ribboned Women in South Memphis. Will you be my Purple-ribboned woman in Byblos?"

He pulled out a bolt of purple ribbon trimmed in gold. "I can cut you a beautiful sash plus a strip to tie your silver hair."

A wide smile came over the woman's face as she stared at the expensive ribbon. "It is beautiful. It would make me feel young and pretty again."

EGYPTIAN GODS: Osiris/Dionysus—Isis/Ariadne/Philyra, Horus, Set/Charon, Nephthys/Dexithea.
CANAANITE GODS: Anath, Astarte, Shalem, Shahar, Moloch, El.
OLYMPIAN GODS: Zeus, Dionysus, Hestia, Ares, Athena, Astraeus, Eos, Hermes.
OCEANIDS: Polydore, Lyris, Acaste, Eidyia, Dione.

They talked on as Djoser fashioned the belt and a ribbon for her hair. There was laughter.

They left the house at sundown. Djoser said—as much to himself as to Horus—"I was in the room when the decision was made. I was in the room."

In silence, they walked to the café, where Hetephe waited sitting cross-legged on a table.

She was jubilant over her afternoon. "It's a wonderful archery field but they have no archers. Two young women watched me practice and wanted to know how I did that! I found some poorly made bows and arrows in a shed. They were adequate for students. Having new students is wonderful. I have put them on the path to glory! How was your day, Ibis Head?"

Djoser answered, "Exquisite. Simply exquisite. I'm thinking I may want to make a side trip to Urfa. Do you want to go with me?"

She answered, "Urfa? Seriously? No one's been to Urfa since before I was born. Only Osiris knows what's left there. No, thank you. I can stay here and teach archery! It's a nice city. More civilized than those Canaanite places."

Horus said, "Father never returned to Urfa. He regretted not returning because he told Urfa Priest Teumessian that he would return from the sky and take Teumessian up with him to meet the gods. I think Father intended to throw Teumessian into the sea to join the remains of the gods. I promised Father that I would someday return. I haven't because ... it's complicated."

Djoser laughed. "It's not complicated at all, Horus. You know what you will find there. You know you can't change it. You don't have an airboat to fulfill your father's promise. You will become an abject failure on all fronts. That's why your father gifted wine to the world. Let's go to Urfa and you can become an abject failure then we can drink a lot of wine."

Hete laughed. "That would be fun. Maybe I *will* go with you!"

Djoser exclaimed, "Done. But I need to find out more about this 'gods commanding princes' nonsense. We will stay here for a few days talking to people about their gods and then head to Urfa! I was there in my youth, you know! I helped Dionysus and Set lead the Ogdoad out of Urfa into Egypt. We had horses, then! Good times!"

Dionysus/Osiris, Ariadne/Isis/Philyra, Charon/Set, Hermes/Tehuti.
EGYPTIANS: Nebka, Djoser, Hotep, Khasek, Rocky
NUBIANS: Nima, Hetephe, King Kerma, Prince T'jaru, Prince Rafah.
CANAANITES: Phoenicia, Serket, Azazil, Jaffa | URFANS: Teumessian, Abram, Sarai, Terah

Hetephe said, "I want a horse. A fast one like Serket's!"

The consensus of most people in Byblos who thought about such things was, "Why, yes. Chiefs were expected to obey living gods. That would probably apply to kings, too. But certainly, to princes."

Djoser was not at all pleased with that kind of talk.

~

They walked the coast, visiting with people, talking about Isis and Osiris, Egypt, trade, the local economy, how their quality of life was, and which gods they admired.

They finally arrived at the small port city of Ugarit from which a road turned northeast to the old city of Urfa.

The local Shaman was delighted to entertain Horus and his friends with an evening meal. They sat at their table drinking what might be called wine. Horus was obviously a Shaman of the highest order and could discuss the gods of old with authority and had a great interest in the newer and local gods.

Horus asked, "And what of talking with the dead? Has anyone ever talked of this?"

The Shaman replied, "No, Master. But I have heard talk of mushrooms in the caves of Alashiya; that's the island to our west. Those who eat these mushrooms leave this world and enter a strange, indescribable world. It is said that the scholars of old ate these mushrooms and it was the source of their knowledge. Whether true or not, I cannot say but I have heard such talk."

Horus replied, "My father told me stories of these mushrooms. He, himself, experienced their effects with Tallstone Shamans. He told me that there are no words to describe what he felt—where he was. He seemed to leave his body and there was no time or separation between him and all things. Strange patterns filled his vision. He did not believe that he had entered the land of the dead but wherever he had gone, was nothing like what we normally experience." *Strange. Now that I think about it, that's how I felt when Anath told me she was leaving me. How strange.*

"The elders say that Alashiya is the remains of fabled Tartarus; that beneath their harbor lies the sunken Godhouse and the ports of the Titans."

EGYPTIAN GODS: Osiris/Dionysus—Isis/Ariadne/Philyra, Horus, Set/Charon, Nephthys/Dexithea.
CANAANITE GODS: Anath, Astarte, Shalem, Shahar, Moloch, El.
OLYMPIAN GODS: Zeus, Dionysus, Hestia, Ares, Athena, Astraeus, Eos, Hermes.
OCEANIDS: Polydore, Lyris, Acaste, Eidyia, Dione.

Djoser answered, "That's exactly true, Shaman. I was there. We are leaving for Urfa at sunrise. Do you have any wisdom for us?"

The excited Shaman chattered on, including, "Leave the woman here, Lords. She will not be welcome in Urfa. Our women avoid their missionaries and certainly would never venture into Urfa."

His guests responded in unison, "Oh? Tell us more."

The Shaman replied, "Urfa men want their women to stay in their place—speak when spoken to—do as commanded—show subservience in all things—those sorts of things. The women of Ugarit do not tolerate that attitude. I am told that once, some young women actually set upon three Urfa missionaries and beat them. A missionary had called them whores, sluts, and fallen women for some perceived slight the women had unknowingly committed. One said, 'Call us that again, and we will keep your precious testicles as our playthings.' The confused men ran back toward Urfa. I can't say that we have good relations with Urfa. Certainly, Lord Hetephe would not be welcome. She appears to consider herself equal to men."

"More equal, actually," Hetephe replied. "Meeting such men might be fun! I may go disguised as a man. Djoser, Sweet, cut off some of your hair so I can fashion a mustache. I wonder what I can get a man to say about women. Are men ever vulgar when speaking of women behind their backs? I will gain firsthand knowledge! Men cannot be as simple as they appear! I will find out all your secret information!"

Hetephe, Azazil, and the Shaman chatted on amicably.

Djoser and Horus retreated into quiet contemplation.

Dionysus/Osiris, Ariadne/Isis/Philyra, Charon/Set, Hermes/Tehuti.
EGYPTIANS: Nebka, Djoser, Hotep, Khasek, Rocky
NUBIANS: Nima, Hetephe, King Kerma, Prince T'jaru, Prince Rafah.
CANAANITES: Phoenicia, Serket, Azazil, Jaffa | URFANS: Teumessian, Abram, Sarai, Terah

15. Return to Urfa

The four adventurers performed their sunrise ceremonies and set off east toward Urfa.

As they walked, Horus and Djoser walked in front discussing the purpose of their visit—what did they wish to learn?—what did they hope to accomplish?—what did they wish to leave with?—what did they wish to leave behind? Assuming Teumessian no longer lived, who replaced him? How did he think?

Hetephe bound her breasts and glued on her new mustache. She wore a loose-fitting tunic with her bow and dagger displayed prominently. She rubbed dirt into her hair and onto her face to roughen her soft features. She might not appear to be a man to be feared but no one would see an attractive woman. She and Azazil walked behind discussing the ruses they could perform. What if Hetephe revealed herself as a woman? If she did, how would she do it? Should she just strip down naked or maybe perform a Nubian fertility dance? Did she want to liberate the women? "How do you do that? Surely, with a little teaching, they can liberate themselves!"

Soon enough, they came to the gateway outpost of Riverport. It was a burned-out shell. The once-large dock was in ruins. Only a single barge remained.

Djoser was solemn as he said, "Polydore once told me, 'I have no sisters in Riverport!' I should have pursued that statement." *Why not, Polydore? Why not?*

Azazil swam the swift river, returned with the barge, and carried the others across. Everyone studied the ruined port trying to imagine what had happened there. They made camp well before nightfall.

The men explored the dock area.

Hetephe walked to the south. She found a tranquil pond beside a large, beautiful tree. An ancient bench sat facing the pond; a perfect place to sit and be with oneself. She sat. Memories of her life suddenly flooded her mind. *Am I happy or sad? Have I done well? Have I failed? I am the best archer in the world. Everyone says so. I led the Egyptian Army to clear the Sinai of bad men and received some awards. I'm pretty and I can attract any man I want. How could I possibly be sad?*

EGYPTIAN GODS: Osiris/Dionysus—Isis/Ariadne/Philyra, Horus, Set/Charon, Nephthys/Dexithea.
CANAANITE GODS: Anath, Astarte, Shalem, Shahar, Moloch, El.
OLYMPIAN GODS: Zeus, Dionysus, Hestia, Ares, Athena, Astraeus, Eos, Hermes.
OCEANIDS: Polydore, Lyris, Acaste, Eidyia, Dione.

She smiled. *I'm happy when Djoser holds me close after we couple—and before. Really, just being with him makes me happy—and sometimes listening to Horus. He is so strange, but I love listening to him get carried away when he talks about things only he cares about. But I DO like being the best archer and all the medals and everything.*

She reflected for a moment and thought, *But without someone to share it with, what difference?*

She shrugged, rose, looked at the pond, then at the tree, smiled, and leisurely returned to the camp.

Sunrise

Horus stood waist-deep in the river looking toward the sun which would soon breach the horizon. *You told me many stories of this place, Father—of the love and the warmth of the Oceanids who lived here—of the horror of their slaughter—of the disfigurement of Clymene—It appears that Riverport was revisited—by gods?—or maybe worse.*

He felt the weight of what had been done here. The sun breached the horizon. He stared into the rising sun. *Father help ... me help me understand ... help me to change the nature of evil ... help me understand the hearts of men ... help me teach them the path of Kiya ... help me make them whole ... help me .... help us all!*

He waded from the water to join the others as they prepared morning meal. Djoser greeted him with, "We have a big day today, Son. This will be your first visit to where it all began! I am returning to the source of my grand adventure with your father, Set, and the Ogdoad. I was still a child at the time—innocent—I had not even yet met this lovely creature ..." He spread out his arm toward Hetephe, who had bound her breasts, glued on a mustache, wore a loose-fitting tunic with bow and dagger prominently displayed, and had rubbed dirt onto her face.

She asked, "Shall I flick your Ibis while I'm dressed like this? Would that excite you, Master?"

He laughed. "You always excite me, woman—no matter how unattractive you might be!"

Horus said, "Let's eat and get on with it. There is much serious work to be done this day!"

As they sat down cross-legged in front of the small cooking fire, Hetephe suddenly grabbed for Djoser's groin. He slapped her hand away. "Enough

Dionysus/Osiris, Ariadne/Isis/Philyra, Charon/Set, Hermes/Tehuti.
EGYPTIANS: Nebka, Djoser, Hotep, Khasek, Rocky
NUBIANS: Nima, Hetephe, King Kerma, Prince T'jaru, Prince Rafah.
CANAANITES: Phoenicia, Serket, Azazil, Jaffa | URFANS: Teumessian, Abram, Sarai, Terah

of that young man! Save your energy for the women of Urfa that may attack you!"

She laughed. "I might like that!!"

Horus rose, left them, and began walking toward Urfa without eating.

~

They found Horus sitting on a bench, under a large apple tree, staring at the well-marked entrance to the city. He said to no one in particular, "There are boys roughhousing around some kind of fountain. They are fairly noisy. They don't look this way. This is probably the best entrance we can make. Let's get on with it."

With that, he rose and started walking toward the entrance to the city. The others fell in behind him. He stopped at the gate to survey the area. A young girl watching the boys play saw them, immediately turned to face them, and curtsied. Three other girls saw their friend's actions and they, too, turned and curtsied. They then stood facing the visitors with straight backs and hands folded in front of them. They made no attempt to greet the visitors. Hetephe saw them, smiled, and waved. One girl looked at the other two, tentatively raised her hand slightly, and gave a little wave back.

The smallest of the six roughhousing boys noticed the visitors, stopped dead in his play, and stared with wide eyes at Horus. Horus raised his right arm with the universal, "Greetings!"

The other five boys fell upon the small boy and began beating him unmercifully. With his loudest voice, Horus commanded, "Cease!" The five boys stopped the beating and, for the first time, saw Horus and his friends standing at the gate. The largest one turned to face them with a wide stance and his hands on his hips. He bellowed, "Whadda *you* want?"

Horus, quickly accessing the subservience of the girls and the belligerence of the boys, made no recognition of the boy's inquiry. He merely began walking toward the four girls. The other three followed and thought variations of *this is your show, Horus. Have fun!*

Horus arrived and stood facing the slightly more outgoing of the girls. He said, "Greetings. My name is Horus. I am a Shaman. We come in peace from the land of Egypt and wish to learn the people and customs of your city. What is *your* name?" He addressed her as if she were an official emissary from Greece.

EGYPTIAN GODS: Osiris/Dionysus—Isis/Ariadne/Philyra, Horus, Set/Charon, Nephthys/Dexithea.
CANAANITE GODS: Anath, Astarte, Shalem, Shahar, Moloch, El.
OLYMPIAN GODS: Zeus, Dionysus, Hestia, Ares, Athena, Astraeus, Eos, Hermes.
OCEANIDS: Polydore, Lyris, Acaste, Eidyia, Dione.

The girl replied, "I am Asherah—the chosen one, Great Lord. If I offend you in some way, please beat me immediately so that I may learn the correct response."

Horus replied, "You will not offend me, Pen Asherah. And if you do, it is my nature to counsel you—not beat you."

In the distance, the boys, being ignored in favor of the girls, began making catcalls toward the group.

Horus asked the girl, "You are the chosen one? For what were you chosen?"

The girl replied, "To provide pleasure to the men who I will fornicate with during the great festival, Great Lord Shaman Horus."

"You do not yet appear to be a woman full grown. Are you older than you appear?"

"Great Shaman Horus, I am ten years in age and have not yet entered the sisterhood of women."

"Oh. And what happens after the men have finished taking pleasure with you?"

"I will be thrown into the great fire as a sacrifice to the glory of God Ares and as atonement for the sins of all women."

"I see. Who makes such decisions about the festival?"

"The-Living-Word-of-the-Gods whose name I may not speak, Great Shaman Horus."

The conversation went on along these lines for a while. Finally, Horus said, "I have a friend named Hete. Will you counsel with her—I mean him?! He turned to Hete and said, Friend Hete, counsel with these fine young women. Perhaps have a small party of some kind."

The girls were not at all at ease having a small party with a male.

The three men then left the girls and approached the boisterous boys. Djoser said, "You manly men seem to be in control of everything in this land. Are you the leaders of Urfa?"

All but the leader were bewildered by such talk. The leader said, "Who are you and what are you doing here? I should get Enforcers to come and beat you up!"

Dionysus/Osiris, Ariadne/Isis/Philyra, Charon/Set, Hermes/Tehuti.
EGYPTIANS: Nebka, Djoser, Hotep, Khasek, Rocky
NUBIANS: Nima, Hetephe, King Kerma, Prince T'jaru, Prince Rafah.
CANAANITES: Phoenicia, Serket, Azazil, Jaffa | URFANS: Teumessian, Abram, Sarai, Terah

"Oh, don't do that, please! I'll be good. But how does one 'be good' around here?"

"Don't be a smart anus, for starters!"

Djoser replied, "I don't think I like you. You are an obnoxious, disrespectful piece of dung! Smelly dung, at that! Do you ever bathe, little piece of dung?"

The boy instantly took a swing at Djoser who skillfully threw him off balance, delivered a hard blow to the boy's chest, threw him to the ground, put his foot on the boy's neck, and asked the other five boys, "Now, who wants to urinate on this piece of dung to clean him up a little bit?"

The boys looked at each other in horror, turned, and ran south, presumably to their betters.

Djoser removed his foot from the boy's neck, and said, "Run along home to your mother, little piece of dung. Have her clean out your pants and wipe your bottom for you!"

The men walked back to the group of girls who were nervously talking with Hete. Djoser casually asked Asherah, "By the way, what is an Enforcer?"

The girls froze, stricken with fear.

Hete asked, "Enforcers hurt people, don't they?"

Asherah violently shook her head, "Yes."

Hete said, "I have enjoyed talking with all of you. Now, hurry home and stay out of harm's way. Stay safe, my young friends." With that, she shooed them away with hand motions. The girls scurried away.

Hete then commanded, "Djoser, you and Horus sit at the fountain and wait. Azazil, you take up a position out of sight between the fountain and the road south. I will stand out of sight on the other side of the road. They will be facing Djoser and Horus. We can surprise them from behind or else I can kill eight of them in that many heartbeats. If there are more than eight, then be prepared to fight or run. Djoser, raise an arm high if you want me to kill them. If they do not come by Highsun, let's meet and discuss our options. Go!"

All four went to their assigned positions. Djoser and Horus were sitting at the fountain when five Enforcers came from the south.

EGYPTIAN GODS: Osiris/Dionysus—Isis/Ariadne/Philyra, Horus, Set/Charon, Nephthys/Dexithea.
CANAANITE GODS: Anath, Astarte, Shalem, Shahar, Moloch, El.
OLYMPIAN GODS: Zeus, Dionysus, Hestia, Ares, Athena, Astraeus, Eos, Hermes.
OCEANIDS: Polydore, Lyris, Acaste, Eidyia, Dione.

The lead Enforcer demanded, "Who are you? What are doing here?"

Djoser replied, "We are travelers from Egypt who come to learn of the gods and customs of Urfa."

"Terahson said that four of you set upon him and beat him unmercifully."

"Terahson is both a liar and an obnoxious brat. I only threw him on the ground and insulted him."

"It is not for you to educate Terahson. He is a high-born, head-strong young boy used to getting his way."

"I am higher-born, more headstrong, and *always* get my way. You understand my disagreement with the young dung-in-training, I'm sure." Djoser smiled but did not break the man's cold stare.

"Young Terahson said there were four of you! Where are the other two?"

"One is behind you with an arrow pointed straight at your neck. The other one, I don't know. I can't keep track of Azazil the Merciless."

"You would attack an Enforcer of The-Living-Word-of-the-Gods?"

"No. My archer would kill you. Then I would explain the necessity to The-Living-Word-of-the-Gods. He would understand, I imagine."

"You must remain under my escort when you enter the city. I will tell you where you may go."

"I would hope so. Someone must protect us from the likes of the little pond-scum Terahson. Are there others like him?"

"Respect the son of Terah"

"No."

"Then remain here while I return to the temple for further instructions. The-Living-Word-of-the-Gods will not want me to kill you until he understands why you are here!"

Soft-speaking Horus calmly replaced Djoser in the conversation.

"Is the name of this The-Living-Word-of-the-Gods, Teumessian?"

"YOU MAY NOT SAY HIS NAME! IT IS FORBIDDEN!"

"Tell Teumessian that I have come to judge him. And, so far, I am displeased. Even as my great-grandfather sent the Great Flood so can I

Dionysus/Osiris, Ariadne/Isis/Philyra, Charon/Set, Hermes/Tehuti.
EGYPTIANS: Nebka, Djoser, Hotep, Khasek, Rocky
NUBIANS: Nima, Hetephe, King Kerma, Prince T'jaru, Prince Rafah.
CANAANITES: Phoenicia, Serket, Azazil, Jaffa | URFANS: Teumessian, Abram, Sarai, Terah

send fire raining from the sky. The wrath of the gods is a terrible thing to behold; far worse to experience. Go now. Tell Teumessian that Horus—son of God Dionysus—Son of God Zeus—Son of Titan Cronus—Son of Queen Kiya has come to judge him. Return at sundown with a plan that pleases me. If the plan is not pleasing, I and my company will leave you to die in agony beneath my rain of fire. You tarry. GO! NOW!"

"*You* do not tell *me* what to do!"

Horus stood, reached, and pulled the man's ear away from his head while simultaneously pointing to Hete, behind them. An arrow separated the ear from the man. Horus handed the ear to the man and quietly said, "By sundown—a plan that pleases me. Go now."

The dumbfounded Enforcer stared at the ear, said, "Y-yes, Lord Horus," and left with his men to consult the The-Living-Word-of-the-Gods."

After the Enforcers were out of sight, Hetephe and Azazil rejoined the group. She said, "I wasn't sure if that's what you wanted, Horus, but I decided it couldn't hurt."

Horus replied, "It was perfect, Hete. Exactly what was needed. Now, do we prepare for their army to try to kill us or a delightful reception with the chief or priest, or whatever?"

Djoser said, "At this point, we either run away or plan to be treated with great respect. I prefer the latter. Maybe I shouldn't mention it, Horus, but you responded exactly the way your father did. Quiet, self-confident arrogance must be in the bloodline. The last time we were here, it got us the Ogdoad, settlers, and five wagons of supplies pulled by some fine livestock. Whatever do we want this time?"

Horus muttered, "To save them!"

Azazil said, "We must respect their gods and their customs."

Hetephe retorted, "Yes, as long as they respect ours."

Horus responded, "Do you not understand? They will not respect anything that is not exactly according to their beliefs. They will kill anyone different from them. These people will not tolerate beliefs different than theirs. Do not speak of our gods and customs. Women are seen as inferior creatures, here only at the pleasure of men, and, unfortunately, seemed to have convinced the women of this—at least the young ones. There is no hope in this place."

EGYPTIAN GODS: Osiris/Dionysus—Isis/Ariadne/Philyra, Horus, Set/Charon, Nephthys/Dexithea.
CANAANITE GODS: Anath, Astarte, Shalem, Shahar, Moloch, El.
OLYMPIAN GODS: Zeus, Dionysus, Hestia, Ares, Athena, Astraeus, Eos, Hermes.
OCEANIDS: Polydore, Lyris, Acaste, Eidyia, Dione.

Djoser replied, "Don't roll around in despair, Horus. Your orders are simple—do what's right!!"

"There is no 'right,' Father. Whatever I do is wrong!"

Hetephe grew impatient with this talk. "Stop it, you two! Horus, talk to the people. Share your wisdom. If they don't believe it—fine. If they do believe it—fine. You will influence some people, maybe even change one. I doubt if they will kill us no matter what we do. Horus put the fear of Zeus into that Enforcer. They may ignore us and be happy when we leave, but they won't kill us—I don't think. I'm going exploring. This place must have been magnificent in its day. The buildings are still magnificent, even in their state of disrepair. Urfa—Mother of Cities!"

Azazil said, "I'll go with you. Let's take the road east. The road south apparently leads to their settlement. We will see that soon enough."

Hete and Azazil left for their exploration. Djoser and Horus walked through the ruins of the city as they discussed what it was they wanted, and how they would get it.

~

The young boy, possibly eight years in age, tentatively entered the ruined city toward sundown. He approached the four who had just sat down around their cooking fire to share their day's experiences. Horus stood to face the approaching boy. The boy began his obviously rehearsed speech. "G-greetings, Great Lords. I am Abram, youngest son of Terah, Chief of the city of Urfa. I am sent to invite his gracious and illustrious visitors to be entertained by Father at tomorrow's Highsun meal. Will you accept his invitation?"

Horus replied, "I am Shaman Horus, son of Dionysus. I and my friends are delighted to accept your father's gracious invitation so expertly delivered by his youngest son. We, ourselves, are preparing to eat our evening meal. Will you be so kind as to join us?"

The boy, at first elated and overwhelmed with Horus's response, grew confused and agitated by the invitation. He stammered, "G-great and Magnificent Son-of-a-God Horus, Father didn't tell me what to do after I delivered my message. I don't know what to do!" No one mentioned the urine running down the boy's leg.

Horus answered, "Messenger Abram, making a decision is simple. Consider all the information available to you at the time you must make the decision. Make the best decision you can. It is that simple. Now, what would Messenger Abram like to do? Perhaps that will assist in your decision-making."

Abram stammered, "I-I want to stay here and watch you, Great Lord."

"Done, Messenger Abram! Azazil make another place for our new friend Abram. He is an expert Messenger and decision-maker. We will do well to listen to his counsel!"

Abram sat at his appointed place, between Horus and Djoser, nervously looking around.

Hete spoke, "You said your father's name is Terah. Azazil met an interesting young man earlier today whose name is Terahson. Do you know of him?"

Abram replied, "He is my oldest brother. He is my father's favorite. He will someday take over Father's market selling idols and make many Shekels. Father will become even richer."

She asked, "But why did he not send Terahson with his invitation? Are we not important enough for him to send his favorite son?"

"Oh, no, no, no. You are TOO important and powerful and fearsome. Terahson displeased you greatly. He has been sent away until you are gone. Father wanted to come himself, but the The-Living-Word-of-the-Gods commanded that he send the invitation by someone who is not impressive. Father will look better when you get there."

Hete said, "How wise. But if your father is more impressive than his Messenger, we may all run away in fear!"

Abram silently, proudly accepted a roasted vegetable from the offered skewer.

Sweetly, Hete asked, "Now, Messenger Abram, tell us about the girls and women in your city and especially about this 'Chosen One' I have heard so much about."

Abram was a wealth of information. Once started, he became a nonstop torrent of words. He explained, "Most women are respectful and obedient and that's the best way to get a husband and if you aren't you're sent away

EGYPTIAN GODS: Osiris/Dionysus—Isis/Ariadne/Philyra, Horus, Set/Charon, Nephthys/Dexithea.
CANAANITE GODS: Anath, Astarte, Shalem, Shahar, Moloch, El.
OLYMPIAN GODS: Zeus, Dionysus, Hestia, Ares, Athena, Astraeus, Eos, Hermes.
OCEANIDS: Polydore, Lyris, Acaste, Eidyia, Dione.

to the pastures to be kept away from decent men and women. But sometimes, if a woman is especially disrespectful, she will be taken to the Sacrifice Field and men will plow her until she dies. Or sometimes, the other women will throw rocks at her until she begs for forgiveness."

He continued, "Asherah is the Chosen One for this year's festival. We hold it in the Sacrifice Field. Everybody comes to watch. Men and women can stand together to watch Asherah get plowed by three men and then by my father. The-Living-Word-of-the-Gods used to finish her off but he got too old, so now Father does it. When Father's finished, Asherah will be thrown into the sacred fire and burned up so the crops will grow. Then, an Enforcer guts the first three men as a love offering to God Ares."

Abram paused for a long time, lost in thought. No one spoke. The boy continued. "Asherah and I used to be friends and play together when we were younger. She was older than me, but she liked me because I was the only boy that would play with girls. After she was The Chosen One, we couldn't play together anymore. She had to visit The-Living-Word-of-the-Gods every day to practice her teachings about the male body. I asked her if she liked it, but she wouldn't answer and always turned and walked away. I don't think she liked it. But we weren't allowed to be friends anymore, so I never found out."

Horus stood, said, "Excuse me for a moment," walked away from the fire, and vomited. He returned, laughed, and said, "And we haven't begun learning of your gods yet, have we?!"

Excitedly, Abram said, "I can tell you about the gods. Any righteous person in Urfa can tell you of the gods; Zeus—Ares—Dementer—Dionysus—all of them! If I convert a nonbeliever, I get an extra star in my crown after I die! Will you let me try to convert you?! Father would like me better if I did!"

Horus nodded, "Yes."

Djoser pulled a flask from his traveling sack and poured four and a quarter cups of wine. To the quarter cup, he added three parts of grape juice and handed it to Abram.

Hete said, "Oh, Sweet. That may make him talkative!"

Abram tasted the fruit-wine, decided it was acceptable, and launched into converting his new friends. The wine, even though much diluted, made

Dionysus/Osiris, Ariadne/Isis/Philyra, Charon/Set, Hermes/Tehuti.
EGYPTIANS: Nebka, Djoser, Hotep, Khasek, Rocky
NUBIANS: Nima, Hetephe, King Kerma, Prince T'jaru, Prince Rafah.
CANAANITES: Phoenicia, Serket, Azazil, Jaffa | URFANS: Teumessian, Abram, Sarai, Terah

him more talkative. "In the beginning, there were the glorious gods." He continued with his rote recitation of the teachings he heard after each quarter moon. Horus became more attentive when he heard the words, "Then God Dionysus came unto 'He Whose Name May Not Be Said' and said these words unto Him, 'With you, I am highly pleased! You will be my voice unto all people of righteousness. I shall lead the few unrighteous remaining in your lands to purify it even further even as the Gods lovingly purified the lands of Tallstone and Urfa with their wrath!'"

Horus interrupted, "Teumessian teaches that Dionysus appointed him The-Living-Word-of-the-Gods?!"

Upon hearing the name that must not be said, Abram covered his ears and began some kind of sing-song chant.

Djoser glanced at Horus as Horus rose and walked from the gathering. *My father caused all of this. He empowered Teumessian to believe that Teumessian spoke for the gods. Whatever perverted, contoured, despicable beliefs Teumessian has, it was legitimized by my father's blessing. How can this be? Father?*

Hetephe reached and took Abram's swaying shoulders and forced him to look at her. He stopped his chants and looked at her in sheer terror. She said, "I apologize Messenger Abram. My friends and I can use the actual name of 'The-Living-Word-of-the-Gods' because we are not yet converted. But your ears are unfamiliar with the sound, so we won't say his name again in front of you. We will use another title like 'El' when referring to him. Is that all right?"

Abram meekly asked, "Could you use the name, The-Living-Word-of-the-Gods?"

Hetephe glanced at the others but shook her head, "Yes."

Abram ceased being talkative and sank into fearful silence.

Djoser rose and said to Abram, "Messenger Abram, your visit has been most pleasant. Tell your father that you have interested us in your gods and we will certainly consider converting to the path of righteousness as taught by your righteous teacher The-Living-Word-of-the-Gods. It's getting late, now. Your father may be concerned about your safety. Be careful on your way home."

After Abram had gone, Djoser poured cups of wine for the two remaining in the circle and caught up with Horus with a cup for him. "Horus, my

EGYPTIAN GODS: Osiris/Dionysus—Isis/Ariadne/Philyra, Horus, Set/Charon, Nephthys/Dexithea.
CANAANITE GODS: Anath, Astarte, Shalem, Shahar, Moloch, El.
OLYMPIAN GODS: Zeus, Dionysus, Hestia, Ares, Athena, Astraeus, Eos, Hermes.
OCEANIDS: Polydore, Lyris, Acaste, Eidyia, Dione.

son, you aren't as accomplished as your father in concocting wild stories that enrapture your listener. We four need to make up your story tonight!"

"No, Father Djoser. It will be *my* story. I alone will invent it. I cannot save these people but maybe I can influence the thoughts of those who one day might. Tell Azazil to work on making Abram one of my followers and to accompany us on our travels. Convince his father of the riches that will follow if Abram makes many contacts with the outside world. And tell Azazil to find out what he can about 'the pastures.' Hete said that the Sacrifice Field is down this path. That is where I shall be listening to Father Osiris do a lot of explaining. Then he and I will concoct our story."

Horus turned and began walking down the path toward the Sacrifice Field.

Djoser called after, "He did the best he could at the time he had to do it!"

"So he will say!"

Sunrise

Azazil made a small cooking fire and prepared the morning meal as Djoser and Hetephe sat around it and talked.

After greeting the rising sun, Horus returned from his night at the Sacrifice Fields.

As Horus approached the fire, Djoser looked up and asked him, "Did you have a good conversation with Osiris?"

Horus answered, "Dark clouds obscured the sun this morning. He is ashamed. I suppose." Horus hesitated. "I shall ask all of you for your subservience while we are in Urfa. When I meet with Teumessian today, I will be representing the gods and each of you should support this fabrication for the sake of our success. The only discussions I wish to have with you should relate to this meeting."

He sat and joined them around the fire. "When I meet with him, my first goal is to change his mind about the desirability of killing the woman and men participating in fertility rites. His view and teachings about women appear to be nonsensical but we have no firsthand knowledge of what he teaches and the consequences of his teachings. Maybe we will gain some insight before the meeting."

As they continued their talk, all understood the seriousness of Horus's upcoming discussions and honored his request for their total focus on his

Dionysus/Osiris, Ariadne/Isis/Philyra, Charon/Set, Hermes/Tehuti.
EGYPTIANS: Nebka, Djoser, Hotep, Khasek, Rocky
NUBIANS: Nima, Hetephe, King Kerma, Prince T'jaru, Prince Rafah.
CANAANITES: Phoenicia, Serket, Azazil, Jaffa | URFANS: Teumessian, Abram, Sarai, Terah

project. After finishing their meal, Djoser and Hetephe excused themselves and left Azazil and Horus to talk of gods—living and dead.

~

As Highsun neared, the four explorers heard marching drums in the distance. They gathered at the fountain to await he who soon arrived. Abram, who led two rows of six drummers followed by two dozen girls in festive long dresses, wearing matching hats, and carrying baskets.

Abram commanded his entourage to stop and then stepped forward to bravely address Horus. "Son-of-Dionysus Horus, I am commanded to escort you to my father's house and then to the humble hovel of The-Living-Word-of-the-Gods. Please follow me."

Abram smartly turned, walked to the front of his entourage, and signaled all to follow him. The drummers began drumming. The girls began throwing flower petals from their baskets to line the path of their guests. They broke into a marching song.

"Zeus so loves the women and the children.
He loves them more than they can know.
His love is great as all men show.
Obey your man; your love will grow.
Obey your father; grow straight and strong.
Obey a man; receive his love.
As Zeus so loves the women and the children."

The four, led by Horus, fell in between the two rows of drummers. Hetephe did not like the marching song, which was repeated many times, louder each time. They marched past the fields that contained the livestock that Djoser remembered from his childhood. It was from here that the Ogdoad had set off with their five wagons of supplies contributed by Teumessian at Dionysus's request. There appeared to be watchers in the far distance.

Further down the road, they came to Terah's house where the group would be entertained. The flower girls discreetly disappeared.

They were enthusiastically greeted by the outgoing Terah. His wife, Amathlai, stood discretely behind him with her hands clasped in front of her. Terah rushed to Horus, bowed, and gushed, "Welcome to the pious city of Urfa, Great son of Dionysus. In the name of The-Living-Word-of-the-Gods, I welcome you! Come with me, bring your friends. I will show

EGYPTIAN GODS: Osiris/Dionysus—Isis/Ariadne/Philyra, Horus, Set/Charon, Nephthys/Dexithea.
CANAANITE GODS: Anath, Astarte, Shalem, Shahar, Moloch, El.
OLYMPIAN GODS: Zeus, Dionysus, Hestia, Ares, Athena, Astraeus, Eos, Hermes.
OCEANIDS: Polydore, Lyris, Acaste, Eidyia, Dione.

you the greatest selection of idols in the world—all available for trade at a modest price. I have arranged a wonderful selection of statues of your father for your enjoyment—Dionysus the naked youth—Dionysus leading a parade of wanton drunken revelers—Dionysus playing his aulos—with his Thyrsus—holding grapes—every representation imaginable." He leaned over, and in a conspiratorial voice whispered, "I keep some of his statues in a private backroom along with some of Goddess Aphrodite. We don't want the women or overly pious men seeing them. I may even have one of Dionysus plowing Aphrodite. I know that I have one of Aphrodite pleasuring all of the main gods at the same time. It's a beautiful piece—very expensive. But well within your means, I'm sure."

To everyone gathered, Terah loudly said, "Well, let's go have ourselves a magnificent Highsun meal! If there's one thing Amathlai knows how to do, it's how to prepare a fine meal!" He looked at Abram and said, "You can join us Abram, if it pleases Great Lord Horus."

Horus nodded affirmatively. Abram was thrilled to be allowed to join the adults at a meal, but he wasn't sure he would know how to act.

Terah turned and led his four guests toward his impressive home. Upon entering, a girl, younger than Abram, began collecting her guest's traveling bags and outer apparel to be stored away while they visited. The girl commanded Abram to assist her with their guests.

Abram obediently answered, "Yes, Sister Sarai," as he began helping her.

Horus impulsively said, "Abram is an intelligent, resourceful, and superior young boy. I wish him to be my personal assistant if it pleases him."

Abram's family was shocked. His father, surprised that anyone thought his dullard son to be worth anything; his sister, with the pride that her big brother was worthy of such attention; his mother, with fear that such forwardness would in some way upset her husband.

Terah replied, "Of course, Abram will be overjoyed to be your servant, Lord Horus!"

Horus calmly replied, "I await your decision if you wish to become my follower, Young Abram."

Amathlai grew more fearful that Terah might lash out at Lord Horus for his insolence. She waited in fear.

Terah was magnanimous. "Well, come on, Abram. Answer the man!"

Horus held out the palm of his hand for silence until Abram made his decision.

Abram was in turmoil. He had no experience with dealing with adults other than staying out of their way. His father might lash out at him at any moment for something Abram didn't even know he had done. Across Abram's mind flashed the words *"Making a decision is simple—consider all the information—make the best decision you can—now, what do I want to do?"*

Abram swallowed his fear and very maturely answered, "I would like to be your follower, Great Lord. Tell me what I should do."

"Sit at my right side when we eat. Advise me if I inadvertently do or say something that Hostess Amathlai might find offensive. I don't know your customs and a refined person must always obey the local customs of the people. You must not allow me to do something offensive to my hosts."

Djoser held back a chuckle. *Other than correct the host, tell him to keep his mouth shut and that his younger son, who he considers to be worthless, is twice the man as his beloved older son, and you showed respect to a woman—his wife, at that—you didn't say anything offensive. But you did it all with a purpose, Horus. Your Father would be proud!*

Abram, suddenly filled with newfound power and candor he did not know he harbored, said, "My Lord, don't worry about offending a woman, their glory is in serving their husband and children. If you find your meal to your liking, the praise belongs to my father who gives his wife everything. If it is not to your liking, then tell my father so that he can beat my mother for being inadequate."

Horus replied, "I understand Disciple Abram. I shall do these things. But, from the aromas coming from your cooking area, it smells as if your father has the best cook in all of Urfa! I shall begin my praises now!"

Both host and hostess relaxed. Everything was going to go well, after all.

Terah led his guests into the eating room which contained a long table that would seat up to twelve people. Terah sat himself down at the head of the table and motioned for Sarai to seat Horus at the foot with his friends on either side—but not before Abram rushed to claim the chair at Horus's right.

EGYPTIAN GODS: Osiris/Dionysus—Isis/Ariadne/Philyra, Horus, Set/Charon, Nephthys/Dexithea.
CANAANITE GODS: Anath, Astarte, Shalem, Shahar, Moloch, El.
OLYMPIAN GODS: Zeus, Dionysus, Hestia, Ares, Athena, Astraeus, Eos, Hermes.
OCEANIDS: Polydore, Lyris, Acaste, Eidyia, Dione.

Abram had never sat at the big table with adults. *My teacher commanded me to sit to his right. Father will not beat me in front of my master—maybe after he is gone, but not before! Terahson will beat me when he finds out, but it will be worth it! I will get to sit at the big table with my father and beside a master who likes me!*

Terah signaled for Amathlai to begin serving drinks and food. Sarai served drinks according to perceived rank, beginning with her father, then Horus, and then her little brother. Sarai thought, *Now I know that I will marry you when we grow up, Abram! I will give you so many children that we will start our own nation! I'm so excited for us. My body will give you a nation!*

She stroked his shoulder after serving him his drink. It was not a sisterly stroke.

The men, primarily Terah, talked of the weather, the wickedness of men outside Urfa—of women—and of those who lived in the pastures—not good enough to live with righteous citizens but not bad enough to stone to death. The guests took note that what they considered to be demeaning talk about women did not appear to register with either Amathlai or Sarai; both went happily about their duties.

Azazil asked, "Is it permissible for me to visit the people in the Pastures?—to learn about their nature?—their depravities, I suppose."

Hetephe interjected, "I want to go with you!"

Terah was elated. "Yes! Both of you go and see the lowest form of humans! When you return, tell me if anything can be done to rid the world of such creatures. I will have Abram show you the way!"

Horus replied, "Abram will be with me." He left it at that.

Terah was startled. "Oh well, then Haran can take you there! Where is that boy? Go find him, Sarai! Get him here right now!"

Sarai scurried off to find her brother.

Terah said, scornfully, "Children these days are useless! Not like back when I was a boy!"

Amathlai wrung her hand nervously until Sarai came running back with Haran.

Haran ran and stood before his father awaiting instructions.

Terah commanded, pointing toward Azazil and Hetephe, "Haran, take those two people to the Pastures and show them the disgusting people that live down there. Don't let one of their whores seduce you. Zeus only knows what kind of diseases she would have! Be useful for a change. Don't foul this up like you usually do! Do you hear me?!"

"Yes, Father! I will make you proud of me. And I'm not old enough to fornicate and don't have a wife, anyway! Father!"

"Well, those whores down there don't care about that. They just want their hands inside a righteous man's loincloth. Stay away from them!"

"Yes, Father. I will!"

Terah said, "Well, good then. Get them on their way. Abram, you take Lord Horus up to the Grand Temple. Somebody will meet you at the gate and take Lord Horus to be introduced to The-Living-Word-of-the-Gods, himself. Fortunate man! I'll show Lord Djoser around the city. Well, are you waiting for God Zeus to come down and kick you in your butts! Get on with it!"

Everyone rose from the table. The guests quelled their need to thank the hostess for a lovely meal. Djoser simply said, "Wonderful food, Lord Terah. We all thank you."

Terah said, "Well, I got a good cook!"

Amathlai beamed with pride.

Abram led Horus toward the door and on to the Great Temple.

Haran led Azazil and Hetephe out the door and on to the Pastures.

Terah put his hand on Djoser's shoulder and said, "Let me show you all the idols I got for trade!"

Amathlai and Sarai watched everyone depart, smiled at one another, and began to clear the table.

EGYPTIAN GODS: Osiris/Dionysus—Isis/Ariadne/Philyra, Horus, Set/Charon, Nephthys/Dexithea.
CANAANITE GODS: Anath, Astarte, Shalem, Shahar, Moloch, El.
OLYMPIAN GODS: Zeus, Dionysus, Hestia, Ares, Athena, Astraeus, Eos, Hermes.
OCEANIDS: Polydore, Lyris, Acaste, Eidyia, Dione.

16. The People of Urfa

Djoser and Terah

Terah led Djoser to the large room containing all manner of idols. He narrated, "I already had a lot of idols before the great flood—my predecessors traded directly with that Athena god at Tartarus, so the story goes—I don't really know—but I do know that after the flood, these things could be found for the taking—and I and my friends took everyone we could find. What we found up in the mountains was unbelievable—warehouses full of things like this—enough idols to trade for ten lifetimes. This one is said to be Zeus, himself. Friendly looking, isn't he? This one is supposedly Ares—evil-looking, I think. And that one is Poseidon, and that one is Demeter—I trade a lot of Demeter's for the Winter Solstice Festival. I don't believe any of that god nonsense…" Terah froze and exclaimed, "… Don't tell anyone I said that. It just slipped out. I really do believe everything that The-Living-Word-of-the-Gods teaches. I really do—their unconditional love and vengeance if you disobey them and all the gifts they shower on the righteous—it's all true—every word!"

They came to a small door at the back of the idol room. Terah said, "I don't show the cellar to many people—just The-Living-Word-of-the-Gods and his priests. They are the only ones righteous enough to see it without becoming unrighteous. You seem to be high-born and will be leaving soon enough. These idols command a trade of great value. Perhaps you will see one that attracts you."

He opened the door to a landing which led to a large cellar. He poured oil into a trough leading downward and lit it. The resulting flame traveled to oil-filled troughs which lit the cellar. They walked down the steps into a scene only the gods could have imagined.

Terah said, "This section is mostly Aphrodite—that's a statue of her and a goat—and this is one of my favorites—Aphrodite servicing Zeus, Areas, Poseidon, Hades, and Heracles all at the same time—amazing what she could do, isn't it?—and those are her in unusual positions with different gods—the one of her on her knees with her mouth open looks like a man could—well, never mind—I'll leave you alone with it if you like. And this one, the story goes, represents a historical event—that's Ares and Zeus raping a god by the name of Selene at one of the first Harvest Rites. Wild, isn't it? Ares threw her into a big fire and burned her alive when they were finished with her—that's a favorite of The-Living-Word-of-the-Gods. See anything you like? Aphrodite on her knees, maybe? I could let that go for as little as a thousand pieces of gold. I wager she is worth it!"

Djoser laughed, "I'm afraid that I am an Egyptian!"

Terah had no idea of what that meant but it sounded like a no. He said, "Well, enough of this ... the oil is about to burn out. Come on, I'll show you around the city." He led Djoser back up the stairs and into the afternoon light.

They walked down the path between large communal buildings. Children played outside. Women tended gardens behind the buildings. Men sat around long tables talking and drinking. One of the men called out, "Ahh, Great Terah, come, bring your friend and join us!"

Terah asked, "Do you have an afternoon drink you can serve me and my new high-born friend?"

The man turned and screamed out toward the gardens, "Woman! Bring me and my high-born friends a beer! Right now! We are waiting!" Under his breath, he muttered, "Women! Useless except for bringing beer and plowing!"

Djoser laughingly replied, "In my country that can also cook and have babies and smell nice."

The man responded, "Yeah, well, I suppose so." His woman came hurrying up bringing three beers. She curtsied to Terah and then, seeing Djoser, deeply curtsied to him, flashing her brightest smile. "Welcome to our modest home, Lord. I hope you are having a pleasant visit."

The man waved her off but not before Djoser ventured, "Your home is exceedingly lovely. Your husband does a fine job of keeping it so. That, plus, he had excellent taste in selecting a woman to provide all the exquisite comforts he demands!" *Did I say everything correctly, Abram? Did you instruct me well?*

The man was somewhat taken aback by such praise; he did not notice that it was the woman being praised. He said, "Well, Yeah, she's a good one—righteous and everything. I suppose I'll keep her."

The woman beamed with pride.

EGYPTIAN GODS: Osiris/Dionysus—Isis/Ariadne/Philyra, Horus, Set/Charon, Nephthys/Dexithea.
CANAANITE GODS: Anath, Astarte, Shalem, Shahar, Moloch, El.
OLYMPIAN GODS: Zeus, Dionysus, Hestia, Ares, Athena, Astraeus, Eos, Hermes.
OCEANIDS: Polydore, Lyris, Acaste, Eidyia, Dione.

Djoser thought, *Hetephe, I'm glad you're not seeing this. You might be inclined to kill all the men so this attitude doesn't spread. This is the result of Teumessian teachings.*

Djoser said, "How do you keep your women in line, so well?"

The man answered, "All our women are righteous. They listen to the teachings of the priests and understand that the way to happiness is by being a loving wife—obeying her husband—not being a whore—understanding that the man knows what's best for his family. Our children are raised from birth to listen to the teachings of the priests and that their teachings are the words of the gods, themselves. Disobey the teachings of a god and you will be thrown into the fire. It's hard being the master of a household, I guess you know that. Sometimes you have to slap the wife and kids around to keep them in line—but that's a husband's duty!"

Djoser's only response was, "You serve a good beer." On impulse, he asked, "Do you have any of Lord Tarah's idols?"

The man laughed. "Of course. I keep one of Zeus to remind my family of the boundless love the gods have for us and one of Ares to remind them of what happens if you disobey the husband." He looked around, leaned over, and conspiratorially whispered, "And I keep a special one of Aphrodite back in my quarters to try to inspire my wife, but my wife always says that the priests teach them not to do anything but get on their hands and knees and wait for their husband to finish—that that's the only godly way." The man sipped his beer as he stared at Djoser. "Say, Brother, you're a little on the dark side. Where did you say you're from?"

Djoser attempted to mentally second guess the implications of the question but decided there *were* no implications. *I'm half Nubian—of course, I'm darker than you people.*

He answered. "I'm from Egypt. We get a lot of sun. You should see my friend—she—I mean—he is Nubian and is a beautiful black."

The man jerked back in his chair. "Nubian, you say. Aren't those people all black-skinned? You're not one of those Nubians, are you?"

Djoser found the man's words confusing—his tone was accusatory but there was nothing to be accusatory about. *You sound upset, Friend. But upset over what? That I'm from Egypt?*

He temporized. "Are Egyptians not welcome here?"

The man stared at Tarah and said, "This man *is* a friend of yours, isn't he? Did you know that he is friends with a black person? He *is* righteous, isn't he? I don't want any non-believers drinking my beer!"

Terah panicked. The man was a good customer—but always filled with righteousness and a little on the mean side.

Djoser considered going into full domination but decided to see how Terah handled such insolence.

Terah stammered, "L-lord Djoser is v-very high-born and friends with the living son of God Dionysus. The-Living-Word-of-the-Gods sent word that they and their friends should be treated with respect. The high priests are probably teaching them how to be Righteous. His b-black friend is very courteous and shows respect, as he should."

"Humph, I'm sure The-Living-Word-of-the-Gods knows what he is doing. But black people—we aren't even certain that black people can achieve Righteousness!"

"Why is that?" Djoser innocently inquired.

The man became even more pompous. "Well, the gods were all Lilly white, you know—the purest white possible. The further people get from the gods, the darker their skins become."

Djoser asked, "Oh, I didn't know. Which of the gods taught that?"

"They didn't have to teach it! It just stands to reason. Only the Righteous people of Urfa have pure blood. We have never rejected the wonderful love the gods give to us. We keep our thoughts and our women pure!"

Djoser replied, "Well, that is wonderful. As I said, you serve an excellent beer. Which statue of God Aphrodite do you have?" *You probably have a short attention span.*

The man was placated. "Well, even if you are dark-skinned and not totally righteous, at least you don't look down on righteous people like we aren't as good as you."

He screamed out over his shoulder, "Woman, bring us another beer— and while you're at it, bring my statue of Aphrodite to show my friend!"

Soon, the woman hurried out bringing three more beers and an item covered in cloth. She delivered the beers, handed the package to her husband, and turned to hurry off.

EGYPTIAN GODS: Osiris/Dionysus—Isis/Ariadne/Philyra, Horus, Set/Charon, Nephthys/Dexithea.
CANAANITE GODS: Anath, Astarte, Shalem, Shahar, Moloch, El.
OLYMPIAN GODS: Zeus, Dionysus, Hestia, Ares, Athena, Astraeus, Eos, Hermes.
OCEANIDS: Polydore, Lyris, Acaste, Eidyia, Dione.

The man said, "Not so fast, woman. Unwrap this idol and show it to my friend. He's never seen such a thing."

The woman was conflicted, "Oh, Husband, you know I don't like to look at that thing, especially touch it!"

The man raised his voice, "Woman!"

Djoser stared into the woman's eyes and softly said, "It would mean a great deal to me if you would show me your idol. In my country, we do not connect the naked human body with a lack of righteousness. We see the beauty in each person as they are. Let the two of us look upon this statue and decide for ourselves if it is a thing of beauty or of unrighteousness."

The woman, shocked by actually being noticed and addressed by a man in such a manner, stammered, "It's a n-naked man and a naked woman, Lord, and they are n-naked and they are t-touching each other."

"You hold it out for me while I unwrap it." Djoser removed the wrapping from over the statue and stared at the idol admiringly. *Aphrodite, you insatiable god, you. I wasn't told you could be so demure.*

He said to the woman, "It is exquisite! I have never seen the love between a husband and his wife captured so Righteously. Do you agree? Look at how she lays in his embrace—in his protection—in his adoration as he holds her perfect female body and suckles the very breast that delivered the milk to his babes. Look at how she grasps his manhood, recognizing his strength, and bringing him unknowable joy—and, of course, his manhood can bring unknowable joy to a woman when she is married to the man and obeys the gods to abandon all self-restraint when she couples with her husband. Be careful not to touch Heracle's gigantic, erect manhood until you are ready to enter your husband's full embrace. It might inflame you too quickly. This is a Righteous, loving idol. Thank you for sharing it with me."

He covered the statue back up, looked condescendingly at the man, and said, "I don't know what your priests teach but I *do* know what Heracles and Aphrodite teach. Heracles teaches the husband to treat his wife with tenderness and respect. Aphrodite teaches us that mutual exploration is a wonderful, righteous thing, and the husband should always ask the wife what she likes and doesn't like." *I hope I have helped you, Sweet Woman. There is no more I can do.*

Dionysus/Osiris, Ariadne/Isis/Philyra, Charon/Set, Hermes/Tehuti.
EGYPTIANS: Nebka, Djoser, Hotep, Khasek, Rocky
NUBIANS: Nima, Hetephe, King Kerma, Prince T'jaru, Prince Rafah.
CANAANITES: Phoenicia, Serket, Azazil, Jaffa | URFANS: Teumessian, Abram, Sarai, Terah

He said to the man, "I have enjoyed your company. You have been most enlightening."

Djoser looked at Terah and suggested, "Shall we leave and let this husband and wife go exploring?" *So, the gods were lily-white, were they? That's where everything went wrong!*

Djoser and Terah returned to Terah's house.

Horus and Abram

As Djoser and Terah had left the house earlier in the day, Horus and Abram had set off to the Grand Temple. Horus instructed Abram on how to present himself—how not to be cowed in the presence of his betters—what to say if spoken to.

Abram absorbed every word.

They eventually arrived at the gates of an immense estate.

Abram gathered his courage, walked to the guards at the massive gates, and announced, "I am Abram, son of Terah. I bring the great Shaman Horus to meet with The-Living-Word-of-the-Gods."

The guard rang a loud bell. Six uniformed escorts marched in double file from a nearby building and lined both sides of the entrance to the wide walkway from the gate to the temple. The guard opened the gates and said, "You may enter. Stay with your escorts."

The man and boy were escorted into a small anteroom outside the main temple. The attendant, an Enforcer, instructed, "Leave all daggers, swords, and other sharp instruments and weapons with me. You may pick them up when you leave."

Horus removed his dagger and gave it to the seated Enforcer. Another Enforcer walked up behind Horus and ran his hands over Horus's body checking for any other potential weapons and then Abram's. Finding none, he nodded to the first Enforcer, who said, "You may enter the Temple. Someone will meet you."

Horus observed all of this without comment or expression. Abram mimicked the posturing of his Master.

Someone opened a door for them to enter a massive nave. A pleasant priest greeted them. "Ah, the great and formidable Shaman Horus finally joins us! Greetings Horus, son of Dionysus. The-Living-Word-of-the-

Gods has long awaited this reunion. He is so disappointed that your father did not come as he had promised to do."

Horus processed the magnificence of the room in which he stood while parsing the man's words and demeanor and extrapolating implications. *My first look—my first words—my first gestures must establish my dominance. And I am walking into a situation for which I had not supposed and planned. Father—be with me!*

Horus merely nodded to the priest without expression.

The priest said, "Follow me, Shaman Horus. You may bring the boy."

They walked to the center of the nave where large transepts on the left and right intersected. The priest turned them into the right transept where Teumessian sat on a large throne wearing his robes of office including a tall hat. He held a scepter in his right hand. He did not rise as Horus approached. Horus reached the foot of the throne. The two men locked stares. Teumessian held out his right-hand palm down upon which he wore a large ring. The gesture was obvious—"Kiss the ring!"

Father—be with me!

Horus stared at the ring. His mind churning with options. *He does not fear me as a representative of the gods. I am in his house—he is surrounded by his people. He is confident –arrogant—defiant! He figured out Father played him! He intends to dominate me. The best I can do is …*

"Greetings. Teumessian, Father didn't come back because he was never able to commandeer an Airboat to take you up into the sky. He was ashamed, I suppose. But he made me promise to fulfill his promise to return to Urfa. So, I return only to fulfill his promise."

The old voice broke with anger. "Kiss my ring!"

"Go fornicate with yourself. Teumessian. I will wander off and tour this monstrosity of a building on my own while you pleasure yourself."

"Silence your insolent tongue. Kiss my ring or I will have you killed!"

Horus laughed, "You would kill the son of Dionysus—the grandson of Zeus, himself? You are funny, old man. Go find a young girl to frighten."

Teumessian stood in a rage. "Enforcers. Enforcers. Come and behead this insolent wretched man!"

Two Enforcers came running up, swords unsheathed.

A large, self-confident man stepped from behind the throne, laughed, and said, "Hold off, Enforcers. Father never learned the art of negotiation. Let me try."

The man walked to Abram, knelt beside him, removed his dagger, held it to Abram's throat, looked up at Horus, smiled, and quietly hissed, "Kiss the ring!"

Horus knelt, looked Abram in the face, and said, "Are you prepared to die in my name, Abram?"

"Y-yes, Master. I am ready."

Horus stood, looked down at the man, and quietly said, "After your hands are wet with his blood, I will take your dagger, cut your throat, then the old man, and then your two Enforcers. You will win, unfortunately, because Urfa will have lost nothing of worth, but the good earth will have lost a boy of great value. Why do you tarry, dung-head? Kill him so that I can get on with purifying this wretched land of yours." He stared at the kneeling man without blinking.

The kneeling man laughed, withdrew his dagger, stood, and said, "I am Deoares. The loss of my father and our two Enforcers is not too great a price to pay—but my life, too, you say? You are not negotiating fairly, my friend."

"I am not negotiating, you are not my friend, and the two Enforcers are merely good men trying to do what they see as their duty. Let us leave your father to his ravings and find a quiet place to talk. You may serve me wine but only if I select which of the two cups to drink from. You will drink the other cup."

Deoares walked to the old man, knelt before him, and kissed his ring. He said, "Father, you heard, I'm sure, that the vermin does not feel worthy to kiss your ring. He sent me in his stead. He whimpers and begs that you will find this gesture satisfactory. I will now escort him out of your sight."

The old man vigorously shook his head, "Yes."

Deoares rose and gestured to a far corner of the transept. A young woman came running up. Deoares said to her, "Baalat, Father is greatly agitated. Calm him as only your sweet lips can do. I will take our guests to the Children's Transept to visit." He glanced at one of the Enforcers. "Have

EGYPTIAN GODS: Osiris/Dionysus—Isis/Ariadne/Philyra, Horus, Set/Charon, Nephthys/Dexithea.
CANAANITE GODS: Anath, Astarte, Shalem, Shahar, Moloch, El.
OLYMPIAN GODS: Zeus, Dionysus, Hestia, Ares, Athena, Astraeus, Eos, Hermes.
OCEANIDS: Polydore, Lyris, Acaste, Eidyia, Dione.

the priests send serving girls with wine to the Children's Transept." He turned to Horus and said, with charm, "Shall we retire to other quarters for a game of who will get the poisoned wine?"

Horus did not lower his guard but nodded in agreement.

The two men and boy walked from the transept, across the nave, to the other transept. Deoares sat down at the long table upon which set a large vase of flowers. "Have a seat, Horus. Anywhere you like. Do with the boy as you will. My sisters will be joining us, so they said. Women! Who knows what they are doing when men are waiting? Ahh, here comes the wine." He looked at the girl arriving with the tray of drinks and nuts. "Wench! Which cup contains the poison?"

The girl was indecisive only for a moment. "Why, all three, Lord Deoares. Lady Deoathena commanded me to rid the world of all worthless men at my earliest convenience."

Deoares shook his head in disgust. "They always get the last word, don't they?

A large woman wearing a metal helmet with horns walked in.

Deoares greeted her. "Ahh, Sister Deoathena. Come and meet the great Shaman Horus—the nemesis of our missionaries—undoer of all the progress they make—the great pain in our butts."

Deoathena walked up to Horus, hit her chest over her heart in respect, and said, "Lord Horus, son of a bastard child of Zeus. Our lives would be so much easier if neither of you had ever existed but what would be the challenge of that? I follow your exploits closely. You are peskier than your father was. Our missionaries are angry with you. They want you killed."

An attractive, older woman entered the room. "Men are so short-sighted, don't you think, Sister Deoathena? They would kill the very ones that will give us even more power. I'm late to meet our very important guest, I know, but I was having my nails done. He understands, I'm sure." She stopped to study Horus. "My, you are a handsome one. I'm glad I didn't let them kill you. Do you like to fornicate with older women?"

Horus coldly stared back without responding. *My father. I am in the land of the insane. You did not prepare me.*

He then turned and said to Deoares, "I am sure you are all terribly amusing. To yourselves, at least. When you get through amusing yourselves, if I am still awake, I will talk with you."

The woman purred, "Ohh, he is a mean one, isn't he? Kill him, Deoathena. I will go get my toes done, now." She turned to go.

Deoares said, "All right, Sister Deohestia. Sit down and let's get our work accomplished, then we can rid ourselves of the commoners."

Deohestia turned deadly serious, sat down, selected a cup of wine, sipped, and stared at Horus for a while. Finally, she said, "We have decided to peacefully coexist with you even if you do cost us a great deal in lost revenue and loss in control over the masses. The simple reason is that you are one of us. We could corrupt your Prince Djoser, or if not him, some other Egyptian with power. There is always someone willing to serve us. But why go to all that trouble when you will one day come to us? With all your power—with all your control—with all your influence—with all your followers. You will one day come to us because you are one of us. You simply haven't realized it yet. Now, what can we do for you?" She clasped her hands together and leaned forward waiting for his answer.

Horus studied her. *Never let them see you unsure of yourself. Do for me? What?! She asked the question. Give her the answer.*

"Stop the human sacrifices at the Solstice festivals."

Deoares joined in, "Oh, but that's my favorite part!"

Deohestia said, "Quiet, Brother!" To Horus, she said, "Done. It will take at least a year to reach all our temples, but our missionaries will be instructed to immediately start preaching the significant disgust this practice brings to Demeter, or whatever the local god's name is. Is this satisfactory?"

Horus answered, "What do you demand in return?"

"You made a request. We will fulfill your request. We did not ask for anything."

"So, you will leave it to me to deduce what it is you wish from me?"

"Don't be dense, Horus. Deduce? I just gave you a list of the things you take from us."

"And if I will not stop doing that which I do, what then?"

EGYPTIAN GODS: Osiris/Dionysus—Isis/Ariadne/Philyra, Horus, Set/Charon, Nephthys/Dexithea.
CANAANITE GODS: Anath, Astarte, Shalem, Shahar, Moloch, El.
OLYMPIAN GODS: Zeus, Dionysus, Hestia, Ares, Athena, Astraeus, Eos, Hermes.
OCEANIDS: Polydore, Lyris, Acaste, Eidyia, Dione.

"I don't understand."

"What will you do if I do not agree to stop doing the things I do?"

"I will do that which I said I would do—stop the human sacrifices within a year."

He asked, "Without concessions on my part."

She answered, "I did not ask for concessions."

Horus thought, *She plays some hidden game.*

Horus said, "I look forward to the cessation of human sacrifices. If you are finished with me, I will go."

"Did you kiss Father's ring?"

"No."

"Good. I was correct. I was sure you wouldn't. Goodbye, for now, Horus. I am going to get my toenails done. Show him out, Deoares." She rose and abruptly left.

Deoares called after her, "I haven't finished my wine yet, Sister."

He looked at the remaining sister and said, "Baalat should be finished with Father by now. One of us has got to take him back to his bedroom to rest. Meeting Shaman Horus was more difficult for him than I had anticipated. Horus evidently isn't as smooth as Dionysus."

Deoathena answered, "I will take care of our sweet Father. You deal with the bastard's son. Dionysus wasn't an Elder Olympian, anyway. Just a latecomer with wine." She gulped her wine, rose, and left.

Deoares stared at his wine as he swirled it in his cup. "I will welcome the day you join us, Horus. There aren't that many of us here at the top. I enjoy your company. We Kyrios Olon must expand our membership if we are to be masters of all humanity, you know. We are doing alright, for now, but the world keeps on growing."

"Why should humanity wish to serve such self-centered, arrogant, non-nurturing masters such as yourselves?"

"Oh, Sweet Horus, since the beginning of time the masses have had a chief to tell them what to think—what to do. Now, everything has grown too big—too complicated. They don't have their chiefs, anymore. They don't know how to change from the way things have always been done. They *need* us to be their Masters. Besides, they never blame us for their inconveniences. That's why we have missionaries and priests. The masses simply aren't smart enough to figure out that someone is controlling the people who are controlling them. The masses don't even know we exist. It's a great system."

Horus listened intently but with feigned disinterest. He replied, "They learn quickly enough, Deoares, but admittedly, not in the once grand city of Urfa. Enjoy yourselves."

Deoares replied, "Oh, we do, and we will, but no, the masses will not learn—ever! So go try to teach them and when you get tired ...," he raised his glass of wine in salute, "... come see me! By the way, the poison is in the cup with the engraved skull. He finished his wine and asked, "Do you want to leave now, or shall I show you around?"

Horus rose, looked at Abram, and asked, "What do you recommend, Abram? Go or take a tour?"

Abram panicked. *Me? I don't know what to do. Let's get out of this place as quickly as we can!*

He replied, "Y-you have taught me to obtain knowledge wherever I can."

"Good answer, Abram!" Horus turned to Deoares and replied, "We accept your gracious invitation to tour your wonderful temple."

Deoares motioned for them to follow him as he said, "Oh, this is much more than a Temple. The temple is just for controlling the masses. This is actually our home. I mean the home of all my brothers and sisters and cousins. Well, my half-brothers and sisters. We all have different mothers—I think. Keeping with the spirit of things, the woman doesn't really matter. We figured out quickly that if we are going to control the world, we must neutralize the females. They have too much natural empathy for other people—nurturing—teaching—picking you up when you fall—caring for others—that sort of thing. Oh, look ...," he said, stopping to point toward the ceiling, as they arrived in the nave,"... our ceiling is made of colored glass. It's impossible to get any more. Father took all that he could back in the old days when the Oceanids were reclaiming what they could from the sea. They worked at it for years. Everything of value had been submerged. All the nice things—all the valuable things—all the technology. Well, not all of it, but a large portion.

EGYPTIAN GODS: Osiris/Dionysus—Isis/Ariadne/Philyra, Horus, Set/Charon, Nephthys/Dexithea.
CANAANITE GODS: Anath, Astarte, Shalem, Shahar, Moloch, El.
OLYMPIAN GODS: Zeus, Dionysus, Hestia, Ares, Athena, Astraeus, Eos, Hermes.
OCEANIDS: Polydore, Lyris, Acaste, Eidyia, Dione.

That's how our missionaries came to be—men talking sweetly to Oceanids, telling them what they wanted to hear, taking everything they had, amassing the riches of the lost civilizations. Did you know that the Tartarus workshops and warehouses at Phlegethon Mines were simply abandoned? Just like that! Their warehouses were on higher ground in the mountains. A missionary force stumbled across them. Warehouses full of priceless treasures. Immense—unknowable—immeasurable—gold—Alburun—all the bright and shiny things of the greatest civilization that will ever be. All there for the taking. It took Father an entire year of dedicated scavenging to retrieve everything. Your friend, Terah, was still a boy, but he commanded all the younger, strong-backed boys and he knew enough to negotiate all the idols for his own. Terah was our first Useful Fool. Father set him up very nicely, don't you think? He did all the work and all he got was the idols—of which we let him take care for us—for now. We are Kyrios Olon, from us all power flows. We do not deem ourselves to be kings or monarchs or worshipped by the masses. Those things are our playthings. We control them all. We do not need 'things.' Only raw power over those that have 'things.' It's best that the masses don't know we exist. We need only control those who control the masses. Gods are such a wonderful tool for this, don't you think? Gods keep the masses mad at one another and divided. Give them someone to hate—somebody not like themselves. They don't seem to ever develop enough sense to be mad at *us*. It's all so delicious, isn't it?"

His dissertation was interrupted by the young woman who had soothed Teumessian. "Great Deoares, your father is calm and in his quarters. Do you still require me?"

"Yes, sweet Baalat. Take us to visit good old Cronus." Deoares said to Horus, as an aside, "We call Father 'Cronus' because Cronus fathered the Elder Olympians—the very ones we Kyrios Olon replaced. Except, this time, we know exactly what we are doing, thanks to Sister Deohestia."

Horus knew enough to simply respond, "I understand."

"I'm talking too much, aren't I? But my siblings are not as quick-witted as you. They are so boring. But never mind, you know enough to get you started on your journey back to us. Let's go visit Father."

Horus said, "I understand." *I don't understand at all. What journey? Should I ask and appear ignorant? Never let them see you unsure!*

Dionysus/Osiris, Ariadne/Isis/Philyra, Charon/Set, Hermes/Tehuti.
EGYPTIANS: Nebka, Djoser, Hotep, Khasek, Rocky
NUBIANS: Nima, Hetephe, King Kerma, Prince T'jaru, Prince Rafah.
CANAANITES: Phoenicia, Serket, Azazil, Jaffa | URFANS: Teumessian, Abram, Sarai, Terah

Baalth led them down a long opulent hallway and into a massive room. She loudly announced, "Great and well-endowed The-Living-Word-of-the-Gods, you have visitors. Shall I allow them to enter into your magnificent presence?"

A frail voice answered, "Are they righteous? Are they worthy?"

She replied, "Your son, Great Deoares, is with them, God-father Cronus. The other two appear worthy enough."

He answered, "Very well. I will deem to meet them."

She led them to face the old man sitting in an oversized chair staring at nothing.

The usual honorifics and pleasantries were exchanged. Teumessian appeared not to remember his earlier confrontation.

Horus listened to the old man blather on. *Father, your ancient nemesis has come to this! He has nothing I want. His daughter said that she would stop the solstice sacrifices. I believe her. I don't know what she will demand from me, but I will bear it. The old man is only decoration. Who will replace him? What will be his goal? Power? Tribute? Who controls the temple? Not Teumessian and not Deoares. Deohestia? Someone not yet known?*

As Horus started to take leave of Teumessian, he impulsively asked, "Does Baalat please you satisfactorily?"

Teumessian wrung his hands and said, "In the beginning, before she became a woman, she was extremely satisfactory. But she has grown old and I suspect she has turned into a whore." He hesitated a moment and loudly exclaimed, "Yes, she has become a whore! She must be stoned! All whores must be stoned to death!"

Deoares motioned for Baalat to leave immediately, which she did. He said to his father, "I will send the girl before the council for their decision, Father. Do you wish to witness her stoning? It may be bloody."

"YES! YES! I WISH TO SEE HER PUNISHED FOR HER WICKEDNESS. FIND ME A NEW SERVANT. One that isn't a grown woman yet. One that is pure and innocent and isn't a whore."

"Should she be pretty, Father?"

"Yes, yes. A pretty one."

EGYPTIAN GODS: Osiris/Dionysus—Isis/Ariadne/Philyra, Horus, Set/Charon, Nephthys/Dexithea.
CANAANITE GODS: Anath, Astarte, Shalem, Shahar, Moloch, El.
OLYMPIAN GODS: Zeus, Dionysus, Hestia, Ares, Athena, Astraeus, Eos, Hermes.
OCEANIDS: Polydore, Lyris, Acaste, Eidyia, Dione.

"It shall be done, Father. Now let me show our guests the magnificent treasures you saved from the flood. They will be impressed just as the old gods rejoice in your service to them."

"Yes, yes. Show the nice young man everything!"

Deoares led Horus and Abram from the room where outside waited a concerned Baalth. "Am I to be stoned to death, Great El Deoares?"

"We will see, Sweet Baalat. You have served Father well and I have seen no signs of your whoring. In the meantime, select three of our youngest maidens for the Kyrios Olon to consider as your replacement."

She curtsied and bowed to him.

Horus blurted, "I will take her as a follower!"

Deoares said, "You would take a woman as a follower? How absurd. Besides, we may want her stoned to death for Father's pleasure."

Horus replied, "I have many women followers. She could learn all my plans and secrets and report them to Urfa Missionaries we will undoubtedly cross paths with. You would have your personal spy embedded with my real followers." He turned to the young woman and asked, "Would you like to be my follower, Baalat?"

She was confused. "I have not yet been told what I would like, Shaman Horus."

Abram shivered and blurted out, "You must decide now! Make the best decision you can."

Deoares commanded, "Silence, boy!"

Horus commanded Deoares, "You shall not command my follower! He is mine to command!"

Abram felt a rush of pride.

Baalat felt a rush of confusion. *Me decide?—A woman is not allowed to decide— Decide? I am a woman. They are men. Yet a boy challenges me to decide in front of men. How can any of this be?*

Deoares surged with fury at being so addressed by a commoner. *YOU COMMON BASTARD I WILL …*

Dionysus/Osiris, Ariadne/Isis/Philyra, Charon/Set, Hermes/Tehuti.
EGYPTIANS: Nebka, Djoser, Hotep, Khasek, Rocky
NUBIANS: Nima, Hetephe, King Kerma, Prince T'jaru, Prince Rafah.
CANAANITES: Phoenicia, Serket, Azazil, Jaffa | URFANS: Teumessian, Abram, Sarai, Terah

But he immediately remembered the agreement. *Sister Deohestia, MUST I show respect to this vermin? He tried to command me—a god!*

Deoares said, "Very well, Shaman, if you cannot control your follower, I will allow it!"

Baalat thought, *"Follower?" I know what THAT means. I will supply you with what all men want. Cronus casts me off but I will be caught by a young, powerful shaman. And two men—two men and a boy—have exchanged words because of me. Who do I please? Who is the more powerful? Deoares just backed down from the Shaman. What do I want? If I stay, I will probably be stoned to death. If I go then …*

Baalat blurted out, "I would be pleased to be your follower, Great Shaman!"

Each male reacted differently, but only Horus spoke, "Excellent. I will provide whatever considerations the Kyrios Ono require for your release, Pen Baalat."

Deoares shook off his tremendous irritation and laughed. "Having a personal spy reporting back all the actions of the great Shaman Horus— we not only allow it, Baalat, we command it. You will provide reports on Horus to every Missionary that you may see. This is a most excellent trade. Most excellent, indeed. Give us the great tour, Horus-follower Baalat. Show your new master that you are worthy of his attention! Most excellent, indeed!"

Baalat overcome with confusion, said, "F-follow me, M-master."

As they began their tour, Abram leaned over and whispered into Baalat's ear, "Never let them see you unsure."

Azazil and Hetephe

As Djoser was being given a tour by Terah, and as Abram and Horus had set off to the great Temple, so it was that Haran had led Azazil and Hetephe to the Pastures.

Haran idolized his older brother, Terahson. Terahson was everything a father wanted in a son—dominating, loud, manly. Haran imitated Terahson as best he could, in words and projected attitude. "These people down here are disgusting—not allowed to live with righteous people like us. Don't let them touch you—they are all filthy. The women are all whores—whatever that is. I won't play with the boys because they are so

EGYPTIAN GODS: Osiris/Dionysus—Isis/Ariadne/Philyra, Horus, Set/Charon, Nephthys/Dexithea.
CANAANITE GODS: Anath, Astarte, Shalem, Shahar, Moloch, El.
OLYMPIAN GODS: Zeus, Dionysus, Hestia, Ares, Athena, Astraeus, Eos, Hermes.
OCEANIDS: Polydore, Lyris, Acaste, Eidyia, Dione.

different than me. I would catch their diseases and everything. But if either of you want a good time, this is the place to go. Terahson says he sneaks down here sometimes to see naked women. I don't want to see a naked woman because they're whores." Haran babbled on to the gates of the fences surrounding the Pastures. "I'm not going any farther. I cannot take care of you after you go through those gates!"

Azazil said, "Actually, Guide Haran, sophisticated men know few women are actually whores and the ones that are, are usually nice people. You have been an informative guide. Thank you for your expert leadership. We will be careful inside but hope to meet some people as good as you are. You are extremely righteous. Stay safe on your way home."

Hetephe opened the gate. She and Azazil entered the Pastures, leaving Haran behind to consider the words he had just heard.

As they continued on the path leading to a large barn, Hetephe observed, "These people have a thing about whores. They must be terrified of them."

Azazil replied, "They use it with a derogatory connotation. Ishtar would not be pleased. She and her daughters always give more in return than they receive. Maybe it's a derogatory word to intimidate the local women."

They heard sounds in the distance and looked up to see what appeared to be people on galloping animals coming toward them.

Azazil asked, "Do you have those arrows ready?"

She laughed. "Always!"

The horsemen came pulling up and jumped off their horses—two young men and two young women. The leader asked, "Are you here to stone us to death or to have a party?"

Azazil risked a laugh. The six entered an engaging conversation that grew more delightful as they talked.

One of the young women insisted, "Someone will be having a party tonight. There's always a party—with beer and wine and even more intoxicating beverages. If you want to get to know the Pasture people, you simply *must* come to a party. We always have delicious food. We dance and sing and drink and sometimes get too friendly. I have many girlfriends that would be elated to meet such handsome foreigners." She looked at Hetephe and said, "You will be quite the center of attention with that black skin of yours. Look how good it looks against light skin like mine." She held her arm against Hetephe's in comparison.

Hetephe interjected, "I already have a special man-friend, thank you."

"Oh, then I will find a nice man to entertain you, but the women will be so disappointed."

Hetephe, realizing her verbal lapse of disguise, wanted to undo what she had done but decided there was no easy way to unsay it, and besides, such conversations might be entertaining, anyway.

But for now, their hosts were thrilled to tour them through the pastures. As they passed an apple tree, one of the women picked four apples and handed two each to her guests. "Our horses follow us because they know there will be apples. Would you be so kind as to oblige them?"

Hetephe laughed out loud when the smallest of the horses came trotting up to her with an expectant look.

A female host said, "Look, this one likes you."

Hetephe asked, "What's its name?"

First Female: "Name? We don't name horses. There are too many of them."
First Male: "When we need one, we simply take the nearest one."
Second Female: "They are all acclimated to humans."
Second Male: "Yes, they are happy enough when we mount them."
First Female: "They like the stroking, I suppose."
Second Male: "They have learned that they will get an apple for their service."
First Female: "You may have that one if it pleases you."

Hetephe exclaimed, "You will give me a horse?!"

The first woman replied, "As many as you like. We have hundreds of them in the Pasture. They eat our resources and must be tended to. Can you start with a hundred? They grow to all sizes."

Hetephe's eyes glazed over. *General T'jaru with a hundred horses? They could carry men into battle. They could pull chariots. Traders could ride them across Horus's Road from Canaan to Egypt and back. I could travel from Memphis to Abdju in a day! I would have a horse like Serket's!*

EGYPTIAN GODS: Osiris/Dionysus—Isis/Ariadne/Philyra, Horus, Set/Charon, Nephthys/Dexithea.
CANAANITE GODS: Anath, Astarte, Shalem, Shahar, Moloch, El.
OLYMPIAN GODS: Zeus, Dionysus, Hestia, Ares, Athena, Astraeus, Eos, Hermes.
OCEANIDS: Polydore, Lyris, Acaste, Eidyia, Dione.

She finally stammered, "My man friend is here. He is a master trader. I am sure he and your traders can reach a mutually satisfactory agreement."

The two men laughed. "Trade? You sound like the men of Urfa! 'Give me something and I will give you something!' If you need horses, take what you need. Leave for others what you don't need. It's not complicated! Now, come with us! We will find out who is having a party tonight!"

They walked down a trail that led to a good-sized river. There were men fishing from flat-bottomed boats and children splashing in the water. Women were washing clothes. One of the women said, "If you want to go for a swim, there are two swimming places; upstream if you want to go naked; downstream for the more modest. For some reason, the young go upstream and the older go downstream but young boys, for some reason, always go upstream although they never seem to take their tunics off. But whatever pleases you."

A breeze came off the river. The smell of fish being cooked on an open fire drifted past them. One of the men volunteered, "Some fisherman had a good day. Let's find him and share his bounty." They walked upstream in search of a free meal, which they found.

The day wore on. A party place had been identified—the old woman of the Pastures known for her cooking expertise—as well as being old. Hetephe found herself surrounded by a bevy of women; all under the impression that she was a man—although a man who preferred men— but it never hurt to be friendly. "You just never know."

As nightfall approached, Azazil volunteered to find Djoser and Horus. "Tonight's party would be an excellent opportunity to observe the attitudes and traditions of this part of Urfa. If their day had yielded as fine people as these, Urfa would be an excellent trading partner for Egypt and all the lands between."

Hetephe observed, "There has been no mention of gods—that's interesting in itself. By the way, tell my consort that I am surrounded by attractive, vibrant, willing women. I'm beginning to like this being a man thing and that he had better show up soon or I might take a special liking to my new friends."

Azazil laughed, excused himself, and set off to Terah's house to bring his friends to a party in the Pastures.

Dionysus/Osiris, Ariadne/Isis/Philyra, Charon/Set, Hermes/Tehuti.
EGYPTIANS: Nebka, Djoser, Hotep, Khasek, Rocky
NUBIANS: Nima, Hetephe, King Kerma, Prince T'jaru, Prince Rafah.
CANAANITES: Phoenicia, Serket, Azazil, Jaffa | URFANS: Teumessian, Abram, Sarai, Terah

Party at the Pastures

The party was well underway—the three-quarter moon rising—the main course almost roasted. There was beer and laughter. Hetephe sat close to Djoser; both surrounded by vibrant, chattering, hopeful young women. Azazil sat next to Horus; they, too, were of local female interest. The local men sitting around the fire kept shooing the women away. "Let the men talk for now. You can have them later." Children played by the river.

Abram and Baalat could have joined Horus around the fire, but Abram chose, instead, to lead Baalat to the river to talk. Shy, reserved Abram felt a kindred spirit with the woman and, even though she was fully grown, and he was still a child, he had the advantage of being Horus's follower for two full days longer than Baalat and was filled with the self-worth Horus had instilled into him. She was overwhelmed with the concept of self-actualization. Abram felt as if he were her big brother—teaching and protecting his sister.

Baalat remained confused—having no knowledge or experience with such relations. She assumed she knew what her duties were to be, but none of the men had called for her.

Azazil was the center of attention after casually saying, "My master Horus, the son of Dionysus and educated by his esteemed father, teaches that the gods of old were no more than self-important, high-born, people with no more innate power than the average man—they were just vicious and wielded the power they had for their own good rather than the good of the people."

The hostess, the Pastures Elder Woman, took notice and interjected, "He teaches that which the Oceanids taught. Who taught who, in this matter?"

Azazil hesitated.

Horus cut in, "The Oceanids knew these things before I was born. These things were seen by their sisters from the beginning even as they were seen by my father from the beginning."

The Elder Woman said, "The Oceanids taught me these things at Riverport many years ago. They are all dead now—I still feel their deadness. I will talk with you, young man. Come to me."

Horus rose and approached the old woman who leaned in to see him closer.

EGYPTIAN GODS: Osiris/Dionysus—Isis/Ariadne/Philyra, Horus, Set/Charon, Nephthys/Dexithea.
CANAANITE GODS: Anath, Astarte, Shalem, Shahar, Moloch, El.
OLYMPIAN GODS: Zeus, Dionysus, Hestia, Ares, Athena, Astraeus, Eos, Hermes.
OCEANIDS: Polydore, Lyris, Acaste, Eidyia, Dione.

She asked, "Have you been taught by Oceanids?"

Horus replied, "Yes, Grandmother. My father surrounded himself with Oceanids. In my youth, there were Oceanids everywhere. My uncle Djoser—there, sitting by the fire—is personal friends with many influential Oceanids whom he hoped to meet again at Riverport."

The woman gasped, "He knew Lyris and Acaste and Eidyia?"

"Yes. He knows them well." *Knew? This can't be good.*

"Send him to me! Alone!"

Horus nodded, went to Djoser, talked with him for a few moments, and sent him to talk with the Elder Woman. Horus replaced Djoser next to Hetephe as he joined in the chatter while trying to keep an eye on Djoser, deep in serious conversation with the Elder Woman.

As the night wore on, Azazil and Horus, the two men who appreciated women, became the center of attention. Horus politely declined all offers to go upstream and swim with the women.

After the moon was past its zenith, Djoser rose, kissed the hands of the Elder Women, said a sweet goodnight, and returned to the dying fire where he signaled the seated Horus and disguised Hetephe to join him. Hetephe jumped up and embraced him as she grabbed his crotch to the shocked delight of the women and the rolling eyes of the men.

Djoser did not respond. "There will be a place to bed down in one of the barns. Horus, go find your disciples and join us there."

Horus walked upstream to retrieve his three followers.

Four of the horses, including the one taken with Hetephe, rose and followed Hetephe and Djoser back toward the barns. She said, "Apples must be a love potion in the Pastures. Can we take them back to Egypt?"

"Yes. I would like that."

"You're somber after a night of partying. Your visit with the old woman wasn't good, was it?"

"It's been a long day. Let's get some sleep and we can talk in the morning."

They came to the orchard. Hetephe reached high to pick some of the remaining apples. She said, "Morning light will make things better. But tonight, I need to show *somebody* a little love!"

Dionysus/Osiris, Ariadne/Isis/Philyra, Charon/Set, Hermes/Tehuti.
EGYPTIANS: Nebka, Djoser, Hotep, Khasek, Rocky
NUBIANS: Nima, Hetephe, King Kerma, Prince T'jaru, Prince Rafah.
CANAANITES: Phoenicia, Serket, Azazil, Jaffa | URFANS: Teumessian, Abram, Sarai, Terah

Pre-Sunrise

Hetephe rose first, walked outside, built a small cooking fire, and began preparing the morning meal. She heard a gasp and turned around to see wide-eyed Abram and Baalat staring at her almost naked body.

"Oops. I should have dressed before I started our meal. Excuse me, children. Abram, you continue making our meal. Baalat, you come and help me put on my boy disguise. We can talk."

Hetephe led the incredulous Baalat to her sleeping area where the two of them disguised Hetephe as a man. Baalat didn't talk. She processed this new information into the already unknowable nature of these people— her new "friends." *Nothing about these people is as it should be. Lord Horus has not even made me undress for him. His friend spurned my offer to fornicate with him in the river. A little boy treats me like his big sister. A woman is a man. I have been taken into an unknowable world. Am I to be happy? Am I to run away in terror?*

She considered her situation. *I will make the best decision I can.*

The three men began stirring as Hetephe finished dressing. Hetephe loudly said, "Men are so lazy! Get up. Let's eat!" She looked at Baalat and whispered, "Men are all pigs! Even the good ones!"

Baalat, stunned by such words from a woman, could only nod in agreement.

Sunrise

Horus called his two disciples and faced the rising sun to greet his father.

His new followers observed in reverent but confused silence.

The group then gathered around the cooking fire and began their morning meal. All waited in silence for Djoser to begin their discussions.

He began. "The Riverport Oceanids are dead, ordered slaughtered by Teumessian. I know where their bodies were thrown to rot."

He said to Hetephe, "Get with the locals. Prepare a coffin to transport them to a suitable burial site. Their remains will not be left behind in this Osiris-forsaken land. Find someone knowledgeable about our horses. Learn how to properly ride and care for them. Pick out a stallion that would like to join our four mares and immigrate to Egypt."

EGYPTIAN GODS: Osiris/Dionysus—Isis/Ariadne/Philyra, Horus, Set/Charon, Nephthys/Dexithea.
CANAANITE GODS: Anath, Astarte, Shalem, Shahar, Moloch, El.
OLYMPIAN GODS: Zeus, Dionysus, Hestia, Ares, Athena, Astraeus, Eos, Hermes.
OCEANIDS: Polydore, Lyris, Acaste, Eidyia, Dione.

He looked at Azazil. "Take our two new followers to say goodbye to their appropriate village elders. Make sure they know Horus will train and educate Abram and let him return to Urfa when he is a man. Find out Baalat's desires for her coming life. She is as unsophisticated as Ishtar's daughters were and she doesn't have any concept of what opportunities are open to her. Begin her education. Horus and I will tour the Pastures. We meet back here tonight and leave after sunrise tomorrow."

The group dismissed, Hetephe found her horse expert. She learned proper care of horses quickly. Hetephe and the expert selected a stallion appropriate for the four mares that had taken up with Hetephe. Hetephe harvested all available apples, even those high in the trees.

The day passed quickly.

Sunrise

The group rose.

Horus welcomed the sun, and they ate their morning meal. As they prepared to leave Urfa, Hetephe introduced the five horses to the group. She expertly mounted her steed and said, "Her name is 'Arrow,' and the stallion is 'Djoser the Horse.' Nobody knows the names of the other three." She kneed Arrow to command her to raise her forelegs high into the air and to whiny.

The group muttered humorous things.

Djoser walked to the stallion. "I suppose Horse-Djoser is mine."

Hetephe ordered, "No, no! Djoser-the-Horse is large enough to carry two people—Abram and Baalat in this case. You men fight over the remaining mares. Baalat, show Abram how to mount a horse. If you don't know how, make something up. He will believe you. It's time for us to ride!"

Arrow pranced to the front of the procession. Djoser-the-Horse followed last—carrying his two riders plus pulling a buggy fit to carry Oceanids of Consequence.

~

In a grove, before Riverport, the horses received their love offerings and a rest. Djoser found the remains. The two women watched in reverence as Djoser, Azazil, and Abram retrieved bones, artifacts, bits of clothing, and hallowed ground and placed these things into a coffin fit for Oceanids.

On his knees, Horus wept.

EGYPTIAN GODS: Osiris/Dionysus—Isis/Ariadne/Philyra, Horus, Set/Charon, Nephthys/Dexithea.
CANAANITE GODS: Anath, Astarte, Shalem, Shahar, Moloch, El.
OLYMPIAN GODS: Zeus, Dionysus, Hestia, Ares, Athena, Astraeus, Eos, Hermes.
OCEANIDS: Polydore, Lyris, Acaste, Eidyia, Dione.

17. The Making of a Living God

Using the decrepit barge at Riverport to finally get everyone across, the troupe began their leisurely, chattering ride back to Ugarit.

Hetephe: "That Sarai girl didn't want to see her big brother leave. I think she wants to fornicate with him."
Abram: "Women in Urfa don't fornicate. They are all pure!"
Hetephe: "Oh, I forgot. But she wants you to pollinate her so she can have your babies!"
Abram: "What's pollinate?"
Baalat: "Fornicate!"
Azazil: "You are experienced to be so young, Baalat. You need to learn to be purer."
Baalat: "Do men in your country not like to pollinate?"
Azazil: "If we make it back to Jaffa, I will introduce you to Astarte. However, if achieving purity is your goal, emulate Serket. She is purer than new snow. Astarte is as pure as a lump of coal."

Horus interrupted. "Student Baalat, in Egypt and the civilized world, women are equal to men and are not commanded around by men like animals. They may lie with whom they wish, when they wish, and are not looked down on by other people for the doing—other than special friends whose trust or affection may have been betrayed. The civilized world does not use sex to control women. Urfa is the other end of the scale. Canaan is somewhere in between. As a woman, you must learn to navigate this treacherous landscape."

Hetephe piped in, "Which is easy enough because men are so easy!"

Baalat asked, "And pigs, Archer Hetephe?"

"And pigs! Young Baalat."

~

They came to Ugarit where they retained a stable for their horses and rooms for the night.

Baalat and Abram were enchanted with the city. They walked hand-in-hand wide-eyed through the city looking at the buildings, listening to the chatter, and seeing all manner of people.

Dionysus/Osiris, Ariadne/Isis/Philyra, Charon/Set, Hermes/Tehuti.
EGYPTIANS: Nebka, Djoser, Hotep, Khasek, Rocky
NUBIANS: Nima, Hetephe, King Kerma, Prince T'jaru, Prince Rafah.
CANAANITES: Phoenicia, Serket, Azazil, Jaffa | URFANS: Teumessian, Abram, Sarai, Terah

Djoser and Hetephe found a patio that appealed to them and told Horus that this was where they would be. "Take your followers, educate them, and pick us up on your way back."

Life was good.

~

Sunrise. On toward Byblos. They chattered.

Baalat: "Did you hear that woman telling a *man* what he did wrong?!"
Abram: "He didn't even hit her or anything!"
Baalat: "That place was so big and people didn't sound Righteous at all!"
Abram: "Where were the Enforcers? Who beats people that need beating?"
Baalat: "And the Priests. Where were the Priests?"
Abram: "They may not be a godly people!"
Baalat: "And the girls got to talk to people just like a real person!"

Eventually, Byblos came into sight. Byblos was far larger and more cosmopolitan than Ugarit. The two young ones were mesmerized. The others strolled the city but Horus and Djoser excused themselves to call on an old friend.

Horus knocked on her door. They heard her make her way to the door and open it; a look of extreme pleasure overtook her.

Horus said, "Young woman, you should not be so beautiful with your purple sash and ribbon in your hair when you open your door. Some men might try to take advantage of you!"

She took their hands, led them inside, sat them down, and brought them sweet drinks. "I should have accepted your wine and then I could be serving it to you except I would have already drunk it all and perhaps found a man who would have me. But then I would not have my purple sash and ribbon. Life's decisions can be hard, sometimes. Was your adventure fruitful?"

They talked on.

She said, "No. There are no Oceanids nearby. Lyris and her sisters were the last ones through. They would always stop to visit on their way to and from Riverport. I knew they would be dead. I hope they weren't tortured. I won't ask you the truth about their dying. I will be with them soon enough to share their story."

EGYPTIAN GODS: Osiris/Dionysus—Isis/Ariadne/Philyra, Horus, Set/Charon, Nephthys/Dexithea.
CANAANITE GODS: Anath, Astarte, Shalem, Shahar, Moloch, El.
OLYMPIAN GODS: Zeus, Dionysus, Hestia, Ares, Athena, Astraeus, Eos, Hermes.
OCEANIDS: Polydore, Lyris, Acaste, Eidyia, Dione.

Horus picked up on words and asked, "Who taught that to you?".

She laughed, "No one taught me these things, young man. The knowledge comes with the living. I believe there are still some Oceanids in Greece and Crete. If you find practicing Oceanids, return them to me. I will hire us a nice boat and have us taken to the middle of what was once Oursea. The boat can return as I escort the remains of my sisters to the bottom. Perhaps we will find Tartarus."

She glowed with anticipation of returning to her old world with her sisters.

Horus said, "Oceanid Polydore lives in Jaffa. I will tell her about you, Grandmother. Perhaps she will find time to visit."

The very thought softened the woman's features.

They talked on for a while then the men bid farewell and set off to find the others.

They spent, for the young ones, an exciting evening in Byblos. Later, Azazil found the local Disciples of Horus and took them to a quiet park to join Horus and hear the stories of Osiris and how to walk the righteous path of Kiya. Abram and Baalat listened with wide-eyed fascination.

Djoser sat on the ground listening to the old stories from the back; Hetephe was cradled in his arms.

Life was good.

~

Meanwhile, in the south, three followers of Horus tread northward to find their beloved teacher. To warn him.

~

Horus performed his ritual sunrise ceremony on Middlesea Beach. His dozen Byblos followers had invited friends and acquaintances to observe and be part of this uplifting experience of renewal and homage to an important god. Azazil stood beside him. Abram and Baalth sat at his feet and soaked up every word.

Horus taught them how to be good and what it means to be good.

"The Path of Kiya is worthy, as are they who find and follow it.
Honor your ancestors. They are your past. You are their future.
Kill nothing you do not consume. Each life is precious unto itself.

Honor your vows. Do that which you say you will do.
Take nothing that is not yours.
Say nothing that is false.
Pick up those who have fallen.
Give to those who ask.
Love everyone, even those who despise you.
Be worthy."

Horus presented the "how" nicely but, as usual, a member of the crowd asked, "But why be good?"

"Your question is a good question. But if you don't feel the answer inside you, I cannot answer it for you. Osiris says that the dead know the reason, but I still search for it. But know this; if you ever fall, I will pick you up. If you ever need, I will give. Decide for yourself the why of it."

They talked on. Azazil eventually took over the answering of questions as Horus retired with the two young students. Leaving the circle, Baalat observed, "The gods do none of those things, yet they remain gods. They have everything and I have little."

Horus asked, "And who, Student Baalat, had you rather be?"

"I had rather be a god that follows the Path of Kiya! You told me Osiris followed her path! And Isis, too! So there! That's what I'd rather be!"

Horus laughed his sad laugh. "You are correct, Student Baalat. You are wiser than I. I must think upon your young wisdom."

Baalat was pleased with herself. Abram was impressed. Confidence grew in both.

Horus said, "Let's go find Djoser and Hete. Azazil will be along later. He enjoys long, drawn-out discussions."

They found Hete on the archery field teaching five young women the joy of archery. Baalat ran over to maybe learn how to shoot an arrow.

Djoser leaned against a tree munching nuts. "Horus, my son. You had a large turnout this morning. Your reputation grows."

Abram piped in. "My master and I do not know why we should be good. We know good is better, but we don't know why!"

Djoser chuckled. "Dionysus was convinced, and convinced me, that good came to the good and bad came to the bad. What you sow, so shall you

EGYPTIAN GODS: Osiris/Dionysus—Isis/Ariadne/Philyra, Horus, Set/Charon, Nephthys/Dexithea.
CANAANITE GODS: Anath, Astarte, Shalem, Shahar, Moloch, El.
OLYMPIAN GODS: Zeus, Dionysus, Hestia, Ares, Athena, Astraeus, Eos, Hermes.
OCEANIDS: Polydore, Lyris, Acaste, Eidyia, Dione.

reap. That works most of the time; not all of the time, but most of the time. Look at Egypt. We try our best to be good and my country receives the bountiful blessing of good fortune. Did you notice the joy of living in Jaffa has increased since Polydore has cleaned things up? I suppose that I, myself, could have accumulated a lot more wealth for myself at the expense of others, but, what's the fun in that?"

Horus muttered, "The old woman said, 'I will be with them soon enough to share their story' and that 'the knowledge comes with the living.' Perhaps they will know the why of it."

They chattered on. Azazil walked briskly toward them followed by his local disciples and the three disciples from Jaffa.

Djoser said, "A problem comes to greet us."

Azazil and his group arrived.

Azazil stood facing Horus. "There is a problem waiting for you in Jaffa. God Set has become even mightier. He believes he is mightier than Anath. Everyone in Jaffa, including Anath, accepts that he is. He waits for you to return to command you to do humiliating things. He intends to command Prince Djoser to do humiliating things. He believes himself to be equal to Zeus and Ares and Poseidon—and certainly mightier than Dionysus. It is said that he demanded Serket to fornicate with him; that she withdrew her dagger, pressed it into his crotch, and said, 'I will be delighted to fornicate with your penis, Great Lord. But not if it is attached to you! What do you wish to do? Decide! NOW!' He is said to have stormed off in a great fury. Things will not go well when you return. Burlyman is protecting the dock as best he can."

Djoser said, "This is *my* problem. He will command *me*. I will refuse and cause a division among the people. The influence of Egypt in Canaan will be reduced not to mention the turmoil when word of such a confrontation got back to South Memphis. I explained to Set what would happen if he challenged me. He must be extremely confident in his influence. This confrontation must not be allowed to happen. I must think!"

Horus said to no one, "Forgiving him—understanding him—nurturing him—not attacking him—not challenging him—to what end?—Is this the reward for 'being good?' Is it?!"

The thought of Set's body entering Serket's was repulsive. The thought of Set commanding Djoser was repulsive! *Do you wish to see how far you can push me, Uncle? Is that your purpose? Well, I will not break—"Love everyone, even those who despise you." I love you, Uncle Set, and I will NOT break.*

Hetephe and Baalat, seeing the commotion, began walking toward the group.

Djoser waved them away, and quietly said to the disciples, "Leave us."

Everyone departed, leaving Azazil, Abram, Horus, and Djoser. No one spoke for a long time.

Djoser said, "For Set to challenge you is madness. You have more followers, better followers, more enlightened followers, and a massive following from Abdju, through Memphis, into Canaan, Phoenicia, and Urfa. You have a network of priests and teachers across the land. He is mad!"

Azazil jumped in, "Master Horus could publicly command the prince not to accept the command of any god! That would solve the prince's problem!"

Horus laughed. "Now, that's an idea! A shaman commanding a prince! A shaman telling a god that he cannot command those that the shaman commands. Nice suggestion, Friend Azazil. But neither Prince Djoser nor God Set is likely to agree."

Djoser said, "There is a way. My son. All it requires is for you to abandon every principle you have based your life upon."

Horus stared at Djoser with trepidation.

Sunrise

The crowd to watch Horus greet the sun was a significant size.

Horus had spent a sleepless night. He had decided.

The sun came. To himself, Horus said, "Father, forgive me for what I am about to do …"

You will do that which is right.

"I will tell the smaller lie to prevent a larger lie …

Both good and bad will flow from the smaller lie.

EGYPTIAN GODS: Osiris/Dionysus—Isis/Ariadne/Philyra, Horus, Set/Charon, Nephthys/Dexithea.
CANAANITE GODS: Anath, Astarte, Shalem, Shahar, Moloch, El.
OLYMPIAN GODS: Zeus, Dionysus, Hestia, Ares, Athena, Astraeus, Eos, Hermes.
OCEANIDS: Polydore, Lyris, Acaste, Eidyia, Dione.

"I will diminish myself so that others will not be diminished."

Love is hard.

"Baalat told me that she wished to become a god that walks the Path of Kiya."

So, she may. And you.

"Father, forgive us all."

There is nothing to forgive.

Horus raised his head and turned to face his disciples and congregation. With certitude, he addressed them all. "I am Horus, son of Isis and Osiris; blood of Zeus, blood of Kiya."

Speaking louder, he said, "I left you a simple man. I return a god. I am God Horus. The mightiest of all living gods. I am mightier than Anath; mightier than Set; mightier than the lesser gods of Canaan. All that hear my words will obey me for I am God Horus, son of Gods. All men and gods, weak and mighty will obey my commands. Go forth into Jaffa. Tell my priests these things."

He raised his arms into the air, his voice loud. "Tell my followers to spread the good news throughout all cities; that all people should rejoice for a living god comes to bring them love and hope and peace. A god that does not obey me will be torn to pieces by my loving people. I shall return to Jaffa with the quarter-moon. Prepare the city for my arrival."

He thundered, "Go now—all my disciples—spread my gospel—make these things so!"

He said quietly to Azazil, "Go to Serket. Tell her she did well; she brings me peace. Then to Set; tell him what has come to pass; that I will come under the half-moon for him to kneel before me."

He then dismissed his disciples, turned, and melted into the horizon.

~

Djoser walked the beach looking for Horus.

Abram came running to him. "He is this way, my prince. He will not talk. He stares at the sea; just sitting there."

Dionysus/Osiris, Ariadne/Isis/Philyra, Charon/Set, Hermes/Tehuti.
EGYPTIANS: Nebka, Djoser, Hotep, Khasek, Rocky
NUBIANS: Nima, Hetephe, King Kerma, Prince T'jaru, Prince Rafah.
CANAANITES: Phoenicia, Serket, Azazil, Jaffa | URFANS: Teumessian, Abram, Sarai, Terah

Djoser walked with Abram to the solitary figure "just sitting there." He sat beside Horus but did not speak.

Eventually, Horus said, "Father told me Hathor invented 'The Word of Isis' from only her imagination. That she told and wove the story until people believed it."

"Yes. That's true. I was there."

"Hathor told the story so often that the story became true."

"In her mind and the mind of the masses. Yes."

"She invented the lie about my father becoming 'King of the Dead' and her calling him forth as the sun each morning to become Ra."

"She did."

"In the end, she believed all her lies to be true. Even today, there is no doubt in her mind that her lies are truth."

"She no longer even questions it."

"Oceanus had a chance to kill the Olympians before they began. He waited. What *should* he have done?"

"He made the best decision he could. Whatever he decided was correct."

"I could have Set killed and yet I wait. What would Kiya have me do?

"Your duty."

Horus laughed a bitter laugh. "It is only a small lie. Less than Hathor's."

"Yes. Everyone must now obey you; even kings and queens and princes."

"It is the only way. When we arrive in Jaffa, my first commandment will be that Prince Djoser will obey no living god but me. Too, your family. Can you do this thing?"

"I have no choice. I may have a problem in the future; like if Set kills you or something. Someone needs to establish that the King of Egypt obeys no one but Osiris and everyone must obey the King of Egypt. But in the meantime, do you think you can handle this being a god thing?"

"Hathor was born a simple gutter girl. I can handle 'this being a god thing.' Can you handle it, young Abram?"

EGYPTIAN GODS: Osiris/Dionysus—Isis/Ariadne/Philyra, Horus, Set/Charon, Nephthys/Dexithea.
CANAANITE GODS: Anath, Astarte, Shalem, Shahar, Moloch, El.
OLYMPIAN GODS: Zeus, Dionysus, Hestia, Ares, Athena, Astraeus, Eos, Hermes.
OCEANIDS: Polydore, Lyris, Acaste, Eidyia, Dione.

Abram was shocked to be addressed in the midst of these deep discussions. "M-me Great Shaman Horus? What difference what I think?"

Horus spoke sharply, "You are the future of civilization, Abram. I will die and turn to dust. I will live on only through you and your words. What will you say of me?"

"I will say the words you have taught me and all you have done and all things I have seen and experienced. I shall say what is right to say. Great Teacher."

"Call me God Horus."

"Yes, God Horus."

The three remained on the beach for a while—"just sitting there."

Dionysus/Osiris, Ariadne/Isis/Philyra, Charon/Set, Hermes/Tehuti.
EGYPTIANS: Nebka, Djoser, Hotep, Khasek, Rocky
NUBIANS: Nima, Hetephe, King Kerma, Prince T'jaru, Prince Rafah.
CANAANITES: Phoenicia, Serket, Azazil, Jaffa | URFANS: Teumessian, Abram, Sarai, Terah

18. The Penultimate Contesting

Polydore and Astarte

They sat at the table. Polydore drank a Bitter. Astarte drank a Sweet. Jaffa the Eighteenth lay on his bed, exhausted.

The two women had become confidants and had shared their professional love-making techniques. Each had become the better for the knowing. Jaffa was the great beneficiary. Polydore lay with Jaffa because it was her duty; Astarte, because he was a path to power.

They chattered with one another.

Astarte: "God Set is so sad. He may do something bad."
Polydore: "Why is that and what?"
Astarte: "Have you not heard that Horus is now proclaimed a greater god than either my sister or Set? Horus is said to be a god greater than the gods of old. The word is in everyone's mouth."
Polydore: "Serket said something this morning about Horus being pleased with her. She had eaten morning meal with his friend, Azazil. Is there more happening?"
Astarte: "Oh, yes! Azazil and the disciples of God Horus are spreading the Gospel of Shaman Horus becoming the supreme living god."
Polydore: "Who anointed him?"
Astarte: "They don't say, but he traveled to the ancient city of Urfa and had all manner of adventures. I imagine it happened there."
Polydore: "I would imagine. What does Set plan to do? Why is it sad?"
Astarte: "I probably shouldn't be telling his plans. Anath and Set forget that I am around sometimes. I'm such a fixture at their place. Set is losing his interest in Anath. She usually needs me to help with him. But Set heard the gospel of Horus and was furious. So, they made a plan."
Polydore: "What's their plan?"
Astarte: "I can't share their private discussion, Polly."

Polydore leaned across the table, placed her fingers on Astarte's cheek, pulled Astarte's face to within an inch of her own, and drippingly said, "We are Consort Sisters. Tell me!"

"Astarte pulled back, and with exasperation said, "Very well! But just because you won't tell anyone!"

Polly listened with fascination.

EGYPTIAN GODS: Osiris/Dionysus—Isis/Ariadne/Philyra, Horus, Set/Charon, Nephthys/Dexithea.
CANAANITE GODS: Anath, Astarte, Shalem, Shahar, Moloch, El.
OLYMPIAN GODS: Zeus, Dionysus, Hestia, Ares, Athena, Astraeus, Eos, Hermes.
OCEANIDS: Polydore, Lyris, Acaste, Eidyia, Dione.

After hearing Set's plan, Polydore asked, "Can you get me some of that cave-mushroom sweetbread? I may want to experiment with Jaffa. It sounds like it might turn him into Jaffa the First!"

~

And so …

God Horus triumphantly entered the City of Jaffa! He wore a purple cloak and a crown of flowers holding a staff given to him by the highest Shaman in Byblos. Abram marched on one side, and Baalat, dressed in white and wearing a necklace of flowers, marched on his other. Two dozen disciples followed behind; four dozen disciples waited in the city. Behind the disciples came Nubian Archer Hetephe, in her old army uniform, riding upon a horse. And behind her, Prince Djoser of Egypt, riding a great stallion. Following faithfully behind were three more horses. All horses wore garlands. All had been promised apples.

Polydor provided a reception to greet the arrival of Horus, the greatest living god. Jaffa the Eighteenth, sober and chiefly looking, stood between his two consorts, dressed in full finery.

Behind them, stood God Set and God Anath. Polydore, with the wisdom of an Oceanid, the scheming of a prince, and the shared secrets of women, decided hers would be the very best plan. She had suggested to the two resident living gods that if they were quick enough and warm in their greeting, God Horus wouldn't have enough time to *command* them to do anything. Anath, not competing with anybody, thought that to be the gracious thing to do. Set, in death-battle competition with Horus, considered the possibilities.

When Horus arrived, Polydore bowed deeply, held out both hands, and leaned in to kiss him on his right cheek. She whispered, "We need to talk." She then leaned in to kiss his other cheek and whispered, "Greet them both with respect."

God Horus nodded in Godly acknowledgment and then moved to bless Jaffa the Eighteenth.

Approaching Horus, Set fell to one knee, placed his forehead on Horus's hand, rose, and loudly proclaimed, "I salute you great God Horus, greatest of the living gods. You learned all that I taught you well! You are a worthy son to Osiris and the Bit … Isis. I look forward to helping and advising you any way I can." *"Greet them both with respect."*

Horus did not speak. Instead, he leaned over, embraced Set, smiled, and acknowledged Set's words with a Godly nod. Then he took Anath's hands, brought them to his lips, and kissed her fingers; a little too long. Anath's heart fluttered.

Set said, "Nephew, when all your festivities are over, bring your lovely woman to my place and have evening meal with Anath and me. We have so much to catch up on. I want to hear about how you did this thing. Will you dine with me, Nephew?"

"Of course, Great God Set. Tomorrow evening at sunset. I and Serket look forward to it."

Next, Horus moved to Djoser and proclaimed for all to hear, "I supreme Living God Horus command you, Prince Djoser of Egypt and your kin, to obey no living god but me!"

His glorious day of coming continued.

The Plan

Djoser, Hetephe, and Polydore sat on the beach, a small fire behind them.

Polydore took a container of sweetbread from her basket. "Well, here we have it. Set's plan to glory. He intends to feed cave-mushroom sweetbread to Horus and Serket at tomorrow's meal. Set will have his way with Horus first, and, then his sweet revenge with Serket as Horus happily cheers him on. But what he will really have is his seed inside Horus's body. He will present this fact to Hathor and the other powers that be. Horus will be stripped of all power and be made the vassal of God Set. A simple plan; good and effective.

Hetephe asked, "What do these sweetbreads do?"

Djoser replied, "For one thing, you feel no pain when a woman pulls your eye out and throws you onto rocks. Osiris spoke of these things. He ate them in his youth at Tallstone trying to find the land of the dead. It's powerful stuff. Eat it and go to lands beyond our imagination. I can believe that Set can make Horus and Serket do anything Set wants them to do."

"I want to eat one!"

EGYPTIAN GODS: Osiris/Dionysus—Isis/Ariadne/Philyra, Horus, Set/Charon, Nephthys/Dexithea.
CANAANITE GODS: Anath, Astarte, Shalem, Shahar, Moloch, El.
OLYMPIAN GODS: Zeus, Dionysus, Hestia, Ares, Athena, Astraeus, Eos, Hermes.
OCEANIDS: Polydore, Lyris, Acaste, Eidyia, Dione.

233

"That would not be wise, Hete. We don't know what we are dealing with. Horus, at least, had the experience when Anath took his eye out. That is the only first-hand experience we have to go on."

"His eye was removed, and he doesn't even remember it. He won't provide any good intelligence. But very well, I will eat only half of one. I may be able to remember it but you two can observe what I will and won't do. I'll let you know if I had fun or not!"

Polydore said, "We should wait on Horus and Serket. We need to work together on this."

"They are going to be a while yet. Besides, I may be fully recovered by the time they get here plus I may do or say things that would embarrass me in front of Serket. A quarter of one! Give it to me!"

Polydore and Djoser looked at one another. Djoser suggested, "Half a quarter of one. We can test her tolerance for pain and receptiveness to suggestions. That will be a little knowledge. We can save the big questions for Horus and Serket."

Polydore broke a sweetbread in half, in half again, and in half again. She handed one piece to Hetephe. "I will protect you, Hete."

Hetephe ate the sweetbread, waited, and said, "I need more."

Djoser said, "All the better. We can find out how much you must eat before it affects you. Wait a few minutes and eat another piece."

Hetephe sat back down on the beach, looked up at the moon, and said, "That's the biggest target I have ever seen."

Djoser handed her an imaginary bow and arrow and said, "Hit it looking back between your legs!"

Hetephe accepted the imaginary bow and arrow, ran to the beach, bent over with her bottom toward the moon, and loosed her imaginary arrow between her legs toward the moon. She followed the path of the imaginary arrow until she fell over onto the beach giggling with delight. Djoser rose, lifted Hetephe to her feet, and slapped her hard across both cheeks. She laughed hysterically and said, "I didn't know you enjoyed rough foreplay, Big Man. Here, let me show you rough foreplay. She attacked him trying to remove his clothes."

Polydore commanded, "Archer Hete. Make love to the sea!"

Hete stopped, turned around to look at the sea, and frantically asked, I don't see its penis! Where's its penis?!"

Polydore said, "The sea is not a man, Hete. Go lie down in the surf and let her wash over you."

Hetephe ran toward Middlesea, strewing her clothes as she ran. She lay down in the tide and let the sea embrace her.

Polydore said, "You may not want to witness this, Prince. I will protect her if you wish to leave."

He looked at Hete, writhing in the tide, soft sounds coming from her throat, and said, "This is a private time for her. I don't wish to violate her privacy. Protect her, Polydore, while she cannot protect herself."

He rose and walked off down the beach to wait for the arrival of Horus and Serket.

Polydore looked at Hete, rolling in ecstasy. *You would have been a fine Oceanid, Lord Hetephe.*

~

Horus, Serket, and the young followers found Djoser waiting on the beach. Djoser said to Horus, "Perhaps Abram and Baalat could explore the city on their own tonight, God Horus."

Horus said to Baalat, "You and Abram tour the city but stay alert. There are many here who would hurt you. Protect each other and carry daggers."

The two students scurried off, proud that they were being treated as responsible adults.

As the three walked back down the beach, Djoser explained the coming problem as he nervously looked to see if Hete remained in the tide. He was relieved to see two figures sitting side by side.

As they approached, Hete saw Djoser and ran, only half dressed, to jump on him, her legs wrapping around his body. She nuzzled his neck, saying, "I know exactly what I'm doing Immature Boy. I just don't care who sees it or what they think. You have an ibis head on you somewhere. I know you do. Let's go find it."

EGYPTIAN GODS: Osiris/Dionysus—Isis/Ariadne/Philyra, Horus, Set/Charon, Nephthys/Dexithea.
CANAANITE GODS: Anath, Astarte, Shalem, Shahar, Moloch, El.
OLYMPIAN GODS: Zeus, Dionysus, Hestia, Ares, Athena, Astraeus, Eos, Hermes.
OCEANIDS: Polydore, Lyris, Acaste, Eidyia, Dione.

Djoser just kept walking down the beach with Hetephe pawing his body. He said, as he walked, "Serket, this is what Set plans for you to do to him after you eat his sweetbread tomorrow night."

Polydore presented the plan. The plan revolved around Serket and her actions. Polydore held Serket's full attention. Both Djoser and Horus were suspect that Serket could ever do any of these things. Neither had any idea of what a sweet unassuming little hen would do to protect her nest.

The Cabbage

They arrived at sunset. Phoenicia answered the door. "Good evening honored guests. Come in. Set and Anath have been waiting for your gracious arrival." A woman from the port café brought each a glass of fine wine and led them to a sitting parlor. Anath gushed in. "Welcome to our home. Phoenicia volunteered to prepare her most delicious meal for us to end with wonderful, delicious sweetbreads made with my very own recipe. Fine wine, fine friends, and fine conversation. We are going to have a night to remember."

Serket gushed, "Yes, we are. And I will do everything I can possibly do to make Set's night memorable!" *Polydore's Oceanid outfit I wear is so revealing. I can't believe Oceanids wore these things everywhere.*

Anath smiled. *You didn't even fight for me, Love. After tonight, you are going to be so low on the man scale that you may fall off completely.*

Set walked in and saw Serket sitting there in her translucent form-fitting dress. He was mesmerized. He had intended to closely monitor the kitchen to make sure the two platters of sweetbreads weren't inadvertently interchanged. *Ah, you really did want me to take you that day I found you alone. You just weren't brave enough yet to let me do it! I knew it!*

Phoenicia and her helper happily worked away in the kitchen preparing a delicious meal. *Very good, God Anath. I believe you said the platter with the beautiful flower must be served to your guests and the one without the flower must be served to you and God Set. And then I and my staff must leave immediately after serving sweetbread and wine. Very good. But it would be so much prettier if I took the flower from this platter of sweetbread and put it on this platter.—There! That does look better.*

Fine conversation ensued. Who knew that Set could be so gracious?

Dionysus/Osiris, Ariadne/Isis/Philyra, Charon/Set, Hermes/Tehuti.
EGYPTIANS: Nebka, Djoser, Hotep, Khasek, Rocky
NUBIANS: Nima, Hetephe, King Kerma, Prince T'jaru, Prince Rafah.
CANAANITES: Phoenicia, Serket, Azazil, Jaffa | URFANS: Teumessian, Abram, Sarai, Terah

Horus knew. He had been sparring with his uncle all his life. The Competitions. The derogatory comments. Set could be anything Set needed to be necessary to achieve his goals. Anything!

Serket carefully sipped her wine as she chattered with Set. It was hard to believe Set had any dishonorable intentions. She wore this little almost-see-through thing because Polydore told her to, Djoser encouraged her to, and Horus said she should; but sitting here in her almost-see-through tunic, warmed with wine, she thought she could handle anything. Nothing bad could happen.

And then she remembered, *"Serket, this is what Set plans for you to do with him after you eat his sweetbreads tomorrow night."*

The main meal over, Phoenicia refilled wine glasses, and announced, "Here come the sweetbreads."

The sweetbreads arrived.

Serket accidentally spilled water on the front of her tunic; converting it from almost-see-through to see-through. She laughed. "Oh, how clumsy of me. I'm glad no one is here to see me other than my dearest friends."

The attendant set two plates of sweetbreads on the table. Anath remembered to ensure her guests received the sweetbreads from the flowered platter. The attendant spoke to Horus, "Your sweetbreads have been inspected and approved by the cook. Enjoy!"

Almost salivating, Set exclaimed, "Now, Servants, leave us to our merriment!"

Phoenicia replied, "Yes, Great God Set. It has been our pleasure to serve you. There will be a delicious breakfast cabbage waiting to delight you in the morning. Good night."

Phoenicia and her assistant let themselves out, greeted Djoser and Hetephe waiting outside the door, said, "All is going exactly as planned," and happily scurried back to their quarters. *I can't wait to hear about this.*

~

Horus shared wine with Serket, picked up a sweetbread, offered it to Set, and said, "Let's sweeten the evening."

Set picked up a sweetbread from his own plate and said, "I have my own! Come, God Anath. Let's eat our sweetbreads as our guests eat theirs."

EGYPTIAN GODS: Osiris/Dionysus—Isis/Ariadne/Philyra, Horus, Set/Charon, Nephthys/Dexithea.
CANAANITE GODS: Anath, Astarte, Shalem, Shahar, Moloch, El.
OLYMPIAN GODS: Zeus, Dionysus, Hestia, Ares, Athena, Astraeus, Eos, Hermes.
OCEANIDS: Polydore, Lyris, Acaste, Eidyia, Dione.

Set and Anath made a show of eating their sweetbreads and demanded their guests join them. Horus enthusiastically ate his. "Your sweetbreads are delicious, Anath. I will have another if Set joins me."

Anath laughed. "Oh, Set will join you, Horus. Eat another, Set. Let's get our guest ready for his joining!"

Serket said, "Will you have another, Anath? If you will, I certainly will!"

Serket said, they really are delicious, if you each eat your last one, I will take this wet tunic off!"

Set and Anath looked at one another, smiled, and devoured their last sweetbread. The effects had already begun and would grow more severe.

Serket looked at Set and sweetly asked, "Will you take Horus first so that I may lay naked on his back and watch you as you enter his body?"

Set was no longer in the room. He was in clouds somewhere. *His whore wishes to watch me as I sodomize her male. I am all-powerful. All desirable. I am a man. Horus is an impotent boy!*

Anath was excited. Somewhere she heard something like, "Do you have ointments so that Set's entry into Horus will be pleasurable?" *Ointments? I am Anath—I have ointments for everything. I will get us some and we can both watch the humiliation of Horus. We can both apply ointments to Set and fondle him while he dominates Horus!*

Serket, seeing things were going as planned, walked to the door, and let Djoser and Hetephe enter to stand in the shadows as witnesses. Hetephe handed Serket a cabbage and a red blanket.

Serket took a deep breath. *Grandfather—these people are different—I do what I must do. Please do not judge me—It will be best not to look.*

Serket removed her tunic, walked to Horus, and removed his clothes. Horus leaned over the table, presenting his rear to Set. Serket climbed onto the table and lay, face down, naked on his back, looking at Set.

"Hurry Anath, bring the ointments. Prepare Set to plow my husband while I watch!" She had never referred to Horus as her husband before. *I hope he doesn't mind. This is getting me excited!—Grandfather, forgive me!"*

Set floated down from his clouds leaving Philyra there begging him not to leave. He sensed Anath run up to him and begin applying ointments to his erect penis.

Anath heard the command for her to stand behind Set and rub his shoulders to help him as Serket guided Set's penis into her husband's waiting body. Both Set and Anath were in their different worlds with colors and sounds swirling around them; through them, over them. They could not see but the voices kept telling them that they were doing glorious things.

The voice told Set to put his hands on Serket's head as he plowed Horus. "Here, I will guide your penis into his waiting body! You are magnificent!"

Serket placed both of Set's hands on her head, made sure Anath was standing behind Set messaging his shoulders, took the cabbage, oriented it so that the hole was properly positioned, held her breath, seized Set's penis, stroked it several times, guided it into the cabbage, and began moaning like Phoenicia had taught her to do.

Horus added a few grunts to the festivities. *My sweet, innocent Serket, you are a world-class weapon of war. Mother Nephthys is going to be so proud of you. The two of you could hire yourselves out to destroy countries. You called me "husband."*

He reached above his head, found her ankles, and gently messaged them. *I love you.*

Serket was keeping all the balls in the air, so to speak. It was hard work keeping the cabbage positioned and she would sometimes have to help Set and she was supposed to moan and things. All the while keeping Set and Anath preoccupied so that they would not notice Set was humping a cabbage instead of Horus. And now, the love of her life was tenderly messaging her ankles. *This moan is for you, my husband.*

All the sounds emanating from the women were turning into mountains flying through the sky penetrating the soul of the colors wrapping themselves around the bodies of armies shouting "Plow her, plow her" on a mountain of red warrior bodies lying beneath the glory and power of mighty gods flying through the sky surrounded by adoring masses of screaming colors. Colors shouting, "I am Set, mighty conqueror of all things, lover of Philyra, dominator of Horus, builder of mountains, admired by all people; praised, glorious."

Set released himself. Somewhere a voice said, "Rest, while I prepare my wife so you can plow her while I watch."

Serket confirmed that she really had Set's semen inside the cabbage, quickly rose, got Horus out of the way, spread the red blanket across the

EGYPTIAN GODS: Osiris/Dionysus—Isis/Ariadne/Philyra, Horus, Set/Charon, Nephthys/Dexithea.
CANAANITE GODS: Anath, Astarte, Shalem, Shahar, Moloch, El.
OLYMPIAN GODS: Zeus, Dionysus, Hestia, Ares, Athena, Astraeus, Eos, Hermes.
OCEANIDS: Polydore, Lyris, Acaste, Eidyia, Dione.

table, went to Anath, led her to the blanket, and whispered, "Look, Dispatcher Anath. Dead warriors. A mountain of dead warriors. The gods cry out for you to lie upon them and fornicate for their glory. Hurry. I will get someone for you!"

Upon rising, Horus walked to Set and whispered, "I will get Serket for you. I will lay her down on this table so you can plow her. I want to watch you while you plow her!"

But it was Anath that lay upon the table. Serket guided Set into Anath. The colors of Anath's emotions were an ode sung by a thousand Oceanids.

Before she dressed, Serket went to the kitchen with the cabbage. She motioned Djoser and Hetephe to witness the making of the breakfast salad which was a semen-filled cabbage garnished with condiments and a dressing. Satisfied, she dressed and joined Horus.

He said to her, "You bring me peace. I love you."

She replied, "You bring me peace. I will not leave you until you do not return to me."

They left and returned to sit on the shore of Middlesea.

Djoser and Hetephe remained behind, their arms around each other, standing close. They watched the unfolding majesty of gods flying through the firmament on glory-colored carpets.

Too, unseen on a high shelf, watched the "Eye of Horus"—seeing all.

Sunrise

Horus thought it best not to stay in Serket's quarters as long as such notoriety surrounded him. Azazil had set up their camp in a secluded area of public space.

Living God Horus performed the sunrise ceremony with more pomp and ritual than usual. Azazil was inspired by the new-found authority of his god. His congregation had grown. Abram and Baalat sat beside their teacher as he taught his word. Everyone was pleased but Horus, who felt a little more of himself slipping into some kind of black pit. *Serket— Father—Mother Nephthys—Mother Hathor—I need you.*

Horus took his morning meal on the beach surrounded by his disciples and the curious. Baalat served him food and drink. Azazil and Abram

Dionysus/Osiris, Ariadne/Isis/Philyra, Charon/Set, Hermes/Tehuti.
EGYPTIANS: Nebka, Djoser, Hotep, Khasek, Rocky
NUBIANS: Nima, Hetephe, King Kerma, Prince T'jaru, Prince Rafah.
CANAANITES: Phoenicia, Serket, Azazil, Jaffa | URFANS: Teumessian, Abram, Sarai, Terah

walked through the visiting multitude answering questions and providing bread to the hungry. Djoser and Hetephe stood at the edge of the crowd silently watching.

Finally, Horus left the gathering, went to his tent, and collapsed onto his makeshift chair. He was exhausted from a long intense night and highly structured morning; all piled on top of his newly self-appointed godhood.

Azazil led Djoser, Hetephe, and Serket into the tent.

Horus rose and embraced Serket. "We said words last night that need discussing."

She stepped back from his embrace, took his hands, and said, "That you love me? That you bring me Peace? Are those the words, Horus? Don't be concerned. I, Serket of Rusalem love you, Horus, but you owe me nothing. You are not in bondage to me. You will always do what you must do. My love will be with you no matter where you are, no matter what you are doing. I think and speak of you as my husband. But I need not be called your wife. Are those the words that need saying, Horus?"

He embraced her, buried his face into her tunic, and sobbed. After a moment, he said, "We had an exciting night didn't we, Serket?"

Serket asked, "Who would have thought a little girl from Rusalem could do all those things? Are you proud of me?"

Djoser laughed. "Both of you were superb. That was the most enjoyable spectacle I have ever seen. Perhaps Set and Anath would agree to perform it again in a stadium filled with the people of Jaffa; maybe even Memphis."

Horus sat back down and pulled Serket into his lap. "I doubt it, but now what? Azazil and I will work on this living god personae but what is it we need to accomplish, and did we accomplish what we needed to?"

Djoser became serious. "Yes. Set is now figuring out that his plan didn't work; that you somehow bested him once again. He may be furious; he may be resigned to failing once again. Regardless, I need a plan to eliminate this idea that a living god can command a king. I'm going to discuss it with Hathor. I will propose that when she anoints the next king of Egypt, she also anoints him the supreme Living God of Egypt. That will eliminate that other nonsense."

Azazil suggested, "Have the supreme living god do the anointing. That will add even more legitimacy to the anointing."

EGYPTIAN GODS: Osiris/Dionysus—Isis/Ariadne/Philyra, Horus, Set/Charon, Nephthys/Dexithea.
CANAANITE GODS: Anath, Astarte, Shalem, Shahar, Moloch, El.
OLYMPIAN GODS: Zeus, Dionysus, Hestia, Ares, Athena, Astraeus, Eos, Hermes.
OCEANIDS: Polydore, Lyris, Acaste, Eidyia, Dione.

"Yes, except who legitimizes living god claimants as the supreme one. But that's a good suggestion. I'll discuss it with Hathor. And now, there's a little matter remaining in Byblos that needs to be addressed. Excuse me all. I will be at the port patio."

With that, he held out his hand for Hetephe to join him and they headed out to the port.

19. Oceanid Songs

Djoser and Hetephe walked, first, to Chief Jaffa's headquarters. Chief Jaffa was out inspecting wine houses but his assistant, Polydore, could meet with them. After the exchange of pleasantries, Polydore would be delighted to join them for an early Highsun meal to catch up on non-official business. "I can hardly wait to hear how you handled that little welcome party I told you. That was told in confidence, wasn't it? Astarte would be horrified if she thought I broke a confidence."

Hetephe said, "Oh, assure Astarte that we kept her gossip in complete confidence! Just between us girls! Come as soon as you can. I can't wait to tell you! Invite Astarte to join us! She would love this story!"

Djoser and Hetephe left to get their favorite table at the patio café. They were drinking fine wine when Polydore and Astarte arrived. Astarte was delighted to be invited to eat with the prince! "However are you and Archer Hetephe doing?"

Djoser replied as they sat down, "Oh, I'm afraid, Archer Hete has done a bad thing!"

"Oh? Whatever could that be?"

"Well, Phoenicia catered a major dinner hosted by the great Living Gods Set and Anath. Hetephe showed up to help Phoenicia clean up. As Set's dinner was going on, Phoenicia called Hete back to see the sweetcakes Anath had prepared. One platter had a beautiful flower arrangement on it. While Phoenicia was doing something else, Hete decided the flower would look better on the other platter; so she moved it. Phoenicia was upset with Hete when she found out, and Hete was just trying to help! Life is so unfair, sometimes, isn't it?"

Astarte was sympathetic, "Oh, I'm sure no harm was done. Was it a nice party? They made me leave for the night!"

Hete replied, "Oh, you just wouldn't believe how nice."

As the meal was finishing, Djoser invited Polydore to walk down to the beach with him.

Polydore said, "Whenever I walk on the beach with you, Prince, my life gets more complicated. What do you want this time?"

Djoser replied, "To complicate your life."

EGYPTIAN GODS: Osiris/Dionysus—Isis/Ariadne/Philyra, Horus, Set/Charon, Nephthys/Dexithea.
CANAANITE GODS: Anath, Astarte, Shalem, Shahar, Moloch, El.
OLYMPIAN GODS: Zeus, Dionysus, Hestia, Ares, Athena, Astraeus, Eos, Hermes.
OCEANIDS: Polydore, Lyris, Acaste, Eidyia, Dione.

"Oh, well then, let's walk on the beach."

They walked to the beach and walked on.

He said, "There is an older Oceanid in Byblos."

She said, "Dione?"

"She never told me her name."

"Dione survived the flood."

"Yes, Dione. You know of her?"

"Very little. We never met. The people who survived the inundation never really recovered. Dione was made an Oceanid, but never returned to the water. She turned to too much wine—too many men. She stayed at Els End—Byblos—whatever. Lyris and other Sisters would visit her on their way to Riverport. So now, tell me …"

"Dione watches over your sisters. Horus and I discussed what was appropriate to do with their remains. It was obvious to both of us, that Oceanids should care for their sisters. Dione said she was not worthy. I come to Polydore."

"How many?"

"Many. We believe Lyris, Admete, and Eidyia are there plus the other Riverport Oceanids. The carrying box is full."

Polydore did not speak. She removed her clothes, walked into the surf, dove in, and swam to forever and back.

Djoser stared out over Middlesea after her.

When she returned, she walked from the water, donned her tunic, and said, without slowing down, "You did well, Prince Djoser. I shall do that which is appropriate." She returned to the dock.

Djoser followed.

~

The next morning, Djoser did not attend the Sunrise Ceremony. He sat alone on the Dock Patio sipping a fruit wine concoction.

Dionysus/Osiris, Ariadne/Isis/Philyra, Charon/Set, Hermes/Tehuti.
EGYPTIANS: Nebka, Djoser, Hotep, Khasek, Rocky
NUBIANS: Nima, Hetephe, King Kerma, Prince T'jaru, Prince Rafah.
CANAANITES: Phoenicia, Serket, Azazil, Jaffa | URFANS: Teumessian, Abram, Sarai, Terah

Astarte was the first to drop by the dock to see what was happening. "Prince Djoser! May I join you? Set and Anath kicked me out—and after I helped get God Set calmed down again this morning!"

"He was upset?"

"Yes! And he couldn't even explain why. He was just upset over his party for Horus and Serket. I told him that Serket had spoken highly of the party, but she wondered why they were invited to leave after they ate their sweetbread. But, anyway, they both had a delightful time."

"Oh?"

Astarte said, "Yes. Set was interested in the fact that Hetephe had dropped by and helped out by moving that flower from one platter to another. Anath said, 'Well that explains it!' Set was not happy, but Anath and I did some things to him to make him a little bit happier. I left them talking about what they should do now. People get upset over the strangest things, don't they?"

"Yes, Astarte, they do. Luckily, they have you and me to keep everything moving along."

She laughed her "delighted" laugh.

Soon after, Phoenicia walked by on her way to find Serket. Phoenicia stopped to talk. "Serket has a big project coming her way. Polydore told me that she plans to make trade calls at Byblos and then Alashiya. Serket must retain a ship. Polydore may find traders for some of her shipment, but I think she will return with a ship half-empty. But Assistant-Chief Polydore usually knows what she's doing!"

"Yes, she does," said Djoser.

Serket was not far behind Phoenicia. Serket had left Horus and his followers after the Ceremony had been completed. She joined them and said, "I am so fortunate that Horus always returns to me after his travels. He will always return to me except the day he doesn't. He will be leaving after services in the morning to spread his gospel along the Way of Horus. His followers are so excited. They expect to reach Memphis itself in five or six seasons."

"I will be there when he arrives," Djoser said. "I imagine he will make an appearance at the Winter Solstice Season."

EGYPTIAN GODS: Osiris/Dionysus—Isis/Ariadne/Philyra, Horus, Set/Charon, Nephthys/Dexithea.
CANAANITE GODS: Anath, Astarte, Shalem, Shahar, Moloch, El.
OLYMPIAN GODS: Zeus, Dionysus, Hestia, Ares, Athena, Astraeus, Eos, Hermes.
OCEANIDS: Polydore, Lyris, Acaste, Eidyia, Dione.

Djoser sat at the table with, other than Polydore and Anath, the three most prominent women in Jaffa; Astarte, Phoenicia, and Serket.

The three women talked about how their women trainees would learn and advance and then leave for greater opportunities in the various businesses opening around the city because of the increasing trade. In fact, two of Serket's employees had immigrated to Damascus with a significant increase in responsibility. Men trainees tended to work, collect their wages, and invest in wine and women at the wine houses. Astarte was ecstatic that her students so quickly grasped the fundamentals of being invested in. More and more rural people were immigrating to Jaffa, even from Rusalem and Tophet. The world was changing. Women seemed to be at the forefront.

The women would visit more with Djoser but, unfortunately, they all had pressing business to attend to. "We will see you later, Prince!"

After they departed, Djoser switched from fruit-wine to real wine. *Where are you when I need you, Friend Osiris?*

Horses

Shalom had such a nice time with Djoser the Horse; he was so attentive to her needs. But now she must bid farewell to her new friends. Djoser the Horse and Arrow were needed to carry their people along the Way of Horus so they could visit the people at the various forts. The other three horses would travel with them, but Shalom expected to see everyone periodically as she carried Serket to visit Horus along the road. Apples were usually involved.

The man and woman came and bridled Arrow and Djoser the Horse and mounted them. Arrow was signaled to stand on her hind legs and whiny, which she was always happy to do. Then they were off; their three herd-mates followed.

~

Djoser and Hetephe were greeted with pomp and fanfare when they arrived in Fort Rafah. There was much business to conduct and advice to solicit from both the prince and his consort. Growth was sometimes difficult to manage. Improvements and upgrades were needed in many areas. After the official meetings were concluded, it was suggested that the prince and retired general might want to be entertained with God Set and God Anath; both of whom were in temporary residence in the fort.

Djoser: "What a fine idea! May we invite them to join us at an official dinner?"
Official: "Yes, of course! I will send them invitations and have the cook prepare something special for us!"
Djoser: "Splendid. We look forward to evening meal!"
Hete: "Do you have apples for our horses?"
Official: "Of course, Minor-general. Very fresh apples!"
Hete: "Wonderful. We will see you at sundown! Now, excuse me. I must go find an ibis."
Official: 'I'm so sorry Minor-general, but we don't have ibises along the coast; only seagulls and pelicans."
Hete: "My loss. I always enjoy inspecting local ibises; they grow so large in Canaan, don't they Prince Djoser?"
Djoser: "Not as large as the ones in Abdju, I'm told. But perhaps we can find something to occupy your time until mealtime."
Hete: "Oh, I do love being occupied. Now, let's get out of these busy people's way so they can get to work!"

Hetephe and Djoser rose, bid farewell, and walked to their guest quarters.

~

Hetephe lay nestled in the crook of his arm. "We haven't had a peaceful time alone in a long time. I miss that."

"We have had a lot going on. We still do. It's hard to keep track of who's doing what to whom and where. And we need to stay on top of it."

"I'm so glad you suggested that!"

~

Mealtime came. Djoser greeted Set and Anath. "God Set. How good to see you! Do you have anything you intend to command me to do?!"

Set, ever conscious of who had control, laughed his laugh, and said, "Prince Djoser, we both know that you are commanded by God Horus to obey no god but him. I may be an opportunist, but I am not foolish. Neither I nor Anath can command you, not at this time, anyway. But Anath grows stronger in Canaan, and I am returning to South Memphis and the Western deserts. I hope to continue my growth as a worthy god.

EGYPTIAN GODS: Osiris/Dionysus—Isis/Ariadne/Philyra, Horus, Set/Charon, Nephthys/Dexithea.
CANAANITE GODS: Anath, Astarte, Shalem, Shahar, Moloch, El.
OLYMPIAN GODS: Zeus, Dionysus, Hestia, Ares, Athena, Astraeus, Eos, Hermes.
OCEANIDS: Polydore, Lyris, Acaste, Eidyia, Dione.

Perhaps Horus and I will someday meet as equals and let a contesting decide who is more powerful."

"Perhaps so, God Set. Have you and Horus had a contesting since the Tophet challenge?"

"Ahem. Not one to speak of. Maybe in the future."

"Maybe so. But God Set, as delightful as you are to talk with, you are distracting me from your glorious and powerful companion. How are you, God Anath?"

Glorious?—Powerful?—I do love compliments from powerful men.

"With God Set gone, I will need someone to join me in my Dispatch Ceremonies! Would you be available, Prince Djoser?"

"Well, I don't know, God Anath. Let me ask. What about it, Consort Hetephe? Would I be available for that military duty?"

"Oh, no. God Anath. He would not be available at all. I'm sure you would want someone with bigger credentials. The prince is just too young and immature for such an important role!" Hetephe smiled. "Perhaps God Horus would plow you!"

A chill swept over the gathering.

Djoser quickly interjected, "No, Horus is busy trying to save the world. Now, shall we join our hosts for evening meal? I suspect it will be spectacular considering who our special guests are. God Anath, may I escort you?" He held out his elbow to her.

Hetephe looked sweetly and expectantly at Set who had no choice but to offer his.

Sisters

In the meantime, Polydore's ship anchored off Byblos. A small amount of trade was boated to shore and only one container plus a passenger were returned to the ship. The ship then sailed to a spot southwest of the island of Alashiya. She requested a raft be lowered along with cargo they had picked up in Byblos. She and a woman wearing a purple scarf debarked onto the raft containing the cargo. Then, unbelievably, Assistant-Chief Polydore commanded the ship's captain to set sail for Port Jaffa and leave the two women and cargo alone on the raft. Reluctantly, the Captain did

Dionysus/Osiris, Ariadne/Isis/Philyra, Charon/Set, Hermes/Tehuti.
EGYPTIANS: Nebka, Djoser, Hotep, Khasek, Rocky
NUBIANS: Nima, Hetephe, King Kerma, Prince T'jaru, Prince Rafah.
CANAANITES: Phoenicia, Serket, Azazil, Jaffa | URFANS: Teumessian, Abram, Sarai, Terah

as ordered. He told his crew, "Polydore is an Oceanid. They are different than other people."

As the ship disappeared, Polydor and Dione began singing songs; The Song of Lyris, the Song of Admete; the Song of Eidyia, Ode to the Sky, and the overpowering Ode to the Sea. They sang and laughed, sang and cried, sang and sang their songs. Toward sunset, Polydore faced Dione and asked, "Are you ready, Sister?"

Dione replied, "I am ready, Sister."

She and Dione pushed the coffin into the sea. Polydore embraced Dione as they followed close behind the sinking coffin. They stroked one another's hair as they descended to the ocean floor. Polydore took Dione's purple sash and tied it to the coffin keeping her secure near her sisters. Polydore stroked Dione's hair until Dione no longer reciprocated. She stayed a while longer, still stroking her sister's hair. Then silently said, "Soon, my sisters. I will see you soon," rose to the surface, lifted herself onto the raft, rested, and then dove into Middlesea to begin her long swim to Jaffa.

~

The nights became the days became the seasons.

EGYPTIAN GODS: Osiris/Dionysus—Isis/Ariadne/Philyra, Horus, Set/Charon, Nephthys/Dexithea.
CANAANITE GODS: Anath, Astarte, Shalem, Shahar, Moloch, El.
OLYMPIAN GODS: Zeus, Dionysus, Hestia, Ares, Athena, Astraeus, Eos, Hermes.
OCEANIDS: Polydore, Lyris, Acaste, Eidyia, Dione.

20. The Season of Winter Solstice

Priestess Hathor began the Winter Solstice season by hosting a reception for the king and his family. It was held on the patio of the Mastaba of Osiris and laid out so that the people of Memphis could observe the well-lit, heavily decorated platform with all their dignitaries on show for their pleasure. Amid the decorations and tables piled high with food, near the Mastaba entrance, sat the unadorned table once favored by the living Osirus. Upon the table lay only a crook, a flail, and an Ankh.

At the long table best positioned for the appreciative audience in the streets, revered King Khasek and Queen Nima sat facing their subjects. Across from them, back to the crowds, sat Prince Djoser, Chief Rafah, and General Sanakhte. It was not lost on the crowd that these men were the leading contenders to someday inherit the kingship.

On the right the Priestesses, Priests, and support staff, mingled with proper pomp and regality as they sipped their drinks and sampled the food. On the left, the kingdom officials, including Hotep, Set, and Tehuti, displayed their pomp and dignity as they munched and drank. At the rear, near Osiris's table, Hetephe, Dexithea, Halia, Seshat, Anubis, and Snefru stood laughing and carrying on. Anath and Astarte had a vested interest in all three tangential groups; they flitted around.

Khasek leaned to Nima and loudly whispered, "Our times draw near, my queen. Who shall I name as my successor?"

The table went on high alert. *So, it begins.*

Nima laughed. "Whoever is best suited, my king. Have you considered Archer Hetephe?"

Khasek laughed a genuine laugh. "No, but I may well add her to the list of candidates! What of you, Prince Djoser, would you be a good king?"

He thought, *Ahh. Go first. The embrace of the defeated. Speak first so the others can disembowel you. Oh well. I am resigned.*

He said, "Yes. I would, King Khasek. I am my mother's son and grandson of Chief Kerma. It is in my blood. But Mother is correct. Choose whoever is best suited. Without a doubt, that is Chief Rafah. He would unite the upper and lower kingdoms into a solidified nation. Egypt would be viewed as the most culturally diverse kingdom in the world. We would become a role model for other nations. Your son is more able in the understanding of military matters which is important but even as you were the power behind King Nebka, so world Sanakhte be the power behind King Rafah. I am better suited solving the many small problems facing the kingdom; not facing the larger ones."

Khasek said, "You did not speak with the diplomatic evasiveness of a king, Prince Djoser."

"There, you have it, my king!" Djoser laughed. "It is time to add Hetephe to your list!"

"Perhaps, but what of you, Chief Rafah, what do you say in this matter."

Rafah replied, "I sit between the son of the queen and the son of the king. I hold no illusion of ever becoming King. I will gladly serve the Kingdom of Egypt, whomever the king."

Khasek said, "Spoken like a true diplomat, Chief. And you, General Sanakhte, what say you?"

"I have studied your techniques and decisions and have learned from the best, King Khasek. If I am chosen, I shall endeavor to be the greatest king to ever live!"

Khasek sighed, "I cannot fail when choosing my successor. I am cursed with too many excellent choices." He made a motion to retire for the evening.

Djoser cut in. "My king, there is one small problem you might consider this evening."

Khasek relaxed back into his chair. "That being …?"

Djoser quietly explained the issue of living gods gaining so much power that they could actually command a king and expect obedience.

Khasek considered the issue and quietly asked, "And would one such living god be nearby?"

"Two."

"I see. But I will wager that you have a solution, Prince."

"I have discussed the issue with Priestess Hathor. She has a proposal for your consideration."

"Should I discuss this proposal now or another day?"

EGYPTIAN GODS: Osiris/Dionysus—Isis/Ariadne/Philyra, Horus, Set/Charon, Nephthys/Dexithea.
CANAANITE GODS: Anath, Astarte, Shalem, Shahar, Moloch, El.
OLYMPIAN GODS: Zeus, Dionysus, Hestia, Ares, Athena, Astraeus, Eos, Hermes.
OCEANIDS: Polydore, Lyris, Acaste, Eidyia, Dione.

"A mighty source of the king's power lies in his mastaba. This might be a good time for the Priestess to escort King Khasek to visit God Osiris."

The adoring crowd watched as their king and queen stood and were joined by the High Priestess herself. All watched in awe as the three entered the sacred mastaba of Osiris, King of the Land of the Dead!

The three king candidates stood, talked among themselves, and melted into the festivities.

Djoser joined Hetephe and said, "Hetephe, King of Egypt! How does that sound?"

"Not the title I was hoping for, but I'll give it a try! Why?"

"Mother suggested you someday be crowned the King of Egypt. Nothing special. What title are you hoping for?"

"Don't worry about it!"

They were interrupted when Hotep and Halia joined them. The two brothers and their companions visited until a slightly inebriated Astarte joined their group.

Astarte asked, "So, Halia, what does Hotep think about raising that gigantic penis even higher?"

Halia answered, "Sweet Astarte. You are drunk. That's not something we discuss in polite company!"

Astarte said, "Oh? Mother tells me that all the women in Memphis discuss it every morning. They are so happy when the sun hits the top of that thing. They know another day is about to begin when the sun shines on the top of Osiris's penis. That thing gets first light, you know. I say, make it even taller. It can be seen farther away. Let the women in Ogdoad Town see it and admire it! It's a big thing."

Djoser was incredulous. "The women view the obelisk as a penis?"

Hetephe asked, "What else would we think? It's certainly not a cabbage!"

Djoser and Hotep looked at one another and then at Halia.

Hotep asked Halia, "You have been discussing this 'thing' with Astarte?"

"It's women's talk, Husband. Nothing a man would be interested in."

Astarte chirped in, "That's right! It would make men feel unworthy and we can't have that, especially when they are trying to perform their duty!"

Hotep: "Unworthy? Do you mean women are aware of these things?"
Astarte: "Only when we are looking around deciding who to mate with!"
Djoser: "Women judge us on that?!"
Hetephe: "Not exactly. It doesn't matter most of the time."
Djoser: "It matters some of the time?"
Halia: "You men are making too much of this."
Djoser: "I am beginning to understand why those Urfa men don't want their wives to know about other men."

Halia snapped, "We are talking about God Osiris. He is a god. He can have a big penis. Let's drop this disgusting subject!"

Hotep glanced at the Mastaba with the obelisk on top of it. "It *does* appear to be rising out of his mastaba, I suppose."

Djoser offered, "If you add another level, you could raise the obelisk even higher, and the women would start saying, 'Isis is inspiring him!' "

Hetephe said, "The women of Egypt are inspiring him! He loves us so!"

"Or, it is a new Winter Solstice, Osiris grows stronger, each year!"

The conversation once more degenerated into the discussion of the pros and cons of sexual organs and the best use of them including influencing the people of Egypt. It was probably the wine.

Eventually, Djoser asked, "So, Hete, what title were you hoping for?"

She gave him a look of disgust.

Winter Solstice, Year 155

Shalom arrived in Memphis the morning before the coming calling of the Winter Solstice sun. Arrow and Djoser the Horse were overjoyed to see her. There were apples.

Horus and Serket visited his Mother Nephthys, and his many friends gathered in Memphis for the yearly ceremony. South Memphis bustled with seasonal attitudes and fellowship. Many had already forgotten the despair and hopelessness of the city before the coming of Set and his bringing forth the House of Ishtar and all that came after it. This, however, was something of which Mother Nephthys, who some referred to as a living god, continually reminded her people. Nephthys was the

EGYPTIAN GODS: Osiris/Dionysus—Isis/Ariadne/Philyra, Horus, Set/Charon, Nephthys/Dexithea.
CANAANITE GODS: Anath, Astarte, Shalem, Shahar, Moloch, El.
OLYMPIAN GODS: Zeus, Dionysus, Hestia, Ares, Athena, Astraeus, Eos, Hermes.
OCEANIDS: Polydore, Lyris, Acaste, Eidyia, Dione.

good wife and good steward even if her husband roamed the countryside plowing, or in the current, more genteel nomenclature, humped—any person who could advance his power and godhood. Nephthys was content with the station in life she had achieved—even if her mind sometimes enjoyed remembering her days of glory.

Nephthys was overwhelmed with joy when Horus introduced Serket as his wife. She insisted Serket go into detail about the ceremony performed by her grandfather in the village of Rusalem at sunset and how they had talked throughout the entire night watching the children play across the sky. Serket blushed when she told the part of the next morning when she insisted that the entire village witness the sunrise consummation of her marriage. "No one in Rusalem had ever heard of anything like that! They all thought it an act best performed in the privacy of one's home. I shocked everyone by insisting they be a witness—but Grandfather approved. I told him that it was not *always* inappropriate and that I wanted to show Horus that I could be as sophisticated as those high-born women from Memphis. I enjoyed it more than I thought I would. Everyone was so nice and complimentary about it!"

Dexithea shared stories of her youth. The two debated the desirability of "peace" versus the experience of "excitement."

Horus felt a degree of happiness as he listened to his mother and wife lost in the common sea of women's joy.

~

So came the time for the rising of the sun on Winter Solstice Day.

Horus stood with the dignitaries so that his wife could have the heady experience of standing with world powers and witnessing the most important event in the world.

Serket was overwhelmed. Horus was underwhelmed.

Horus *did* note the changes Hathor had made in the ritual. This season, she and her priestesses and priests stood on the roof of the mastaba; the highest point they could access. As usual, they stood, in their royal garb, facing the crowd except, in this ritual, Hathor stood with her back to the crowd, facing the obelisk. And, curiously, King Khasek sat in a high back chair directly in front of the obelisk. Hathor was staring at the obelisk.

Suddenly, the top of the obelisk reflected the brilliance of the sun. *Was that a collective sigh from the street?*

He continued to study Hathor as the reflection from the sun slowly crept down the obelisk. Suddenly Hathor turned, stepped forward, and with raised arms, greeted the sun exactly the moment it breached the horizon. The ceremony began! *Good timing, Mother! How did you know when to turn?*

It was glorious. Five women and one man fainted.

After it was completed, Hathor's yearly reception on the patio of Osiris's mastaba began. Before she joined the festivities, she went to Osiris, laid her head on his chest, and sobbed. *You have lifted me to the highest of the high— if you cast me down, still I shall sing your praises until I am no more—but you said you would not cast me down. I pray that I am worthy. I have been the best priestess I know how to be. My Friend—My Lord—My God—Make me worthy!*

She rested for a moment, rose, put on her hostess face, and left to lead the festivities of another happy new year.

Horus held back, giving Hathor time to greet the king, queen, and other dignitaries.

He then took Serket and greeted High Priestess Hathor. He said, "Mother, this is my wife—Serket of Rusalem and Jaffa."

Hathor asked, "Is the boy worthy of you, Serket of Rusalem?"

Serket replied, "Mightily, Great Mother. He brings light where there is darkness and peace where there is chaos."

 "Welcome to my Heart, Sweet Serket." Hathor grasped Serket by her shoulders and kissed her on both cheeks. "We will visit and share stories after the madness." She turned and strode off to visit Egyptian officials.

Much later, Horus sat by candlelight next to the body of his father, talking to him. Serket stood by his side, listening.

Horus said, "It is worse than you could imagine, Father. The evil you unleashed with Teumessian is spreading across the lands. Their teachings inundate Canaan and the eastern cities. My disciples cleanse our trade route of their teachings, and all along the route honor the gods of Egypt. But in cleansing it, I have become a bad thing. I live a lie and teach lies. My life is a lie. I teach that you and mother are gods, and I know full well—you are dead. I know full well, too, that there are no gods, nor were

EGYPTIAN GODS: Osiris/Dionysus—Isis/Ariadne/Philyra, Horus, Set/Charon, Nephthys/Dexithea.
CANAANITE GODS: Anath, Astarte, Shalem, Shahar, Moloch, El.
OLYMPIAN GODS: Zeus, Dionysus, Hestia, Ares, Athena, Astraeus, Eos, Hermes.
OCEANIDS: Polydore, Lyris, Acaste, Eidyia, Dione.

there ever, only legends of people who called themselves gods and a land full of ambitious, arrogant fools who call themselves gods and a land full of ignorant people who need there to be gods. The words I teach fall on ears that cannot hear; the 'Path of Kiya' and the 'Path of Osiris' are 'hoo-rahed' and then they say 'Now, tell us of the gods.' "

Hathor, arriving, had stood in the shadows near the door, listening. Finally, she walked to Serket and said, "He was a dark child from the beginning. I would come to him bathed in sunlight carrying moonbeams in both hands. Horus would find the darkness between my toes. But he is sweet, isn't he? He needed me—now you—so badly. He is what makes us whole. And we, him. Come with me, my daughter. We shall talk of many things."

Serket rose and left with Hathor to walk and talk of many things.

Sunrise

Horus and Serket watched the ceremony by the river, behind the still massive crowd, which was mesmerized by every word, every gesture. He stood with his arms wrapped around Serket; his cheek pressed against her head. He did not listen. He was lost in remembrance of time past.

Horus had asked his father, "The sun is not the light you wait for, is it, Father?"

"-- *breathe*—no—*breathe*—the light I wait for is—*breathe*—The One—*breathe*—The All—*breathe*—Each Thing—*breathe*—All Things—*breathe*—you have only to die to join it—*breathe*—it is a place without time—*breathe*—call it the land of the dead if you wish—*breathe*—but it is really—*breathe*—the land of the living—*breathe*—Ariadne waits for me there—*breathe*—I have only to release this body from my service—*breathe*—I long for my release—*breathe*—to join The One—*breathe*—"

"Tell Mother I love her."

"-- *breathe*—I will—*breathe*—"

"I love *you*."

"-- *breathe*—as I you—*breathe*—"

Horus had stood holding the wine-red pillow.

"Love is hard."

Dionysus/Osiris, Ariadne/Isis/Philyra, Charon/Set, Hermes/Tehuti.
EGYPTIANS: Nebka, Djoser, Hotep, Khasek, Rocky
NUBIANS: Nima, Hetephe, King Kerma, Prince T'jaru, Prince Rafah.
CANAANITES: Phoenicia, Serket, Azazil, Jaffa | URFANS: Teumessian, Abram, Sarai, Terah

"'*-- breathe*—I know—*bre…*'"

Back in the moment, Horus choked back a sob.

Serket patted his hand. "It's all right, Horus. You did right. You honored your father, and he rejoiced in the honoring."

Horus said, "He didn't even jerk; hardly at all."

Horus wept.

~

After the ceremony, Horus sent Serket to join the others at the Mastaba. "If you see Djoser, tell him where I am."

Horus enjoyed walking along the river, watching the crowd honoring his father and mother. *Father, I never knew Mother. Mother Dexithea says she was a better person than you. That her love for you was greater than the Ocean she so loved. That her unbendable will did not allow her to profess her love for you until she was cast down from on-high by the gods themselves. That she breathed life back into your dead body. Does Mother Dexi remember well or remember things that never were? And does it matter? Are you a god? Do you still live but in the Land of the Dead? I am no closer to finding you than the day I was born. Oh, and I just realized, I killed you too, didn't I, Mother? Along with Father—"Horus, bringer of death"—"Horus, bringer of lies!"—I am nothing!*

Djoser found him. "Hello, Son. Your Aunt Amphitrite would tell you that when you finish rolling around in it, to make a plan. You make good plans!"

"You lie, Uncle. That's what she said to Father; not to me."

"Only because she's not standing here. Obey her, anyway. Are Abram and Baalat learning your teachings well?"

"Yes. They are lost in the crowd somewhere; taking care of each other. They listen to my words but speak my words mixed with their own experience. The Path of Kiya somehow always includes gods in their telling. But still, they understand the need to lift those who have fallen; to give to those in need; to not judge others based on their own beliefs. Even Azazil mixes in Father every now and then—for emphasis, he says. After the Festival ends, we will go to Canaan and counter the Teumessian missionary teachings. There is much to be done. Baalat knows all the missionaries and visits them when we cross paths. She tells them everything I do even as she is finding out everything they are doing. They are now teaching against human sacrifice for the Fertility rites. A large victory for us even as she fulfills her commitment to the Kyrios Olon in Urfa. She continues to learn the path of righteousness. She will be a good teacher to the Phoenicians. I noticed Hathor rearranged the presentation since I last saw it."

"Yes, she added some new features—looking into the future. Did you know that women view the obelisk as a giant penis?"

"No. But now that you mention it, it *is* rising out of the Mastaba in a suggestive way."

"Well, apparently the women in Memphis see it that way. And first light hits the top of it even before the sun breaks over the horizon. I am told they watch the light slowly slide down the obelisk. I'm not one to miss an opportunity to impress my subjects. Hotep is going to add another level to Osiris's Mastaba every year to be completed by the Winters Solstice. He is going to ask Set to help him figure out a way the obelisk can be raised and stabilized in the darkness before the sun rises. Get it? Winter Solstice—Osiris rises higher in the sky; the obelisk rises higher each solstice. I think the women will notice. And even if they don't, once the Mastaba is completed in a few years, it will be one of the wonders of the world. A 'First Mother' but for men. I like it! But there's more. The 'more' probably involves you. I don't see how it won't!"

Horus asked, "Me?"

"Yes. The little problem you brought me of gods commanding kings. Remember?"

"I do. I thought I resolved that issue."

"Oh, you did. For the short term. However, your innocent but infinitely manipulative Mother Hathor saw the ultimate resolution."

"Which is?"

Djoser answered, "King Khasek's successor will be crowned King of Egypt by Hathor. The new king will then be anointed the living embodiment of Osiris by the most powerful living god in Egypt. Hathor will then blow the sacred breath of Isis into him. He will become 'Pharaoh!'—God-King of Egypt. Do you like it?!"

"More lies? How can I *not* like it?"

"I will pay close attention to Set. He will have the ear of both Hotep and Hathor. His ultimate success in life would be to be chosen to anoint the king of Egypt as a god. You have bested him in every contesting plus you still have your secret which Hetephe and I can attest to—by your doing, Set ate his own ejaculate. That alone should be enough to disqualify him in the eyes of the people. But your uncle has risen from the gutter many times. He is a worthy competitor, Horus. Be wary of him."

"Let Set have that which Set desires. It costs me nothing."

"Let Set anoint a god in the name of Osiris? In the name of Isis? An agent of the gods? A god equal in name to Osiris?"

"It's all lies and illusions, Uncle. Let Set have what Set desires."

"Khasek has a few more years—but only a few—before he must name a successor. We will see how things progress."

"Will he name you?"

"I don't think so. He will not favor his wife's son over his own, but I believe Mother may convince him to name Rafah; a compromise that is best for the kingdom." He laughed. "Were we crowning me, I would insist that you perform the anointing. My almost-son, son of my mentor and almost-father, son of the throne of Greece. No, Djoser. Were it me being crowned, Ma'at would become chaos were it not you to anoint me. If it is Rafah, then perhaps Ma'at would be better served by Set."

"Ma'at is more real than gods. I will serve Ma'at before I serve the gods!"

"Good. I, myself, will serve the wine. Osiris will be pleased. By the way, your wife is making quite a good impression; many believe she is Greek high-born. Do you find marriage to be a good thing, Horus? I look at Hete and I can't think of life without her by my side. But she is so independent—so much her own woman—I fear she would not have me as a husband. Now, she can go anywhere and do anything with any man she wishes. Being my wife would be boring."

"Were you not at Urfa? She was your shadow. You show fear! The man who *should* be King of Egypt is afraid of a woman. Be brave, Uncle. Do brave things! Now, let us join our women! Let us drink your wine!"

The crowd parted as the Prince of Egypt and the son of Osiris walked through their midst—talking with them, touching, being touched, laughing with them, loving them. Only two people fainted.

EGYPTIAN GODS: Osiris/Dionysus—Isis/Ariadne/Philyra, Horus, Set/Charon, Nephthys/Dexithea.
CANAANITE GODS: Anath, Astarte, Shalem, Shahar, Moloch, El.
OLYMPIAN GODS: Zeus, Dionysus, Hestia, Ares, Athena, Astraeus, Eos, Hermes.
OCEANIDS: Polydore, Lyris, Acaste, Eidyia, Dione.

They eventually made it to the Mastaba patio where the reception was going full force. Djoser stopped at the edge of the patio and stared over the crowd. By the table of Osiris, Hete stood laughing with Serket. Her lean, trim body stood ramrod straight with total confidence; powerful, beloved, the greatest archer in the world; Djoser's epitome of the glory of a woman. She could make him laugh; she bought him excitement; she bought him peace.

The Universe mused, *Love—what is love, Djoser? Does love even matter? What do you think the nature of love? Love by any other name is …?"*

Djoser displayed no emotion. He walked straight to Hetephe. People instinctively moved out of the way for a man on a mission. He stopped directly in front of Hetephe and stared at her.

She was suspicious. "Yes, Prince Djoser. How may I help you?"

He did not answer. He grabbed her. He kissed her for a long time. She did not resist. The patio saw and became quiet. He released her. He stared at her. He said, "You are my life. Will you marry me?"

Does time ever stand still? Can a moment last forever? What would Hetephe say?

Hetephe said, "Yes."

"Hathor will marry us tomorrow at Highsun on the roof of the Mastaba in front of the obelisk with Horus and Serket and Mother and Dexithea standing with us."

"Yes."

"Then we will ride Arrow and Djoser the Horse to visit First Mother"

"I will have the title 'Wife?' "

"Yes."

"I will be complete."

They kissed again.

The wedding was viewed by tens of thousands. People fainted. It was magnificent. The ride and visit to First Mother were glorious.

There were apples.

21. Scenes from a Nation

So it was that Prince Djoser accomplished more than he had ever set out to do. He now found peace with his constant companion—Archer Hetephe, once of Nubia. They were both content roaming the halls of power but were now no more than courtly background players.

In the machinations of the powerful, not only must King Khasek begin the long process of selecting his successor, but High Priestess Hathor must also begin the process of selecting the most powerful living god to anoint the new king as Pharoah—the living god-king. In Hathor's mind, her responsibility was the heavier. Many men could be a good king. Only one person could be the most powerful living god in the world.

And, as was his curse, Horus, with his followers, must continue his search for the land of the dead and, perhaps, to save civilization.

Machinations and searches progressed. As did the days and the seasons.

Hotep and Nima

In Egypt, Priest-Builder Hotep and his mother stood looking out from the great concourse discussing Mastabas.

Hotep suggested, "It would be better to build Father his own Mastaba. His being under Osiris's has always bothered me. I could build adjacent mastabas for Father and King Khasek with a connecting walkway. You could move between them now and after you join them in death."

"I would like that, Son. I must respect my present husband's wishes, but Nebby always held my heart. Resting beside him would please me—in this life and the next. Have you discussed King Khasek's Mastaba with him?"

"Yes. He told me to 'do whatever needs doing.' I don't think he cares much one way or the other. He will pass soon enough, leaving you once more a widow. You can choose to rest in whichever Mastaba you wish."

"I yearn for my youth, Son. We don't even perform the sunrise ceremony well anymore. Fortunately, Egypt now has High Priestess Hathor to call forth the sun. But it was such fun when it was the king and queen's duty."

"Things change, Mother. We must change with the times."

"Perhaps you are correct, Son. But then again, we can choose to die. Build the two Mastabas side by side with a walkway between."

EGYPTIAN GODS: Osiris/Dionysus—Isis/Ariadne/Philyra, Horus, Set/Charon, Nephthys/Dexithea.
CANAANITE GODS: Anath, Astarte, Shalem, Shahar, Moloch, El.
OLYMPIAN GODS: Zeus, Dionysus, Hestia, Ares, Athena, Astraeus, Eos, Hermes.
OCEANIDS: Polydore, Lyris, Acaste, Eidyia, Dione.

King Khasek and General Sanakhte

The party was tremendously successful. There was much boisterous talk and laughter among the men among men. General Sanakhte shared his many triumphs with the group. Assistant-General Khaba usually led the applause and accolades. But they were all men of substance; high-born, wealthy, thought-leaders, doers of great deeds.

Young women drifted among them serving food and drink and sometimes being slapped on their butt.

King Khasek laughed, drank, and complimented one-and-all, observing everything.

King Khasek and Chief Rafah

Chief Rafah's reception for his older sister, Queen Nima, and her husband, King Khasek, surpassed all other festivities ever held in the city of Abdju. The city had grown richer through trade, their association with Ogdoad Town, and with their tight connections with Memphis. Even the Kushites in the south began thinking of Abdju as part of Egypt and not a city to annoy. Rafah was in his glory and his people glorified him; worshipped him; shouted "Glory to Chief Rafah" and "Glory to Egypt!"

All knew why the King had accepted the invitation to make a state visit to Abdju. Brother and sister were pleased with King Khasek's inability to hide the wonder and pride he felt watching the majestic land of Nubia display its glory and its love of their beloved great ruler, Chief Rafah of Nubia. A man fitting to be named the successor to the King of Egypt.

King Khasek and Prince Djoser

Khasek said, "You seem resigned, Prince Djoser—that you will not be named King."

"As I should be, my king. Had Father not died early, there would be no decisions, I would be designated his successor. I am trained. I am worthy. I am prepared. There is but one problem. My father died early. Such is the way of gods and men. Their plans twist and turn and do not find their way to the place we had planned. But I am not only resigned, I am also well pleased. Especially if you name a Nubian your successor. But whomever, I will serve them well."

"Before your father died, he named you his successor, not me."

Dionysus/Osiris, Ariadne/Isis/Philyra, Charon/Set, Hermes/Tehuti.
EGYPTIANS: Nebka, Djoser, Hotep, Khasek, Rocky
NUBIANS: Nima, Hetephe, King Kerma, Prince T'jaru, Prince Rafah.
CANAANITES: Phoenicia, Serket, Azazil, Jaffa | URFANS: Teumessian, Abram, Sarai, Terah

"We both understand that would have been a disaster; not for me but for Egypt. The time was not right. There is no doubt that you were the better choice. You have raised Egypt to its full glory. I have no regrets."

"You and Hetephe appear to be happy."

"Yes. There is happiness other than being the ruler of the world. I finally have that happiness. You *will* select Rafah?"

"Perhaps. That would please you?"

"Yes. That would please me."

Set and Priestess Hathor

Set said, "We both love Horus a great deal, don't we Hathor?"

Hathor answered, "We do, God Set. But let us talk plainly why you have come to me. You wish me to favor you over Horus in choosing who shall anoint the king of Egypt as a god. And it is to you to whom I owe everything. Tell me plainly what you wish me to do."

"My dear, dear Hathor. I would never remind you of the infinite debt you owe me. No, you must choose wisely. I come to remind you of your oath—to counsel with Tehuti and choose the strongest god to do the anointing! That is your oath, isn't it?"

"It is, God Set."

"That is all I wish. Let me present my case. Horus is more caring. Horus is wiser. Horus had bested me in almost every contesting. Horus raises the people. Horus teaches. Horus does more glorious and wonderful things than I do. Are we in agreement?"

"You, too, have done these things, God Set."

"Yes, but I will not contest that Horus has done these things better."

"Then you acknowledge that Horus should be selected over yourself."

Set leaned over, took her hands, and said, "No, my dear Hathor. I do not— because I am the *stronger* god!"

Set and Nomarch Tehuti

Seshat knew both men well and knew why Set had come. She had been the wife of both men. And now they talked and laughed and guffawed

EGYPTIAN GODS: Osiris/Dionysus—Isis/Ariadne/Philyra, Horus, Set/Charon, Nephthys/Dexithea.
CANAANITE GODS: Anath, Astarte, Shalem, Shahar, Moloch, El.
OLYMPIAN GODS: Zeus, Dionysus, Hestia, Ares, Athena, Astraeus, Eos, Hermes.
OCEANIDS: Polydore, Lyris, Acaste, Eidyia, Dione.

over man-things. They talked of their conquests, women they had lain with, who could do what more often with how many women. Man-things.

Set said, "Yours is a heavy burden, Lord Tehuti. Deciding who is the most powerful god in the kingdom; other than your illustrious, powerful self of course. You, yourself, could be a great powerful god if you would only accept your godhood. You are, after all, one of the magnificent gods of old. You just don't bring it up."

Tehuti was ecstatic with the recognition and the remembrance of "the old days." He rambled on and on. And on. Finally, he asked, "You weren't a god in those days—or were you? I don't remember exactly. But I do remember you were a powerful lord! Lord Charon, wasn't it? Back then."

"Ah, yes. Those were the days, weren't they? Before the Flood. I was cast down to the gutter after the flood, but I used all my power to climb back to the top. Your decision is of the utmost importance to the future of Egypt. To the future of the world, really. You and Hathor must decide whether I or my sweet little nephew is more powerful. You might discuss the nature of a man's power with God Anath. She is a living god herself in the lands of Canaan. She has fornicated with both me and Horus, you know. It might be interesting to know who she considers to be the more powerful man. She would be a good judge. All I know is how much she says I excite her, and she would rather me be plowing her than any other man in the world. I don't think a woman would lie about that sort of thing, do you?"

They lied on.

Hathor and Tehuti

Tehuti and Hathor had met, discussed, debated, and argued over which man was more powerful, Set or Horus? Which man would best serve the destiny of the office?

Hathor strongly favored Horus. He had disciples from the Sinai into Canaan and beyond. His words were discussed and debated across the Road of Horus throughout the Sinai and into Canaan and beyond.

Tehuti strongly favored Set. Set was of the old world—the time of the original Olympian gods. Set had walked with Zeus and all the great figures of the time before the great flood. Set was revered by all the people of South Memphis as their savior, he was honored by all the tribes of both

Dionysus/Osiris, Ariadne/Isis/Philyra, Charon/Set, Hermes/Tehuti.
EGYPTIANS: Nebka, Djoser, Hotep, Khasek, Rocky
NUBIANS: Nima, Hetephe, King Kerma, Prince T'jaru, Prince Rafah.
CANAANITES: Phoenicia, Serket, Azazil, Jaffa | URFANS: Teumessian, Abram, Sarai, Terah

the western and the eastern Red Lands. He was considered virtually a god like the gods of old. Set always walked and talked and presented himself as a great, powerful lord. Horus rejected all these trappings. True, Horus had bested Set in all of their little contests, but still, Tehuti insisted that God Set was the more powerful man and should, therefore, be the one to crown the King as the Pharaoh.

Djoser had told Hathor about the incident with the cabbage Horus had lovingly prepared for Set's breakfast. She discussed this event with Tehuti, insisting that this disqualified Set from consideration. Tehuti was discouraged by the story but remained adamant; "He ate his own stuff through trickery. That doesn't count."

Hathor said, "So, Set came to you to talk of his power."

Tehuti was extremely old. He was not as adept at intuiting ulterior motives as Hathor. He had never had a devious thought cross his mind. He said, "How did you know? We have talked a lot about what power means and who gets to have it. God Set claims he is more powerful than Horus and I believe him. But he said we should ask Anath for her opinion."

"Ask Anath?"

"Yes. She has been plowed by both of them a lot of times. Anath is a god, herself, you know. She would be a really good judge of which man is more powerful. Let's ask her to help us judge!"

"We will judge a man's power by what he does in bed?"

"Well, I guess. But I bet it's more complicated than just the physical part of it. I mean, don't women look at some kind of total picture of a man? I mean I will never be as good a fornicator as some of those giant Nubian men, but I believe that Seshat sees me as more powerful and that's why she married me instead of one of them. I don't know. You are a woman. What do you think?"

She thought, *Power? What is power? What is its measure? He is correct. It is not their physical strength or their aggression in bed. It is everything they do. Every word they say. Everything they think. Their approach to all things. What is power? How will we measure it? You told me these things yourself, Set. Horus is better than you in all things—except one—power!—But Isis told me that men confuse power with the power to bring death and destruction—that true power is the power to create and nurture—Still …*

EGYPTIAN GODS: Osiris/Dionysus—Isis/Ariadne/Philyra, Horus, Set/Charon, Nephthys/Dexithea.
CANAANITE GODS: Anath, Astarte, Shalem, Shahar, Moloch, El.
OLYMPIAN GODS: Zeus, Dionysus, Hestia, Ares, Athena, Astraeus, Eos, Hermes.
OCEANIDS: Polydore, Lyris, Acaste, Eidyia, Dione.

She said, "Very well. God Anath is a highly respected woman thought of as a god, at least in Canaan. When the time comes, we will ask Anath to join us for our final decision. It's too important to be wrong."

Hathor and Anath

The sisters met in the Mastaba with Osiris's body. They had begun life as gutter girls, sexually taken by any passing man who might want them, having nothing, expecting nothing. Set had given them opportunity. From nothing they started, to the heights of glory they had risen.

The sisters talked of their beginnings, of their lives, of why they were here.

"What is the nature of power, Sister? How shall I measure it?"

They talked and compared and discussed. It came to this.

"A woman knows power when it lays on top of her; when she watches the man walk; when she sees him deal with other powerful men; when she sees his dealings with children and the weak. Not his physical dominance but the entirety of the man. I have lain with both Horus and Set. I loved and respected Horus the most. No man approaches Horus in the goodness of a man. But you ask me who is the more powerful of the two. You and I owe Set everything we have. Set gave us the opportunity to raise ourselves most high—that is power. Set has raised himself most high, beginning, as we, in the gutters of South Memphis—that is power! I sat with Horus. Set came and took me, virtually mounting me in front of Horus. Horus did nothing! That is power! Horus was a loving, tender, caring, and understanding lover. Set? Fury and power!"

Hathor responded, "I see."

Hathor and Set

Anath had suggested to Set that he might get an invitation to visit Hathor. Set remained vigorous for a man his age, but when the invitation came, he drank every manly potion Anath could concoct just in case ...

An invitation came. Upon arriving, Set was shown to the Mastaba inner chamber where Hathor sat on a sofa visiting Osiris, drinking fine wine. She wore a simple white tunic.

The gracious Hathor served wine to her mentor. Refined and dignified High Priestess Hathor was above-reproach. She was also an accomplished sacred High Priestess who would do what must be done.

Two of her sisters, Anath and Astarte, had become living gods—gods of death, war, and sex. Their mother Ishtar was referred to as the embodiment of God Aphrodite. Hathor was not without knowledge in the arts of controlling men. She knew how to raise their combative instincts. She knew how to make their testosterone levels rise. She would give Set an opportunity to impress her. She chatted about how Osiris was watching them and how powerful she found Horus to be when she lay with him. She knew how to make herself the sacred prize of Egypt.

She laughed. She may have flirted. After their third glass of fine wine, she stood, lovingly looked at the groin of Osiris and stoked it. Hathor turned to Set, and asked, "Do you think you're as powerful as Osiris?"

He took her.

Meanwhile, in Urfa …

Horus took Abram and Baalat to their ancestral home; there for Horus to thank Deohestia and to give his two students a chance to take measure of their lives.

Abram and Baalat

Abram and Baalat entered the ruins of Urfa with Horus walking far behind. This was as much their journey as his.

Abram took Baalat's hand.

It had been several years since the two had left their home to become followers of Horus. They had learned and grown and expanded their understanding of the world and the people in it. They had mixed emotions about their visit. Abram's family awaited him. Baalat had been taken by the priests to be a bedmate to Teumessian when she was eight years of age. Her mother was a forgotten memory. Their strength was now in each other; both orphans after a fashion; following a strange man who taught them the nature of all things; of life; death; gods; man; woman; peace; war; hope; and despair. They were eager students, and they had each other.

The road to their people pointed south. They set upon the road and passed the Pastures. They came to the house of Abram.

Young men, rough-housed in front of his home. The oldest one saw them standing there. He especially saw Baalat, fully developed, watching them roughhouse. The older boy leered, walked to face Baalth, and said, "Hey, you good-lookin' whore! What's yore name, Bitch?"

Abram, a head shorter than the man, stepped forward, shoved him to the ground, and said, "You will speak to Baalat with respect, or you will not speak at all!"

The man jumped up in fury!" Nobody does that to Terahson! I'm gonna rip you ta pieces!"

"My big brother has learned nothing! He remains an ignorant bully. Come to me, Terahson. I shall teach you manners becoming a man!"

Terahson was surprised. "Abram! Is that you? My little brother? You growed up a little bit. I figured you would be dead by now. I won't kill you this time, but you better show me more respect!"

"I shall, big Brother. And you will show women more respect. My friend is Baalat; a woman of great worth and to be respected. We understand one another in this matter, do we not?"

"Oh, yeah. Sure. Baalat. 'Don't mess with her.' I can do that! You from around here, Pen Baalat?"

"You are Abram's brother; Terahson? He has spoken of you. You will inherit your father's idol business and become rich and famous."

"Ah, Yeah. But the old man don't show no signs of lettin' up. That'll take a long time."

"I see. In the meantime, how do you live your life?"

Terahson was confused. "Live ma' life? I don't unnerstand!"

The three talked on; Horus remained far in the background.

Eventually, Terahson turned and led the three into his father's house. Horus found a nice shade tree and sat beneath it. Waiting.

After a long time, Amathlai came rushing out of the house exclaiming, "Lord Horus! Why did you not join us? Am I not a gracious enough wife? I will have my husband beat me for my inadequacies."

They would remain in Urfa for a quarter moon. There would be more of the same.

Horus and the Gods

Horus did take a morning to visit the temple. After many refusals, Horus was escorted to the center nave where they turned into the right transcript to face the throne. Deoares slouched on the throne, leg thrown over one arm, a glass of morning wine in his hand. "Welcome back, God Horus. I'm the best we can do right now. The Living-Word-of-the-Gods whose name may not be spoken died of old age. We didn't start him on Ambrosia soon enough, I suppose. It's a bother. Do you want the position? I can make it happen! Oblate Asherah, bring our guest some wine! Our disciples tell us you are doing well. The little Baalat girl was a stroke of genius on my part. A wonderful spy."

"Hello, Deoares. You are as charming as ever. But I came to thank your sister. Is she available?"

"Yes, she will join us momentarily. She is getting her nails done, right now."

Asherah brought him wine. Horus said, "I don't see a skull on the cup. Is it safe to drink?"

"Yes, indeed. We don't want you dead, or at least Deohestia doesn't. We are a patient family, living forever and all that. She monitors your progress. Married now, are you? Finding peace—teaching the good news of how to be a good person. You are going to be a wonderful addition to our family, Horus. Deohestia is sure of it. I, at the least, will get a new drinking companion and someone worth talking to. It gets lonely around here sometimes, Brother. I don't know how you stand it—out there in the field—trying to teach those people. It keeps you busy, I suppose."

Deohestia strode up, "God Horus. You return more quickly than I thought! Are you ready to bed me?"

Horus replied, "I am married, Deohestia. Perhaps I could find you a goat."

"Goats aren't too bad, Horus. You should get one for your faithful wife since you are never there to service her."

Horus, seldom without words, merely shook his head in resignation.

"You'll get over it, Horus. I accept the thanks you are about to give me. Most human sacrifices will be forsaken in the coming year. Of course, some of the savages enjoy hearing them scream. Just like the original Ares did. These days, we want them to scream if we are getting something out of it. Otherwise, it's just loud noises hurting our ears. Do you understand what I'm saying?"

"All too clearly, Sweet Deohestia."

EGYPTIAN GODS: Osiris/Dionysus—Isis/Ariadne/Philyra, Horus, Set/Charon, Nephthys/Dexithea.
CANAANITE GODS: Anath, Astarte, Shalem, Shahar, Moloch, El.
OLYMPIAN GODS: Zeus, Dionysus, Hestia, Ares, Athena, Astraeus, Eos, Hermes.
OCEANIDS: Polydore, Lyris, Acaste, Eidyia, Dione.

"I'm not your 'sweet,' Dung-head. I'm not anyone's 'sweet.' "

"You are just and merciful, sweet Deohestia."

"Deoathena, come kill this insufferable dung-head!"

Deoares offered. "Go get your toenails done, Sister. I will take him out back and gut him."

"No. Let the dung-head live, Little Brother. He will someday sing our praises."

She left. The two men chatted until Horus grew tired, left the temple, and found Abram.

Abram was thrilled to hear that his once-friend Asherah had not been sacrificed during the Winter Solstice Festival and appeared to be a person of rank, perhaps a Church of Urfa priestess-in-training.

On their way out of Urfa, Horus allowed his followers to spend a day and a night in the pastures. There was laughter and renewal.

~

The years passed. Rulers ruled. Living gods did living god things. People lived their lives until they died. The Step Mastaba grew taller each year. Inspired by the women of Egypt, the Obelisk rose ever higher.

The day came.

Dionysus/Osiris, Ariadne/Isis/Philyra, Charon/Set, Hermes/Tehuti.
EGYPTIANS: Nebka, Djoser, Hotep, Khasek, Rocky
NUBIANS: Nima, Hetephe, King Kerma, Prince T'jaru, Prince Rafah.
CANAANITES: Phoenicia, Serket, Azazil, Jaffa | URFANS: Teumessian, Abram, Sarai, Terah

22. Gods

Decision

King Khasek said, "Nima, I cannot stand."

"I will help you husband. Take my hand."

"I don't feel well Nima. Call my physicians."

"Immediately Husband, but it is only a passing weakness." She called the physicians. It was not a passing weakness. His days could be counted.

The King, Queen, Vizier, and Hathor candidly discussed his coming death. After all the ifs, ands, and buts, it came down to the needs of the kingdom that would be best served if the King announced his successor, and then fell over dead. There were better words to frame it, but Khasek was, at heart, a general, and preferred plain talk. A known date of death would allow their allies to be notified, and plans made properly rather than haphazardly. All that needed deciding was to select the date and begin preparing.

Hearing the plan, Djoser could not help but remember the agonizing decision made by Horus long ago. *We govern nations. That is why we are the way we are. Love is hard!*

The word went out to the kingdom and all its allies. The King of Egypt would soon join his ancestors for the glory of his people. A new king of Egypt would be crowned under the next full moon.

Horus was called to Memphis immediately, as was Anath.

The king's Mastaba was prepared. Priests and Priestesses were interviewed and selected.

The mighty gathered.

Hathor commanded Tehuti to counsel with her.

Both Djoser and Hotep saw the emptiness in Queen Nima's face.

~

The appointed time came. King Khasek sat on a throne in front of the obelisk and faced his people. Nima stood beside him. Sanakhte, Rafah, and Djoser stood facing him.

Everyone in the world stood silently watching.

EGYPTIAN GODS: Osiris/Dionysus—Isis/Ariadne/Philyra, Horus, Set/Charon, Nephthys/Dexithea.
CANAANITE GODS: Anath, Astarte, Shalem, Shahar, Moloch, El.
OLYMPIAN GODS: Zeus, Dionysus, Hestia, Ares, Athena, Astraeus, Eos, Hermes.
OCEANIDS: Polydore, Lyris, Acaste, Eidyia, Dione.

The sunrise came. The players played their parts. Osiris came. No sound arose from those gathered below.

Queen Nima helped King Khasek rise. He held his Crook and Flail before him. He took one step forward. That which was to come was obvious. The king would announce his successor. No one knew, or even suspected, who it would be. Not even his beloved wife and confidant. Even as he stepped forward, it could be any one of the three candidates standing before him.

The world was hushed except for the calls of the river birds.

King Khasek handed his Crook and Flail to the next King of Egypt.

King Khasek then gave the King-designate his instructions. The King-designate followed King Khasek to the edge of the Mastaba. King Khasek raised his arms to his people.

To the roar of the loving people, the King-designate pushed King Khasek off the ledge to his death.

The King-designate heard the soft thud of his predecessor hit the floor below and gave his incredulous subjects a few moments to comprehend what they had just witnessed. He then walked to the throne in front of the obelisk, sat down, crossed his Crook and Flail, and stared out over the vastness of Egypt.

A vast roar erupted as Sanakhte and Rafah came and kneeled before their king.

The Final Contesting

The priests scurried around the Mastaba of Osiris. They were prepared. Even if Osiris returned from the Land of the Dead at this moment, which he might well do, all was prepared for him.

Too, the unimaginable glory of their kind was in the room. High Priestess Hathor stood at the head of the body of the sleeping Osiris. Great Lord Tehuti, old and feeble but wielding the power of great decisions, sat by her side. At the foot of Osiris stood the two contenders for the honor and the power and the immortality—the powerful God Set of the Red Lands and the loving God Horus.

Watching in the background stood King-Mother Nima, King Djoser, Queen Hetephe, Set's wife Dexithea, and Set's consort God Anath.

Djoser was now the King of Egypt and would soon be publicly crowned.

It was a given that the new King of Egypt would be anointed as the physical manifestation of God Osiris and would become the most powerful Living God on earth.

It was a given that the anointing would be performed by the current most powerful living god in the world.

It was a given that High Priestess Hathor would perform the sacred ritual and blow the life and spirit of the eternal Osiris into the king, making the king a god.

It was a given that the most powerful Living God in Egypt would then place the Pschent Crown upon the king anointing him Pharaoh of Egypt.

What was unknown is this: Who is the current most powerful living god?

Hathor and Tehuti had debated and discussed this question with everyone whose opinion mattered. This they had done until it could be done no more. The decision must be made. Hathor had decided.

The two candidates stood before their judge.

Hathor spoke. "My decision is who is the most powerful living god—not the most influential nor who is the better man—only who is the most powerful."

Set trembled with excitement *Is this to be my moment? The moment that I best the great bitch Philyra—the moment I become equal with Dionysus?—when I stand with Zeus and Aphrodite and Athena and all the other gods? Make this my moment! Choose me!*

Horus stood with humility and trepidation. *How difficult this decision must have been for you, Hathor—and Tehuti. How do you choose what is right in a world where no decision is right? Only degrees of right and wrong. But this I know quite well, to anoint Set would be a travesty of justice. I may not be worthy, but Set would be an abomination to the memory of my father. I care not to be selected for this sacred honor, but I care beyond bearing that Uncle Set NOT be selected for this sacred honor. Djoser prefers me! In my father's name, I claim this thing!*

Hathor said, "Tomorrow, I shall blow the living spirit of Osiris into Djoser, and he will then be crowned the supreme God-King of Egypt by the current most powerful living god in the world—Living God Set.

EGYPTIAN GODS: Osiris/Dionysus—Isis/Ariadne/Philyra, Horus, Set/Charon, Nephthys/Dexithea.
CANAANITE GODS: Anath, Astarte, Shalem, Shahar, Moloch, El.
OLYMPIAN GODS: Zeus, Dionysus, Hestia, Ares, Athena, Astraeus, Eos, Hermes.
OCEANIDS: Polydore, Lyris, Acaste, Eidyia, Dione.

Living God Anath was beside herself with excitement. Her powerful consort was now even more powerful and of the highest rank. She ran and embraced him. Set trembled as he urinated upon himself, his mind reeling with his triumph.

The others walked to Set to congratulate him. Djoser cast a sidelong glance toward Horus, who stood motionless, staring back at him. Djoser could do no more than shrug in sad resignation.

Hathor announced, "We will have a long difficult day tomorrow. All meet before sunrise at the top of Djoser's pyramid to be ready for the sunrise and crowning ceremonies." She looked at Horus and said, "I invite you to stand in the background to watch if it pleases you. Otherwise, watch from wherever you wish."

The announcement concluded, Tehuti was wheeled to his visitor accommodations inside Osiris's Mastaba. Everyone left with him, save Hathor and Horus.

Horus stared at his father laying in his sarcophagus. *So, it will be my uncle that escorts your spirit into Djoser? Uncle Set? The ultimate coarseness of a man shall merge the two most perfect examples of men to ever live. Not Horus—the son—the one who tried with his every breath to emulate the two of you—not Horus who tried to make life better for everyone he met—but Set—the evil—the self-absorbed—the profane—the user of people.*

Hathor walked to him and put her hand on his shoulder. "Come to me in a while. We will drink a glass of wine. If it helps, you may lay with me, tonight. Your father would like that, I think."

Horus stared at his father a moment more. From deep within his body, he growled, "This thing shall not be."

Hathor softly replied, "It *shall* be, Horus. Set is simply more powerful than you. You bring respect, understanding, and nurturing. But when the lion comes for a woman and her children, it is power that protects them. When another man comes to take her, will her man fight to defend her? The crowning must be a thing of power. It simply must!"

Horus growled, "Power?! Is that the nature of your kind? Who is most powerful? Who can take what they want when they want it? Who can inflict the most pain on you and make you want even more? Who can have their way without regard for the consequences to others? Power?!"

He stopped, looked at her, and with quiet menace growled, "I shall challenge Set to a contesting. It is my right. You shall honor that right. Bring Tehuti to Set's chambers. I demand it. I go to challenge Set to a contesting of power! Bring Tehuti to watch with you! NOW!"

Horus stormed from the room.

Hathor stared after him. *Yes. It is your right, my child. And I will bring Tehuti to witness. But this I know—nothing will change.*

The Seduction of Anath

Horus stopped before the door to their chambers. He stared at it in cold fury. Every slight came to him. Every hurt that each had inflicted upon him. *I took it all. I took abuse without returning abuse. When given pettiness, I returned love and understanding. Fool! I was a fool! I was born a fool! I lived a fool! I am a fool! Power?! What they want is unbridled hatred. Father, forgive me. I am broken!*

Horus violently kicked the door open and stood motionless framed in the doorway staring at the two of them. She was in bed. Set was undressing. Both stared back at him, speechless.

Horus said, "I, Horus, son of Osiris challenge you, Set, to a contest of power. Your whore shall be our judge!"

Set said, "See here, Horus. This has been decided. I am the winner; not you!"

Horus walked to Set, took him by his throat, and slammed him against the wall. He turned to Anath and began removing his clothes. He said, "Prepare to judge, woman!"

She did not speak. She had seen this look in the eyes of the men who had forcibly taken her when she was still a child. *They will not listen because they cannot hear. Very well, Horus. I suppose I owe you one last time. You were good for me once. Before Set took me from you.*

She stared deeply into his eyes as she slowly removed her nightgown. She lay back as she invitingly spread her legs wide apart. *I will make this really good for you, Sweet.*

Horus stared at her parting legs. *bitch whore betrayer pond-scum i respected you above all others entrusted you with my heart my mind my thoughts my soul.*

Testosterone flooded his body. He ripped his pants off, fell upon her, and entered her. *BITCH WHORE BETRAYER I LOVED YOU*

He pounded her. *anath ... sweet loving whore anath ... sweet loving dispatcher anath ... i understood you before you understood yourself ... i loved you before you understood love ... I taught you ... I nurtured you*

Just then, Hathor arrived with Tehuti in his wheeled chair followed by Djoser. They saw Set standing terrified against the wall. His eyes glued to Horus plowing Anath.

Hathor casually asked Set, "Horus said he would challenge you to a competition of power? Is this it?"

Set could only stare with disbelief at the two thrashing on his bed.

Horus pounded Anath. *set moves his little finger to call to you and you are in his bed writhing moaning screaming with pleasure under his body as he plows and plows and plows you*

Anath was taking his fury. *you are angry my love ... are you angry with me or set or the world? ... you were never this angry before ... this full of being a man ... i loved you horus but that didn't matter ... set took me ... you didn't even try to stop him*

Horus pounded her, his fury growing with each stroke. *i tried hard to do right ... to help those around me ... to be the man I thought my father and djoser wanted ... but they did not want that ... they wanted POWER*

She took his thrusts, growing more and more aroused with what he was doing with her, to her. *i own you horus ... you are thinking of nothing but me ... i am your world ... i anath poor little girl from south memphis control the body and thoughts of the most powerful man on earth ... plow me, horus ... come on ... give me everything you have ... i want it*

His fury was not abating. It was growing. Harder!!! Faster!!! He growled, "Is this what you want, woman—to be plowed by raw power?"

"Yes yes yes yes yes yes yes yes."

"Did respect and love not count?"

"No no no no no no no no no."

"You are MINE Anath."

"Yes yes yes yes yes yes yes yes."

At some point, Anath could no longer think. She could only experience his raw power. Her raging physical pleasure expanded into overwhelming sensual pleasure expanded into intense emotional pleasure expanded into an all-encompassing spiritual being. *I, ANATH, COMMAND THE MOST POWERFUL MAN IN THE WORLD. HE WILL GIVE ME HIS SEED!* I AM HIS! HE IS MINE! WE ARE ONE!

Horus was not close to his release, but she could wait no longer. The trembling and the sound began low and worked their way up her body. Her body convulsed as the moan exploded from her throat.

I win, bitch. You gave it up and I'm still plowing you! I win!

He continued for a while and then noticed his conquest was unconscious. *If I don't win, I will destroy the world!*

He released himself, allowed himself a moment of fulfillment, then withdrew, stood, stared at Set, and said, "I believe I win, Uncle." He paused. "Wait a minute!" Then, with his left hand, he picked unconscious Anath up by her ankles, lifted her, and with his right hand, slapped her rear as hard as he could. "Wake up, sweet Anath. God Tehuti wants to ask you something!" He threw her back down as she was returning to consciousness.

As he dressed, he noticed that, high on a shelf, his missing eye looked down upon everything—seeing all. "Well, well. So this is where it went."

He walked to the shelf, took the eye, and handed it to Hathor. "The Eye of Horus wishes to see me anoint King Djoser as God as you blow the spirit of Osiris into him. I believe you said that the honor goes to the most powerful. Ask sweet Anath the nature of power!"

Hathor, Djoser, and Tehuti parted to let Horus walk between them, unimpeded, out the door. Horus turned back toward them, and said, "Father commanded me to do this thing—if I were powerful enough!" He turned again and left them.

Baptism

Horus walked outside where his disciples patiently waited. They had had no word on any of the events since Horus left them much earlier in the evening. Azazil opened his mouth to speak but, seeing the expression on Horus's face, decided not to.

Horus said, "We will walk to the river. You will wash away my sins."

None knew exactly what that meant but remained silent as they walked with him.

They arrived at the river. Horus removed his clothes. "These are covered with filth. Burn them. Bring me clean clothes and a washing cloth."

Abram took the clothes and hurried to the trading store.

Horus stared into the heavens for a while and said, "I descended into one of them. I now know the extent of their pain, their inadequacies, their insecurities. I did not know these things before I descended into their depths of madness. I became one of them—how else can I understand those who I try to teach? I do not wish for my father's forgiveness. I am what I am. They are what they are. Now, you must wash away my sins."

Abram returned with a change of clothes and a washing cloth. Horus walked into the river up to his neck and held his arms to the sky. "Wash my body. Let the river take away my weaknesses—my inadequacies—my shortcomings—the evil within my mind—the wrongs that I have done to others—make me worthy."

Azazil took a cloth and washed the body of his master. He then took Horus's head and pushed it under the flowing water.

Horus felt the water flow over his body. *I tried so hard.*

He felt all empathy wash from his body; all care of what others thought, wanted, or needed washed away.

Azazil raised Horus to the surface and announced, with a degree of uncertainty, "The water has washed away your sins, Teacher."

Horus stepped from the water and looked at his followers, what he had been now washed away.

He looked at his wife. *Serket—my loving, caring wonderful Serket. You love me so. I am your world. My innocent, loving, naive Serket.*

He looked at the boy Abram. *Abram. You trust me so. You believe my every word. You would follow me into the fires of Hades. My Abram. My sweet, innocent, naive Abram.*

He looked at wide-eyed Baalat. *Baalat my sweet, innocent, whore. A woman-in-full. A child waiting to become what you shall become.*

Dionysus/Osiris, Ariadne/Isis/Philyra, Charon/Set, Hermes/Tehuti.
EGYPTIANS: Nebka, Djoser, Hotep, Khasek, Rocky
NUBIANS: Nima, Hetephe, King Kerma, Prince T'jaru, Prince Rafah.
CANAANITES: Phoenicia, Serket, Azazil, Jaffa | URFANS: Teumessian, Abram, Sarai, Terah

And Azazil. *You have moved mountains for me. Done everything I have asked of you. Converted untold people to the Way of Kiya. Made this world a far, far better place. My faithful, innocent, naive disciple Azazil. I weep for you and your kind.*

He looked upon all those gathered around him—those who believed his words—who trusted his guidance—who relied upon him, to differentiate the good from the evil. *You trust me—you look to me to show you the way—you believe that I can see farther than you—you are all fools—some useful—some not— Father, it was Hestia that you loved. Did you know that? Mother brought you joy— peace –but it was Hestia that challenged you—pushed you—intrigued you. Hestia was your equal if not your better. You never realized this, but the Kyrios Olon do. You were never an Elder Olympian, just the bastard son of Zeus who came late and brought the wine. You were never one of us.*

Horus told them the story of his evening.

Hearing him speak, the quiet assurance in his voice, Serket exclaimed, with joy, "My beloved, you are finally at peace!"

Horus finally bid them good night and walked with naive Serket toward his chambers in his father's Mastaba.

Upon mounting the Great Concourse, he was met by a furious Set who hissed, "I should have killed and eaten you at the moment of your birth! You have defeated me, yet again. DEFEATED ME!!!"

Horus looked upon him as an adult would look upon an enraged four-year-old who had not gotten his way. "Why, Uncle Set, that would have made Aunt Nephthys and Mother Isis exceedingly angry. You really didn't want to do that. You will tell Anath that you rejoice in my union with her and that she should not displease me in the future. I was angry with her. Now, leave me, old man. I may deem to speak to you in the warmth of the sunrise."

EGYPTIAN GODS: Osiris/Dionysus—Isis/Ariadne/Philyra, Horus, Set/Charon, Nephthys/Dexithea.
CANAANITE GODS: Anath, Astarte, Shalem, Shahar, Moloch, El.
OLYMPIAN GODS: Zeus, Dionysus, Hestia, Ares, Athena, Astraeus, Eos, Hermes.
OCEANIDS: Polydore, Lyris, Acaste, Eidyia, Dione.

23. Pharoah

High Priestess Hathor stood on the roof of the eight-step pyramid Mastaba in the predawn light, the sun still well below the horizon.

She had never performed a ceremony of this magnitude. Already, the people were coming. She had added thirty-six drummers and announcers to her usual cadre. A drummer would stand behind her and beat soft metronome beats of the heart so she could time her proclamations. Each proclamation would have to be repeated and repeated twelve times so that her words could filter down to all people. Even thirty-six more would not be sufficient for the crowd that was already formed.

Her people began walking to their positions. Her priests and priestess, wearing robes, crowns, and necklaces of power, slowly took their positions on the roofs of the mastabas below her. Her drummers and announcers began taking their positions. The crowd grew.

Her people finally in position—she judged the time remaining before the sun would breach the horizon—she calmed herself. The crowd extended as far as she could see in every direction and still it grew. *No, thirty-six more announcers will not be enough.*

She gave the signal to her Master Drummer. The drummer rim-stroked his drum with all his strength. The sound resonated over the land.

Djoser stood with Hetephe at the base of the Mastabas pyramid.

He looked into her eyes and said, "So, it begins. Let us do well, Hetephe."

She reached up and affectionately kissed his lips. "We shall, Djoser."

Djoser took a deep breath, composed himself, and turned to face the walkway which circumvented the pyramid seven times to the top where Hathor waited. He nodded to the first firelighters, who lit the torches on both sides of the walkway to supplement the predawn light so that all people could see their King as he climbed his great pyramid. Djoser began his walk to the apex of all things. Torches were lit to illuminate him as he progressed. *Mother, thank you for what you did. You guided me well and gave me all that I needed. Father, thank you for all the things you taught me. Grandfather, you gave us a chiefdom that became a kingdom that now becomes the stuff of legends. For this, I thank you. Brother Hotep, you built this empire for which I shall receive the credit. I love you. Thank you for this gift. Hetephe, my love, you gave me everything. For this I thank you. Set, as evil as you are, you inspired the people upon which I have built an empire. I am commanded to love you. So, I do. You alone conceived of the House of Ishtar and saved South Memphis and the Gods of Egypt.*

Djoser continued his slow march up the Mastaba; Hetephe followed three steps behind. The crowd watched in silence, mesmerized.

Cymbals clashed after each turn in the pathway—as Djoser rose higher—closer to his destiny. *Little hostess girl—who could believe that which you now are? How can this even be? By your own will—by your own determination—by your own nature—Hathor—High Priestess to the gods themselves—dedicated—unpresuming—commanding—High Priestess Hathor of South Memphis!*

The cymbals clashed. *Ariadne and Dionysus—the catalyst that unified my lands. I cannot think of you either together or separately—my legs would not hold firm—my eyes would not remain dry.*

Without looking back, he whispered, "Hete, are you there?

From three steps behind him, a voice replied, "I am here, Husband!!"

The cymbals clashed. *There are so many of you. Each one critical to that which we have brought forth. How do I remember all of you? How can I forget any of you? I love you all.*

The cymbals clashed. *And so, Dionysus, did we raise your son well? Is he the man you wanted him to be? Did I do my part? Did I make him a better man or a lesser man? His teachings are celebrated throughout many lands—he lifts the fallen—the masses love him—he has become a living god—is that too great a title?—or too small? He waits for me with Hathor to infuse me with your divine spirit—to make me the supreme living god of all things.*

The cymbals clashed. *The contestings of Set and Horus worked out well—Horus is the most worthy and powerful living god in the world—what price did he pay?—there is always a price to pay—will you tell me, Horus, if I ask?—do you even know?*

On the apex of the pyramid, in the still-predawn light, Hathor and Horus, arms folded at their chest, stood side by side, staring, unblinking, over the untold masses below, awaiting Djoser and Hetephe. Behind them, the sun illuminated the top of the obelisk and slowly began traveling downward. The large oil-filled jars surrounding the massive, jewel-encrusted throne patiently awaited their flame. The sun neared the horizon. Djoser stepped upon the roof.

Everyone of importance stood on the Great Concourse watching; the once-Queen Nima, Chief Rafah of Nubia, his younger brother General

EGYPTIAN GODS: Osiris/Dionysus—Isis/Ariadne/Philyra, Horus, Set/Charon, Nephthys/Dexithea.
CANAANITE GODS: Anath, Astarte, Shalem, Shahar, Moloch, El.
OLYMPIAN GODS: Zeus, Dionysus, Hestia, Ares, Athena, Astraeus, Eos, Hermes.
OCEANIDS: Polydore, Lyris, Acaste, Eidyia, Dione.

T'jaru, and all Nomarchs. Snefru stood beside this father, the elderly Hotep. Tehuti and his wife Seshat were there, of course. Nephthys stood beside Nima. Set chose not to attend but Dispatcher Anath stood with her mother and all her sisters, save Hathor. The military, the advisors, and everyone of importance were there. Greece had sent a delegation as had governments now rising in Canaan. The gigantic crowd now stood in absolute silence. Only the calls of the river birds were heard. A cool breeze flowed across the land.

Hathor took one step forward and raised her arms toward the horizon.

Osiris came.

She called out, "Osiris, you have become Ra—the Living Sun. Deliver your blessings to your people!" Her drummer signaled. Her announcers repeated her words to the masses.

She called out, "Merciful Ra, we beseech you to imbue your divinity into the worthy King of Egypt and make him a living god!" Her drummer signaled. Her words were repeated.

She called out, "Through the sacred ritual of Isis, enter into your faithful servant!" Her drummers and announcers responded. Hathor then fell to her knees, arms outstretched. She bowed toward the empty throne so that her forehead touched the Mastaba, her arms still outstretched.

Slowly walking across the Mastaba toward the throne, came Djoser, King of Egypt.

Some fainted.

Djoser reached the throne, turned to face the crowd, and held out his arms. Hetephe came to him and removed his royal robe. Djoser stood before his people naked, unclothed, with enormous erection.

More fainted.

Horus walked to Djoser standing before the throne. In Djoser's right hand, Horus placed a Crook, and in his left, a Flail. Holding both Crook and Flail, Djoser folded his arms across his chest. Horus stepped away.

Hathor raised her head from the mastaba floor and, on her knees, faced Djoser. Djoser took one step forward so that Hathor could begin the sacred rite—Isis returning life to Osiris.

Hetephe stepped behind Djoser and messaged his shoulders.

Dionysus/Osiris, Ariadne/Isis/Philyra, Charon/Set, Hermes/Tehuti.
EGYPTIANS: Nebka, Djoser, Hotep, Khasek, Rocky
NUBIANS: Nima, Hetephe, King Kerma, Prince T'jaru, Prince Rafah.
CANAANITES: Phoenicia, Serket, Azazil, Jaffa | URFANS: Teumessian, Abram, Sarai, Terah

Horus retrieved the Pschent Crown from behind the throne and stood beside Djoser.

Hete whispered, "You are doing well, Husband. Now give unto Hathor that which Hathor demands."

Djoser did not hear. He stared unblinking over the masses, over Egypt. His mind filled with kaleidoscopic images of his life—each one too fleeting to savor—too many to comprehend—faces of his people—his friends, confidants, lovers, enemies, failures, triumphs, despair, joy, Tartarus, Canaan, Urfa, Memphis, Nubia. *OSIRIS, ENTER INTO ME! MAKE ME EGYPT! MAKE ME A LIVING GOD!*

Djoser released his mortality into the demanding Hathor. It was replaced by the omnipotence of God.

Hathor stood. The pots of oil received their flame. The entire mastaba was brilliantly illuminated with early-morning sunlight mixed with the bright light from pots of burning oil.

The sound of singers, drummers, and cymbals burst forth as Living God Horus, only son of God Osiris and God Isis, placed the Pschent Crown of unified Egypt on King Djoser's head.

Djoser sat down upon his throne—arms crossed—holding his Crook and Flail—wearing the sacred crown and symbol of his godhood. The omnipotent God-King Pharaoh stared, without expression, over the land of Egypt.

~

In the multitude below, gazing up in wonder, stood followers of Horus.

Serket was enthralled. "Oh, Abram. Isn't it glorious!? And our Horus helped make it so! My love flows over them like the heavens embracing the children of Shahar!"

Abram wasn't sufficiently developed—emotionally, mentally, spiritually, or intellectually—to process that which he saw. He could only stare in open-mouthed, wide-eyed wonder.

Baalat struggled to make sense of it.

From near the throne, watched the Eye of Horus—seer of all things.

And from on-high—Ra, the Living Sun.

EGYPTIAN GODS: Osiris/Dionysus—Isis/Ariadne/Philyra, Horus, Set/Charon, Nephthys/Dexithea.
CANAANITE GODS: Anath, Astarte, Shalem, Shahar, Moloch, El.
OLYMPIAN GODS: Zeus, Dionysus, Hestia, Ares, Athena, Astraeus, Eos, Hermes.
OCEANIDS: Polydore, Lyris, Acaste, Eidyia, Dione.

Book 5. *The Beginning of Civilization: Mythologies Told True*

###

The Beginning of Civilization: Mythologies Told True
continues in
Book 6. *The Patriarch and the Lord*

which tells the stories of Horus, Abram, Ishmael,
the rise of misogyny,
and the culmination of *The Beginning of Civilization.*

Dionysus/Osiris, Ariadne/Isis/Philyra, Charon/Set, Hermes/Tehuti.
EGYPTIANS: Nebka, Djoser, Hotep, Khasek, Rocky
NUBIANS: Nima, Hetephe, King Kerma, Prince T'jaru, Prince Rafah.
CANAANITES: Phoenicia, Serket, Azazil, Jaffa | URFANS: Teumessian, Abram, Sarai, Terah

APPENDIX

Note: im means "in mythology"

Abram was a follower of Horus and the son of an Urfa idol merchant.

Abram's family was Terah, Amathlai, Terahson, Haran, and Sarai.

Acaste was one of the three Oceanids living in Memphis.

Alashiya was the unflooded, surviving highlands of Tartarus.

Amathlai was Terah's wife and Abram's mother.

Anath was the second daughter of Ishtar and became the Sinai god of war and strife. She was consort to God Set.

Ares was one of the major Egyptian Gods noted for his cruelty.

Ariadne, aka Philyra aka as Isis. See Philyra. See Isis.

Asherah was a child prostitute in the Church of Urfa. *Im, she is the consort of the Sumerian god Anu, and Ugaritic El, the oldest deities of their respective pantheons. She was also the wife of the Canaanite god Yahweh and was highly regarded by the women of Canaan.*

Astarte was the oldest daughter of Ishtar.

Athena was a major Greek God and half-sister of Dionysus.

Azazil replaced Rocky as Horus's leading disciple.

Baal was an honorific title meaning "Lord." *Im, Baal is the God of the Sky and is the equivalent of the Greek God Zeus.*

Baalat was a girl concubine to Teumessian in the Temple of Urfa and a subsequent follower of Horus.

Ba't was the third oldest daughter of Ishtar and eventually became the chief hostess in South Memphis.

Brown Wine was brandy.

Charon was the chief builder in Tartarus before the Great Flood. He immigrated with Dionysus to Egypt where he was renamed Set by Isis. See Set.

Cities - Canaan: See Damascus, Jaffa, Megiddo, Rusalem, Sur (Tyre), Tophet.

EGYPTIAN GODS: Osiris/Dionysus—Isis/Ariadne/Philyra, Horus, Set/Charon, Nephthys/Dexithea.
CANAANITE GODS: Anath, Astarte, Shalem, Shahar, Moloch, El.
OLYMPIAN GODS: Zeus, Dionysus, Hestia, Ares, Athena, Astraeus, Eos, Hermes.
OCEANIDS: Polydore, Lyris, Acaste, Eidyia, Dione.

Cities—Phoenician: Byblos, Ugar, Alashiya

Crook and Flail were symbols of pharaonic power. The Crook represents the staff used by shepherds to protect their flocks and the flail represents the tool used to thresh grain.

Dexithea, aka Nephthys, was the executive assistant to Ariadne and the love interest of Charon. She became the nurse mother to Horus and consort to Set. See Nephthys.

Dione was a fallen Oceanid that settled in Byblos. She was a survivor of the Great Flood.

Dionysus, aka Osiris, was a Titan, Olympian, and god. He was eventually renamed Osiris and became husband to Isis, father of Horus, and upon his death became Ra, the Living Sun.

Disciples of Horus were the ardent followers of Horus who formed in each camp along the trade route from Kemet through the Sinai. Rocky and then Azazil were their leaders.

Djoser was a student of Dionysus and became the first God-King of Egypt. He built the eight-step pyramid. He was the husband of Hetephe.

Drink referred to in this series—**Bitter,** a nonalcoholic drink made by mixing various herbs with water,—**Sweet**, a nonalcoholic drink containing honey --- **beer—wine—fruit-wine**, wine mixed with fruit juices containing only a little alcohol—**brown wine**, brandy—**Red Elixir,** Kiya's secret potion extending life by a factor of two—**Ambrosia**, Demeter's secret potion extending life by a factor of ten.

Eidyia was one of the major Oceanids living in Memphis.

El's End is a fictitious name for the Oceanid's tent city which became Byblos. "El" is a reference of unknown etymology to Elder Titan Cronus. "End" refers to the end of all his Olympian children.

El was used as a title but evolved into the name of a specific god. *Im, he is the supreme Canaanite God. He founded and was the shrine god of Byblos and was associated with the Greek Cronus. His consort was Asherah.*

Eos was a minor Greek god.

Eye of Horus was the eye that Set commanded Anath to remove from Horus while Horus was under the influence of drugs. *Im, it is a concept and symbol that represents well-being, healing, and protection. It derives from the mythical*

Dionysus/Osiris, Ariadne/Isis/Philyra, Charon/Set, Hermes/Tehuti.
EGYPTIANS: Nebka, Djoser, Hotep, Khasek, Rocky
NUBIANS: Nima, Hetephe, King Kerma, Prince T'jaru, Prince Rafah.
CANAANITES: Phoenicia, Serket, Azazil, Jaffa | URFANS: Teumessian, Abram, Sarai, Terah

conflict between the god Horus with his rival Set, in which Set tore out one or both of Horus's eyes. The eye was subsequently healed or returned to Horus with the assistance of another deity, such as Thoth. Horus subsequently offered the eye to his deceased father Osiris, and its revitalizing power sustained Osiris in the afterlife.

Forts along the War Road were 1. T'jaru 2. Haboua 3. Dispatcher Anath 4. First Egyptians 5. unnamed 6. unnamed 7. unnamed 8. unnamed 9. Kerma 10. unnamed 11. Unnamed, and 12. Rafah. See War Road.

Gods - Canaanite: In Canaanite Mythology—Anath, Shahar, Astarte, Shalem, Ba'al, Moloch, El. The word El was originally a word meaning god but evolved into a title that evolved into the name of a specific Canaanite God.

Gods - Egyptian: In Egyptian Mythology—Osiris, Isis, Horus, Set, Nephthys, Anubis

Gods - Olympian: In Greek Mythology—Zeus, Hestia, Ares, Athena, Dionysus, Astraeus and Eos

Gods - Urfa: In this series—Deoares, Deohestia, Deoathena.

Hathor was the youngest daughter of Ishtar. She eventually became High Priestess to Osiris. *Im, she was a major Egyptian God.*

Hermes, aka Tehuti, was the messenger of the Olympian Gods. In this narrative, he survived the Great Flood and immigrated to Egypt where he took the name Tehuti. See Tehuti.

Hestia was the oldest Olympian and, in this series, their leader.

Hetephe, aka Hete, was the best archer in Nubia, the home to the finest archers in the world. She became a Major in the First Egyptian Army and finally became the only wife to Djoser.

Horus was the son and heir to Dionysus in the fight of the enlightened against the powerful gods in the fight for the minds of the people. *Im, Horus's contestings with his uncle Set was the basis for major Egyptian religious beliefs and myths.*

Hotep was the brother of Djoser and chief builder in Egypt.

Jaffa was a seaport in Canaan and the southernmost major town in Canaan.

Jaffa the Eighteenth was the Chief of the town of Jaffa

EGYPTIAN GODS: Osiris/Dionysus—Isis/Ariadne/Philyra, Horus, Set/Charon, Nephthys/Dexithea.
CANAANITE GODS: Anath, Astarte, Shalem, Shahar, Moloch, El.
OLYMPIAN GODS: Zeus, Dionysus, Hestia, Ares, Athena, Astraeus, Eos, Hermes.
OCEANIDS: Polydore, Lyris, Acaste, Eidyia, Dione.

Kerma was the Chief of the upper kingdom. See Nubians.

Khasek was general to King Nebka and father to future leaders.

Kyrios Olon means 'Master of All" and is the name Teumessian's children gave themselves as the self-proclaimed heirs to the dead Olympian gods, Deoares, Deoathena, and Deohestia.

Lyris was one of the major Oceanids residing in Memphis.

Megiddo was a major trading city in Canaan.

A **Marzeah** was a Canaanite wine-drinking event celebrating any special occasion. The men drank copious amounts of wine served by nubile young women. Women had separate Marzeahs, away from the men. This was prevalent throughout Canaan.

Moloch, im, was the Canaanite god of fire and is associated with child sacrifice, perhaps by "passing through fire." Current thought is that this may be the name of the sacrifice rather than the name of the god.

Murex was the owner of the dye manufacturing facility in Jaffa.

Nebka was the first king of Kemet, husband to Queen Nima of Nubia, and father of Hotep and Djoser.

Nephthys, aka Dexithea, was stepmother of Horus and became consort to Set. She was the revered Lady of South Memphis.

Nima was the daughter of the Chief of the Upper Kingdom and married Nebka, Chief of the Lower Kingdom, to form an alliance uniting the two kingdoms.

Nubians were the people of the Upper Kingdom. Notable Nubians in this story are Kerma, Nima, Rafah, T'jaru, and Hetephe. Djoser and Hotep were half Nubian through their mother, Nima.

Oceanids were Eidyia, Lyris, Acaste, and Polydore.

Osiris, aka Dionysus, was the consort to Isis. Their love story provided the unifying tradition Djoser needed to meld his people into a united people. See Dionysus.

Philyra, aka Ariadne aka Isis, was the chief of Port Olympus before the Great Flood. She was presumably killed by Hestia but, instead, escaped and fled to Crete where she renamed herself Ariadne. She subsequently married the king of the united cities of Greece and eventually became

Dionysus/Osiris, Ariadne/Isis/Philyra, Charon/Set, Hermes/Tehuti.
EGYPTIANS: Nebka, Djoser, Hotep, Khasek, Rocky
NUBIANS: Nima, Hetephe, King Kerma, Prince T'jaru, Prince Rafah.
CANAANITES: Phoenicia, Serket, Azazil, Jaffa | URFANS: Teumessian, Abram, Sarai, Terah

queen. She was the love interest of Dionysus and upon his dismemberment by Set, brought the armies of Greece into Egypt to reclaim his body. There she was referred to as Isis, "The Throne."

Phoenicia, the color, is purple.

Phoenicia, the country, becomes a powerful region north of Canaan.

Phoenicia, the person, was the sister of Serket and received her name from the purple dress her mother made for her. She became a powerful leader in Port Jaffa.

Polydore was an Oceanid who came early to Kemet (Egypt) and returned later as Portmaster of Jaffa in Canaan.

The **Pschent** was the crown of the Pharaoh which combined the white Hedjet crown of Upper Egypt and the red Deshret crown of Lower Egypt. It bore two animal emblems; the striking cobra symbolizing lower Egypt's Wadjet goddess and an Egyptian Vulture symbolizing the Upper Egyptian goddess Nekbet—the Two Ladies.

A **Quarter-moon** was the period between each phase of the moon and was approximately one week.

Rafah was the son and successor of Chief Kerma of Nubia. He was a supporter of the concept of a unified Egypt.

Rocky was Horus's chief disciple until he settled in Port Jaffa with Phoenicia. Rocky was replaced by Azazil.

Rusalem was a small town in the Sinai outlands whose gods were Shalem and Shahar.

Sarai was Abram's beautiful half-sister and wife.

Sanakhte was the son of General Khasek who became General of Kemet when Khasek became king.

Serket was consort to Horus.

Set, aka Charon and other honorific names, continually contested with Horus to be the supreme Living God of Egypt. See Charon.

Shahar. See Shalem.

Shalem was the god of sunset. His twin sister and consort was Shahar, the god of sunrise. Shalem is the root word of Shalom, "Peace."

EGYPTIAN GODS: Osiris/Dionysus—Isis/Ariadne/Philyra, Horus, Set/Charon, Nephthys/Dexithea.
CANAANITE GODS: Anath, Astarte, Shalem, Shahar, Moloch, El.
OLYMPIAN GODS: Zeus, Dionysus, Hestia, Ares, Athena, Astraeus, Eos, Hermes.
OCEANIDS: Polydore, Lyris, Acaste, Eidyia, Dione.

Snefru was Hotep's son and a master builder.

Telchine was the tribe from which Dexithea and Halia originally came.

Tehuti, aka Hermes, "He who is like an Ibis." Also known as Thoth in Greece. See Hermes.

Terah was Abrams's father, idol merchant, and the titular chief of Urfa.

Terahson was Terah's oldest son and heir apparent.

Teumessian became the High Priest of ancient Urfa after the Great Flood and sent his missionaries into the world to preach his version of the will of the gods. See The-Living-Word-of -the-Gods.

The-Living-Word-of-the-Gods was one of the titles assumed by Teumessian, the high priest of Urfa. See Teumessian

T'jaru was Nubian Chief Kerma's youngest son and Major of Archers in the First Egyptian Army.

Tophet is a city in the Valley of Gehenna outside Rusalem where child sacrifice by "passing through fire" was practiced.

Way of Horus, aka War Road, is a road across the upper Sinai desert linking Egypt with Canaan. Horus established his teachings along this road.

Way of Horus Teaching:
"The Path of Kiya is worthy, as are they who find and follow it.
Honor your ancestors. They are your past. You are their future.
Kill nothing you do not consume. Each life is precious unto itself.
Honor your vows. Do that which you say you will do.
Take nothing that is not yours.
Say nothing that is false.
Pick up those who have fallen.
Give to those who ask.
Love everyone, even those who despise you.
Be worthy."

Zeus was a major God in Greek Mythology, father of Dionysus, and the equivalent to Ba'al in other Pantheons.

Dionysus/Osiris, Ariadne/Isis/Philyra, Charon/Set, Hermes/Tehuti.
EGYPTIANS: Nebka, Djoser, Hotep, Khasek, Rocky
NUBIANS: Nima, Hetephe, King Kerma, Prince T'jaru, Prince Rafah.
CANAANITES: Phoenicia, Serket, Azazil, Jaffa | URFANS: Teumessian, Abram, Sarai, Terah

www.ingramcontent.com/pod-product-compliance
Lightning Source LLC
Chambersburg PA
CBHW060435310726
48977CB00001B/190